BORDERLAND

BORDERLAND

STRANGER THAN FICTION
— BOOK 2 —

T. B. MARE

Podium

BORDERLAND

PROLOGUE

Death in this forsaken place could come in many forms. From the ever-constant stormy clouds raining lightning upon the terrain to the icy chasms and crevasses lying in patient wait for the unfortunate trespasser that wandered in, this place had it all. Trapped amid several mountain peaks, it was a living nightmare.

Ultaf had spent most of his adolescence here, trained in the arts that allowed him to wear the mantle of the Lord of the Shimizu, and yet, nothing could prepare him enough to set foot inside these barbarous walls again. As his four igriotts pulled his sledge across the tundra, the canines suddenly slowed, looking skyward.

"What is it?" Ultaf asked, stepping off and glancing at the storm clouds above. They had begun to rotate, and he knew exactly what that meant. Tornadoes were a fact of life in the Northern Dominion, but up here, they held an altogether different meaning. He could hear the igriotts howl across the ridges, followed by a roar of thunder that sounded weirdly musical, like the after-tone of some vast gong.

He's awake. That's . . . good, I suppose.

The rest of his thoughts perished as his igriotts whined again, looking around warily.

He couldn't blame them. They had reached the outer periphery of the Peak. From this point on, even the very air would be hostile to them unless they had permission to breathe it in.

"Do not worry," he calmed the canines, crouching as he caressed the thick fur above their ears. "I'll have to make the rest of the journey alone."

Ultaf stood up and looked at the surrounding mountains. There were 361 checkpoints within the Peak's peripheries. Every single one of them had restrainers on duty, along with beasts at their command. Ultaf had seen igriotts, abominables, and even some himthursars here, all of which were magically

enthralled to serve as protectors of the Peak, utterly committed to destroying anything that stepped within this dominion without permission. Even the
Wind would fight you—aeromancer or not. All of this savagery around called
on his instincts to flee this place and never return.

Don't trust your eyes. Don't trust your instincts. The path is safe, Ultaf repeated
inwardly.

Pouring lifeforce into his feet, Ultaf shot through the black rocks amidst
the ice, stamping his way through vegetation, crumbling rocks, and . . . bones.
The ground was littered with them, courtesy of the man-eating monstrosities
guarding the area. Every breath, every step, every rasp of bones rubbing against
one another, multiplied into a thousand echoes that almost seemed to grow
louder than fading away. The black ice walls shone in the Eternal Light, the
ever-present whirlwind making it difficult to see ahead, but Ultaf kept moving.

He had to reach the Peak. He had information to share. This couldn't wait.

He emerged from the outer gates into the courtyard. The insides of this
sprawled-out fortress were bleak and beautiful in their simple symmetry. Every
room, every chamber was built into the very mountain itself, with stairs leading
inside cavernous corridors and open spaces. The courtyard was flat, smooth,
dark ice, and at its center, a single spire rose from the ground and pierced into
the mountain peak above it.

This place was the highest point in the entire Northern Dominion, and
somewhere deep within these crevasses was the infamous Shimizu Well. A
portal that connected to a vicious borderland filled with aerial, eldritch monsters. And Ultaf was here to meet the most dangerous monster among them all.

Son of the Wind King.

The Shimizu Warlord.

And his own grandfather, Mujin Shimizu.

The sounds of igriotts growling brought him to a pause. With steady, mist-
filled breaths, Ultaf waited as five restrainers, with an igriott and an abominable
in tow, shimmered into existence. Even in the surrounding blizzard, he could
spot that two of them were wearing gray wristbands, projecting their ability as
aeromancers.

"Trespassers are not welcome on this land," said one. "Walk away."

Wasn't that a surprise? He'd have expected them to attack first, ask questions later. Had they somehow recognized him? No, that wasn't it.

He removed the covering from his face. "I'm Ultaf, prince of Shimizu."

Technically, he was the lord, but here he was still a prince. Those at the
Peak only accepted the command of one man, and Ultaf was not him.

"Prince," the man bowed instantly, and the other restrainers took a step
back. "They did not inform us of your arrival."

"I need to meet Grandfather. I come with news."

"But—"

Ultaf eyed him. "He did not know of this. Time flies, and it's urgent. Where is he?"

"At the mountaintop." After a momentary hesitation, the restrainer added, "I should warn you that the Beast is awake. To traverse to the top in such conditions is . . . not recommended."

Ultaf snorted. That was an understatement if he had ever heard one. The Beast was a reference to his grandfather's kami, a gargantuan winged demon that he had only heard tales of. He remembered seeing clouds of power circling around his grandfather, creating a radius so intense that just stepping inside it was enough to obliterate anyone. A world of pain that Mujin Shimizu could manifest into this mortal world, thanks to the impossible power of this monstrosity.

And to think, there could be something greater than that.

Closing his eyes, he spoke. "Sigrun, fly."

A surge of mana erupted out of him, forging a mini whirlwind around him. His feet left the ground, and he shot upwards. Within minutes, he had crossed the Peak and stood on the black-iced mountaintop.

And winced.

Across the length of the terrain, his grandfather's sheer presence drew the eye with a terrible fascination. He sat cross-legged, levitating in midair, an orb of pure power surrounding him. The eye of the storm. The soft, bluish light emanating from the haze that was his power bathed the icy crust below. His presence was a kind of weight on Ultaf's mind, a gravity that strained space around it and could not be ignored. It was utterly magnetic and yet fundamentally repulsive at the same time. His power burned, an existence far older and deeper and deadlier than anything he had known. Compared to that power, even Sigrun felt little more than a transient breeze.

And rising above his grandfather was a gigantic outline. A maw that could swallow an entire city in one go. Claws that could slash mountains apart. This wasn't a kami. This was—

"Ultaf." His grandfather's voice tore through his thoughts. Even from a distance, he could hear it—baritone, deep, and thrumming with power. The very air felt alive with it.

"Grandfather." He took a tentative step forward, shielding himself from the wind. "I bring news. Cyffnar located some readings from the Desert. We sent a party, and they reported a powerful anomaly. Lord Straff was pleased. He wanted to get an edge before we were bound to report it to the Empire, so he hired professionals to loot it during the period of the Black Moon Rising."

His grandfather closed his eyes. "I have no time for your despotic nonsense, boy."

Had it been anyone else, Ultaf would have trapped them inside a circle of pure void for calling him that, watching as their bodies imploded like so much waste meat. But when his grandfather said it, all he could do was try his best to remain firm and not flinch. To the world, he was the lord of Shimizu, but here, he was little more than a child who had just learned that there was a monster beneath his bed.

"This—this will be worth your time. This can change . . . everything."

Grandfather opened a single eye. The force of will that condensed on him in that one movement would have instantly killed a lesser man, crushing his mind into something too dense and inert to function.

"Then speak your fill and be gone."

"After the Waning concluded, I visited the Desert." Ultaf shuddered. "It was . . . terrifying. Just like the myths. Dreary. Burning rays of sun in the day. Pitch-black demonic shadows beneath my feet. And that horrible, evil darkness—"

"You are wasting my time, boy."

Ultaf flinched. Maintaining control wasn't easy in his grandfather's presence, not even with Sigrun's power flooding through his veins.

"The adventurers found a rare form of featherglass inside the anomaly. An incredibly pure form. Purer than the Emperor's crown."

That caused Grandfather to pause for a moment. "Purer than . . ."

"The Emperor's. I checked. It's not a fabrication."

"Where is this anomaly?" Grandfather asked. "Featherglass that pure would have an inestimable number of applications."

The wind orb around him dissipated and the elderly man stood on the ground on steady legs. "Tell me you're already harvesting all the featherglass out of it?"

Ultaf swallowed and shook his head. "That . . . is no longer possible, Grandfather."

The winds blew faster, harsher, a manifestation of the man's fury.

"Why?" he asked. Silent, composed.

"Someone massacred our troops during the Black Moon. When I visited there after the Waning, all I found were the destroyed remains of the camp. Someone went in there and killed most of them."

"Who?"

"A girl. Blonde-haired."

Grandfather tilted his head slowly, studying him. "Few in the kingdom can trounce an entire battalion. And a girl, you say?"

"Yes. An aeromancer. This girl decimated tents with a single blast. Took out the entire battalion, without a single wound."

A psychic pressure erupted out of the man, making it hard to breathe. It was dense and horrible and reminded him exactly why he hated interacting with his grandfather.

"So," the man heaved, "the *creature* lives."

Ultaf took a step ahead. "And she has *Ezzeron*." His lips twisted in derision. *"Father would be so proud!"*

He uttered the word "Father" like it was the vilest curse imaginable.

"Do not delude yourself!" Grandfather snapped. "Ezzeron was lost to the very winds during that . . . incident. She has never been able to bind with it. You *know* that."

Anger flooded through his veins. It gave Ultaf strength to stand up before this man he had a healthy fear of.

"Then tell me this, Grandfather," He nearly snapped, "Can an ordinary kami massacre one of our battalions? She blitzed in, slaughtered them all, and destroyed the anomaly."

". . . What?"

"The anomaly," Ultaf replied coldly. "It's destroyed. Collapsed. There's nothing inside. No featherglass. No monsters. Nothing. Except for— well, one issue." He shifted his balance to his right foot. "The Core was undamaged."

"Have you lost your mind?" Grandfather rebuked. "The only way to destroy an anomaly is to destroy its Core. The metaphysical potential returns to the Great Mother and punishes the doer with Sin. That's the rule of the world."

"Well, somebody's ignoring the Rules," Ultaf replied, feeling slightly courageous. He took another step. "The Core was untouched, but the anomaly collapsed. I'm—not sure what happened, but someone achieved exactly what you think is impossible."

"And she's an *Aeromancer.*"

He took another step forward. "She entered the Desert during Black Moon Rising. She found the army, infiltrated it, and massacred them all. They say she flew like the wind, struck like the storm. And then there is . . . this."

He pulled a small contraption out of his pocket. Then he opened its lid, revealing a canister within. Inside that was a zigzag-shaped cluster of crystals. It was expanding throughout the canister, like thin tendrils of rime.

And it was crimson. As rich and dark as bremetan blood.

"Is that . . . ?"

"Frost," said Ultaf. "It was growing on one corpse. It absorbed every bit of lifeforce from the body, becoming large enough to encapsulate it. Frost that feeds on lifeforce. Does that ring any bells?"

Grandfather said nothing.

"She is out there," said Ultaf, grinning through his eyes. "And she has Ezzeron with her. She had him all this time."

"And the Frost—"

"It's grown stronger." Ultaf replied. "A power so staggering that it nearly caused the Great Goddess's demise. A power older than this Empire. A power that can kill an anomaly without destroying its Core."

"I searched around," Ultaf went on. "There was another piece of news. Another anomaly, destroyed. No one knew how. The only evidence they had was one girl, laden and dripping with Sin. Blonde hair, lithe figure. Aeromancer."

His eyes glinted as he extended his hand due east. "She's out there, experimenting. And she has Ezzeron and the Frost. So, I came here to inform you I'm going to the Llaisy Kingdom. To find her. To meet my long-lost *sister.*"

"No."

Ultaf paused. ". . .No?"

"No," Grandfather exhaled, as power whirled around him so fast that it was practically tangible. "I cannot afford any mistakes here. This time, I'll do it myself."

PART I

TRIAL BY CONTACT

CHAPTER 1

A CONFUSING REBIRTH

It
t

b
u
r
n
s

The unleashed wave of power rages through him. The inky blackness stains his mind like a curse. His life is ephemeral compared to the surrounding eternity.

It's not there.

She's not there.

Who is she?

His vision is painted black. How is he able to perceive?

His torso—what happened to it? Melted down? Probably.

He does not feel. He does not see. He does not hear. All he does is say: "In—a—nn—a—"

He's trapped. A plague of insects is trying to devour him all at once. Or is it the heat?

He recalls the ghol. Or was it the bat? It seems like something from another life.

—It burns.

The heat melts his mind. The power is great. Slow. Fast. Terrible. Impossible. The tide crashes against him, shattering him.

Yet he re-forms.

He's remade.

He's destroyed.

Remade.

Destroyed.

The cycle continues forever.

—It's burning.
—It's burning.
—It's burning so much that he might just—

"You cannot die, mortal. If you do, you will break your word."

It's—
He remembers the voice. Does he?
Yes, he does. But then, why can't he remember her name?
Her?
He knows it. He knows it. HeKnowsItHeKnowsItHeKnowsIt—
If he can remember the name, everything will be fine. Everything will be fine. Everything will be—
But he doesn't. He cannot recall her name. But he has to do it. He has to.

"Be the Invader."

He has to call her. Else she will disappear. He knows this, and from the bottom of his heart, he wants her to stay, for she is—

"Be the Conqueror."

He needs to reach her. He can't reach her.
He hears her voice. But she is too far away.
He can't see her. He wants to see nothing else.
He can—
Light.
He can see the Light.
She is disappearing into it.

"Be the Tyrant. and do not forget, you made a promise."

A promise.
He raises his hand. It touches empty air.
There is nothing left in him. There is more energy than he can use in a hundred lifetimes.
The dichotomy is tearing his reality. Mortal, yet divine. Fragmented, yet whole. Human, yet anomaly. He's—he is changing.
Changing.
Becoming. More.
He has knowledge that isn't his.
He has memories that aren't his.
He has skills that aren't his.
"I—"

His heart burns, but the pain does not lessen. He stands, his body scorching in the light, created and destroyed in every fraction of every second.

He takes a step forward.

The power slams into him.

Another step.

Then another.

And another.

The light—he has to reach it.

His hand stretches out and he yells—

"INA—"

. . .

. . .

. . .

"NNAAAAAA—"

Lukas thrashed himself awake, screaming a scratchy, hollow scream that made little more noise than a whimper. Breathing hurt, yet all he could do was sob.

He lay there, naked, undone, his right fist stretched upwards, trying to grasp the emptiness above him. Breathing came first, and he forced himself to control it, to stop the racking sobs, and to draw in slow, steady breaths. Next came the terror. The pain. The realization of what had happened. What he had lost. He wanted to crawl into a hole and pull it closed behind him. He wanted to not *be*.

But he *was*. He hurt too much. He was painfully, acutely, very much alive.

He was lying on the fabric. Soft fabric.

He was in bed.

Wait.

How did he get in bed? When had he fallen asleep? He couldn't remember. He couldn't even recall where he was, or the last time he ate, either.

His throat was tight and burning, as if he had swallowed an entire mug of boiling coffee. His legs felt like someone had switched them for dense lead bricks. He had the same arms he always had, but fewer of them. His belly twisted as if he had been working out for a long time.

It was almost a surprise he hadn't started crying again. But he just didn't want to die. Or find himself back in that darkness.

"Ah," came a familiar voice. "You're awake."

He lifted an arm and rubbed his coarse, gummy eyes. Something was odd. Like there should have been a baby elephant sitting on his chest but wasn't.

Weird.

Lukas opened his eyes.

He pushed himself up and glanced around the room. It was . . . large and empty. Light pink was clearly the default color scheme. Pink curtains, pink rug, pink furniture. Even the beds and lights. The bed he was in was big enough to fit four people. King size? Queen? He didn't know. A second bed lay next to his, with neatly arranged pillows and covers. A large ornate mirror hung on the opposite wall, next to an equally ostentatious dressing table and a lavish wardrobe.

This was a girl's room.

"Do you like it?"

Language Identified — Ualbesh
Replicating . . .

Lukas blinked and turned towards the source of the sound.

A lovely young woman close to his own age stood before him. High cheekbones gave her an aristocratic look, with exotic, almond-shaped blue eyes. Her silvery blonde hair was pulled back into a single ponytail, and she wore a boy's shirt.

He recognized her.

"You . . ." Lukas croaked, his voice rough and unfamiliar. "You're—"

"Tanya," she said, pointing a single digit at herself. "Do you know who you are . . . ?"

"Lukas," he automatically responded. Tanya. He remembered the name. Tanya. Blonde. Frost. White. Tanya. Promise. Tanya. Asukan. Wind—

"I remember you. You—" Lukas broke into a coughing fit. "You—you tried to kill me."

The blonde sported an amused smile. "Yes. You tried to kill me, too."

"You—you tried to kill—"

"Yes, yes." She casually waved it off as she sat down on the bed. "We've tried to kill each other multiple times in the past, but we've also fought together to destroy the anomaly."

Anomaly?

Crypt of Fiendish Worms

Now he remembered.

"You—" He tried speaking again, but getting the word out was too much for him in this state. Lukas fell into another coughing fit.

"Drink something first to wet your throat." Tanya fetched a cup of water and pushed it towards his trembling lips. "Speaking will be easier."

He supported it with his shaky hands and drank from the cup.

"Do not overexert yourself, mortal."

The cup slipped from his grip.

"Shit!" Tanya exclaimed. With a quick wave of her hand, she raised the cup, and the spilled water was suddenly levitating in midair. A casual flick vanished the water, while she caught the now-empty cup with her other hand. After filling it up again, she raised it to his lips.

How did she do it? *Aeromancy*, his mind supplied. Lukas gratefully accepted her aid. But that other voice he'd just heard . . . Who was she?

Inanna?

He called out into the void that was his mind.

Inanna?

Nothing responded. No quip. No condescending response. Nothing. Only cold, brazen emptiness.

"Any better?"

He slowly nodded. "I remember you. You're Tanya."

She smiled. "Yes, I introduced myself. Just now."

"No, I mean . . ." His head swayed. "I recognize you."

"Do you remember what happened to you?"

A frown rose to his lips. "I did something to the anomaly. I think I was dead? I was—"

"What else do you remember?" Tanya asked, curiosity clear in her voice.

"Empty. I recall feeling . . . hollow."

I will find you.

His last words. To Inanna. A big promise, but ultimately meaningless. She was gone. He had lost her. Their one chance to get things right had failed spectacularly. He was alone in this alien world. His all-knowing, all-powerful goddess was gone.

No matter the consequences.

Lukas gave a pain-filled groan as he held the sides of his head. It brought him a momentary respite against the sense of acute loss that was drowning him.

"Guess you're still healing." She sighed. "Lie down for now."

"Where am I?"

"You're at Zuken's mansion. Well, one of them anyway. It's difficult to tell with that guy," she answered with the slightest bit of exasperation in her voice, taking the cup from his hands and placing it on the dresser. "You weren't breathing, but you still had lifeforce and mana coursing through your body. We didn't know if you were dead or . . . and then suddenly, after a month, you took a breath."

A month. He was dead for a month? Why did that sound so familiar?

Instinctively, his fingers found their way to the pendant.

"Ah, that thing." Tanya gave it an intrigued look. "I don't think I noticed it on you when we first met."

An ice-cold shiver ran down his spine.

"...You can see it?"

Tanya arched an eyebrow. "Was I not supposed to?"

Dammit. Dammit. Dammit. The shiver went down his throat, spread through his chest, and made his heart quiver. Tanya could see the pendant. As could the others. That meant the Veil of Ignorance was no longer there. Inanna had cast that spell, and with her gone, it had faded. How long before the translation stopped?

"...Kas?"

What would happen to him? Without the ability to speak or understand this world's languages, he'd be stuck.

"—even listening?"

They had his body for an entire month. Inanna was gone, and now—

"LUKAS?"

Her raised voice halted his inner panic. "...Yeah?"

"You have this—I don't know—strange, angry look on your face."

He schooled his features quickly. "Sorry. It seems the spell on it faded when I was—you know—unconscious."

"That doesn't surprise me," she replied. "There are some serious enchantments on it. We tried everything we could, but it wouldn't come off. Olfric burned his hand in the process! We stopped trying after that."

"It is *my* pendant," he said.

He hadn't meant for the words to come out that cold. That hard. The anger surprised him, but it still bubbled and seethed within him. Some part of him was furious at Tanya for tinkering with *his* pendant without *his* permission. It was *his,* his sole connection to Inanna and *he'd be damned if he let this blonde bimbo and her merry band to mess with his—*

He closed his eyes and clenched his jaw. Pride. Possession. Territoriality. Those emotions, they weren't his. What had caused them?

Tanya hadn't reacted in any way, to his snarl, or his anger. She just studied him.

Lukas's lips twitched. Obviously, his expressions had given away his innermost thoughts. Wordlessly, he composed himself. Hastiness would not get him anywhere. Inanna had used her divine powers to dominate Tanya back then. If nothing else, that was one card he had in his favor. There was no point in making a mess of things with her.

Inhale, he told himself. Inhale and exhale.

Inhale and exhale.

Slowly, he moved his right hand and rubbed his thumb across the surface of the pendant. The familiar azure sheen had faded, now replaced by a dull blue. And yet, the translation spell was active. How else would he be able to understand what Tanya was saying?

How long, though?

"Tell me, Lukas Aguilar, where are you from?"

"From Earth."

"And that is a different world?"

"Yes." He paused. "I . . . I think so. It's a lot similar to this one, but there are some differences."

Like the absence of floating Screens. Or quantized potential. Or monsters roaming around . . . unless, that is, you lived in Australia, from what he'd heard.

"What did you do back there?"

"I was a student. Of the law."

"Are you here to kill me?"

Lukas stared at her.

"Are you here to kill me?" she repeated.

"No. No, I'm not."

"What was the spell you cast back in the anomaly?"

He looked away. "I don't want to talk about it."

"Why not?"

"Because I *don't*."

The words that left his lips sounded far sharper than they did in his head. He saw Tanya's posture stiffen in response. After several tense seconds, she spoke again.

"Ugh, fine. For the record, we brought you back with us to Haviskali."

Haviskali? Llaisy Kingdom, his mind supplied. Haviskali was the town on the western end of the Llaisy Kingdom, bordering the Desert of Namzuuhuu. A town in a different world. People that looked like humans but weren't. Where magic existed, as did monsters and gods. He wondered what he'd tried to make of himself in this world, apart from gaining strength and trying to figure out a way to fulfill his bargain with Inanna. Did this world have practicing lawyers too?

So many questions. It was finally time to get all those answers. He should have been all hyped up.

Instead, he just felt cold.

Tanya rose from the bed. "I should let the others know that you've woken up and remembered." She flashed him a bright grin. "Are you hungry? I can get you something to eat—"

"Leave me alone." The words had left his mouth before consulting the rest of him. He tried to do damage control, but found Tanya staring at him, stiff as a statue, her face blank.

". . . Sorry," he apologized. His emotions were still running rampant. "I mean, I have a lot to process. Why don't you give me some time before bringing the others?"

Tanya folded her hands in her lap and pursed her lips. On the surface, the expression seemed calm and controlled, but Lukas had the sudden instinct that she was concealing unease. It reminded him of their first interaction back in the crypt.

"Did something bad happen back there?"

He knew what she was talking about.

"Yes."

"You look like someone who's lost someone precious."

Lukas lowered his eyes. "I did."

Tanya stiffened. "I thought—" She paused, as if reconsidering her words gravely, "I thought you were all alone here, and there was always a chance that you'd—"

"Have to stay, yes," Lukas replied. "I didn't plan on things ending like that."

"And who's she?"

Lukas stiffened and stared up at Tanya, unblinking. "What?"

"I said who's she?" Tanya paused. "The person you lost," she clarified.

"I never said it was a woman."

"You did actually," she replied, the hard lines on her otherwise smooth face slowly easing, "Over the last week, you've been constantly murmuring about 'finding her' and 'getting her back.' Also, something about 'promises' and 'bargains.'"

Lukas carefully did not move or answer.

"So, who's she?" Tanya tried again. She sounded jealous. Almost.

There was another moment of stillness, before she spoke in a bare whisper, "I know how it is to lose someone precious to you, too. So if you want to stay alone for a bit, I understand."

She stood a little straighter. "I'll get you something to eat. You must be hungry." She turned around and started walking towards the exit. She had barely crossed the threshold when Lukas surprised himself by speaking out.

"You worship the Asukan gods, don't you?"

Tanya stilled. "Why do you ask?"

"Have any of your gods ever . . . died?"

She whirled around, eyes widened slightly. There was a growing wariness in her features. Like a cat about to bolt. She didn't move for several heartbeats. Finally, a false smile appeared on her face, and her shoulders relaxed.

". . .That's a very strange question to ask, Lukas Aguilar."

His brain started gibbering and running in circles as he struggled to think of an appropriate response. It was reckless and stupid of him to say that aloud.

". . . Lukas?"

". . . Sorry," He looked away. "It's nothing. Forget it."

Tanya didn't buy it for a moment but consented, anyway. "Sure. I'll inform the kitchen you're ready for some food."

Translation: she was going to go inform the others about his latest slip-up.

Lukas returned a tentative smile. ". . . Sure."

He needed to get up. Nothing would come from sitting and moping around. He had to get Inanna back. Preferably before his provisional allies acted against him, or worse, came after him like Solana and her ilk probably would.

Tanya spun around and walked towards the door, closing it behind her. He heard her footsteps slowly vanish. This was the time for action.

One.

Two.

Three.

Lukas threw the covers off him and jumped off the bed . . .

And promptly hit the ground face-first.

"Fuck!"

"Oh." Tanya's voice came from the doorway, utterly amused. "I forgot to mention. You have that metallic band stuck to your feet. Really, if you want to get up, you could've just told me."

His face burning in a mix of shame and embarrassment, Lukas turned over and rested on his back, spotting the strange heavy presence on his legs, no doubt placed there to wound his pride. Why hadn't he sensed it before?

Gods. He hated himself sometimes.

He paused and stared at the offending piece of garment on his legs. It was dark gray and placed right above his ankles, covering his knees. There was something incredibly familiar about it. Cautiously, Lukas forced himself up, touched the band with his arms, and—

Snap!

The band blurred into motion and literally jumped off him, condensing and contorting into dozens of metallic tendrils, writhing as it took shape. It shot up into the air, contorting itself mid-flight, into a strange blob-like figure. Its outer metallic surface shone malevolently as two shiny tendrils rose, ready to pierce him at the slightest display of hostility.

Lukas pushed himself back, fascinated and alarmed, watching the still-morphing blob swaying back and forth in the air, before dropping to the floor in a loud splat. A slime? Not that slimes were weak or anything. Given their ability to shape-shift and their monstrous strength, they were frankly nightmarish to face in combat.

But this wasn't like the ones he'd encountered. This wasn't a humanoid monster of a worm.

It was a blob.

A metallic, shiny blob.

He tried to extend his finger.

"No, don't!" Tanya yelled.

Too late. The blob shifted again, but instead of striking, it rolled onto its back almost . . . lazily? Tiny tentacles wiggled out of its end, and Lukas scrambled backward, fearing retaliation.

It never came. Instead, a mouth tore itself open across its face. And with nothing short of utter malevolence, it opened its newly created maw—a lazy, dark tongue slithering out and sweeping across the floor—and spoke its first word.

"MEOOOOOW?"

CHAPTER 2

SLIME OF THE LIVING METAL ALSO CAT

It was a sentient blob of aqāru. With a large, purple tongue.

And it was purring like a cat.

"Uh," Tanya asked, "why is it purring?"

"No clue," Lukas murmured, silently petting it. The thing swept its long, wide tongue out and licked his palm before rubbing its "face" against his skin and purring. No, he wasn't imagining it. This thing was *purring*. It was a walking, talking, *meowing* mass of contradictions. Naturally, it fit right in place with all the madness that seemed to constantly be happening around him.

Inanna would have laughed her head off. And then made a sarcastic-sounding quip about vermin that was most likely entirely serious.

"Well?" asked Tanya. "What is it?"

Lukas smiled. "My new pet."

"Does it have a name?"

His smile widened. "Its name . . . I think I'll call it . . . *Blob*."

"*Blob?* What kind of name is that?"

"A simple one," he said. He knew what this metal was and how he had gotten it. And if his theories were correct then . . . . He grabbed it with his fingers, and Blob instantly twisted, forming a perfect copy of his dagger in less than a second. The length-to-weight ratio felt perfectly right.

And then it went right back to being a rather stylish pair of wristbands and latched on both of his arms. Like it was the most natural thing in the world.

I shouldn't have known it would do that.

He paused and stared up at Tanya, who was gawking at him, unblinking.

"I swear I didn't know it'd do that."

"... *Sure* you didn't."

Her voice was laced with disbelief. Not unexpected. Not after what happened with the crypt's Guardian.

He regarded Blob, now his armbands.

What are you?

Nexus Established
Accessory Confirmed

Reading Data . . .

A rush of images and alien perceptions sandblasted his head. There were flashes of processes in action, and images of monsters, both complete and in progress; images of featherglass crystals, their constituents forged by a power so intense and coherent that it had individuality and awareness. He saw the ponderous dance of the atoms and molecules, inorganic and organic structures, rearranged and twisted to serve the purpose of this alien awareness, and assimilation of not a hundred or thousand, but tens of thousands of monster prototypes—crafted or assimilated, ready to deploy or left incomprehensible; vast reserves of impossible soul information, whole and broken, and so much more.

Lukas fought to contain those impressions, struggling to see beyond this tumultuous wave. But the more he tried, the more he sensed its futility. It was like looking at the world's greatest garbage dump. A disorganized mess without any structure or clarity. Information on modulating rock composition somehow became a blueprint of a species of moss. Knowledge on how to craft vatuatil lay smashed with stuff on netopyr goo.

It was like taking Wikipedia, randomly translating each line of text into a different language, shuffling it all, then trying to track down a single specific fact. The information was technically still there but finding it would be the equivalent of locating a needle in the world's largest haystack.

And he didn't have a magnet.

"It's from that anomaly, isn't it? That metal?"

"Yes."

"Thought so."

Lukas looked up at her.

"We thought the Guardian-monster had latched onto you. But it didn't react to anything, so we assumed it dead and left it as it was."

She wasn't wrong. Not completely. This wasn't the doppelgänger he had fought and tried to siphon at the end. This was—

The *Crypt of Fiendish Worms* itself.

Or whatever remained of it.

When a monster died within anomaly territory, its soul returned to the omphalos that created it, while granting a certain amount of Experience to the killer. The monster's data was then reused over and over. Or maybe combined to make something else. Nothing was lost, only transformed from one state to another. Much like the law of the conservation of energy.

Omphaloi were no different. When the crypt's omphalos was destroyed, all that information had to go *somewhere*. If a monster's soul returned to its "mother"—the omphalos—then logically, the omphalos's data must revert to *its* mother: the world itself.

Unless there was an alternative. A perfect recipient that was readily available for absorbing the spiritual data.

Like the aqāru.

An entire anomaly's data, thousands of monster prototypes, jammed into a purring metal blob. If knowledge is power, then this is a fucking power station. Now if only I could learn to use it.

Analysis Complete **Rendering . . .**

What he saw next sent him choking. Hard.

Type	Heteromorph
Constituent	Aqāru
Deciphering Spiritual Constitution . . . **Decoding . . .** **Rendering Complete.**	
Nature	Conglomerate
Number of Skills	16159
Number of Monster Prototypes	Null
Information Corrupted	

Sixteen thousand skills? Is this for real?

Reversing Corruption will require +597,531,354 units of power. **+47% chance of success.** **Initiate Rollback Protocol?**

No. No way. All that power for just 47% chance? And if I failed then . . .
No.

He scowled. He should have known. It wouldn't be easy. He'd need to find a way to absorb power first. Capacitance was an option. Using it had attracted the Guardian's attention. If he used it directly upon the world and if it treated him as an invader then . . .

He shook his head. *Risk all that for a 47% success rate? No way.*

"Where is your sense of adventure?"

He inhaled. That voice again.

He looked around.

Inanna?

And around.

Inanna?

. . . .

No. It wasn't her voice. Just—just what she'd say. He was hearing things. She was gone. She—

Lukas paused and waited. Maybe he'd hear it again?

He didn't.

Disappointed, he regarded the Screen.

Command Acknowledged
Rollback Protocol Deactivated until further prompt from
PRIME HOST

". . . even listening?"

Lukas blinked and turned around. "I'm sorry, what?"

"I asked, what is it?"

"I told you. It's my new pet, Blob."

"I meant what kind of creature?"

"Oh. It's . . . uh, a fragment."

"Of what?"

"A greater whole," he said, his eyes fixated on the sentient piece of metal on his arms. "But the 'whole' is a broken, disorganized mess, so this 'fragment' is being . . . erratic."

"Are you being intentionally cryptic?" Hard lines appeared on her otherwise smooth features.

Lukas tilted his head up and looked at her. "When I killed the Guardian, I didn't do it neatly. Part of it remained and latched on to me."

"Oh," she said. "Doesn't that bother you?"

He blinked. "Should it?"

"It tried to kill you."

"You tried to kill me, too. You don't see me holding that against you."

Tanya let out a quick breath that might have been hiding a laugh. She tried to grab for his hand, but then stopped midway at the sight of Blob and stood back straight. After a moment of reconsideration, she held her hand out.

"Come on. You need a meal and a bath."

Lukas grinned and grabbed it.

The meal was a ripe assortment of saffron, green, and pink, with a healthy bit of what tasted like an exotic mesh of tomato salsa and avocado. Lukas put all of that on a large, round flatbread and rolled it up, a far cry from the meaty, greasy tacos he used to feed himself every morning back home.

He inhaled it within a minute.

Realizing that she had underestimated how hungry he was, Tanya gave him over half of her breakfast while she went to get some more.

It was gone before she got past the door.

Tanya took it as a challenge and raided the kitchen, returning with a monster-sized breakfast. There were a lot of soft grains in the main course, giving the plate a soft pink background, with another assortment of leaves, petals, and what looked like blue roots. The accompanying beverage was like a mix of milk with cinnamon and turmeric but carried a wild aroma that flared his nostrils.

This was enough to feed an entire party.

Lukas demolished it by himself.

"Huh . . ." said Tanya, watching him continue to shove food into his bottomless pit. "I'm so glad I don't have to pay for your meals."

Lukas grinned. During his month of being dead, his body had had to survive on pure anomalous energy. Now that he was awake, it wanted the real thing.

Tanya watched him, amused.

"Got it all over my face?"

"It means you enjoyed the cooking," she said, handing him a napkin. "It's nice to see you come into focus."

Focus. Yeah. That was one way of putting it. He had taken a nice, long bath earlier. His legs were still weak, and he needed her help to walk to the bathroom and back. He wondered if she had taken care of his bowel issues when he was unconscious but hadn't quite worked up the nerve to ask her about it.

Some things were better left unsaid.

"I hope you haven't gotten rusty. That would irritate Zuken."

Lukas chewed silently. Zuken was a poor man's Solana. Weaker than Ryu or Quonnan, but Tanya claimed he had some political power.

"I'll manage," he murmured, focusing on the blend of sweet and sour. And was that a bit of grapefruit he tasted?

Absently, he thought of his Schema.

SOULSCAPE	
NAME	Lukas Aguilar
Type	Prime Host
Level	8
Experience	239
Current Threshold	2560
Utilized Soul Capacity	14979 / ∞

Mildly slurping through the beverage, his eyes wandered across the information displayed, absently marveling at the unfamiliar words his Schema showed. Nothing particularly interesting. Closing his eyes, he continued to drink with that tiny smile still on his face. Then he swiftly inspected the last line again.

And again.

Lukas choked.

Infinite. Soul. Capacity.

Totally missing the sour look from Tanya, Lukas stared at his Schema and scanned it thoroughly. Prime Host. Not Base but *Prime*. What changed? Were Inanna's actions at work here? He had leveled up again. Not surprising. But *infinite* soul capacity? This was the perfect thing he needed to assimilate—

His expression soured.

Kinetomancy.

He wished he had a knife so he could repeatedly stab something with it.

"Something wrong?" she asked, unable to keep the sourness off her face.

Lukas didn't blame her. He had accidentally spit in her food.

"Just . . . a cruel surprise. But no, it's all good."

And it was.

ESSENCE	
Maximum Lifeforce Output	5075
Replenishment Rate	700 / hour
LEY LINE NETWORK	
Maximum Mana Output	6325
Synthesis Rate	810 / hour

His lifeforce and mana had both grown significantly. The Level Up meant he was more efficient with his skills.

PRIME HOST
Unconditionally superlative among all Monster Prototypes.
Alpha Condition Raised to Maximum (Level 5), granting an absolute
mind free from external influence from Monster Prototypes.
Amplified Resistance to mental intrusion and enthrallment.

Having an infinite soul capacity meant downloading monster prototype skills without limit. In a world where Soul Capacity and skills were everything, he might as well have been handed a Pandora's box.

"You're making that face again!"

Dammit.

"The others," he said. "Where are they?"

The delight faded from her face, replaced by a serious calm. "I thought you wanted some time alone."

"I did, but sitting on my ass won't get me anywhere."

"Well, Zuken's out for some business, and he's taken Elena with him. They'll probably return tomorrow morning. I'm not familiar with Olfric's whereabouts at the moment, since he's usually away on jobs. Apart from the maids and the groundskeeper, I doubt there's anyone else inside the mansion."

"And you stayed behind to play nurse?"

"Someone had to take care of you. Among all of us, I know you best."

Which is true, Lukas mused.

"Can I ask you something?"

"Of course."

"What happened after I fell unconscious?"

"I think you mean *dead,*" she said. "We saw the discharge of raw power. Whatever you did, it was powerful. It nearly buried us alive. We only had enough time to grab you and escape. At first, we thought you were dead. Banksi almost buried you. Then your heart started beating again. It was . . . "

"Spooky?"

Tanya chortled. "You should've seen Olfric's face."

"I can imagine," Lukas said dryly. "What of the others?"

Tanya snorted. "Olfric suggested a Holy Purging. I pointed out it wouldn't work, what with your 'look-at-me-casting-a-shadow-under-Eternal-Light' stunt earlier. Elena's on the fence about you, but only because she can't sense your mind."

He arched an eyebrow.

"Elena?" Tanya repeated. "Brown hair, about yay high. Cute as a button. Remember?"

Lukas nodded slowly. "You said something about sensing minds."

"She's a changeling." Tanya dropped her shoulders. "Elena's damn good at sensing and manipulating emotions. Like, genuinely good. But she can't sense yours, and it pisses her off."

"Sensing and manipulating emotions . . ." Lukas murmured. Inanna's lessons came to mind. "She can read minds?"

"Emotions, not minds," Tanya clarified.

"And Banksi?"

"What about him?"

"What does he think of me?"

"You'd have to ask him. I doubt he wants to purge you. He looked like a kid with a broken toy when we found out you weren't breathing."

"And you? What did you think?"

"Does it matter?"

He nodded.

Tanya didn't move a muscle for several heartbeats. "I thought it was just one of your . . . Outsider things."

He waited for her to continue.

"You've already shown you can ignore the Eternal Light at will. You killed an anomaly. Without amassing Sin. You're not bremetan nor yokai but can use both lifeforce and conjure mana, both in and out of combat. And you've got mad healing skills. None of that is exactly normal."

"So?"

"So if the normal rules don't apply to you, why would death?"

Lukas blinked. Twice. Her logic felt cold and inhuman and much drawn out, but immaculate at the same time. He had proved to be an extraordinary person. It was only natural that even "ordinary" things would take on an "extraordinary" shape around him.

Neither of them spoke for several seconds.

"Lukas . . ."

"Yeah?"

"Why were you inquiring about dead gods earlier?"

"What dead gods?"

She leveled a deadpan stare at him.

He sighed. "Any chance you can forget I asked that?"

"No."

"Yes, I want to resurrect a goddess. From my own world. A goddess whom I consider an . . . associate, of sorts."

Yeah, "associate" was an apt description. Inanna would probably throw a fit if he even so much as insinuated that they were "friends."

She gave him an oblique look. "You're a High Priest."

"I'm not."

"What are you?"

"I told you, an associate."

"What kind?"

"You ask many questions."

"And you don't answer any of them properly."

"Bother!" Lukas exhaled again and squared his shoulders. "We had a bargain. I promised her something and in return, she helped me. But things happened and she, err . . . died?"

"You seem unsure."

"I am. I'm not sure how death works for gods and goddesses. Think you can give me some pointers?"

She shrugged. "I know very little about gods. But I don't think we can revive them after their deaths. I mean, the Asukan Pantheon lost many of its members during the Great War, or so they tell us."

She had a point. But mythology also spoke of gods getting resurrected time and again, often by beings even greater than them. He wasn't sure if Christ's resurrection fit the bill, but other religions had thematic similarities with the process. Baldur was the prime example of that, having been prophesied to be resurrected after Ragnarok. There was also the tale of Zeus resurrecting Dionysus, Shiva resurrecting his son Ganesha, and so on.

But asking direct questions could be dangerous. He needed to carefully tread the line between what was safe to ask and what wasn't. Solana hadn't minded talking about Nordic people. That didn't mean the Asukans would feel the same.

"You could ask Zuken though . . ." Tanya said, her voice hesitant. "If anyone can help you with that, it's Zuken."

Lukas glanced over at the aqāru-slime sitting next to him, rubbing its head against his knee like a kitten. It grazed its metallic tongue across the floor, only to sneeze, morphing into a cone and throwing itself into the air, before finally floating down like a deflated balloon and re-forming on the ground.

Yeah, this thing was going to give him a headache.

"Zuken will love your new pet. I've never seen a metal act like that. The svartalfars have metal golems in their armies, but they're more like automatons and not actual creatures."

Lukas did a double take. "There are svartalfars living in the Empire?"

Tanya gave him a weird look. "In their keeps, yes. Not very approachable either."

Well, wasn't that surprising? So far, it looked like this world had two factions—the Asukans and the Yokai. The former ruled the lands, and the latter survived in cracks and patches, hiding from the Eternal Light and possessing people to survive.

But that wasn't all. There were Nordic elements around. And Elena—Elena was a changeling. Celtic mythos painted her kind as offspring of the fae with mortals. He had yet to hear any references to the Ulster Cycle or the Tuatha, so chances were that the term could refer to offspring between the elves and mortals, too.

And he had entered this mythology carnival with a Sumerian war goddess taking up space inside his freaking head.

Joy.

"What are you scheming?"

Lukas blinked at that. "Who, me?"

"Oh no, I was talking to the wall. It goes all cloudy eyed and stiff from time to time."

He rolled his eyes at her deadpan expression. "Just wondering where to go from here. I know I told you about needing a new life, but I didn't plan on that."

Tanya shrugged. "You're strong. You've got skills. Zuken's interested in hiring you. I don't see how that's a terrible start."

"What does he want from me?"

"I'm unsure. Zuken hasn't sent me on any new missions since the anomaly. On the plus side, I'm no longer hunted."

"Your people hunted you because of your Sin, right?"

Tanya instantly went defensive. "You know *nothing* about me!"

Lukas brought his hands up in apology. Clearly, his mouth had taken on the bad habit of running off without thinking. Another part of his mind carefully observed her reaction and filed it away.

"Not my place to comment, but I find your situation ironic."

"In what way?"

"You got shunned because you committed a Sin. No one wanted to hire you. And then Banksi, an influential man, hires you to commit more Sin. Ironic, isn't it?"

"You're right," Tanya said after a few minutes.

"About what?"

She leveled him a gaze. "That it isn't your place to comment on it."

She straightened her back, her lips twisted in disdain. "I was on the run. Living the life of an outcast. Now? I'm free. I'm not shunned, and my work conditions are better. Many people would call that progress."

"Many people would also call that exchanging one prison for another."

"Why do you care?" Tanya half snarled, half shouted. Clearly he had touched a raw nerve.

"I just think we're kindred spirits, you and I."

"We're nothing but strangers who have repeatedly tried to kill each other."

"Strangers don't nurse each other back to health," Lukas replied in his composed tone.

"You . . . I . . ." She seemed utterly frustrated, before a strange look flashed on her face. "You—you want something from me, is that it?"

His jaw fell open, surprised. "'Scuse me?"

"No, it makes sense," said Tanya, rattled by her own deductions. "We fought. You won. But you've ensured that I'm satisfied. First the frost, and then during negotiations with Zuken. No wonder they think I'm lying about you. They think you and I are old acquaintances. And now this—"

It was like watching glass shatter. Lukas almost winced at seeing her pleasant mask fall away, leaving behind a wary neutrality.

"So what is it? Ezzeron? My Frost powers? Yes, that must be it, isn't it? You did something to me back in the anomaly. It's why when I look at you, all I want to do is to—"

She broke her tirade at the last possible moment and looked away.

Lukas knew he had only a single chance to keep from spoiling his one ace in this new world. And so he acted.

"Yes."

Tanya looked at him, her questions clear on her face.

"Yes," he clarified. "I brought your Frost under control."

She switched her hands, moving the bottom one to the top as if worried about wrinkling her dress. Her mouth twisted. "Of course. I *knew* that was the case."

"I want you to know I will not hold that one over on you."

Her eyes widened slightly. She held completely still. "Why?"

"Why what?"

"Why did you bring it under control? And why wouldn't you hold it above me?"

"Do you want me to?"

"No, of—of course not," she backpedaled. "But I want to know why."

"Because I respect you too much for that."

He couldn't interpret her expression after he said that. There could have been anger in it, or suspicion or terror or blank curiosity.

"You don't believe me."

It wasn't an accusation. The truth was plastered on her face.

"I've lived my entire life in the Empire. I don't believe anyone."

Trust breeds betrayal. I've seen it as a babe. I've seen it in Ereshkigal. Your words will not shake me.

In that one moment, Lukas didn't think he had ever met someone so lovely, yet entirely alone. Call it a hunch, but he *understood* her. On a fundamental level. Not the predator that Inanna had sealed away, but the young girl that was trying to survive against a harsh world outside. Someone that was compassionate, friendly, and caring, but had seen enough ugliness to walk into an anomaly, ready to commit a Sin, believing it was her only choice. But Lukas had learned the hard way that sometimes, a choice wasn't a choice at all. And yet she had done it. And survived. That told him she had a lot of inner strength, and that was a quality he always found attractive.

He could *really* grow to like this girl.

Which, come to think of it, was why Zuken Banksi and the others had left her to care for him. She had admitted that they suspected them to have a deeper and older relationship. Perhaps Zuken Banksi was luring him with Tanya to make him reveal his secrets . . .

Too many questions, and webs of intrigue that kept deepening everywhere he looked.

What would you have done, Inanna?

Silence was the only reply he got.

CHAPTER 3

NEW WORLD CITIZEN

The Banksi mansion stood out boldly against the blue beyond. It stood there as if conjured from a child's storybook. It was perfect. Lukas imagined dragons and wyverns chained in the menageries of the outer courtyard, because if such a mansion could exist, why not? Every single stone was even and square, as if those who constructed it were set on perfection, obsessed with their art. The massive stone edifice was built into the face of a sheer cliff and left to hang in space. Crafted to be a seamless part of the forests and streams penetrating into its heart, the mansion endured the relentless pull of gravity for who knew how long, never slipping from its original purpose—to insulate its occupants from the world around it.

Ironic that the residents are the ones hosting an Outsider while the rest of the world stays ignorant.

"Feel like jumping?"

Before he knew it, Lukas had jumped to his left, away from the source of the voice, fire and lifeforce pulsing on his palms, ready to scorch and blast away the intruder. The moment his eyes landed on Tanya, his brain switched gears and pushed himself out of his fight-or-flight mode.

"Sorry."

"That was some reaction," she observed. "You weren't this nervous back in the anomaly."

Naturally. The anomaly was a wild zone. Neutral territory. The rules were simple—kill or be killed. Plus, wandering through the tunnels gave him an idea of what to expect. He knew what ate what, who hunted whom, and what to avoid and how.

But this place was foreign territory. Living in real rooms, sleeping in clean beds, showering, talking to Tanya, having breakfast—it was a normal, civilized life again. It should've made him feel better. Comfortable.

Instead it psyched him out. Monsters were simpler—he knew how to behave with them. People? They had agendas. Smiles on the outside, daggers on the inside. Hiding their intentions behind a nefarious web of lies. He was an Outsider with unique mysteries and these people wanted it, one way or the other. "New place, new people. It'll take me some time to get used to this."

Tanya smiled but said nothing. Instead, she took a step towards the precipice and stood, gazing at the town below.

"So . . ." Lukas ventured, "what was that about jumping?"

"Oh." She grinned. "Just a bit of trivia from my Aeromancy training. Looking from above disrupts one's mental image of reality. It makes you want to get back to the sense of normalcy that existed when you were on the ground."

Her feet rose from the ground, wind swirling and kissing her toes. The beauty, the grace, it should've left him spellbound.

Instead he suppressed a sneer. He could sense the waves around her feet, feel the pressure of the wind on the floor. She wasn't *fluttering*, she wasn't *levitating*, she was *thrusting* wind downward like a crude space shuttle, using mana instead of fuel. Had Inanna done it, he'd have felt *nothing*.

I'll show her.

Focusing inward, he pushed lifeforce out of his feet, using Kinetomancy to push back against gravity while lifeforce pushed him upward. It was neither subtle nor graceful, but it pushed him up. He staggered and bent his knees all the way until he was squatting in midair, only to lose balance and fall down in an unceremonious heap.

Damn, that was hard.

Tanya chortled.

Lukas scowled at her, and that made her laugh harder. After a few seconds of hopeless glaring, he joined in.

The blonde slowly descended and extended her hand toward him. Lukas grabbed it and stood up.

"That wasn't Aeromancy, I don't think," she said.

He shook his head. "Lifeforce. Pretty lousy first attempt, huh?"

She shook her head. "If anything, it's impressive. Even for aeromancers, stabilizing against gravity is no minor feat."

It was child's play for Inanna. Lukas looked at his hands. *What went wrong? Why did I lose control?*

"Say," Tanya asked, her feigned detached tone fooling no one, "I've been wondering. How do you do it?"

"Do what?"

"You know, use multiple elements. You used fire and ether. At first I thought you were a . . ." She trailed off. "But then Zuken said you didn't have a kami."

He twitched. They had ways to tell if one had a kami? That was problematic. Especially with him using two elements. Tanya's attempts at being casual were clumsy at best. Maybe he was right. Zuken and the rest were using Tanya as bait. Did they think that a pretty young woman would be enough to make him spill his secrets?

What to do?

"Lukas?"

He looked at her. Dammit. He'd have to go with the truth this time around. "I don't have a kami. I can conjure mana by myself."

"Fire and ether?"

"Fire and ether."

"And the others?"

He gave her a half shrug. "Can't. I think. I'd love to channel wind though. Or get a Wind kami, if I can. I'd love to fly really high."

Tanya lifted her nose in mock haughtiness. "You are *high* if you think it's as easy as getting a Wind kami. It took me years before I could do just this . . . "—she did a little jig in midair—"without falling on my butt."

And it's still got nothing on Inanna.

Lukas frowned. Maybe he was being a bit unfair. Inanna was a goddess, and not just any goddess. She was the Supreme Queen. Compared to that, Tanya was just . . . ordinary.

No. He corrected himself. Not ordinary. Nothing about that Frost was ordinary. Inanna had called it a power as ancient as herself. How did this girl get a power like that?

He trained his features to look curious instead of appalled. "Must help that you have a body that matches your style to a tee. You're slim and fast. In perfect shape for an aeromancer, I reckon."

Tanya looked at him strangely. "How else would it be?"

"Excuse me?"

She took a step closer. Blob stirred. The urge to shape it into a dagger was overwhelming. Instead he held back and met her eyes. Blue eyes gazing at his brown ones, they both studied each other intently. After three seconds, she finally replied.

"You're serious, aren't you?"

"I *really* don't know what you're talking about."

"The body reflects the skills."

He gave her a slow nod. "What of it?"

She cocked her head. "So if you level up, your body will morph to accommodate. I favor high-speed blitz tactics. Can't do that with a fat waist and giant jugs, can I?"

Was it just him or had he noticed a sliver of jealousy in her tone? Tanya had a lithe, athletic figure with long legs. A far cry from some of the buxom women he had seen around.

She did have a nice ass though.

"Now that I notice," Tanya said, cupping her chin, "for someone who packs all that power, you're awfully lean."

Am I? He looked at himself. Maybe because, unlike her, he wasn't a specialist. He favored high-powered punches, but with the flexibility of Kinetomancy. Shatterpoint Intuition was a mental skill, and Pyromancy didn't lend itself much to physical changes. Seismic Sensing was less Terramancy and more like a Perception skill from a slime monster.

"Maybe I just . . . function differently? You know, Outsider things?"

She snorted. "Let's go with that. But I digress. Zuken's back, and he's got the overseer of Haviskali with him as a guest. Zuken asked me to fetch you."

"For what?"

She shrugged her shoulders. "No clue. Maybe about your documentation. You need a legitimate history to be a citizen."

"Any advice?"

"Keep your wiseassery to a minimum."

"Eh? That might be difficult. I don't do great with authority figures."

"Lukas," Tanya said, her voice suddenly tight. She put her hand on his arm, and her lean fingers felt like heavy wires. "That man is the *overseer*. He's the one in charge of this town and answers directly to the Shogun, the governor of the entire Llaisy Kingdom. You don't fuck with that guy. I've seen what happens if you do."

Lukas pursed his lips and studied her hand thoughtfully for a moment. Then he nodded. "Okay," he said. "I hear you."

Tanya exhaled slowly and nodded.

"If he's the top dog, why's he here? I doubt he'd come all the way for li'l ol' me."

Her expression cracked. "I . . . don't know. But Zuken holds the ear of the Shogun. You can say he and the overseer are professional peers."

"Big man then?"

"You've no idea."

Lukas had expected this world to be stuck in some pre-Renaissance, swords-and-kings era. Turns out, he was wrong. Sure, they hadn't quite upgraded to night clubs and ripped jeans, but on the other hand, they had *smart* technology.

Like, really, *really* smart tech.

Just one look at a single freaking wall was proof enough.

Potent sigils ran across every single surface, hidden in plain sight by the graffiti and home decor. These sigils stored the energy from Xulp—their *sun* and star—like photovoltaic cells and used it to run a multitude of functions inside the place. The defensive systems built into the castle had been laid by someone who was clearly deranged. Even his analysis tool could only touch the surface of their functionalities. Hell, the only reason he felt like he knew what he was talking about was because of the strange similarity of these sigils with the ones he had seen on the walls in the yokai territory. What those sigils were doing in an Asukan nobleman's house was anybody's guess.

It gave him the feel of living in a smart house. Only *old*. And engraved out of a single stone.

And with no shadows. None.

Talk about a stark, alien dichotomy.

He followed Tanya into one of the waiting rooms, and found several people immediately jumping to their feet, including a couple of warriors, complete with chain mail and swords, and Olfric Bergott, looking like he had seen several miles of bad road recently. He was a bald, fifty-something man with tattoos engraved on his skin, starting from the tip of his scalp and running all the way downward. Olfric was covered in bumps and bruises and still-healing cuts. He looked incredibly wary of Lukas's presence.

And finally, there was the man himself—Zuken Banksi, dressed in robes of Prussian blue, Elena standing right next to him in a tight bodycon of floral patterns.

"Uh, easy," he said. "I won't attack anyone, I promise."

Every single person in the room eyed him warily. They had their hands inches away from the hilt of their swords. Except for Elena, who did her best to ignore his presence, and Zuken, who just looked plain amused.

Lukas closed the door behind him and walked forward, the excessive light everywhere giving his pupils more of a workout than they'd had in a while. He had seriously considered trying to conjure sunglasses, but the entire concept of "sourceless" and "all-pervading" Eternal Light kind of defeated the point.

"Banksi," he replied. The trick to facing a crowd was to ignore everyone else and focus on a singular person. It took some of the psychological advantage of numbers away. "Tanya said you wanted to talk to me?"

"Oh, yes," the terramancer replied. "Lukas, meet Tatun Kinosu, the overseer of Haviskali. Overseer, meet Lukas. He's a private hire from Maluscion. The one I talked to you about."

"The metamancer?"

"Same."

It bore mentioning that this world ran on the *ether* standard. The ability to synthesize ether—natural or otherwise—and contain it in standardized containers governed the Empire's economy. Unlike the other elements, ether signified change, transformation, creation, and a lot of other concepts that led to it being considered the most prestigious element out of the five. Every nation—heck, every town—had a minimal number of ether-manufacturing sites, employing both machinery and metamancers to synthesize raw ether from the natural energy of the world. That ether-type kami were comparatively rare only drove the demand up.

And that was where Lukas had struck gold. Not only was he capable of synthesizing ether, he didn't even need to depend on a kami to do that. His Conjuration skills were still a decent Level 2, but raw ether synthesis? That was way above average.

That made him significant. Significant people stuck out in people's minds. A petty psychological trick, but at least it gave him a decent presentation.

"He doesn't look like much," said the overseer.

"It's part of my super-secret strategy that makes my opponents underestimate me."

The look on Tanya's face was priceless as she realized he had just mouthed off to one of the top brass, even though she didn't have the exact frame of reference to understand how. Lukas had been expecting a similar reaction from Zuken, but his smile widened.

Okay. Yes, Tanya had warned him about trying to be a smart-ass, but that didn't mean he'd succeed at following her advice.

Zuken snorted. "Apologies. My friend here is rather independently minded. You know how it is with Maluscian hires."

The overseer scrunched his nose and replied in the wry tone of a man engaging in understatement. "As always, you bring me the most vulgar of requests, Banksi."

"You know I'm owed a couple of favors, Overseer," Zuken replied. There was an undercurrent of sternness in his voice. "Compared to what I could ask, this is but a tiny little arrangement."

The overseer shook his head like an old elephant trying to shake off fleas. "This is neither tiny nor little. You ask me to make a no-name nomad into a full-fledged adventurer of the Empire and enlist him under the Shrine. That's as close to sacrilege as one gets."

"I do not want you to enlist him as a member. Just enough paperwork to keep the army from interfering."

"I don't see why you're making such a big fuss about it. Metamancer or not, he's just a Maluscian hire."

"A Maluscian hire that can trounce anyone you throw at him."

The man squinted at Lukas, giving him an appraising look. "That's a bold claim you're making, Banksi."

"The only kind of claim there is."

Lukas glanced around to meet Tanya's face. She hadn't told him anything about fighting others. But he supposed in a world where Potential and skill were quantifiable, almost anything could be solved by gladiatorial fights. Everything looked like a nail when all you had was a hammer.

"And would you mind proving it?" the overseer challenged.

Zuken didn't reply. Instead he just turned towards Lukas, his eyes staring meaningfully. Asking him. Quantifying him. Demanding that he prove himself.

"I know this is a little sudden, given your injury," said Zuken, "but do you think you're up for a practice match?"

Good question. Was he? His body certainly felt fine, and stronger than before. A battle would allow him to test out his new abilities and showcase a little Metamancy for his audience. He knew what this was. Not a test of his abilities, but a boast.

Their eyes met.

Can you justify my confidence in your power? his eyes said. Zuken wasn't asking him to win. He was asking him to dominate. To utterly destroy the opponent and make a show out of it.

That was fine. Shows, he could do.

"I can," Lukas replied. "But you know I don't do free shows."

Olfric choked.

"Spirited, aren't you?" The overseer laughed. "Say, Banksi, a thousand mezals should do, right?"

"How about two thousand?" Zuken offered. He turned towards Lukas. "If you win, half of that is yours."

Lukas gave him a brief nod. "When do you wish that to happen?"

Zuken's mouth twitched as if he was about to smile but thought better of it. "Now."

Lukas blinked. "Against?"

"One of my men should do," The overseer replied, giving Lukas a thorough once-over. "Suketh here has been part of security for over three years."

He turned to Zuken. "If your hire survives him, then we'll talk."

"Humph!" said one soldier, whom Lukas recognized was probably Suketh. The hulking, armored man gave him a look dripping with condescension. "I won't blame you if you run away, kid. It's almost impossible to gain status after losing face in front of the overseer. Go back home to your bunch of tree-hugging vagrants and no one will think less of you."

Lukas arched an eyebrow at him but said nothing. He watched as the man walked ahead of him with a strut in his step, no doubt already preparing his victory speech post his supposedly easy victory. He saw Zuken and the rest of the crowd follow Suketh towards the courtyard and sighed.

When in Rome . . . he told himself.

* * *

The dull fight that just occurred couldn't be called a duel. It was too fast and uneventful for that. For the few that were watching the spar, it was all about seeing a thirty-something man, covered in mail from head to toe, fire off some moderately strong Wind-based attacks using his broadsword, at the strange, young metamancer in a sleeveless shirt and pants, missing every time, and then being beaten barehandedly by said young man until he couldn't stand anymore.

Heck, when the elder fighter attempted to stab Lukas with his weapon, it snapped as soon as it came into contact with Lukas's palm. Lukas didn't know if his technique was just that strong or if the blade was simply that fragile, but it was disappointing nonetheless.

He idly watched as the other guards took the downed man away to receive treatment for his bruises and a minor concussion. The last bit was more of a precautionary measure, just in case Suketh turned out to be a stubborn idiot, or worse, a sore loser. Even if you broke their arms and legs, there was always a chance that they'd cast some kind of potentially dangerous hit at your back as a last resort.

Lukas shuddered. Even now, he remembered being caught off-guard by that bastard Olfric's attack.

"You've gotten faster." Zuken walked into the duel zone, as the other guards took away the downed Suketh to get treated for bruises and a minor concussion. "You didn't even need to use Metamancy to defeat him." His eyes flashed knowingly. "No, it was more like you knew what his skill set was before the fight even began. You weren't concerned in the slightest when he attacked you with that blade."

Lukas glanced at Tanya and then back to Zuken. He could lie about using ether to shape Suketh's Wind and use it against him. That Suketh had projected his attacks too clearly. That he had used his lifeforce to fortify himself and pinpointed his blows to shatter Suketh's blade.

Then he opened his mouth.

"What can I say? I mean, really, he's kinda *weak.*"

Tanya's eyes twitched.

It took all his resolve to not chuckle out loud.

In hindsight, now that he was using his siphoned skills against regular people, he was finally beginning to understand why a Level 2 skill was considered such a bigger deal over a Level 1. Even the passive effect of Seismic Sensing told him where Suketh was without needing to look at him. Seeing the bremetan's trajectories through Shatterpoint Intuition felt like watching a snail in action. Especially with tachypsychia doubling his perception speed.

"Well?" Zuken asked.

"I'm not sure I actually heard a question there," said Lukas, more amused than offended. He hadn't expected Zuken and his ilk to just trust him sight unseen. If he had, Lukas would have merely assumed he was naïve at best, a fool at worst.

"The overseer does not suffer fools. Every single one of his security is Level 15 or higher and has enough skill to go toe-to-toe with a Bronze-tier adventurer like Tanya and Olfric. And you defeated one of them without even trying."

Lukas glanced at Tanya, wondering *how in hell* she was placed in the same tier as Olfric. Even without the power of that strange Frost, she was easily leagues above the former aquamancer. Part of him itched to see where he stood against her now that he had leveled up again, with a greater well of power now at his fingertips.

"Well, other than the fact that you're wrong, I didn't actually hear a question there. Again."

He could see that brief twitch in Tanya's body movements. She was barely keeping herself from face-palming.

"Wrong? Wrong in what?" Zuken inquired. "I'm a hundred percent sure about the competence of the overseer's security staff."

"Oh no, you're not wrong about that," Lukas easily admitted, wiping dust off his clothes. "I meant your comment about Tanya being in the same league as him."

He thumbed at Olfric, whose reaction was more muted. Surprisingly, he seemed to accept it.

"When did this discussion become about me?" Tanya demanded. Lukas didn't need to read her mind to sense her growing anxiety. It reminded him of his own situation back at the yokai camp. Just what kind of agreement forced her to play ball with these guys?

Time would tell.

"Ask him," Lukas gestured at Zuken. "Also, about my hiring? I'd like a full accounting. Details of my job, work hours, perks, and benefits. You know, the usual."

"Someone's in a hurry," Elena noted.

Lukas cocked his head and looked directly at her. "It's called taking precautions. So that next time, I have a legal reason to say no, when I'm dragged into someone's freak show."

Elena looked taken aback by the bite in his tone.

It was Zuken who broke the tension. "I agree. You'll get your documentation as soon as we can iron out a few terms."

"I'm listening."

Zuken actually stopped to consider. "Not here," he replied after a moment. "I have some business to take care of with the overseer. "Come to my office in the evening. Tanya can show you the way. And Aguilar, *honesty* is the only thing that works with me. Please keep that in mind."

With those words, Zuken turned around and left, with Elena and Olfric following shortly behind.

"Well . . ." Lukas trailed off, "that went well."

CHAPTER 4

DEMIGOD

You're almost late," Zuken stated dryly as he went over some paperwork behind his desk, not even looking up as Lukas entered the room with Tanya in tow.

The terramancer sat on a plush chair, everything save his head and shoulders obstructed from Lukas's line of sight by the folders stacked upon each other in front of him. Elena sat to the left of him, her brunette hair tied backwards into a single ponytail. She wore a formal white shirt, a black skirt with a slash on one side that showed off a generous portion of her thigh, and shoes that seemed to be a study in high-heeled torture devices.

"Sorry," Lukas replied half-heartedly, "I got lost in a bit of soul-searching."

Tanya made an odd, throaty noise from behind.

"What?" Lukas challenged, glancing back at her. "It wasn't like we agreed to a particular hour."

He had decided to play the game. If Zuken and his crew thought that he shared a deeper relationship with Tanya, then he was going to give them what they expected to see. The entire day he had been acting overly casual with her, as if they were long-term acquaintances, if not friends.

It was driving her insane.

And he loved every second of it.

Zuken looked amused at his scorn. "That is true. Also, my thanks for cooperating earlier. The overseer's presence sped up my plans a bit, especially with your little demonstration."

Lukas nodded.

"Tatun was impressed by your performance. You now have his attention." Zuken paused for a moment. "I'm not sure that's a good thing."

Lukas arched an eyebrow.

"Tatun has this habit of trying to . . . pick a lucky bicorn out of the herd of adventurers. Someone who shows potential. Stamp his own brand on them."

"And you think . . ."

"That he will do the same to you? He will try, yes. You should expect extremely expensive presents from him soon. He's predictable that way. The good thing about this is that your documentation will be ironclad. Tatun wouldn't want the army sniffing around his newest toy. That you work for me only makes him want you more."

"And can I be his bicorn?"

Zuken tilted his head to look at him obliquely. "Sure. Join a person you've never known over a man that knows you're not a bremetan, not even from this world, and capable of manacrafting without a kami. And is getting you everything anyway."

Both Elena and Tanya were giving him odd looks.

A wicked smile played on Lukas's lips. "I see. I'm being intimidated. Are you going to tell me why, or do I get three guesses?"

"Stop being a wiseass, Lukas," said Tanya. "None of us want the overseer's attention on us."

"Then you should've thought of that before throwing me into the fight."

"I admit that was hasty on my part. In my defense, I didn't expect you to trounce his candidate so easily. Tatun will now watch you much more closely. People with your power or skill do not just pop up out of nowhere. This can be a benefit. Or it might prove to be a curse."

"For you?"

"For everyone." It was Elena that answered. "Don't get cocky. Not everything is about you."

"But for that to be true, I'd have to *not* be the center of the universe."

He ignored Tanya's throaty growl and looked around at the room. It was a reflection of the person working within it. Every piece of furniture, every pen, paper, file cabinet, and device needed for the job was meticulously positioned and organized. Granted, a third of this paperwork would have been absent had computers existed in this universe, but he knew better than to make suggestions on that end without getting a better idea of the true potential of the world around him.

"Fine," he consented. "What's the issue?"

Zuken tilted his head slightly to one side. Sitting like that, he wasn't at all imposing to look at. A man in his good shape, probably in his late twenties or early thirties, with a respectable amount of muscle, in the way of a long-distance runner or soccer coach, but too heavy in the shoulders and arms for that to be all he did.

He glanced at Tanya and spoke in a clear baritone, "I need everyone to leave. I have private business with Aguilar."

"But Zuken—" Elena objected.

Zuken raised his hand. "You know the risks and the rewards. This is something I have to do myself."

"Are you certain this is a good idea?" Tanya asked. Lukas wasn't sure if she was worried about Zuken or for him, which felt oddly refreshing. Or maybe that was because after spending an inordinate amount of time in the presence of entities that could have killed him on a whim, he was finally towering over others.

In less than ten seconds, the room was empty save for the two men sitting on opposite sides of the large, wooden desk, gazing at each other with different levels of wariness and expectation, as if trying to figure out what was running through the other's mind. Once again, it was a poetic repetition of the events that had transpired back in the yokai territory.

"Where is that metal band?" Zuken asked after several moments of silence.

Lukas tapped his abdomen. "It reacts to the oddest of things. So I made it into an undershirt."

"An . . . undershirt?"

"It's a slime. It can become whatever it wants."

The edges of Zuken's mouth twisted into a small frown. "Or whatever *you* want it to be."

"That too." Lukas beamed at him. Smiling always seemed to annoy people more than insulting them. Or maybe he just had an annoying smile.

Zuken seemed a little put off by his attitude. "We had some very interesting experiences with that band. I've seen automatons crafted out of metal, as well as sentient weapons that hold many mysteries within them. But a complete living creature? That's new, even for me."

"It's a big world." Lukas shrugged.

The terramancer nodded acceptingly and looked down at the papers in front of him. "Lukas Aguilar. Origin, Outsider. Race, phenotypically bremetan. Eyes, brown. Hair color, black. Assumed age, twenty-one. It is possible your world arose from an Asukan invasion in the past. Estimated lifeforce output, five thousand units. Estimated mana output, 6300 units."

Lukas stood there, suddenly very wary. He had expected this, but the sudden, blunt impact had caught him off guard.

"Nature of mana, fire, and ether. Kami—" Zuken met his eyes. "None."

And right there was the first roadblock. Dead or alive, his body had been under observation for over a month. Spiritism arose out of voluntary sacrifice of Soul Capacity, so it wasn't surprising they had technologies to determine if someone had a kami in them or not.

Kind of like thermal-imaging cameras, only for the soul.

And knowing he was an Outsider was one thing, but him demonstrating the ability to perform manacrafting without a kami? That was something else.

"Are you a deviant?" Zuken asked.

Lukas blinked. "And that is?"

"Someone of mixed heritage. I know the jotun are wielders of Fire and Frost, depending on their origins. The svartalfar's affinity for Terramancy is well-known and feared for good reason. The ljósálfars twist light to their will and the vanir can use the World Energy directly." He paused for a moment. "All of them are physical beings but are attuned to a singular form of mana. But you, on the other hand—" He trailed off.

"I can use multiple elements," Lukas affirmed, wondering where this was leading. "And no, I'm not a deviant."

Zuken cupped his chin. "I assumed as much."

"Are we going to have a problem?"

"Potentially. It's not unheard of for an adventurer to wield multiple kami, or boast enough Soul Capacity to bring out multiple affinities of their kami, but they're rare, and are usually Gold-tier or higher. But not only can you use multiple elements, you do it without one."

Lukas eyed him.

"I have a couple of questions, and I need you to answer them truthfully. Be advised, if you try to lie to me, I'll react appropriately."

"Honestly, that's not much of an incentive for me to be truthful either."

The man narrowed his eyes. "I'm trying to help you, Lukas."

"You're trying to help me help yourself," Lukas shot back. "I wasn't born yesterday. You've had my body sitting in your labs for over a month. God knows what sort of tests you've done on me. So, no, if you're hounding me for questions, it is to seek answers, not help me."

"And you're against this? Us finding out more about you?"

"I'd like you to call a spade a spade."

"I suppose that much I can agree on," the man murmured. "Yes, I have questions, and I'd like you to answer them. Truthfully. In return, I swear I'm not going to act against you."

Lukas narrowed his eyes. "I'll keep that in mind."

Zuken nodded.

"Shoot. What do you want to know?"

"Where are you from?"

"Earth."

"Which is a—"

"Realm, from what I understand. Much like this one."

"And your people travel to this world often?"

"Can't say."

"Why?"

Lukas weighed his options. Tanya's image of Zuken painted him as a man of connections and questionable motives. He didn't consider even for a second that the man was keeping him here because of some misguided sense of fair play. No, Zuken had seen something valuable in him but didn't know his exact worth.

That was what this meeting was for.

Very well. Two could play at this game.

"I have reasons to believe that something destroyed my world, or at least damaged it beyond repair. It is possible that there was an Asukan invasion on my world earlier, and possibly Nordic ones as well, since I recognize species from both, and well—your folks look like mine do."

"Interesting." Zuken crossed his fingers and rested his chin upon them. "And how did you get here?"

"My parents put me on a baby shuttle and sent me to a different world so that I could live a normal life full of sunshine and flowers. Instead, I got stuck in a cave and encountered you folks."

Zuken let out a brief snort of amusement. "I suppose I walked into that one myself. But levity aside, what would you say is the Soul Capacity of the average . . . whatever it is you call yourself?"

"Human."

"Right. That."

"Why do you ask?"

"Humor me."

Lukas narrowed his eyes. This was a trick question, and he knew it. He already knew that lifeforce and mana were measurable, the presence and absence of kami detectable. In that light, how impossible would it be it to measure one's Soul Capacity?

"What's there to think about? Surely that's not a hard question?"

Oh yeah, this was a trap alright. But staying silent would make things worse.

No value, no matter how great or small, would ever match up to infinity. Nothing would explain the impossible amount of Soul Capacity he had within himself. So instead, he went for the truth.

"Nothing."

"Excuse me?"

Lukas smiled. The truth was, at times, stranger than fiction. Yeah, it'd be interesting to see him tackle this one. "Nothing. Absolutely zero. People on Earth *did not have* Soul Capacity. We did not level up. Or have skills."

"No Soul Capacity. No skills," Zuken repeated dumbly.

Lukas beamed. He could practically see the gears running in the terramancer's mind. Seeing him struggle to face a truth so byzantine reminded him of himself when Inanna had first unveiled her existence before his eyes.

"Nothing. We led our entire lives, reliant on our intelligence and technology. No lifeforce, no mana, nothing. At least not in the last two thousand years. Before that, not so sure."

"And why not?"

"Because I have genuine reason to believe that gods and goddesses existed back in my world back then. As did demons. And lifeforce and mana and all that."

"But not any longer?"

Lukas shook his head.

"And yet *you* do."

"Well," Lukas drawled, "all that potential had to go somewhere."

He let that one hang there. And given the gobsmacked expression on Zuken's face, the effect was just as devastating.

"You . . . you can't be serious."

"I'm not," Lukas replied with a straight face. Crossing his arms, he regarded Zuken's growing scowl. "What? You expect me to just *tell* you stuff like that? Nothing is free. You want information? *Pay for it.*"

It was hard not to smile. Zuken was no doubt trying to sort between what was true, and what wasn't. The fact that every single thing he had revealed had been the absolute truth while simultaneously being among the most unbelievable things Zuken had ever heard was not lost on him.

"Do you think this is a joke?" Zuken growled. "The Cobalt Army would be happy to pay a hefty amount to get their hands on you."

"If you tell them about me, then yes."

"And what's stopping me?" Zuken asked coolly.

Lukas pressed his palms against the table and regarded the terramancer. "We had a bargain. I help you with the anomaly, and you get me documentation and a job."

"And I am keeping my word," said Zuken, just as calm. "Keeping your origins a secret was not a part of our deal."

"And thus you'd hold my Outsider status over my head and force me to comply with your new demands?"

"I don't see what is stopping me. Do you?"

Lukas eyed him. Zuken had just established that he *knew* exactly what Lukas was capable of, as well as the towering differences between them. And despite that, he wanted *him* to react with fear and caution.

Why? Because of fear of prosecution from the army? Could the man be betting so much on the army's arrival and their ability to trap him? Perhaps he had already had the army ready to move in if the shit hit the fan? It would definitely explain why he had Tanya and the others leave. Was this what he had meant when he had mentioned "risks" and "possibilities" to Elena earlier?

No.

No, it was too simple. Too . . . direct.

For the first time since waking up, Lukas used tachypsychia. Not to fight but to *think*. The world around him slowed down to a crawl. His initial burst of panic died down, and his thoughts began racing a hundred miles a minute. Zuken had his body for over a month. No doubt he had performed whatever experiments he could, and derived whatever conclusions that were possible. And *after* this period of experimentation, he had practically *showed off* Lukas to the overseer, like a prized object in a collection.

No sane person would do that unless he intended to keep said object for a considerable period of time.

At least, that was how it would have happened on Earth.

The pounding of his heart slowly abated with that thought until it approached something that he could at least pretend was normal.

"Yes," he said at last.

"Excuse me?"

"If you wanted to, you'd have done that already, instead of having this conversation and gloating about it."

The terramancer stared back at him, his face set in a half frown, thoughts indecipherable, before giving a curt nod. Then he calmly raised his right hand and flicked his fingers once, and the ambient energy inside the office room drastically shifted.

"I had estimated a sixty percent chance of you attacking me right off the bat," Zuken said, as he continued to watch him. "I could almost see you considering alternatives, verifying your chances against a possible army onslaught, and every other possibility you could think of. That you could arrive at a satisfying conclusion makes me feel a lot more confident about your involvement in our world."

Lukas's throat constricted at the thought of being so predictable, but he managed to keep his composure. "What do you mean?"

Zuken wrinkled up his face, as if carefully considering what he would say, taking his well-being into account with an almost grandfatherly concern. "I might not look like it, but I have *some* experience dealing with beings that eclipse me both in raw Potential and strength. And I'm certainly not foolish enough to deny the existence of beings above my power, nor their ability to cause unbridled chaos. So far, you've shown no inclination towards disruptive tendencies, bar your unorthodox attitude and outspoken behavior, especially in matters of social hierarchy."

Lukas felt like a kindergartener being condescended to by a teacher. Zuken's words carried with them a sense of finality, but despite that, Lukas wasn't sure what the man was going for.

"Tell me—"The terramancer's eyes drilled into him. "Just why are you hiding the fact that you're a fucking *demigod?*"

From entities such as Perseus and Heracles in Greek mythos to the likes of Cu Chulainn and Scathatch in Proto-Germanic lore, the concept of a "demigod" described those who either were born to or rose to great powers, eventually becoming a beacon of their era. A person whose accomplishments were so above expectation that it was easier to believe them to have a divine origin than to try to explain their otherwise unexplainable conquests.

Had he been back on Earth, Lukas would have laughed his head off and called Zuken a lunatic for suggesting something so insane. But since his arrival, he had met an actual goddess and seen the utter devastation she could cause, even while running on fumes. Sure, he was stronger and far more skilled than ever, but to be considered anything remotely associated with godhood?

Even with a "demi" prefix.

He opened his mouth to respond with a dry retort, but his words died on his tongue. Instead, Inanna's last words resonated within his mind. Words that he had heard but not really internalized back then:

I used my Presence to bind your shattered Soul.

Inanna had used her divinity to resurrect him. Her divinity. Her presence. That which made her a goddess. She used that as a fabric to reforge him, to bring him back and, in so doing, sacrificed herself. But that presence, that divinity—it was still there, immersed in the shards that made up Lukas's soul.

It was still there in him.

Divinity.

Power of a goddess.

Power that belonged to Inanna.

But how did this bremetan find out about that bit? Solana, for all her tricks, hadn't been able to figure out anything about Inanna's presence. Was Asukan technology really so advanced that they could test for "divinity" within a soul? What was this "divinity" anyway?

He really hoped that wasn't the case.

Either way, his mind began to run through worst-case scenarios as fast as he could.

"Demigod," he said slowly. "What makes you think that?"

Zuken began listing on his fingers: "You ignore the Eternal Light and cast a shadow in its presence, and just as easily, allow it to affect you as any of us. You *die* and yet your body shows no signs of rotting. You miraculously resurrect yourself. Even though you don't have a kami, you can conjure both lifeforce and multiple kinds of mana. *And* you've nigh endless Soul Capacity."

Damn it. When put like that, it sounded suspicious. And insane.

"And that makes me a demigod?" he asked. "I also killed an anomaly. Would a demigod do that?"

"No," Zuken admitted. "They wouldn't. No demigod would ever commit that kind of sacrilege. But that's not all, is it? The anomaly's Guardian looked like you. Not just that, it talked to you. Like you share a history. And I remember what it said."

Their two pairs of brown eyes met each other.

"*You still have much to learn about omphaloi.* That's what it said. To you." Zuken relaxed into his chair. "I've spent a long time researching anomalies during your . . . sleep, and from what I understand, the Guardians are manifestations of the anomaly's consciousness. If what you say is true, you're not of this world. So why is—correction, *was*—*this* anomaly so interested in *you?*"

"Even if it was," Lukas murmured, never once looking away, "do you really think I'd tell you?"

"You're evading," Zuken replied, annoyance seeping into his words. "Answer the question."

Lukas crossed his legs and relaxed into his chair. "As I said before, I can't just *give* you that kind of information. It's too powerful."

"What's that supposed to mean?"

"It means I've played ball for quite some time. If you want more answers, I'm gonna start charging."

Zuken folded his arms. "What do you want? If it is the woman you cry out for in your sleep, I'm afraid I cannot get her back to you."

A scowl darkened Lukas's features. "Tanya told on me?"

"No, she didn't. I had you placed under observation. In fact, when Olfric tried to connect this with the yokai, Tanya defended you."

"Oh," he mumbled, caught off guard by her silent show of support.

"I will be blunt, Aguilar. I don't want to lose a rare specimen like you, and you can't desert me. If you do, I've taken steps to ensure the Empire comes after you. Depending on what faction gets their hands on you first, you'll either be executed out of sheer paranoia, dissected for study, or simply made to disappear. Several clans would be ready to sell their firstborns to get a chance to research your 'divinity' and try to replicate it."

Why does that sound so familiar?

"But I can tell that you're a powerful tool. And I'm interested in seeing you grow. Register yourself as an adventurer and demonstrate your true potential before everyone else. Tell me whatever you need—money, resources, information—I'll provide it all. But in return, I want answers. All of them. I want your secrets. I want to study your unique nature, your powers. So I ask, once again, *what is it that you truly want?*"

Lukas froze in indecision. On the one hand, Banksi was a collector and a treasure trove of resources. If he gave up on this deal, he'd likely not get another opportunity like this. With Banksi's support, he had better chances of finding out what happened with Inanna and how to bring her back.

But on the other hand . . .

This was too easy. Too quick. Could he trust him with that information? He might have gained a deeper insight into Zuken Banksi, but that didn't negate the fact that he knew nothing about the man's agenda. It was entirely possible that all of this was simply an act—a planned performance to convince him to trust him and get the information out of him.

But what if it wasn't?

He already had his bodily fluids. Lukas had been dead for a month and then had spent weeks waking out of it. There was no doubt Banksi had already collected all the information he could have from analyzing him physically. No, what the man really wanted was a correct estimate of his Potential. Lukas could already perform Metamancy and Pyromancy. Perhaps Zuken wanted to see if he could repeat that with the other elements as well?

Breathing slowly and closing his eyes, Lukas calmed himself down and emptied himself of his emotions.

He closed his eyes.

He wasn't allowed to lose.

He was only allowed to win. He had to solve this problem.

Being a lawyer was all about problem-solving. Taking a complex situation, pulling it apart, and then putting it back together in a way that benefited one's argument. However, you couldn't always solve the entire thing all at once. You had to look away from the biggest problem and examine the smaller ones. If he focused on the enormity of the former, he'd lose focus and suffer defeat.

In this case, the larger, overarching issue was Zuken Banksi and his motives. There were simply too many variables, too little information, and too many high-risk factors to reach a conclusion.

Lukas ignored that.

The key was to start small. Focus on solving what he could. Build some solid ground beneath his feet. Something to stand on. Something to base his existing hypothesis and transform the impossible problem into difficult-but-solvable. He was looking too closely at the tree's trunk. To see the entire forest, he'd have to take several steps back.

And so he did. He separated himself from the fear, the paranoia, and the confusion burning within him. It was time to consider one question at a time.

Zuken wanted information. He wanted his secrets. The problem was, Lukas himself did not know what he was. Inanna was no more, and he needed information. On the world. On anomalies and omphaloi. On divinity.

No. That was still too broad in scope. He had to narrow it further.

Zuken wanted information. And Lukas needed to find a way to get Inanna back, without revealing everything. And that meant understanding exactly what Inanna did to him.

Better reduce it even further.

What kind of information would solve both his and Zuken's desires?

The answer was simple.

Lukas opened his eyes and smiled. "Fine. You win. But the truth is, there are several things about myself and my powers that I don't yet understand. You want my secrets? Fine. But you'll have to help me decipher them first."

Zuken frowned. Clearly the conversation wasn't going in a direction he was fond of. "And what kind of help would that be?"

"I need information. Texts. Ancient tomes. Grimoires or whatever you call them in this world. Research material."

"On what?"

"An analysis of divinity itself. Gods. Goddesses. What makes them. What kills them. What brings them back. I also want what you can get me on anomalies."

"A demigod, wanting to know more about divinity?" Zuken leaned forward, with a smile that seemed to say, "I have you figured out." "Or . . . is that just you trying to find out what *we* know about divinity? This isn't your research. This is you trying to figure out the limits of our own understanding of your kind."

"Oh my." Lukas gave his best fake smile. "Look at you. You've figured me out completely."

Zuken glared at him.

He casually met his gaze.

Nobody spoke for two long seconds. Then Zuken's evident anger evaporated. His expression turned placid and enigmatic. "You'll give me what I want, but in return, take everything my civilization has on your kind. That's an interesting quagmire you have me in."

Lukas gave him a lopsided grin. "So, do we have an accord?"

Zuken laughed. "It appears we do."

CHAPTER 5

———

ELENA

Lukas Aguilar frowned at the spotless ceiling above him.

For someone used to the infinite blackness of a starry sky, living in a world where the concept of "darkness" and "shadows" were practically anathema was weird as shit. There were no artificial lights—no neons, no LEDs, nothing at all. Every single surface shone, as if light was falling directly on it. No matter whichever way he turned his face, and however much he squinted his eyes, there was absolutely *no shadow*.

Anywhere.

No shadow. No darkness. People divided days and nights based on the color of the sky. When the sun was up, the sky was lit up with vibrant crimson and yellow. Even after sunset, the rest of the world seemed to magically stay illuminated.

Gods, he hated it. He hated it so much that he'd often just shut his eyes to embrace the familiar darkness that provided. At the very least, the damned Eternal Light didn't reach there. He really didn't know what he'd do if it did. There were moments when Lukas wished for the darkness of the decrepit cave he had found himself in. Even the pitch blackness of the yokai prison now felt more welcoming than this byzantine, ever-bright, shadowless world.

If not for his newly gained omphalos functions, he'd probably have lost it already.

Thinking about shadows and the yokai reminded him of a certain black-haired monstrosity.

Solana.

She had promised that she'd kill him if he ever joined the Asukan side. Granted, Tanya and her folks had taken his supposed corpse to Haviskali without his knowing, but his prior agreement kind of implied that they had his permission. Besides, it wasn't like Solana was the goody-two-shoes type either. She might have kept her word about hiring him, albeit it with a literal sword hanging above his head, promising a gruesome death should he ever leave her employment. Also, she had tried to manipulate him into Sinning, making it impossible for him to join the other side. It was this sort of backstabbing politics that reminded him of back home. Humanity might not have had lifeforce, mana, or any of these myriad powers, but their potential for treachery and crimes made Solana look like a newbie.

A knock sounded on the door, breaking him out of his reverie.

Prey Found You

Deactivate Created Territory?

Territory Creation. A brand-new omphalos function he had gained after waking up in Haviskali. A reflection of how his body was slowly changing more and more into an anomaly. He might still *look* human, but the changes were clear if one knew where to look. Increased lifeforce and mana production, increased rejuvenation and physical strength—all of them were impressive by themselves, but the real signs were far more subtle.

Living anomaly—the ability to ignore Rules that were alien to Earth.

Territory Creation—the ability to create a . . . well, a territory around himself, one where only the Rules of *his* world existed, and nothing else. A boundary layer of reality that he could "ship" over the real world outside, where light and shadow were counterparts of each other, instead of this fraud called Eternal Light.

And of course, Soul Siphon.

Not to mention the Screen—which Lukas was slowly recognizing as the interface between his own spiritual existence and the omphalos within him— was becoming more interactive, more responsive to his commands.

Living Anomaly Deactivated within Created Territory
Created Territory Deactivated

And just like that, the shadows around him dissipated, and Lukas got out of bed.

Someone knocked on the door again.

Scanning Registered Prey
Found Matches with "Changeling"

Accessing Monster Prototype Array
Accessing species "Changeling"

. . .

Found NULL

RECOMMENDATION
Soul Siphon?

Lukas rolled his eyes.

Recommendation for Soul Siphon of "Changeling" Rejected
Acknowledged.

Gone were the days where he had to play twenty questions to get the Screen to do something productive. Now? It was literally recommending he act like an anomaly and add as many prototypes as he could. The good part about this was that the Screen was listening to him now. The bad side? It was a pain in the ass.

PRIME HOST has ignored 27 recommendations
Possible Lack of Synchronization between HOST and OMPHALOS
Re-enact Babysitter Protocol?

Yeah, that's what he was talking about.

There was a third knock at the door.

"Coming!" he yelled and strode towards the door. Holding it wide open, he found Elena lounging against the doorframe, her lips twisted in resigned annoyance and a single eyebrow raised, as if demanding an apology.

"Yeah?" he ventured, wondering why the changeling had come for him. At first sight, one would think that Olfric was the one that held maximum animosity towards him. But the reality was that Olfric Bergott was a simple person that liked things to fall into neat boxes. And when he encountered something that didn't fit into his preconceived notions of reality, he tended to react a bit . . . aggressively.

That was all.

Elena though . . .

"Zuken asked me to get you."

Lukas frowned. "For?"

"To begin your training."

Lukas blinked. Surely she didn't mean actual training? Tanya might still be able to best him in a head-on battle, but she was an exception. Compared to her, Zuken was just . . . average.

"What kind of training?"

Elena peered around into Lukas's room, as if expecting someone inside. "I'm not sure of the particulars, but he wants you to get started on the Shikigami Ritual."

"The what?"

"The Shikigami Ritual," she repeated. "It's the spell that spiritists cast to trap kami and use them as forges for manacrafting."

Interesting. Maybe he really was being serious about Lukas being spotted.

"He wants you to learn the spell and see if you can bind a kami to yourself. Preferably one that can perform—"

"Metamancy," Lukas finished for her.

"Right."

"And who's gonna teach me?"

"Mostly Tanya, but Zuken wants Olfric to give you a thorough grounding on the subject."

Lukas arched an eyebrow. The idea that he'd be taught to wield kami by the same person who lost his own to him was ironic on multiple levels. "Olfric? I thought he didn't have a kami any longer."

That removed all expression from Elena's face. "That . . . might be so, but he's trained in the onmyodo arts. Most spiritists just end up mugging the spell and performing it, but not him. Olfric really understands what he's doing."

Lukas frowned. That reminded him of Inanna's words. She had mentioned the difference between spellcrafting and skills, promising to revisit the topic later. She had said that a spell was carried out in the mind of the caster and often employed tools to create suitable conditions for performing it. She might have said more, but he hadn't been in any condition to pay attention.

Having your brain crumble could do that to you.

"And I guess he's terribly enthusiastic about teaching me this stuff."

"Yes." Elena seemed inordinately proud that her voice hadn't hitched at all. Lukas smirked.

The changeling sighed. "Olfric needs a kami, but as he is now, trying to find another one will get him killed."

"And so Banksi wants him to teach me, so that we both go together and help each other. No, wait, he's probably roped Tanya into this just to ensure I don't end up spilling Olfric's guts after he runs his mouth and annoys me a bit too much."

"I wouldn't put it that way—"

"But it fits, doesn't it?"

Elena groaned. "Just come with me, already."

"Tell me this," he persisted. "How does Banksi know that I can even *do* this ritual in the first place?"

"He doesn't, but we can find out if you just get on with it."

"Fine! Fine!"

Lukas straightened his clothing, feeling Blob shift around over his chest. Blob wasn't the most reliable thing he knew, but he could trust the aqāru-slime to instantly react if something tried to physically harm him. How that reaction would turn out though was anybody's guess.

Closing his door from the outside, he joined Elena as she moved down the hallway. If Zuken wanted Olfric to teach him, then he wasn't going to complain, no matter what the hour. They walked down the steps to the first floor, crossing the armory that contained several sets of chain mail and an enormous number of weapons that Banksi had collected for whatever reason. There were a couple of half-finished furniture projects lying in the next room. The kitchen, however, was bustling with activity.

And then Elena paused in her tracks.

Lukas mirrored her.

"Lukas . . . That's what you're called, right?"

"Last I checked, yes."

He wasn't sure what Elena wanted to talk to him about, but he was certain she had planned it out in her head.

She turned and faced him, meeting his eyes. A tingle went through his body. She had sharp cheekbones, and her bright gray-silver eyes seemed capable of boring through plate steel. Long, brown tresses fell on either side of her head, accentuating her slender, elfin ears.

And yet—

There was something odd about her. In the way she carried herself. She did not have the ethereal, impossible beauty that was Inanna, or the cruel, poisonous allure that Tanya's frosty self exuded. Instead it was one of those sensations you have trouble remembering afterward, like the last moments of a dream. The sort that you know you're going to forget once you awaken, and you can't believe you could lose something so significant, so undeniably tangible.

It was simply a *fact*, like gravity, that everyone's attention should be directed to her face. Her eyes. An unconscious act performed, oblivious to the fact that their minds were already captured. As would Lukas have been, if not for the Level-5 Alpha Condition holding vigil at the back of his mind.

The tingling sensation faded and the real Elena came into focus.

He looked at her. Her body language. Her mannerisms. The way she asserted herself.

His mind threw up a bunch of contradictions. For someone capable of ensnaring anyone, Elena appeared like she knew what people found so attractive about her but didn't quite get why it was so. At the same time, she had this bubbly, airheaded facade in front of others. To Lukas, however, she felt different. Not someone who reveled in her power to manipulate others, but one that thought of it as just a big joke.

Lukas gave her an edged smile. "Yes?"

"Why can't I sense your mind?"

"Excuse me?"

She arched an eyebrow. "You know exactly what I mean. And you know *exactly* why it is so. I can read your face just fine, but your mind—your emotions. They just . . . slip away from me, and I want to know why."

Great, and now she expected him to share the reason behind his immunity with her. Lukas wasn't sure whether to laugh or scoff at the lack of professionalism that implied.

"You want me to tell you why . . ." Lukas trailed off, not bothering to hide his disbelief. "When I burst out laughing at you, do you think you'll be offended?"

The look of incomprehension on her face reminded him of a child stuck in the midst of trying to solve a difficult puzzle. Just a little more and she'd be throwing a tantrum.

He let out a harsh burst of laughter. "You . . . want me to . . . I mean, you really *expect* me to tell you why you can't manipulate me into doing what you want? That's so cute I could just put you in my pocket."

Elena bared her teeth in sudden anger and undisguised suspicion. "You may think you're funny, but I know better. There's something *wrong* about you."

Lukas cocked his head. "You're not really going to get anywhere by trying to intimidate me, you know."

"We'll see about that," Elena replied just as nonchalantly, as if discussing the weather. "Get this through your head, Aguilar. I don't trust you. Whatever lies you've fed Zuken, I'll get to the bottom of it. I'll stop you from taking advantage of his weakness."

His weakness?

"—and just because you're an Outsider doesn't mean you're safe."

Lukas narrowed his eyes and activated tachypsychia, allowing his perception to vastly slow down compared to the reality outside. As the time between heartbeats crawled slower and slower, he couldn't help but observe Elena's reactions in a new light. There was no doubt that she had gone out of her way to arrange for this little meeting, but whether these actions were a result of her own inability to read his mind, or a reaction from seeing Banksi's behavior, Lukas couldn't tell. And with that came a second realization that, unlike Olfric, blunt antagonism wasn't going to work on her. She literally read people's emotions as she talked to them. She had probably played every mind game around. No, if he wanted to deal with this mind-bending pixie, he had to play a whole different type of sport.

One that Inanna often played with him.

"I see," he said, meeting her eyes. "You love him."

He had half expected Elena to give an explosive reaction to his crass statement. Maybe a blush, maybe a flustered reaction, or an open denial. There was a chance that she'd even get angry or, worse, attack him—not that it would make any difference.

He certainly hadn't expected her to gaze blankly back at him and say—

"Love? Why'd you think that? Zuken is my employer," she said, the blandness now mixed with resolve. "And it's my job to ensure his well-being."

Huh. What side of Elena had he cracked open now?

"And you think that *I* mean him harm?"

"In what way is my opinion relevant to the truth?"

"Is there any way it isn't?" he shot back.

She let out a soft, musical laugh. "You think you can worm out secrets about my business with him?"

"Was that what I was aiming for?"

"Are we going to stand around answering each other's questions with more questions?" she demanded.

His smile widened. "Would you like that?"

She lifted a hand, capitulating. Lukas inclined his head slightly, a gracious victor. He had endless grueling hours of excruciating wordplay with Inanna on his resume, and she had been a grandmaster of this art.

Elena gave him a look of pure calculation. "I would like to know why Zuken trusts you."

"Why not ask him yourself?"

She eyed him without actually looking at him.

"He wouldn't *tell* me."

His mouth twisted at one corner. "Ouch. That must have hurt."

"Did you psychomance his mind?"

Lukas arched an eyebrow. "What's that?"

"Don't play dumb. I've seen you stiffen and your pupils move superfast from time to time. You can slow or speed up your inner perception. Obviously you have *some* skill in Psionics."

Lukas was impressed. His instincts were right. There was a lot more to Elena than what met the eye.

"Lifeforce. Pyromancy. Metamancy. Regeneration. Psionics," she counted. "Anything you *can't* do?"

"Can't vanish myself off this world, apparently. It'd be nice not to deal with twenty thousand questions for once."

"Aguilar!" she replied sternly.

Lukas blinked and smiled. "Ah, so you do know my full name then. Fun."

Elena narrowed her eyes. "I can't believe I have to ask this. *Can you die?"*

Lukas shivered as the feeling of blackness enveloping him like a blanket came to mind. He couldn't help but also think of the time Quonnan had him possessed. Or the time Olfric had injured him. Or that time when Ryu had nearly skewered him with those fiery swords of his.

Oh hell.

"I don't know," he heard himself say, and it was an honest truth. After all the misses so far, he had no clue anymore.

Elena stared at him blankly. "You don't know?"

"The first few times I died, it just didn't take," Lukas explained lightly, scratching the back of his head. "I guess, I can, maybe. I don't intend to test it out though, if you don't mind."

She nodded slowly.

"You know," Lukas replied, "I'm a 'live and let live' kinda guy. All this antagonism, it isn't scoring any points with me. Whatever it is your employer wants with me, he can have it, but not if he—or you I suppose—keeps trying to step on my feet. I've already told him what I need, and we have an agreement. As long as he sticks to his part of it."

Elena gave him an irritable look. *"Fine!"* She said it like it was the vilest curse imaginable, and turned her back on him. "Follow me."

So he did.

"Does it feel any different?" Tanya asked.

"Is it supposed to?"

"It feels a little weird the first time around. But you'll get used to it."

"Oh."

He was trying out the brand-new wristbands that Zuken had gotten for him. He had seen Tanya and the others wearing them but figured they were a fashion accessory. Apparently they were much more than that.

"What do these even do?" he demanded, looking at the bands on either wrist. Jet black, with seven ornate spirals of silver running through them. Tanya had a similar pair, only hers were gray with five silver spirals. He seemed to recall that Banksi's had a dark, chocolate brown matrix while Olfric had Prussian blue ones. Elena? He doubted he had ever seen her wear any.

"These are fractals," Tanya explained, showing off her own. "You see, our bodies aren't exactly great at conducting mana, and end up getting poisoned or worse, directly affected by the conjured mana we produce—"

The memory of Quonnan incinerating her own host body came to mind.

"—so we use these fractals to amplify mana in our stead, allowing them to take the strain we cannot. Make no mistake, even with these, one can only channel so much mana before our elemental balance goes awry. That's . . . not a pretty sight."

"I hear you," Lukas replied, glancing at his own pair of fractals. "But looks aside, I can conjure mana just fine by myself. So why am I being forced into these?"

"Because even an ordinary pair of fractals increases one's mana output by twenty percent."

That stopped him short.

"And these?"

"Close to ninety percent," Tanya replied, smug little thing that she was. "But these are the most expensive of the lot, and not everyone has Zuken Banksi sponsoring them."

But Lukas was already ignoring her. He could almost *double* his mana output just by wearing these? And considering what he was currently capable of—

Maximum Mana Output	6325

Yeah. This was going to be fun.

"And I imagine the number of spirals are—"

"Proportional to your output."

"What about the colors?"

Tanya gave him an impish grin. "Fashion statements. It takes a rare spiritist to manipulate more than one element. Not all of us can be Outsiders, can we?"

Lukas arched an eyebrow at her but said nothing. He had seen Tanya effortlessly manipulate Frost to do her bidding, despite having a Wind kami at her command. But there was nothing to be gained from letting the others know that.

"You're supposed to be a metamancer," Elena chimed in, her airheaded mask back in place. The expression melted into her face so well that it was almost impossible to think she could be anything else.

"And that's why the black color."

"Why don't you try it out?" Tanya suggested.

Lukas shrugged. Reaching out to his mana was always an instinctive process. He'd never quite understood how he managed to eject flames, or craft ether for that matter, without so much as charring his body. He had seen Quonnan literally immolate herself, but nothing of that sort had happened when he had instinctively channeled fire, even for the first time.

Maybe it had something to do with the ley line network? Time would tell.

Lukas tentatively reached out to his power. He felt the familiar frosted coldness of ether, and the cold, brimming power that came with it. Just by holding that power, everything felt more . . . real somehow. While not the true power of creation that Anomalous Energy was, Metamancy could still be used to materialize some very cool things.

His first instinct was to try and reconstruct one of those vatuatil daggers. He had lost all of his pairs in the final battle with the crypt. Then his mind had shifted towards Olfric's sword, but he didn't want to give the guy an even bigger head. Finally, his thoughts revisited Inanna, and the exemplary weapon of an axe she wielded with impossible dexterity. The things he had seen her accomplish with that weapon were simply mind-boggling.

But Lukas wasn't an axe user, no matter how cool it might've looked. No, he needed to craft something that he *could* use, and preferably something more than a melee weapon. Crafting a bow and arrows sounded useful, but he had no training in archery, though he supposed he could cheat using Shatterpoint Intuition. Maybe a gun? His grandfather did own a Smith & Wesson 460, capable of firing six .44 magnum bullets one after the other. In a world of monsters, it would be exactly the kind of weapon he'd need. Why, with his increased strength, he'd face no problems firing bullet after bullet like action heroes did in the movies. It would be . . .

" . . . stupid," he finished, realizing as he said so how utterly pedestrian he was being.

He exhaled. "All this learning to harness Potential, and I jump to technology the first chance I get."

Guns? Why would he need them? He could develop his Kinetomancy to hurl anything, from tiny projectiles to bladed weapons at bullet-like speeds or faster. Seismic Sensing was his answer to locating targets within his range. Shatterpoint Intuition could add missile-homing technology to his projectiles. Metamancy ensured he could conjure an unlimited number of weapons, which would dissipate the moment they ran out of juice, leaving zero residue. And last but not least, his own reserves and these fractals would ensure he could keep firing for hours. If he could develop his abilities further, he'd be able to conjure a larger number of projectiles and launch them all at once.

Now that would be impressive, don't you think Ina—

He paused. A waft of loneliness hit him all over again.

"Lukas?" Tanya demanded.

"Never mind. These fractals look great," he tried to digress. What else was he going to say? That he was suddenly reminded of the goddess that used to live in his head?

He didn't meet Tanya's eyes but said, "Tell me about this kami business again."

Elena cocked her head in Tanya's direction, who nodded.

"Kami are spirits. Apparitions that have spiritual bodies and a consciousness so alien that it's almost impossible to understand them, except for the most rudimentary impulses. Beings from a world that runs parallel to our own, and yet beyond our perception."

That gained his attention. Tanya was talking about the Haze. A world with broken laws, existing only as an endless labyrinth traversing its entire expanse. A dimension through which the yokai could travel from anywhere to anywhere, disregarding geographic or political boundaries.

"If their world is beyond your perception, how do you catch them?"

Tanya smiled. "There are points where our world meets theirs. An intersection that traverses both worlds and yet belongs to neither. Places that are so saturated with mana that most bremetans would suffocate within an hour. It's where you can find wild kami. Their zone of power, their dominions."

"A borderland," Elena surmised.

"Borderland," Lukas repeated, as if hearing the word for the first time.

"There's more. We have locations in the real world that we call Wells. Through these Wells, one can enter and exit a particular borderland. And if you know how, you can lure a kami out of a borderland—"

"And then catch it when it's on this side of the world," Lukas finished.

"Yes," Tanya affirmed, looking at him with interest. "Kami do not have Soul Capacity. They do not grow, evolve, become anything other than what they were born with. That's why they *need* to possess physical creatures. So that they can use the victim's Soul Capacity to promote their own growth. We take advantage of this behavior, lure it out, and then capture it, binding it to ourselves through the Shikigami Ritual."

Lukas had come full circle. The Shikigami Ritual—this must have been what Solana had referred to back then. One that utilized the power of the Eternal Light and forced the kami into servitude, allowing Asukans to utilize them as tools that allowed them to do the impossible.

Manacrafting.

Solana told me I could get a kami of my choice after I killed the anomaly. Something to keep in mind for later.

He regarded the two women before him. "What about the elements? I assume every kami can use a single element then?"

"Yes and no," said Tanya, tilting her head. "Most kami can, upon being given Soul Capacity, develop skills for multiple elements, with varying degrees of affinity. But in the end, it doesn't matter, because a spiritist would choose a single route and progress along that."

"So it's a matter of choice."

"And Soul Capacity," Tanya reminded him.

That too. He could progress in any element he wanted, but unless he had the required Soul Capacity to burn, his choices meant little.

In that sense, a kami that had attributes for fire and ether would fit him best. Fire, because that was what he had maximum Experience in. Ether, because it was versatile and made him stand out.

Show me information on kami.

Scanning Index for "KAMI"

Searches returned TRUE for Monster Prototype MARID
Continue?

No.

Acknowledged.

But that got him thinking.

"So . . . are all kami the same with just elemental differences?"

Tanya snorted. "The thing is, our own history is filled with multitudes of spiritual creatures that fit the description of 'kami.' By Wind, some of the old legends refer to the kami having their own gods. And then there are folktales about nightmarish creatures that stalked these lands before the Great Goddess illuminated the world with her Eternal Light and rid the world of shadows and dark creatures."

Elena stood up. Something about her posture felt stiff. Too stiff. "I'll call Olfric. He can continue with the ritual while you finish talking through the types."

Tanya paid her no mind, except a casual one-shoulder shrug.

With a single, inscrutable glance in his direction, Elena turned around and left.

"She doesn't really like you, does she?" Tanya observed.

"We all can't be winners," Lukas replied. Something about Elena's behavior bugged him, but he wasn't able to put his finger on it. Deciding to ignore it for now, he turned towards his more affable Aeromancy expert.

"So, you were saying?"

CHAPTER 6

OLFRIC'S WOES

*H*e fell.

It was a horrible, helpless feeling, his body twisting uselessly as he tried to land well—but it was a futile attempt. The metal whip cracked against his back ribs, and he achieved a new personal best for pain.

"You've shamed me!"

No—

"You've shamed us all!"

His screams grew louder and louder. A strange numbness was spreading through him. He tried to move his hands and his legs but he couldn't. Maybe, maybe—

"My great-grandfather raised Shahxith into a monster. Your grand-aunt made it into a weapon fit for a warlord. And I took that gem and handed it to you, and you LOST IT!"

Crack came the whip.

A spray of red spread across his vision.

"In the name of my father, and his father before—"

No. He wanted to say. No, no, no—

"I, Ordo Bergott—"

He tried to raise his arm. He felt nothing. Absolutely nothing. But he had to try. He had to—

"BANISH YOU FROM THIS CLAN—"

Olfric woke up in the familiar bedroom that Zuken Banksi had provided for him. His entire body was covered with cold sweat, and his chest hurt. Breathing in and out steadily, his nose caught some half-remembered scents. Sandalwood, and the scent of tree sap. It reminded him that the floor beneath his bed was consecrated, as was every wall, door, floor, and window, blessed by prayers to

Amaterasu, until the hum of faith permeated every inch of the walls and the very stone from which the room was built.

It made him feel safe. Kept those shadows from returning. It did nothing, however, to keep his mind from troubling him with the memories of his father flogging him, but that was at least preferable to the coldness and the darkness that caught him off guard even now.

When he was alone.

Or he closed his eyes.

Or when he found himself staring into a mirror.

In his memories, a twisted caricature of a girl with crimson demonic eyes leered at him in mad satisfaction and whispered—

Go to sleep. Go to sleep. Sleep and let me inside you.

Olfric shivered and shook the image away. That demon was dead. And if not, it was away somewhere, hiding in the depths of that destroyed cave. It had attacked him back when he had first "killed" Lukas Aguilar and had come within a hairbreadth of corrupting him, twisting his soul into a demonic caricature that knew only of Sin and carnage. Olfric still remembered how those shadowy tendrils slipped into his eyes, mouth, and nostrils as he screamed and screamed endlessly, while every single bone and muscle of his body was stretched past limits he had never known, unleashing a strength that could only have belonged to a nightmarish creature with no place in the land of Eternal Light. *A power so deep and dark, that tasted like black grapes and—*

He shook his head again.

Guess the experience was still able to affect him. The consecration around him could keep away external influences but did nothing against the corruption gnawing within his own heart. For if that wasn't true, then why else was he—

Olfric had dozed off right on his table, with papers strewn all around him. Half of them were filled with sketches of half-drawn pentagrams and endless scribbles, with circles, triangles, and all kinds of shapes and symbols that could only make sense to an insane mind—

Or an apprenticing spellcrafter too traumatized to do anything else.

"Con—constraints won't do it," he mumbled to himself, looking at his jottings. "Constraints won't do it. Need harmonization. Need to harmonize it. But—but—"

He grabbed a new piece of paper and began scribbling across it.

. . . assimilation of mana into the individual will only corrupt it. Five sides, five elements, a perfect balance of the spectrum is required to unleash the power but adding constraint will only lead to explosion. Need harmonization. But how?

Can't find it. Can't find it. CAN'T FIND . . .

Olfric grabbed the page with both hands, twisted and wrung it upside down, and tore it apart, before throwing it away. Seeing the torn fabric slowly float its way down to the ground reminded him of a certain blonde aeromancer and that only made him angrier.

He wanted to blame her.

This mission—it was all for her. She was the reason Banksi had chosen him. She was the reason he had entered that accursed land of shadows and demons. She was the reason he had walked out of the group and attacked the Outsider and—

And he had lost his kami Shahxith.

My great-grandfather raised it to become a Monster. Your grand-aunt made it fit for a Warlord. And You Lost it.

His father's words still rung in his ears. They were harsh, but every word he spoke was true. Ordo Bergott was a rigid man who lived by a code and ruled over the Bergott Clan with an iron fist. Ever since Olfric had been a kid, he had been provided with the best instruction, resources, and the opportunities to become the greatest he could be. Ordo had taken him under his tutelage and made an Adept spellcaster out of young Olfric by the time he had finished his bladecraft and spiritism apprenticeship at the Shrine. And once he was ready, Ordo had gotten the strongest water-type kami in the Clan and offered it to him—all in the hopes that one day Olfric would become a worthy successor to his own name.

Instead—

He had joined a sacrilegious mission.

He had been foolish enough to be possessed by a demon.

And he had lost Shahxith.

Olfric had proven his unworthiness, and Ordo had punished him for it.

By flogging him mercilessly and throwing him out of the compound. No clan to call his own, no home to return to, and no heritage to prove himself against.

He was no one.

A nomad.

Like Tanya.

The irony of the situation was not lost on him.

In that respect, Zuken Banksi had been a miracle in his life. The significant fortune Olfric had gained from the mission, not to mention Banksi allowing him to stay at the mansion and offering him an endless number of "jobs," providing him with much-needed distraction and the opportunity to gain Experience and Level Up.

And now finally, he was ready to get his kami.

And he would get it.

He'd show his father.

He'd reclaim his name, no matter the cost.

Picking up the wad of papers, Olfric began to scramble through them all over again. Corrections. Plans. Equations old and modified. Calculations that followed the Empire's thaumaturgy and those that outright ignored it.

He'd solve it.

He'd find a way.

A way to use the skills he had gotten from Shahxith. Skills that were only useless until he managed to gain a mana-forge of a similar synthesis rate. A way that would allow him to get the best of both worlds—the unleashing of delimiters of the bremetan body as demonstrated by the possession, and the complete control of the possessing spirit through modification of the Shikigami Ritual.

All he needed was—

"Olfric?"

He lifted his head and found himself staring into Elena's face. As if by magic, the unending frustration fizzled out of him, leaving nothing more than a lingering apprehension in its place. That and an abject curiosity as to what she was doing in his room, as well as a sense of self-deprecation at being so unmindful as to not notice the sudden intrusion into his quarters. He stood up, meeting her eyes a second time.

"Sorry, did you need something?"

"Uh . . ." Elena appeared unsure. "I thought Zuken might have mentioned it to you."

"Mentioned what?"

"He asked you to teach the Shikigami Ritual to the Outsider."

Olfric arched an eyebrow. "Are you serious?"

Elena tilted her head curiously. "He really didn't tell you about this before?"

"Must have missed the memo. Came in late last night. But whatever. The Shikigami Ritual is to be taught to Asukans and Asukans alone. Not alien Outsiders dropping from whatever rock in space and thinking they're the next coming of Kagutsuchi."

"He's enlisted Aguilar's help in helping you gain your kami. Plus, it's safer if Aguilar has a kami and not—"

Olfric didn't need to hear any further. It was true that he was an Adept in the onmyodo arts, and the best person to teach the Outsider about Asukan theology, doctrine, and spellcraft, but he wanted nothing to do with that man. At the same time, he was objectively aware that saying no wasn't an option, regardless of how the "request" was made to him. Zuken Banksi was his sponsor and bedrock in the current conditions, and denying him something so trivial would only make things sour between them.

At the same time, he had to grudgingly accept that Banksi's actions made sense. Olfric wanted a powerful substitute for Shahxith, and to capture something of its level, he needed to go into the more dangerous borderlands. Having Lukas Aguilar—as much as he despised the man—to aid him was the pragmatic thing to do. Tanya and Lukas, as much as he hated to admit it, had a far greater mana and lifeforce output than he did. And while Tanya lacked physical strength in general, she more than made up for it with her blitz attacks. Between the two of them, he'd have a much better chance at binding a powerful Water-kami.

"Yeah," he replied, if a bit sourly, "I can teach him, I suppose. But I can't guarantee it'll work for him."

Elena gave him a one-armed shrug. "Maybe it won't, but he can perform Pyromancy and Metamancy. Maybe exposure to the other types of kami could—"

"Cause a reaction and activate his powers," Olfric caught on. "Much like how I have Shahxith's skills in me. Not that I can use them."

"But he can."

Olfric frowned. "Yes. He can."

He thought he saw a strangely amused expression on Elena's face but ignored it. The changeling wasn't his first choice of person to be around but the anomaly mission had given him an acquired taste for her. The fact that he had sought shelter in the Banksi mansion didn't help either.

"Tanya's giving him a general briefing, so I came to you for the details."

Olfric studied Elena with his cold, discerning eyes. He had often wondered if Tanya shared a deeper connection with the Outsider beyond their encounter in the anomaly. For someone who was practically a stranger, Tanya seemed to naturally gravitate towards Aguilar a bit more than what Olfric was comfortable with. Just what was it that she saw in him that she didn't see in—

Olfric paused and immediately perished the thought. Tanya was a Sinner. And her gravitating towards an alien only spoke about her own unnaturalness. That was the reason behind his discomfort. Nothing else.

"Fine," he growled. "Let's get this done."

Olfric paused just outside the threshold of the living room, letting Elena enter the room without him. Sounds of laughter were trickling out. Not raucous laughter, but something softer—something indicative of genuine mirth, of good-natured enjoyment. Whatever it was Tanya was discussing with Aguilar, they were certainly enjoying themselves.

Olfric wasn't certain what kept him out of the room. He hesitated—as if the light-heartedness and the humor were a barrier—and he instead remained in the quiet, solemn hallway. He watched from the door but wasn't able to completely suppress his longing to join in.

"But jokes aside," he heard Tanya say, "Tengu, Marid, and Ghul—those are the three you'd generally see around. Mostly the first two. I think I only met a ghul-tamer once, back in Baramunz."

"What are you waiting for?" Elena called out. Blinking, Olfric shook his head and stepped in.

And just like that, the room fell quiet. He could see lines of tension form around Tanya's face, no doubt forming her own conclusions about what he was about to do or say. The Outsider, on the other hand, lost his jolly mood, and instead took on an indifferent mask. He did not draw power, but the expression on his face told Olfric an entirely different story.

They're tense, Olfric realized. *And the worst part, I can't even blame them. I tried to kill Aguilar, and I didn't score any points with Tanya. And now I need their help to get me a kami. By the Light, I hope—*

The rest of his thoughts flickered out as he felt an overwhelming peace. The emotion slammed into him like a sudden weight, squeezing his emotions dry, as if crushed by a forceful hand. His fear was snuffed out like a candle, and even his inner conflict seemed to go silent.

Slowly, Olfric wondered why he had been so worried. Between the three of them, he was the scholar in onmyodo arts. Without him, the Outsider would fail at getting a kami. Plus, Olfric himself was Zuken's candidate for the Choosing. The only reason he was helping these two was to get needed aid in the future.

This was a bargain. A transaction. Nothing more, nothing less.

"So," he voiced aloud, looking at Aguilar, "I heard you needed some help in getting a kami."

"Really?" the Outsider replied in a half-amused tone. "And here I thought you were window-shopping for one."

"Behave!" Tanya warned Aguilar, eyeing him.

Olfric eyed Elena, who seemed utterly unperturbed, and then back at the bolt door. He was certain everyone in the room was watching him. Not for the first time, he cursed himself for losing Shahxith. Being in a vulnerable state like this was . . .

Insulting.

But he couldn't afford to show weakness either. Weakness killed. He had to pretend to ignore his hesitation. Logic and instinct told him to take advantage of the Outsider's power and Tanya's skills, just like he had made use of Banksi's support and his willingness to keep his word. Calmly, he sat down upon the floor, maintaining a neutral distance from both. This would require some diplomacy on his part.

"You're right." He sighed. "I lost my kami in the anomaly, and I'm looking for one. A strong water-type, preferably another marid if I can help it. And

I'm told you need someone to teach you the ritual so that you can get your own."

"It'd be for the best," Elena chimed in. "We don't want him to get persecuted."

"She's right," Tanya supported. "It'd be safer."

"So, you help me get this down," the Outsider replied, "and in return, I—" He glanced at Tanya. "We help you enter some borderland and get you a new kami?"

Olfric winced. There was bluntness and then there was this.

"Yes," he admitted. "That's exactly what this is about."

Tanya snorted quietly.

"Great," Aguilar chirped. "No point wasting time. Let's get started, shall we?"

Olfric blinked. Maybe there were benefits to being this blunt after all.

CHAPTER 7

TOURING AND TRESPASSING

In hindsight, Lukas supposed he shouldn't have been surprised.

Literal gods or not, the people in this world seemed to have no problem in twisting history to suit their own interpretations, and more often than not, their own egos. He had heard a brief recalling of events of the Great War between the Yokai Kingdom and the Asukan Empire, with Solana painting the Asukans as war-crazed barbarians who couldn't live with themselves upon realizing how becoming an oni was a crucial step towards their own evolution.

On the other hand, the tale Olfric was weaving couldn't be any more different.

One of the benefits of growing up with a religious academic was the ability to see through the curtains of various dogmas and find patterns among them. The concept of transmogrification, or "god-eating," was common in religions back on Earth. He briefly thought of how Christianity had fused the sun-worship of Romans, the Jewish Sabbath, and so on. He thought about the constant recurrences of the concept of the Great Flood in several religions, or gods asking their Chosen Ones for sacrifice in the name of faith.

And now, he had found something similar here in this world. Here, where gods were real, the people, their followers, were all too willing to rewrite history to suit their own opinions. He could not, in this sense, blame Olfric or Solana for this, because it was only natural for them to believe their ancestor's words and dogmas as the "truth."

"As I was saying," Olfric went on, "using the Eternal Light, we purify these malevolent spirits and bring them under our control. The ritual allows us to purify their unnaturalness, and bind them to our own, granting them the benefit of growth and potential in return for—"

"Being a mindless tool for the rest of their lives?" Lukas offered.

Olfric scowled. "Sharing the use of their ability as a mana-forge. The kami are poisonous creatures, and they can twist our elemental balance into complete disarray. The ritual, empowered by the divine light of the Great Goddess, keeps them subdued, and allows us to employ their forge, while granting them the Potential they never had."

Two different versions. Compared to Tanya who seemed to stick with cold, neutral facts, Olfric's explanations were tilted in favor of Asukan supremacy. The belief in the holiness and purity of Eternal Light—something that drove the cruel, malignant darkness away and ensured a world of purity and order.

It definitely fit the classic trope of Good versus Evil. Hell, they even had a freaking Goddess of Light in their favor.

And at the same time, the arguments he was using were the same as the ones employed by fanatics to justify their misdeeds. There was pride in his bearing, clarity in his eyes, and an absolute, serene certainty in his voice as he painted history to suit his own kind. Hitler must have looked *exactly* the same when he had justified the mass killings of Jewish people at the onset of the Second World War.

Be careful, Lukas, he told himself. *You don't know which version is right.*

There were always three sides to every situation. Ours, theirs, and the truth. Often, the truth turned out to be stranger than either of the other two. And as a lawyer, it was his job to seek the truth, and not fall into the prejudices of either.

"And how does that work?" he questioned, silencing his own thoughts. "Tanya was telling me about the types of kami out there."

"There are a hundred different types of kami," said Olfric, "but spiritists mostly go for two types: a marid or a tengu."

"Just those two?" Lukas inquired. "From what Tanya told me, neither of them would be what I want."

Tanya had described the marid race as rebellious and prone to being lone predators. Marid tended to display traits for Aquamancy, Aeromancy, or Terramancy, which probably explained why the majority of captured kami belonged to that category. But their extreme affinity to those elements also came with extreme incompatibility with Metamancy. Only marid with a Level-3 skill or higher could display minor Metamancy, and even that was limited to gaining a temporary physical shell at best.

The marid he had fought and siphoned in the crypt came to mind.

MONSTER PROTOTYPE: MARID		
APTITUDE	**LEVEL**	**SOUL CAP REQUIRED**
Possession	1	50

Water Creation	2	500
Water Manipulation	3	5000
Pressure Modulation	2	500

That reminded him: now that he had infinite Soul Capacity, transforming those Aptitudes into Skills would be no-brainer. He had no use for Possession and he already had Pressure Modulation listed on his Schema, so it was only the other two that were really useful.

Having a Level-3 skill at manipulating water would be wonderful.

Now, if only he could manage to get that done away from spying eyes . . .

As for the tengu-kind, Tanya had described them as docile terramancers with some minor Aeromancy and absolutely no affinity for Metamancy. Zuken's own kami, Avriel, was apparently a tengu, and no, nobody had any idea how it looked in real life.

Neither type would be of any reasonable help for his metamancer status.

"Neither can a ghul for that record," Tanya chimed in, "Ghuls are infamous for their shape-shifting, but that's it. You'd have better luck with being a monster tamer."

Or directly siphoning them and gaining their skills, but there was no need to tell her about that either.

He posed a question to her. "Are you telling me that there aren't any kami that specialize in Metamancy?"

Tanya clenched her jaw. "Only one, I think. But even talking about them is a bad habit. Creatures of fire and ether, malevolent beings that embody the worst traits of the emotional spectrum. Rage, jealousy, hatred, fear. Unlike other kami that prey upon physical hosts to grow, these creatures possess others to cause carnage and terror." She met his eyes. "We call them ifrits."

Lukas wasn't as well read on Islam as he was on other religions, mostly because of the language barrier, but he had, of course, heard of this particular creature back on Earth. Dating back to pre-Islamic cultures, the ifrits were regarded as cruel, self-serving demons that lacked the fire component out of the five elements. But Tanya's description did not seem to match the one he had heard.

"And these fellows can use Metamancy?"

"Yes."

"That'll be enough," Olfric declared, looking vexed, though his displeasure seemed to be focused more on Tanya than on him. "The Empire frowns upon ifrit-kind and any bremetan that fall under its corruptive influence."

He turned towards Lukas and stressed, "Even with the Holy Eternal Light, it is very difficult to control an ifrit's wickedness. You will not make any friends by having an ifrit at your command."

Lukas almost smiled back. Nobody said anything about commanding one. He was simply looking forward to absorbing one. Maybe one of these ifrits? If he got his hands on a powerful one, he could upgrade his Pyromancy and Metamancy both in a jiffy.

But if he couldn't get an ifrit as a kami, then—

"Maybe I'm not made for this metamancer business. Maybe I should tell him—"

"No!" Olfric interrupted. "There is something else."

Elena did a double take. "There is?"

Lukas almost didn't notice the sudden stiffening on Tanya's part.

"There is one more, albeit a very rare kind. It's called a *jann* and is regarded as the most dangerous kind of kami there is. They're destructive beings that manifest a single element, but their affinity is impossibly high. It's possible that you might find a jann that's an expert at Metamancy."

"I sense a 'but.'"

Olfric gave him a mirthless grin. "Not one. Several. Jann are impossibly rare, and only found in the most dangerous of borderlands. And most importantly, the soul capacity required to even bind a low-level jann is more than what most Asukans could muster."

Lukas, without even realizing, pressed forward. "How much?"

Olfric shrugged. "Four-digit figures, at minimum. There's a reason the number of jann in the entire Empire can be counted on one hand. But I think that's enough preamble on kami types. If you want to bind a kami to yourself, what you really need to focus on is the ritual."

"And how do I do that?"

A thin smile tore its way across Olfric's lips. He touched the air in front of them with a single finger, its tip glowing with pure lifeforce. He dragged the finger slowly through the air, leaving a thin mist of lifeforce behind, forming a perfect, five-pointed star.

"Five points," he intoned. "Each signifying each element. Fire. Wind. Earth. Water. Ether. Exactly in that order. A perfect balance of all five elements signifies a healthy functioning of the physical, mental, and spiritual state of an individual. But a kami—" He paused for emphasis. "—is, by nature, a symbol of varying affinity towards the different elements, and ends up making this structure look like, say . . ."

He twisted the structure to an even more bizarre shape and kept on tweaking it further in all directions. "The point is, the more twisted the structure is, the more it signifies an elemental imbalance. Since every element also affects our mental and spiritual state, having a twisted structure could manifest in the form of different attributes. Water, for instance, is associated with thought, defensiveness, adaptability, flexibility, and suppleness. But an improper rise in water components can nearly destroy the positive effects of Fire and very much weaken the aspects of Earth."

"So if a water-type kami gets hold of you and possesses your body . . ."

Olfric flinched, if only for a second. "Yes. If a water-type kami possesses a person, that is what will happen. Which is why, the Shikigami Ritual adds this . . ."

He joined the open ends of the pentagram, forming a pentagon at the center, and drew a perfect circle around the entire structure, forming what people would describe as a pentacle, the symbol of Satan, or a Yantra, depending on whom one asked.

"Using the power of Eternal Light, we place two impediments upon this structure. The first," he said, pointing at the circumcircle, "is the Elemental Constraint, limiting the elements from going out of control."

Olfric paused for a moment, looking strangely conflicted. "This . . . isn't an ideal solution, since it does nothing to stop a particular element from shrinking, but if the other elements are kept within the accepted range, the chances of shrinkage are minimal. As for the other—" He pointed at the pentagon in the middle. "—this is the Spiritual Constraint, one that keeps the kami isolated from the Host, unable to intentionally manipulate the Host's emotions and mental state."

"A prison."

"In essence, yes." Olfric looked like he had swallowed a bitter pill. "Through this ritual, any bremetan can bind a kami to themselves, by sacrificing a portion of their Soul Capacity. Mind you, your Soul Capacity must be proportionally high, or else you'd be consumed by the kami from within. Not even the Eternal Light can save you from that."

"Consumed . . ." Lukas mused. "You mean, like *possessed?*"

He might have been seeing things, but something flickered in Olfric's eyes. "Not . . . not possessed. Kami twist the emotional spectrum. It can render your soul unstable but if you can somehow . . . *amalgamate* it into a second boundary layer, then perhaps . . ."

Tanya cleared her throat.

"Sorry," Olfric croaked. "I was just . . . thinking. Anyway, it's dangerous. *Very.*"

"That's why the Shrines always mandate the capture of weak kami with Level-1 skills," Tanya chimed in.

"Where do fractals come into this?"

Olfric pointed at the circle again. "A fractal directs to the Elemental Constraint, and drinks from it, bringing out far more mana than is physically possible for the bremetan body without adversely affecting itself."

"A shortcut, then."

"Essentially. Good fractals are notoriously expensive for a reason."

Lukas nodded. "What's next?"

"Next, we try to gain entry into a dangerous borderland. That is one thing that Banksi cannot provide us at this mansion. And any clan that boasts a Well would rather go to war than unveil it to others. Fortunately, we have a solution that *might* allow us access some of the most dangerous borderlands in the Empire without starting a war, which is why, starting tomorrow, you and Tanya have a job to do."

Lukas arched an eyebrow. "And what, pray tell, is that?"

Tanya looked at him with a pleasant grin. "How would you feel about joining me on a tour of this town?"

Lukas beamed.

When Olfric had mentioned that he would get a tour, Lukas had expected to be walking, or traveling on monsters—or maybe, just maybe, some unearthly variation of mechanical transport. His time spent with the yokai hadn't instilled faith in this world's ability with technology, unless it was the magical kind. Not that he'd say no to flying carpets, wormhole doors, nor anything fantastical, but knowing his luck, it was probably going to be stranger than fiction.

Still, he hadn't quite expected . . . this.

Tanya grinned at him. "Like it?"

Lukas stared at "it" for a long moment. "Like it? What the hell *is* it?"

The contraption before them was enormous. Vaguely reminiscent of a car, except that the front was so flattened that it might as well be a square, with several pieces of metal protruding out of it from the bottom. There was a single large glass-like, transparent layer covering the upper surface, which probably served as the entry point to the cockpit, which itself had a pair of seats inside.

No wheels. No doors.

Nothing.

"A high-speed Jixin, fully automatic," Tanya bragged like a mother about her child. "Jumps at three hundred miles an hour. You must have done something seriously impressive to get Zuken to lend us this big boy."

Yeah, Lukas inwardly chuckled. *I threatened him, but wait—*

"Jumps?"

Tanya smiled. "Oh, yes." She pressed her fingers against an elaborate graffiti painted in gold and silver near the cockpit, causing it to turn alive and contort into a new shape. The window glass receded, allowing her entry into the contraption.

"Don't worry too much," she said. "Sure, you don't get to see a Jixin out here very often. Zuken's probably the only one to own one of these in Haviskali. The government provides the older platform model for Civil Transport, but just give a few years, and the Jixin will take over the market. You can kiss the conventional platforms goodbye."

Lukas looked warily all around him. "Uh, I think I'd prefer a conventional platform, whatever that is."

Tanya chuckled and began operating the terminal before them. It had no keys or buttons, instead having gold and silver squiggles drawn all over. Daintily, she pressed her fingers on it and dragged the structure into a bizarre shape.

"Now come on in."

The interior was comfortable. Lukas stepped in and strapped himself with the seatbelt, just in time for the windowpanes to close from above. He swallowed hard and waited, hoping he'd survive this. Inanna would laugh herself silly if he got himself killed in a transport accident after surviving everything else he had.

"Comfortable?"

"Not in the slightest."

Tanya snorted. "Just relax. You won't feel a thing."

"That's what they say before killing you."

Tanya beamed.

Roughly ten minutes later, an incredulous and slightly airsick Lukas Aguilar stepped out of the death machine that was the Jixin. He wobbled across the plank and literally threw up the contents of his stomach on the sidewalk.

"Gross!" Tanya scowled at him, before her expression changed to one of concern. "That bad, huh?"

Lukas rubbed his stomach. "Feels like I've been eating mud."

She nodded. "Altitude sickness and gravity shifts. You're lucky we only did a single jump. If we'd gone to another town in this, it'd have gotten your insides rolling."

Lukas gave a wan nod and counted himself lucky. All things considered, it wasn't as terrible as he had expected. The vehicle moved very much like an elevator, only traveling across a trajectory that spanned several miles at a stretch. The surprising part about the entire process was the complete lack of drag, except for the continuous shift in gravity as it traversed a distance of several dozen miles. Lukas had been ready to explode his way out of the machine before it collided with the floor. But fascinatingly enough, the collision had amounted to little more than a bad road bump back on the streets of Ohio.

Friction and Momentum Manipulation seemed to be the likely culprit.

Wiping his face with a kerchief, Lukas stood tall, feeling the crisp breeze rustling the lapels of his sleeveless shirt. He squinted his eyes and tried to take in the world around him. Having a bird's-eye view was one thing, but to be standing in the middle of it felt—

Repulsive.

There was a theory in aesthetics known as the Uncanny Valley. It held that when something looked *almost* similar to a human being—a robot or a mannequin—it generated an innate revulsion in the eyes of the observer, because its appearance was so close to human, yet just off enough to evoke a feeling of uncanniness, a mix of both familiarity and unease. A similar psychological effect pervaded his mind as he tried to grasp the world around him. One that was filled with creatures that looked *like* people, lived in places that felt *like* cities, and yet, this was not Earth. Instead, looming before him was a world of glass and stone, featuring a transparent, minimalist design that bordered on the impossible. Instead of the fixed structure that had been the Banksi mansion, the builders here constructed everything out of moving blocks, seamlessly sliding upon the other, often taking bizarre and physics-defying forms.

Lukas was barely conscious of the fact that a handful of people had scurried onto the runaway where the Jixin had landed and begun tending to it, or of the fact that Tanya had grabbed his hand and pulled him forward on an elevated platform, floating just inches above the ground. All around him were shops and edifices full of people—all of which looked human at first sight.

He turned his head in every direction as he walked ahead, trying to look at everything at once. Gargantuan-sized malls that sold cosmetic products stood next to shops selling armor, gauntlets, and tassets, with the red sun overhead shining brightly on the metal. He could see large buildings that could only be factories on the horizon, the air shimmering above them to create a striking effect of blue and yellow against the sky. And just turning to his left, he could spot two men bickering over a two-headed, horse-sized goat in one corner of a lane.

Talk about dichotomy.

It was only when the floor beneath him started moving that he was finally brought out of his daze.

The floating platform was moving. And yet, Lukas couldn't so much as feel the brush of wind on his face as the platform zoomed its way across the wide lanes of the surrounding town. It took him a second to recognize that an invisible barrier was present along the edges of the platform, similar to the one inside which he had fought Quonnan.

"So, uh," Tanya's words brought him out of his daze, "welcome to Haviskali. It's not as big as some of the other towns and cities, but it's home."

Lukas blinked and looked around. Ryu had described Haviskali as a redneck town. Extreme environments on two fronts, lacking in sophistication and with limited growth offerings, and composed of a small community of people, ruled by a single overseer. Lukas had pictured Oklahoma or Cleveland from the kasha's words.

This? This place looked like New Orleans meshed with a futuristic New York.

And this was a *town?*

"So, where are we heading to?"

"Well," Tanya drawled, "I *am* supposed to kind of show you around the place, but Zwaray Keep is where we're actually headed to."

"Why?"

"To meet the svartalfars."

Lukas did a double take. "Act—I mean, why svartalfars in particular?"

Tanya pushed a lock of golden hair from her face and tucked it behind her ear. "Several reasons, actually. They're the best at making enchanted gear. Anybody with the mezals to pay for fancy and durable equipment always go for the svartalfar-made stuff."

"And people just go there and purchase what they want?"

Tanya snorted. "Hardly. Svartalfars are anal-retentive, bloodthirsty weaponsmiths with a fetish for beheading others. They're also ferocious sticklers for privacy."

"Charming."

Tanya giggled. "Oh, and they loathe Asukans with a passion, and that goes double for nobles."

Lukas arched an eyebrow. "That doesn't seem very conducive to business expansion."

She shrugged. "Doesn't have to be. Svartalfars usually sell their goods through third-party agencies, giving them the peace and privacy they want. It's rare for someone to visit their premises directly."

"Then how are we—"

"You'll see," she replied evasively. "Besides, we aren't going there to buy, but to sell."

"Sell . . . what?"

Tanya must have sensed the stiffness in his posture. "Don't worry. We aren't selling *you.* Well, not directly anyway." She chuckled. "The thing is, these guys have a knack for finding the most dangerous borderlands strewn across the Empire, and they often traverse these lands to extract rare minerals for smithing. And for that, they hire adventurers, mostly non-bremetan."

"What jobs?"

"Mostly security. Especially if the terrain doesn't suit them. What we are going to sell them is a permanent job contract, hiring Zuken's firm Iylaerion for the next ten years."

"And why would they do that?"

Tanya smirked and took out a tiny vial from her pocket. Inside it was a shining, glassy, broken piece of rock fragment. One he recognized instantly.

> **FEATHERGLASS**
> **Crystal Outgrowth. Indicative of stored information.**

But that was not all.

> **Information about Featherglass Synthesis Found Lacking!**
> **Creation of Featherglass within Territory impossible without**
> **further information.**

That was new. Synthesis? Creation? He had created nothing directly before. Sure, he had done some minor ether manipulation, but that was just False Construction, nothing concrete, and certainly not out of Anomalous Energy.

"Featherglass from the anomaly," Tanya showed off, ignorant of his own mental tirade. "One tiny specimen. Unusable, because it already contains information."

"But enough to prove its superiority over commercially produced ones," Lukas finished, mentally reviewing through his omphalos functions. Apart from the recently gained Territory Creation, he had activated nothing new. Perhaps Creation was an attribute within the Territory Creation function itself?

"—*ere* paying attention."

He tuned back in.

"But you're right," she continued, oblivious. "It's enough to get them to play ball with us. Our collection is small, but priceless. The anomaly's destroyed, and that makes the tiny amount we have even more valuable."

Not unless he could somehow reproduce the material from scratch. Anomalies were creators, their ability at forging far beyond even divine powers. That was how Inanna had described it. He suspected that if he reorganized the clutter that was inside the Blob, he'd have access to the featherglass synthesis process.

> **Reversing Corruption will require +597,531,354 units of power.**
> **+47% chance of success.**
> **Initiate Rollback Protocol?**

No.

> **Command Acknowledged.**
> **Rollback Protocol Deactivated until further prompt from**
> **PRIME HOST**

As if in acknowledgment, Blob stirred a little before going silent again.

It made him wonder. Inanna had described Anomalous Energy as the truest form of Creation. The precursor to both lifeforce and mana. It was the thing *souls* were made up of. But the Rollback Protocol wasn't about *creation*. It was about *repair*. Repair of information. And if Anomalous Energy could take the randomized chaotic leftovers of the crypt and restructure it into order, then what *else* could it restructure?

He'd have to think about that.

"Kas? Are you even listening?"

He blinked and regarded Tanya, who was glaring at him, her hands at her hips.

"Sorry."

"You're distracted." Her expression softened. "Is everything alright?"

"Just . . . figuring things out," he replied honestly. "It's a new world. New people. New situations. It'll take some time to get used to things."

Tanya found that acceptable, giving a nod.

"So, why isn't Banksi dealing with this negotiation stuff himself?"

"I can think of two reasons. He's a noble and being caught with this stuff can be dangerous. Especially if the army comes in sniffing. Also, svartalfars would probably throw him out the moment he gave his name. Same for Olfric. And Elena . . . well, we don't know how svartalfars would react to a changeling, so that leaves—"

"You."

"Me, and you get to come along for the ride."

"You're too kind."

"And don't you forget that."

This world was obsessed with understatements.

Back on Earth, the concept of a keep came into use for the European nobility, referring to construction of fortified castles with the provision for emergency rations, usually employed as a last resort or refuge if enemy forces besieged the area. Given Tanya's description, it fit the svartalfars to a tee—sticklers for privacy, shackling up in a fortified tower with dungeons full of armaments, and the sounds of svartalfar craft workers striking the metal with their oversized hammers.

This . . . this was more like visiting an industrial belt.

Easily spanning several acres on either side, there were three parts of this giant complex. The outer periphery, with large, floating stone pillars, each of them situated approximately ten feet from the other, giving a fence-like appearance. Dozens of buildings lay beyond that, constructed using the moving-block architecture he had seen earlier, all of them surrounding what seemed like a giant hill, with the middle portion replaced with an equally gigantic metallic machinery, exuding bursts of steam and purplish light from various exit points. The peak of the hill was still intact, maintaining the overall pyramidal shape.

"This . . . is the Zwaray Keep?" he asked.

"Yup," Tanya said. "The real Svartalfheim is . . . somewhere up there, in the sky. The svartalfars have a contract with the Empire and stay within these keeps. You'll never see them getting out of one, not that they need to. Everything they need is inside."

"You seem to know an awful lot about them."

"I should," Tanya replied confidently. "I've lived here for two months."

Something in her voice told Lukas she wasn't joking.

"It's how I escaped the army. I'd worked on jobs for them before, and instead of mezals, I purchased a favor from them. When the Cobalt Army came for me, I used the favor to buy asylum." Her face scrunched. "It wasn't nice. Svartalfars don't like to be involved in diplomatic conflicts. Hell, even the Empire leaves them alone. You can be the freaking overseer, but you won't be able to take a step inside without their express permission."

Right. The Cobalt Army. The SWAT-equivalent for this world. Utterly loyal, absolutely obedient, the army only moved to fulfill the Empire's will. Composed of high-leveled warriors and spiritists alike, there was no force stronger than them, nor more trusted by the emperor. There was not a thing they would not do. No act was too vile, and no punishment too cruel. Like fanatics fighting for their god, all was justified in the army's eyes. Normally they stayed away from regular bureaucracy but involved themselves whenever Sin entered the picture.

Which was how Tanya had gained their attention.

They answered directly to the emperor himself, who distributed them in small cohorts throughout every kingdom, while a major force remained stationed in the Sovereign, the heart of the Empire. Also, the Sacred Eight and the Shogun of the kingdoms had some control over them, which was how Zuken had called them off.

"Sounds tough."

"You have no idea," she replied dryly. "They granted me asylum but made me go on endless jobs during my stay. Maybe they were expecting me to give up or get killed. Either would keep them from this bureaucratic stalemate against the army."

"And Zuken thinks *you* should approach them with this offer?"

She shrugged. "We don't have anyone else. Besides, they're a stickler for rules. They might burden you with lethal work, but they won't go against their word. I asked for asylum. I got it. They made me work, and in return, gave me rations and living quarters and everything else. And now I'm free, so technically, they *should* allow me in, despite how much they'd loathe my presence."

"And you're expecting the featherglass to turn things in your favor."

"Yes."

"And where do I come into this picture?"

Tanya stilled. "Excuse me?"

"You're already walking into the svartalfar territory in a risky situation. You're hoping to change their opinions by giving them an offer they can't refuse. And if things go south, not even the overseer can do anything to help you. And you're telling me I'm here for *sightseeing?*"

That put a crack in her mask. He saw her eyes flick up quickly to his face for a moment and then back away.

"I'm not saying I want to know everything, but I wasn't born yesterday. You've brought me here for a reason, and I want to know what that is."

There was another moment of stillness. "It's because of my favor. The svartalfars are twitchy about giving out favors, and it took me over a dozen dangerous missions to get them to agree to one."

"And you used it to get asylum against the army."

Her lips twitched. "And that's why they'd be . . . apprehensive about hiring me again."

Oh.

Oh.

So that's how it was.

"The svartalfars respond to displays of strength. And while I've worked for them before and proven myself in their eyes, Iylaerion—that's Zuken's firm—is an unknown commodity. They'd need some confirmation of its ability to get things done."

Which is where Lukas entered the picture. His ability with lifeforce and manacrafting was considerably high, and while he was sure Tanya could still hand his ass over to him, it wouldn't be without taking damage. And if Tanya wasn't an option, then—

"Guess the demonstration against the overseer's security guy wasn't enough. He wants a bigger, better show."

One corner of her mouth crooked up in a smile. "Something like that."

The two of them slowly traversed the outer perimeter of the industrial zone, easily half a kilometer before they stood before the pillars. Even though the stone edifices were floating in midair, they released a constant thrum of power in all directions, making his Seismic senses all charged up and wary. Contrary to how it might look, the power was actually flowing inward, through invisible relay centers beneath the ground.

Energy Drain detected within vicinity

He stopped in his tracks.

"What?" Tanya asked.

"Is it . . . safe to just cross through them?" He gestured towards the pillars. "Those don't seem friendly."

"Don't mind those. They are part of the power grid."

Energy Drain detected within vicinity

"Are you sure?"

"Positive."

Tanya arched an eyebrow, and as if to prove her point, walked ahead. She crossed the barrier without the slightest break in stride and stood on the opposite side.

"See?" She waved her hands. "Perfectly safe."

Energy Drain detected within vicinity

"If you're sure."

Energy Drain detected within vicinity

He took a step forward.

Nothing came screaming out of the pillars at him. Nobody started firing shots either. So far, so good. He took a second step and put one leg past the pillars, wondering if his Schema had run into a glitch because it was unused to this new world. Maybe it was just—

Energy Drain Detected
Omphalos Energy Reserves Draining
1%

A notification blared at him in an alarming shade of red.

Activating Capacitance Function
Reverse Shift

Initiating Energy Absorption

Lukas barely had a second to glance at Tanya's surprised face.

And then the pillar next to him went neon red.

Energy Drain Detected

Omphalos Energy Reserves Draining
1%

Capacitance Function Active
Reverse Shift Active

Energy Absorption
4%

What the hell was happening? Lukas tried to move, but nothing happened. His body wasn't responding, as if frozen between the two pillars, trapped between the invisible radiation around him while the omphalos system within him locked in a struggle with the grid. Really, Tanya had walked through the pillars without so much as a breeze on her face, while he had gotten stuck inside the pillars with everything around him going neon red. It was probably a shock that it hadn't started honking in alarm. That was pretty much proof of what kind of day he was having right there.

On the other hand, he wasn't sure what he'd really do with any other kind of day. He didn't have to like it, but it was the truth—he was a walking, breathing, mayhem machine, backed up by experience and, to an extent, inclination.

Energy Drain Detected

Omphalos Energy Reserves Draining
2%

Capacitance Function Active
Reverse Shift Active

Energy Absorption
7%

Two things were happening. The pillars, and whatever was part of this power grid system, were trying to drain his omphalos energy reserves. In response, the Capacitance function was draining the power grid, only its absorption rate was faster than the grid.

Energy Drain Detected

Omphalos Energy Reserves Draining
2%

Capacitance Function Active
Reverse Shift Active

Energy Absorption
11%

Much, much faster.

Or maybe it was simply the difference between the amount of power both reservoirs boasted. Lukas knew he had more omphalos energy than he could probably use in ten lifetimes, unless he wanted to perform a spell of Inanna's magnitude. But if this power grid was supplying power to this entire zone, then the power reservoir would have to be at least within comparable levels, if not greater.

Energy Drain Detected

Omphalos Energy Reserves Draining
3%

Capacitance Function Active
Reverse Shift Active

Energy Absorption
17%

Or so it seemed.

Tanya had frozen in place for a second, her beautiful face confused. Then she opened her mouth to say something—

At which point two pairs of hands rose out of the ground, grabbing Lukas by his legs and pulling him below with unrelenting force. With a most unmanly shriek, Lukas dropped upon a cold, hard, stone floor in an unceremonious heap, with Tanya landing right on top of him, kneeing him in the groin as she tried to get up. He failed to suppress the whimper trying to escape his lips. Squeezing his eyes and scrunching his face in discomfort, Lukas pushed himself up.

"That," he declared, sneezing loudly, "was the worst experience I've ever had."

He wasn't jesting. From vampire bats sucking his blood dry to being trapped in slime, with acid-splitting fang-worms wrapped around him, Lukas had suffered through a series of unfortunate, awkward, and absolutely mortifying circumstances that made him want to find a rock and hide beneath it. He had been possessed and trapped in an illusion and forced to fight naked in front of an alien audience. He had suffered through Inanna's bone-shattering training regimen. There had been Tanya, ready to skin him alive and make a human-sized Frost mannequin out of him. The crypt was feeling left out, so it mind-fucked him once into becoming a cheesy villain. One would think it was enough punishment, but the crypt had enjoyed it so much it crafted a new Guardian in his image with a serious psychological dysfunction and utterly bullshit powers.

Oh, and being torn apart by a memory of his disintegrating world also counted, he supposed.

But all of that was nothing, *nothing* compared to feeling the rocky crust beneath his feet turning into thick, viscous jelly and being pulled down through it. There wasn't a word in the English language that could describe it. Feeling the earth on every inch of his body, *beneath* the skin, with sand particles traveling all the way upward. He could feel the bitter, metallic taste in his mouth, his throat, and even his ears and nasal passage as something dragged him downwards, deeper and deeper.

He sneezed again. Loudly.

"Terraportation," Tanya replied. "Svartalfars use it all the time. I'm surprised you didn't puke. I was sick for days after my first time."

"Not my first weird trip." Lukas waved her concerns away. "The Jixin earlier caught me a bit off guard. Terraportation, did you call i—"

He bent down and threw up.

"It is," Tanya muttered.

Lukas stood up, wiping his face. Carefully, he took stock of his surroundings. This place was obviously underground, with slabs of smooth rock covering the walls and the floor. It was like a modern basement, minus the pillars. Dimly luminescent bluish crystals protruded at several points on the walls, their positions too perfect to be natural. Obviously, the Eternal Light did not penetrate this far. Maybe the ground itself repelled Amaterasu's fancy lighting on general principle?

Not surprising. As if that fake Truth had any business being called a La—
Lukas blinked.

And just like that, the thought was gone. Like it hadn't even been there to begin with.

It was then that he noticed Tanya was being suspiciously quiet.

"Tanya, where are we?"

The aeromancer let out a sharp whisper. "The dungeons."

"Of . . . what?"

As if to answer his question, the Screen flickered alive.

Prey Found You

The earth abruptly became liquid near his feet, causing him to step back on instinct. And then heads—multiple heads—popped out of the ground. Then came their bodies. Bipedal and inordinately muscular, these humanoids had grayish skin, triangular faces, pupilless black eyes, and large, floppy ears.

Lukas blinked. He had seen Solana perform subtle and powerful Terramancy back in the yokai camp, and Zuken had shown some quick and dirty boulder action as well. Even the khorkhoi had dug in and out of the ground as if they were swimming through it. But this? This was almost like *phasing* through the ground itself, much like the yurei had done. Only in their case, their bodies were fake and were constantly deconstructing and reforging their bodies with self-Metamancy.

Are these . . . svartalfars?

"Um, hello?" he offered. Truly, he was a master of diplomacy.

A dozen melee weapons protruded out from the walls and the ceiling. Swords, spears, and javelins, crafted out of rock, crystal, and metal, with murderously sharp edges—all of them pointing in their direction.

"Lukas," Tanya hissed, her eyes both furious and wide with near-panic. All five floppy-ears were focused on him intently. One of them even carried a massive, double-bladed axe in his hand. It raised the weapon above its head, as if preparing for a blow.

Tanya instantly genuflected before them. "My apologies to your people. We were just—"

"Intruding!" The tone was acerbic and gravelly, the kind that made skin crawl.

Language Identified
Faecani

Replicating . . .

Lukas tried not to gape in surprise. Faecani? Here? Solana, Nihil, Ryu— several of them had spoken in that language. But the svartalfars too? That was one hell of a coincidence.

"Trespassing into our territory and draining the thirteenth ward stone is a blatant crime against our nation."

The large, double-bladed axe shone in the creature's hands.

"The sentence for this violation is death by decapitation, to be carried out at once."

The blade swung high.

CHAPTER 8

TRIAL BY COMBAT

The svartalfar was coming in full swing. Given its monstrous visage, its warbled war cry, the fury of its movement, and the immense momentum behind its swing, it painted a picture terrifying enough to make the strongest of men falter. Just one clean strike, and Lukas would lose his head.

The creature really shouldn't have done that.

Lukas took in a quick breath, getting his emotions under control so he didn't instantly incinerate it to ashes or send it flying backwards by a dozen feet. His experience in the anomaly, especially after his time spent in the yokai camp, had inculcated several *bad habits* in him. Prime among them was the utter lack of sense to run and hide. Instead, he just tried to smash his fist into whatever was making him afraid. It was a primitive sort of thing, and one he didn't question too much.

But reflex-based murder was a tad extreme, especially considering what he was here for. So rather than setting it ablaze, Lukas went for the next best thing. He took a single step backward, shifted his left leg further left, and narrowly avoided the ax's trajectory. He moved his left hand, and with a single finger, poked the svartalfar in the wrist.

The axe was flung out of the creature's hands and crashed against the ground with a loud thud. The svartalfar, on the other hand, was practically folded in half, grabbing its wrist, eyes bloodshot and brimming with tears. The other creatures instantly stepped back, grabbed their weapons, and looked at Lukas with varying degrees of wariness.

"What?" Lukas asked. "All I did was poke him with a finger."

Which was technically true. The body reflected the soul and, with the latest Level Up, his body had gotten better attuned to the flows of motion around him. Stepping out of the ax's trajectory had been child's play. A pinpoint application of Momentum Manipulation, guided by Shatterpoint Intuition, had sent the axe flying out of its hand—inertia at work. The svartalfar's own momentum had done the rest.

The creature's sour, leathery face turned a bit more sour, the lines at the corners of its mouth stretching and becoming deeper. *"Trespasser!"* it growled. "You attacked our wardstone. You. Will. Die."

"The things at the entrance?" Lukas said in what he hoped was a calming voice. "Yeah, that had nothing to do with me."

He looked at Tanya for support but found her surprised and apprehensive. Then he realized he was still speaking in Faecani, and Tanya probably had no clue what he had just said.

"I'm a newcomer to this town." he went on, putting forward his best lawyer smile, the kind you used to disarm hostile witnesses in court, "As weird as it sounds, it wasn't my intention to create a ruckus. If anything, we've come with a proposal that could be very profitable to your nation."

"Profitable," said a new voice, coming from behind the group before him. It was a deep sound, echoing around the room, resonating from the stone. "That is a dangerous word to throw around here, Asukan."

Lukas stared at the newcomer. It was larger and far more muscular than the ones standing before him. Like the others, it too had grotesque features, with a fundamental repulsiveness emanating from it. Its face was covered in old scars that Lukas was convinced hadn't come with the package but had instead been earned in battle. The svartalfar wore armor, and its presence loomed over everyone else, like the naked, sharp edge of a blade.

There was power in that face too. Lukas could feel it in the air and the ground around it, the tension and focus of a pure predator, and one who rarely failed to bring down its prey. It studied him for a moment and then did something unexpected.

"Lord Dvalinn," muttered the guards, genuflecting before his presence. Even Tanya did a tiny bow.

"An Asukan that speaks the ancient tongue? That's a first."

Language Identified – Ualbesh

Lukas instantly shifted to Ualbesh. "I learned it."

"Did you?" the svartalfar challenged, peering at him from those beaded, coal-black eyes. "The Empire purged everything of the Old World. Then how?"

Lukas could feel Tanya's eyes at him. No doubt she was trying to correlate his being an Outsider with these new revelations. Mentally preparing himself for another round of interrogation in the near future, he focused on the problem at hand.

He addressed the newcomer in Faecani. "Svartalfars were also part of the Old World. And yet, here you are." Inwardly, he was concerned. Not because the sudden language translation didn't work, but because *it did.*

He hadn't known if it would work. He *shouldn't* have known that it would work. And yet, he instinctively had. Perhaps there was more to the pendant than he had thought? Inanna had described it as a relic but never really bothered to explain the details. He had let it go, not wanting to owe her a favor in return for irrelevant trivia.

Something to look into later, he supposed.

"Intriguing," said the svartalfar in Ualbesh, "I'm almost inclined to hear your proposal."

"Then—"Tanya began.

"But—"The creature raised a single finger, in a show of gentle reproof, his eyes locked on Lukas. "You've done damage to our national property. Zwaray Keep does not entertain trespassers."

Lukas weighed his options. What was he going to say? What *could* he say? That he was an anomaly and the wardstone was trying to suck out his omphalos reserves? That his Capacitance function had auto-activated and reversed the drain?

And then a *bad* idea came to Lukas. A very, very bad idea. One that could get them what they wanted, but if it didn't, then things could end very badly. It was like reading about how "Russian roulette should statistically work" all over again.

"I'm an adventurer. A pyromancer," he said out loud, changing back to Ualbesh again. "And I specialize in Energy Absorption."

"Absorption," noted the svartalfar. "So you *did* drain our wardstone intentionally."

Lukas frowned, feeling trapped in his own story. "Yes. It was a demonstration. But clearly, you've no appreciation for my talents."

"Lukas!"Tanya hissed, her face utterly white.

"Oh shut up, Tanya!" he retorted, taking a page from Olfric's book and donning the most condescending sneer he could make. "Look at them! Instead of rewarding me, these twits don't mmmhhh—"

Tanya slapped her sweaty hand over his mouth, her eyes widening with growing horror. Clearly, she thought he was just trying to piss them off with no plan and was going to get them both killed in a spectacularly horrible fashion.

He didn't have the heart to tell her how right she was.

"Reward?" asked one guard. "For what?"

"Mmmmbmmm—"

Another guard yanked away Tanya's hand.

"Speak your fill, trespasser."

"Well—" Lukas lightly coughed into his fist. "I believe I've demonstrated some pretty gaping holes in your security system."

"Preposterous! We caught you before you could escape."

"Escape?" Lukas drawled, as if explaining something to a child. "I stood in the same spot and drained the power from the stone. For all that time. Waiting for someone, *anyone,* to show up. And when you did, I had to keep myself from accidentally injuring you." He snorted, shaking his head. "All those walls and pillars and such shoddy security? I couldn't have pulled off a worse setup if you gave me a year to plan."

Tanya audibly sighed. "We're so going to die."

Dvalinn, whom Lukas mentally recognized as the big shot among these creatures, laughed out loud. "Intriguing! Few people have blades as swift as your tongue, Asukan. I'm conflicted over what to do to you."

"I propose a solution," said the guard Lukas had thrashed earlier.

Dvalinn cocked his head sideward.

"Trial by Combat," it said.

The reaction was instantaneous. Half the guards gave their compatriot intense, approving looks while the rest looked modestly apprehensive. Lukas, on the other hand, was doing a decent stunned expression while his mind ran miles ahead.

Trial by Combat. He knew what that was. It was the prevailing system that the yokai employed to solve competing arguments. He had found himself locked in one such trial against the kasha Quonnan. If the svartalfars followed the same rules then . . .

Yes. Yes, that makes sense. Solana had said the svartalfars were part of the yokai kingdom. But in that case . . . .

Quickly, his mind began to run through a worst-case scenario and draw conclusions as to what it could mean as fast as he could. He barely even paid attention to what the svartalfars were saying. A Trial by Combat wasn't just a simple conflict won by strength and skill. It was a political tool, and if he didn't realize what he was playing for, he'd be in a ton of trouble. No, the sensible thing would be to *not* get caught up in this mess.

Not again.

So why was he feeling so excited? A surge of ambitious lust rushed through him, quite the opposite of his general rationality. It was pure and primal and thrummed through his entire body, reminding him of Inanna.

"Trial by Combat it is," agreed Dvalinn, turning to Lukas. "What do you say, trespasser?"

"I accept," said Lukas.

"Wait," Tanya interrupted. "What is happening?" She turned to him and said in a fierce whisper, "Do you even know what they're talking about?"

"A Trial by Combat," said Lukas, "We have competing claims, and so we'll hold a Trial by Combat to see who's correct, or at least most committed to his version of the story. If one party refuses to take part in the trial, then that means they're guilty."

"Oh?" exclaimed Dvalinn. "You know of it?"

"Just in passing." Lukas shrugged.

"That . . ." Tanya brought her voice down to a whisper. "That doesn't make any sense at all."

He shrugged. "Doesn't have to, but the ability to stand by your truth, even when the cost is potential death, demonstrates your conviction. And the svartalfars value conviction on the same altars as strength, cunning, and ruthlessness."

Or at least that was how Ryu had chosen to describe the process to him.

"Quite true," murmured one guard.

"Oh," Tanya echoed, turning to Lukas. "Oh, crap. Don't tell me—"

"I'll have to face one of them, or whoever they select as their champion. A fight to the death. If I win, we can move ahead and forward our proposal. Whether they accept it or not, we'll be free to go."

"And if you lose?"

A shadow of a smile floated on Lukas's face. "Hypothetical question."

"Fair," said the monster, openly grinning at his statement. "Then I, Dvalinn, Second Stag of Yggdrasil, give this trial my consent."

"Let me fight this braggart," offered the axe-wielder from earlier. For a moment, Lukas thought he'd get the permission to do so, but Dvalinn shook its head.

"No, I will not sully our sacred laws like that. Hreidmar will face him."

"The seidmadr?" asked one of the guards in Faecani.

Dvalinn's gaze did not leave Lukas's face. For better or worse, the svartalfar was studying him. Deeply. There was an almost religious fanaticism in his eyes. "Yes. Hreidmar. Face our champion, stranger. Give us a battle to remember. If you please us, we will listen to your proposal."

"And if we lose?" Tanya asked.

Dvalinn showed his sharp teeth. "Then we execute you and leave your corpses rotting outside our pillars. As a warning."

She turned to Lukas, fear vivid in her eyes.

"See?" said Lukas with a jaunty grin. "No pressure."

The Trial Circle was easily the size of a basketball court. If it was anything like the one Solana had used back then, it should hold up against physical and elemental attacks just fine. A horde of svartalfars sat on the outside of the periphery, watching Lukas's every movement as he and Tanya slowly moved towards the circle. One could literally cut the anticipation with a knife.

"This reminds me of Shrine-officiated tournaments," Tanya said, as she walked beside him, "only they use the Shikigami symbol instead of this plain circle."

Or maybe, Lukas thought, the Asukans stole it from the yokai and called it their own.

The more he learned about the Empire, its customs and rules, the truer and more concrete Solana's version felt. The Empire literally thrived on restraining others and grabbing their power. Their signature presence—the Eternal Light—was all about forcing itself upon the world, keeping the concept of "darkness" at bay. Hell, the entire power behind Spiritism, the backbone of Asukan firepower, was based on the subjugation of an entire race—kami—and their utilization, not as sentient beings but as vessels. Mana-forges to synthesize mana, allowing the bremetan host to actualize elemental magic upon the environment.

"If it's anything like those, then the air inside that thing is potent, saturated with mana to help fighters push themselves to their best."

Lukas gave her a half shrug. He could care less about the mana within the area. He had more important things to consider. Like how he had a shirt and pants on.

"Time to go."

"Alright," Tanya said but didn't let go of his hand. "Listen, I know you're hiding many secrets. Knowing the svartalfar's ancient tongues, and their customs—all of this is very freaky but—" She inhaled. "Just—just take things seriously and do your best. That creature . . ." She paused again. "Hreidmar. He's dangerous."

"He," Lukas noted. "They have genders, then."

"Why wouldn't they?"

He shrugged at her query. "This . . . Red Mare, you've faced *him* before?"

Tanya shook her head. "I've seen him fight. Very quick at terraportation. They call him a *seidmadr* for a reason. And it's Hreidmar."

She pronounced it as "writhe-maar."

Seidmadr. The practitioner of the Seidr, the Norse word for magic. In simple words, a *sorcerer.*

He thought back to what he knew of terramancy. Solana had effortlessly manipulated objects on the ground faster than his eyes could track them. Zuken had used the terrain itself as a weapon, altering its shape, size, and density at will. Terramancy was a devastating weapon, both defensively and offensively. And from his limited experience with terraportation, it wasn't anything to scoff at either.

Seismic Sensing could be a good way to locate terraportation but chances were this Red Mare was better and faster at it than he was. He had already claimed to be a pyromancer, which pretty much dropped his chances of claiming to be anything else.

Lukas frowned. The more he thought about it, the worse he was feeling about his chances of winning this upcoming match. Lifeforce wouldn't be of much help against someone traveling beneath the ground. So long as he was standing on the ground, he would be within their range. And flight was not one of his skills.

Not yet.

"Don't underestimate him, okay?"

"Yes, mother."

Tanya rolled her eyes, before her face suddenly scrunched up in concern. "It's a display of conviction, right? They're—it doesn't *have* to end with either person's death, right?"

Lukas thought back to the screaming kasha at the yokai camp. She had incinerated her physical shell in the process, but her ethereal form had not come to harm. Not until she tried to possess him. But svartalfars were physical creatures *and* damn good terramancers on top of that.

"Well, it doesn't *have to*. But given my luck . . ."

He let that hang there and took a step forward into the circle. Yokai or Asukan, anomaly caverns or modern towns, there was always another battle. Lukas held his power around him like a cloak. He took his time to get into an appropriate position, every step unhurried and precise, keeping an eye on the circle around him. Red Mare was nowhere to be seen. The floor beneath his feet was brittle, enough to be turned into a vicious coffin at a whim, but not enough to classify as sandy terrain. He could go out on a limb and say that this kind of terrain was favorable to terraportation, which meant the game was rigged against him from the very start.

That was fine. Red Mare could have his tricks. He had his own.

Find him.

Prey Located within Radius
Found 99.5% spiritual similarity with pre-scanned prey
"SVARTALFAR"

Insufficient Data for Detailed Analysis.

The outcome of Scan and Analyze used in unison. Whether this flexibility was the result of Warmonger Protocol, him absorbing the crypt's omphalos, or something else, Lukas didn't know. And honestly, he couldn't care much about it either. For now, he had a fight to win and a lurker to call out.

"What?" he drawled, throwing his most condescending sneer at the audience. "This is it? The mighty *seidmadr* doesn't even show up for a fight?"

His efforts didn't disappoint.

Around twelve feet or so away, the ground began to liquify as a lean head popped out of it, much like a dolphin raising its snout above the water. Its dark, beaded eyes blinked and stared up at him before the rest of its body followed suit.

"Preemptive aggression is against the law," said Hreidmar, his blackened teeth on display. "Makes victory sweeter."

Lukas arched his eyebrow and gave the creature a thorough look. Tall and lanky, it—or rather, *he*—was the exact opposite of the svartalfars he had encountered so far. There was very little muscle on him, except for his palms and his feet, reminding Lukas of a frog.

"Is that so?" he challenged. "Then how would you describe that murder attempt earlier?"

Hreidmar cocked his head. "You trespassed. You drained our wardstone. You agreed to this trial. I am only delivering." His lips twisted into something dark and malevolent. "Justice."

"Oh?"

"Your mouth lacks elegance," Hreidmar said, bringing his toady fingers above his head. "So I'll get rid of it."

Outside the circle, Dvalinn rose up to a podium and stamped upon the ground. A seismic force of enormous power came rushing out of it and hit the edge of the circle, dividing and spreading across the perimeter, until both waves clashed against each other on the other side. And just like that, the Circle activated.

Hreidmar let out a vicious croak.

Lukas poured lifeforce into his fists.

And then Hreidmar . . . vanished.

Before Lukas knew what was happening, the floor beneath his left foot opened into a narrow chasm, sucking his leg inwards. Lukas threw force downwards, losing his balance and falling to his right, where another chasm opened at the last possible moment, sucking him into it. A layer of earth instantly shifted above him, burying him completely for exactly two seconds.

And then the coffin erupted in a forceful explosion.

Coughing, Lukas climbed out of the trench, mud in his mouth and ears and all over his face. He was lucky he had already begun forming a defensive force shield around him when everything went *boom*. It was all that kept him from being buried underground.

Lukas coughed some more.

And two spikes of hardened, encrusted earth, pierced into his stomach.

It took him a second to notice the growing pain in his abdomen, and another to recognize that his wrists and ankles had been trapped. An earthly chain spun out of the ground and wound around his neck, smashing his face into the earth. The sharp, brittle particles cut against his cheek, rich, crimson blood now oozing down from his stomach and his chin. Lukas lay there, unable to move, unable to escape.

Like a lamb ready for slaughter.

He watched as the earth inches away from him began to furrow, as Hreidmar terraported himself out of the ground, arms crossed, looking at him with quiet disdain.

"Your powers are quaint."

Lukas tried to move, but all that happened was more chains erupting from the ground, piercing his body in several places, and pinning him down to the floor. If not for Neural Suppression, he'd have been screaming his lungs out.

Damnit, he said to himself. *Stop behaving like prey. Think!*

"Well, *animal?*" Hreidmar demanded, his voice barely more than a harsh whisper. "Speak before I tear your tongue out."

Yeah, he'd definitely speak. But first—

**Activating Monster Prototype DRANZITHL
Initiating Consciousness Shift**

Enact

"I . . . will, just . . ." Lukas looked up and gave him a bloodstained grin. "Stay distracted, will you?"

"Distract—" Hreidmar trailed in confusion.

And the entire place went up in a large, cataclysmic explosion.

The very ground was pulled up by the sheer pressure, as the energy exploded upward, carrying earth and debris with it. Everything within Lukas's immediate vicinity was incinerated, as pure Decay, fused with the hottest blue flames Lukas could conjure, detonated out of him in a wave of such breadth and power that the entire circle glowed with dazzling, white light.

And then, there was nothing but dust.

Regeneration Complete

Not for the first time, Lukas thanked his lucky stars for the dranzithl prototype. The immense, organometallic mass of impossibly lethal sludge was an absolute monster for its regeneration ability if nothing else. If not for the fact that it consumed impossible amounts of lifeforce, Lukas would have concluded it as superior to Inanna's Alleviation technique.

As the dust storm dissipated, Lukas looked around for Hreidmar's broken, burnt form. Half of the arena had exploded, throwing dust and earth into the air. Terramancy or not, you couldn't escape from that much heat. He still had no idea why Fire reacted so explosively with Decay, but he really needed to find out someday.

He pushed himself up, feeling his body already healed. The holes in his stomach had been repaired and were now covered by Blob. His own clothes were smoking, the sleeves now in tatters. The dranzithl instincts bayed for blood, but Hreidmar was nowhere to be seen.

"That . . . was . . . surprising," came a croaky voice from above.

Lukas looked up.

And up.

Hreidmar was there, up in the air—safe, unscathed, looking down at him in a new light. Gone was the look of disdain, and in its place was curiosity, resolve, and maybe a little bit of uncertainty.

"White fire that hot. Healing powers," Hreidmar spoke blandly, counting off on his fingers, "and Energy absorption. You are . . . interesting."

"I'm not giving you an autograph," Lukas shot back, carefully observing his opponent. He had seen Tanya fly, seen her levitate in midair, but this . . . this was something else.

Svartalfars didn't do Aeromancy. They physically couldn't. Their body had natural mana forges suited for Terramancy and only Terramancy. And Hreidmar was no different.

His posture was too clean, too precise, too stationary for that. Like there was an invisible pedestal for him to stand upon. This wasn't like dealing with a speed freak like Tanya, nor a master of Shatterpoint Intuition like his doppelganger had been. No, this was almost like . . . *magic.*

Seidmadr. Tanya's words echoed in his ears.

His heart lurched into overdrive. This wasn't the time to be awed by the creature's skills. This was the time to find defects in his combat ability and take advantage of them. He had already written off Aeromancy. Metamancy was off-limits for similar reasons, as was any other form of elemental manipulation. Unless he was dealing with a monster that could literally *freeze* the air molecules together—

Wait. Could he? Terramancy was all about manipulating molecules. So theoretically, if someone could increase attraction between molecules to acquire a semi-solid frame . . .

No. That wouldn't work. He would still need to balance himself and the frame against gravity.

Let's run some tests.

Spreading his palms apart, Lukas conjured a pair of fireballs in each, and hurled the right one at Hreidmar. His opponent didn't so much as dodge as merely float away, allowing the fireball to shoot through the air and hit an invisible barrier at the very top.

He narrowed his eyes. *A barrier. This means there's a boundary on top.*

He eyed the circle all around them. Was this barrier trapping them inside? Like a bowl?

He sent the second fireball, and then the third, and so on, launching a volley of them at the svartalfar, who kept lazily dodging them by floating away. As the creature approached the periphery, Lukas doubled his shelling. He could see the very first signs of irritation on the svartalfar's face as it stopped its linear path and twisted to one side, before traveling along the periphery, avoiding every single one of his volleys.

And then he began *firing.*

The average cost of a fireball the size of a cannon was roughly 150 to two hundred units, varying upon the temperature of the projectile. Given that he could push over *six thousand* units of mana without having to recharge, that meant he could hurl at least *thirty* of them. And that was without bringing the fractals into consideration, which all but doubled his mana reserves.

The battle arena would be consumed by just *ten* of them. He had at least *fifty.*

The reaction force shoved his feet several inches into the ground as the immense burst of fire mana exploded out of his palms. For a second, Lukas was worried about using too much power all at once and damaging his own nerves, never having tried something on this scale before. If he was unlucky, he would be the center of his own spectacular and splintery explosion. But his plan was good and his execution well managed. Lukas held his hands up in the air, using Shatterpoint Intuition to install trajectories into his projectiles and hurling them with Kinetomancy.

Hreidmar recognized the danger a little too late, and that was where his inexperience showed. He might have real skill at Terramancy and a gift with this . . . air-walking, or whatever he was doing, but in a fight, there was no time to think your way through an opponent's attacks. Either you had done your homework or you didn't, and despite the advantage of using his mystery technique, he was not ready for something like this. He was focused entirely on defense, not on offense, and couldn't come up with a counter in time.

He could float. He could evade. But this far away from the ground? He couldn't do Terramancy. He couldn't terraport. He couldn't conjure weapons.

With the addition of those two things, Lukas had changed the game.

He felt a rush of sadistic pleasure as Hreidmar constantly tried to dodge his spells, dismally trying to return to the terrain he had deserted. Svartalfars were creatures of the earth. They terraported their way through it. They crafted weapons of great power with it. They *belonged* there. And for all his sorcerous might, Hreidmar was no different.

On the ground, he was practically invincible. But up there? He was a chicken.

And one about to be roasted for good measure.

"Hey, Red Mare," said Lukas, "you showed me your tricks. Let me show you some of mine."

CHAPTER 9

CONFLICT OF SECRETS

Years of expertise at masking her emotions were the only things that kept Tanya's mouth from outright gaping. The other spectators, however, held no such advantages and were staring stupefied as one of their own fell to their own machinations. The concept of a bounded circle, Tanya knew, was to deter either opponent from leaving the arena until the victor was apparent. It also kept the destruction limited within, allowing all spectators to enjoy the event without fear of getting smacked by stray hits.

This was the first time they had seen one of their own die at the hands of a stranger within the circle.

"Th—that," the spectator to her right mumbled. His voice broke halfway in the attempt, and he needed to pause before carrying on. "Did that really happen?"

"Yea," Tanya responded, when it seemed no one would. Her eyes, however, remained glued to Lukas's form, standing with his fists clenched at the scorched svartalfar husk that had been his opponent.

"Oh," said her neighbor, before silence once again engulfed the chamber.

"But that was Hreidmar!" said someone else. A woman, this time. Almost immediately, she trailed off. She didn't need to say anything else, though. Everyone in the session understood what she meant.

"Yeah," said Tanya's neighbor.

Finally, someone snapped. "But that was Hreidmar! He's—he's a master at—That Asukan is a *pyromancer*. We are svartalfars—" He was at a complete loss for words and whipped his head at her direction, as if expecting a response.

Tanya wasn't sure what she could say but, given the growing number of expectant gazes upon her, she feared they'd coerce her into a trial of her own if she didn't give a satisfactory reply to their unasked question. "I think—" She swallowed, gathering her thoughts. "—I think Lukas found a loophole in Hreidmar's technique."

"What loophole?"

"You'll have to ask him."

Had it been any other svartalfar, they'd have been able to escape Lukas's constant volleys of flame with some burns and scratches. All they would have had to do would be to get to the ground, hide within, and use Terramancy to harden their skin from damage. But Hreidmar was an aberration in this case—his lack of physical endurance proved fatal in the last moments. The unfortunate creature had tried to pass through Lukas's attacks and gotten himself hit in the face with one of them. And once Lukas had made a hit, the next successive hits had tracked their way to his victim during the free fall. By the time his body had hit the ground, the svartalfar was dead.

The only real problem was that Lukas had revealed himself as a pyromancer while Zuken had exalted him as a metamancer. Although it was not unheard of for Spiritists to draw on multiple elements, they were Gold-rank or higher, not some vagrant from Maluscion.

But that was not all. Lukas had used *Decay*. Again. She would never forget feeling that undiluted fear and running for her life with that monster behind her, wielding fire more corrosive than she had ever known. Only this time, he was in absolute control of himself. Had he perhaps gained the skill from that sludge? How?

The more she tried to decipher the enigma that was Lukas Aguilar, the more she found newer questions piling up. Just . . .

What is he?

Her thoughts were silenced as Dvalinn, exalted among svartalfars, stood up from his chair and stamped the floor a second time. Just like before, a wave of immense pressure flowed through the podium and traveled along the periphery of the battle arena, causing the Barrier Circle to dissipate.

"The trial is over!" His voice boomed as he peered at Lukas with an inscrutable expression on his face. "Well fought!"

Tanya suspected that there was more to his words than she understood. Svartalfars were a bloodthirsty lot, but she could trust them on their word. She was certain they'd listen to their proposal now, but how Lukas murdering Hreidmar would affect this process, she didn't know.

No, wait. Not murdering. This was a Trial by Combat. And in combat, there is always the chance of death. And they mentioned no rules about any death penalty.

Dvalinn turned idly towards Tanya. "Your accomplice has stood the tribulations of the trial and come out victorious. As acknowledgement, we'll hear this proposal of yours."

It took a moment for Tanya's brain to catch up with what he'd said. "Err . . . just like that?"

He tilted his head, the way a dog does at a new sound. Maybe he just hadn't understood her.

"I mean . . . Hreidmar died."

"Hreidmar knew the risks," Dvalinn said. "We have lost a great deal today. Damage to the thirteenth wardstone, the public demonstration of a security flaw, the loss of our seidmadr . . . We hope this proposal will be profitable. However . . ."

Tanya didn't think it was possible for his eyes to darken any further, but they did. What were originally beads of black now looked like pieces of flints, sucking in light.

"It had better be worth it."

Tanya hoped her gulp wasn't audible.

The exalted svartalfar gestured towards the buildings further south. "I assume you're familiar with our resting halls, Tanya of the Fierce Wind. Yes, I know who you are. *Svartalfars do not forget.* You and your associate can wait in one of our halls. You'll find every essential amenity inside. I advise you to wait there until further notice. So, eat, sleep, prepare if you can. The council shall grant you only *one* occasion to hear your proposal. I hope you put that to good use."

Every magic trick was composed of two parts. The first being the trick itself and its execution. It was where the magician took something ordinary and performed something extraordinary with it. Like a svartalfar walking on air. But svartalfars were earth-walkers—terraporters, as the term goes. And that led to the second part of the trick.

The secret.

The "how" factor. It wasn't Aeromancy, and neither was it an illusion. Yet it worked, and the svartalfar walked on air. Magic perhaps? An enthrallment of senses? Probably. Maybe one, maybe both, or maybe none. But one thing was clear—once you found the secret, the trick was no longer mysterious.

No longer . . . magical.

MONSTER PROTOTYPE: SVARTALFAR		
SKILLS	**LEVEL**	**SOUL CAP CONSUMED**
Raw Lifeforce Manipulation	1	50

Terraportation	2	500
Friction Modulation	2	500
Earth Manipulation	2	500
Innate Gravity Control	2	500
Seismic Sensing	2	500

Friction Modulation. Such an absurdly lopsided skill. Despite being at a decent Level 2, Hreidmar had used it to devastating effect. Combining it with terraportation made him impossibly fast underground, capable of diving from one spot and appearing far away at impossible speeds. Using it with Earth Manipulation made it easier to create traps to catch Lukas off guard or, worse, bury him underground. Usage with Innate Gravity Control—another interesting skill—allowed him to not just stand on air but float in it with impossible slipperiness.

The Secret.

"I had it with me this whole time," Lukas murmured to himself, "and not once did I even think of its potential applications. All the power of an anomaly—endless skills and monsters to call upon—and despite that, I'd have lost. I *should* have lost if not for . . ."

He gazed upwards at the barrier that was no longer there. The barrier that had been the true game changer in the fight. Without it, his defeat would have been imminent.

This. This was what Inanna had warned him about. The consequences of spreading oneself too thin, the insane obsession over absorbing other skills to grow powerful instead of taking what he had and going ahead with it. But no, he had always been charmed by the newer skills and the applications he could derive from them, forgetting the ones he already had up his sleeve. Somewhere along the line, he had become a one-trick pony, focused more on winning fights and siphoning monsters rather than evolving himself.

In Inanna's words, a *leech.*

Lukas clenched his fists.

Not any longer. He'd still siphon but only to add to his development. An anomaly grew differently than a human. Its priorities were different. Its growth and nature were different. Forgetting his humanity to embrace being an anomaly wouldn't get him what he wanted. His current methods wouldn't work, not if he wanted to get Inanna back. He needed to do more. Become *more.*

"Lukas?"

He looked up and saw Tanya walking towards him. Hreidmar's charred body was still smoking—an aftermath of being hit by a combination of Decay and Fire. No longer would the creature be able to perform his magic, having lost it to Lukas just after his spirit left his body.

I'll continue where you left off. Lukas promised the decaying creature. *I'll use everything in my arsenal to take your skill to a level even you'd never have dreamed of. Thank you for teaching me this lesson.*

There was no response. After all, dead men told no tales.

"Lukas?"

"Yeah?"

"You alright?" She took another tentative step forward.

He shook his head. "No, but I will be."

He met her eyes and found them shining with intrigue and concern. "I was afraid things would end badly. Especially in the beginning. And then when that explosion happened and he went up in the air—"

"You saw him do that before?"

Tanya bobbed her head. "I could never figure out how he did it. It wasn't Aeromancy but . . ."

"Something stranger than that."

". . . Yes."

Lukas said nothing, looking down at the scorched corpse.

"Did you figure it out?"

"What?"

"His secret."

"I suppose . . ."

"And?" she drawled, arching an eyebrow. "How did he do it?"

A mirthless grin floated on Lukas's lips. "The secret impresses no one. It's the trick that matters."

"Doesn't matter. I still want to know."

Lukas shut his eyes. "I didn't figure out his secret. Only a momentary loophole. A smidge of sheer, dumb luck acting in my favor. That's why I'm standing and he's a corpse. I didn't win it."

"A victory by luck is victory too."

"No." He remembered Inanna's green eyes. "No. It is not."

She touched his arm. "It's a start. You'll get better. Stronger. And I'll help you."

He blinked.

"You will?"

"Of course. We're on the same team, remember? You . . . you used Decay on him, right? The same one from that sludge in the anomaly?"

Lukas didn't react, instead trying to understand her hesitancy. She had seen him kill that monster and then gain its Decay powers. She had seen him kill his doppelgänger and end up with an aqāru familiar. And now, this was the third death by his hands. Was she—did she think he had siphoned its powers too?

"Yes," he replied, wondering what she'd do next.

"Back then, it turned you into an insane monster. Do you . . . you know, feel any different?"

It took every ounce of control to not blink in surprise. He had been thinking solely out of paranoia. Approaching problems from a more logic-based perspective, with his own biases working against him. He had to shift perspective and reapproach the problem by viewing it through an additional emotional layer.

Then he understood.

It wasn't that she was thinking he had absorbed new powers. She was just afraid he'd turned into that monster from before.

"I won't be turning into that monster again."

Tanya caught his gaze and looked away, demurely.

"Good." She let his hand go. "Now all that's left is getting you prepped up."

"For what?"

"For the meeting, dummy," she said. "The svartalfar council will see us soon, and I've got loads to teach you about featherglass before you can explain it to them."

Lukas blinked at her. "Say what?"

Her voice turned wry. "I'll tell you everything about feather—"

"Not that bit." He interrupted her. "Why am I the guy doing the explaining? You've been here before. You know the rules. You know about the featherglass and adventuring. So why am I the scapegoat?"

"Because—" She studied him with a critical expression. "—it'll give us a greater chance of success."

"I don't understand."

"Appearances and impressions are powerful things, Lukas Aguilar," she said. "Used correctly, they're weapons in their own right. I don't know about you, but I want every weapon I can get."

Lukas scowled at her.

"You're right. I've been here before. I've lived here, worked for these people, and forced them into a diplomatic struggle against the Cobalt Army. They know who I am, and they know what I've done. And despite that, I've brought into their territory a stranger whose immediate first action was to find a flaw in their security system, followed by the death of one of their own."

"Uh, doesn't that make me a worse candidate for the job?"

"Hush. Now you, on the other hand, your first actions were proving a security flaw, under the guise of proving your worth in front of them."

"Which everyone with two brain cells knows is bullshit."

"The trial said otherwise," Tanya countered. "You said it yourself. It's a test of conviction. Truth or lie, you proved your worth in their eyes twice, while not breaking a single one of their rules. *And* you've communicated with them in their own tongue, which is another freaky jar of worms I don't want to touch right now. You've stood by their stipulations and come out ahead. That gives you a very different first impression."

She looked him in the eye. "Svartalfars do not forget. I think Dvalinn was trying to give me a hint there. I've a bad track record with them and have done nothing to improve that. He said we have only one chance to offer our deal, and I don't want to waste that."

His scowl deepened. "If I fuck up and they bury us six feet under, I'm blaming you."

"If you fuck up, being buried would be the last thing to worry about. Pissed-off svartalfars usually involve sharp weapons, evisceration, and a lot of screaming."

Lukas gave her an appraising look. "Fine. What happens now?"

"Now, you negotiate."

The room was positively swamped.

Lukas found himself in a rectangular chamber whose high walls were filled with ancient, leather-bound tomes. Additional freestanding bookshelves jutted out of the walls like ribs, interspersed with metallic radiators that clanged and hissed, giving the room the eerie sense of being alive. The hall, if it could be called that, was only moderately sized. Shadows sprawled across the room, the bluish lighting from the crystals only exacerbating the Asukan nightmare. But Lukas was no Asukan, and he hadn't sent these guys the memo, so there they were. He could compare the scenery with a badly-lit motion picture of the sixties.

He stood before thirteen svartalfars—all of them looking nearly if not equally monstrous as Dvalinn—sitting on majestic thrones placed in a semicircle. Dvalinn sat third from the extreme right. Behind Lukas stood an entire cohort of soldiers, armed and ready, with their pointy weapons aimed for his vital points. Tanya stood several feet away from him, surrounded by soldiers—their deterrent against him trying to pull off something reckless. Lukas could understand all that, but seriously, couldn't these guys have arranged for a chair for him?

Talk about being uncouth.

Feeling more amused than intimidated by their methods, Lukas strode up towards them, entering the private space, just enough to be recognized as an intrusion but not one that should have generated immediate concern.

Pausing a moment to breathe in deeply, Lukas gathered his power. Both lifeforce and ether rose in him, generating an instant apprehension among the audience. A petty psychological trick, but one that reversed the intimidation on these old men. Not that he was planning on taking any of them head-on. No sir, Tanya had drilled that sort of Earthly foolishness out of his remarkably dense skull.

Rule Number One of living in this world—*Never fight an old man.*

Back on Earth, old age represented a loss in physical prowess and a dimming of intellect, stamina, and perception. But in this world, age was literal proof that the guy in front of you had leveled up for longer than you had, and probably had far greater skills and Experience than you did. Old people were the ones who had been there, done that, and lived to tell the story. It didn't automatically translate to strength or power output, but chances were that an older opponent was better, more energy-efficient, and, in general, more experienced than a younger guy.

"Gentlemen," Lukas commenced, turning abruptly towards Dvalinn. Focusing on one of them took away the advantage of numbers. Another petty psychological trick, but one that worked in his favor. Also, he had held conversation with the guy before, so he could address him without giving the impression of targeting him from the entire group.

"I believe you already know what I'm here for. But before we continue, I just want to clarify that what I am to share with you must be kept in the strictest of confidence. Are we in agreement?"

"Even from the Empire?" one of them asked.

"Yes."

The councilmen gave tacit acquiescence. Lukas didn't really care, especially given that this was all for show.

"I am here today, with my associate," Lukas began, "because we made a discovery I believe you'll find startling, and, might I be so presumptive, very profitable. It is something that can drastically change everything for both myself and my associates, and your nation. If this information were leaked, it could affect the world in a—shall we say—*profound* manner, causing a shift that could only be described as *disruptive.* At this moment, there are only *five* people that have the information I'm about to reveal to you."

One of the councilmen sighed loudly, sounding more bored than concerned. "Very intriguing, but get to the point."

Lukas glanced at the soldiers all around him and reached into his pouch to pull out a tiny, stoppered vial, containing a single shard of featherglass inside it. As it turned out, the crystal was ferromagnetic, and a proper application of mana was enough to keep the crystal floating in the middle without touching the surface.

Terramancy was useful like that.

He appraised the creatures before him. "This is featherglass. The commercially available variant is usually sixty-two to sixty-nine percent pure, depending upon how much you're willing to spend."

Blank, bored looks met him.

Time for the show.

He raised the vial above his head. "This one in my hand is more than that. *Much* more than that."

Dvalinn squinted at him. "That is impossible."

"Only until you verify my statements." Lukas matched his gaze. "Surely that is within your power?"

An oppressive silence settled over the room. Lukas felt several penetrating gazes centered on him, in a sudden, pointed silence. Finally, one of them spoke in a low voice. "True. That can be determined."

"Wonderful!" Lukas replied in mock cheer and flung the vial towards them. Every single svartalfar in the room inhaled loudly, several of them reaching out to it. A female member among the council raised her hand and it froze in midair before floating towards her.

"Careful," she hissed. "If what you say is true, this is priceless."

"Yes," Lukas said. "I'm glad you agree."

He thought he heard a choking sound somewhere. He wondered if it was Tanya.

The old svartalfar looked at him a long moment before grunting. Then she tapped the vial and muttered something under her breath. Lukas strained his ears but the loud mutterings across the room made it hard to catch. The pendant tried to translate it and threw up a bunch of contradictions. Lukas wasn't sure if it was a flaw in the enchantment design or simply because of his own limitations.

"This is impossible—"

"Where did you get this?"

"Has to be a trick—"

"Goddess-Chosen, playing us for fools—"

And so it went.

Lukas looked around dispassionately, waiting for the mutterings and exclamations to settle down. Svartalfars, by nature, were rather fussy so getting into even one of those questions would get him stuck in a twenty-thousand question and answer session, and he wanted to avoid that. Plus, he wasn't an expert, so the less he spoke, the less chance for him to say something contradictory.

Finally, Dvalinn stood up, and the rest of the room fell into silence.

"This is quite unexpected, stranger," he said. "You show us something we didn't believe existed. That shouldn't exist." He met Lukas's eyes. "What do you wish for? Weapons? Armor?"

"An agreement."

"What sort?"

Lukas folded his arms. This could make it or break it. Clearing his throat, he addressed the svartalfar. "It's true we hold more of it. And unlike the sample your people have verified, our collection is pure and untainted by any kind of spiritual information."

Dvalinn tilted his head and regarded him in perfect silence, somehow implying his annoyance. "Do not waste our time. How much do you have, and what do you want in return?"

Lukas smiled through his eyes. "As I was saying, my associates discovered this featherglass. Because of unforeseen circumstances, we only managed to procure a limited amount of it."

"Fine then," said someone among the council. "The location, then. What do you want in return?"

Hasty, aren't they?

"I could tell you the location, but it means nothing. The origin of these priceless crystals is now gone, and whatever we have is the last of it, making it even more rare."

"And how much is that?"

And there was the first obstacle. "Around half a kastrian."

Assuming the value for gravity wasn't different and all of this Leveling Up hadn't fucked up his perceptions, one kastrian was roughly equivalent to a little more than maybe fifteen pounds.

"Half a—" Dvalinn snarled. "What travesty is this? I warn you that this mockery—"

"It's no mockery," Lukas said quickly. "I know perfectly well that the content we have is . . . far from abundant. But you are svartalfars, the most industrious craftsmen in the world. If there is anyone that can reverse engineer this and mass-produce it, it's you. All we ask is a percentage of the production."

"If it happens," said the female svartalfar.

"*When* it happens," Lukas corrected her.

The female svartalfar looked at him and snorted. "I'm not sure whether to laugh at you or take offense at such a display of blatant stupidity. You want us to reverse engineer an impossible specimen like this, from such a minuscule amount, and then divide whatever success we have, if any at all, with your kind?"

"This is a waste of our valuable time," said another member, standing up. Lukas felt his mouth getting drier by the second. Clearly if he didn't say something useful, the situation would get out of hand. But trying to *convince* these guys wasn't going to help. If he wanted to get something, he'd have to play hardball.

And he had definitely learned the hard way, more than once, that all work and no play made Lukas a merciless bastard. Was that a bad thing? Maybe yes, maybe no—likely somewhere in between, in the details, alongside the Devil and his deep blue sea.

"Fine!" He tried to look crestfallen. "You got me. What was I thinking? Clearly this featherglass isn't as great as we thought it to be. Good thing I asked my associates to give the rest to the Empire in case they didn't hear from me in four days. I mean, *really*, maybe the emperor will find it more worth his time."

That got a reaction. Lukas made sure there was a smile on his face.

"I imagine whatever little you have could be exchanged for a price—" someone began.

"Oh, come now," he said cheerfully. "I'm offering you something priceless. You said so yourself when you caught it, remember? The least you can do is *stop trying to pretend otherwise.*"

He cut the councilman short, eyes blazing, voice strong and sure. Power surged within him, flaring all around him like a protective cloak. Blob moved restlessly, shifting over his front and back, stirred by his heightened emotions. The svartalfar he was dealing with had eyes as wide as saucers, and his mouth worked soundlessly even as his clawed fingers twitched madly.

"And listen," Lukas snapped, "there are two ways we can go about doing this. The first is the messy way, where you can pretend this is all useless and try to attack me and Tanya. In which case, all of this place—" He twirled his finger above his head. "—is going to be one big mess. Maybe you've the home advantage and maybe your army can overpower us, but what then? Do you think it's worth risking the Empire knowing about it?"

He let that one hang for a moment.

"Or—" Lukas breathed "—we can all behave in a civilized manner and discuss how we can *possibly* try to make this deal beneficial for both parties, preferably before you attempt to have me hung, drawn, and quartered."

The svartalfar closest to him was glaring with pure, unguarded hatred.

"Lukas!" he heard Tanya hiss. *"What are you doing?"*

An entourage of several soldiers moved in, swords and spears drawn, while the sudden shuffling behind him indicated similar movements there as well.

Lukas didn't care. Lifeforce surged within him again, as did mana, only twice as much, thanks to the uber-costly fractals. He was not the young man they thought he was. He was something more, something *different*. He was the Warmonger, a title bestowed upon him by an entity larger than these *creatures* had any right to comprehend.

He was the *power* in this room, and he made sure the svartalfars knew it.

"Wait."

It was Dvalinn. The creature took a step closer towards him. In response, Lukas put on his most uncaring facade.

"Tell me, stranger, do you think it wise to make an enemy of our nation?"

"With all due respect, *svartalfar*, all I've done is offer a proposal. Do not blame me for your men trying to turn me into dinner."

He thought of using the dranzithls' murderous aura, but it'd probably be overkill at this point. Seriously, he was getting overdependent on slime-based skills. The dranzithl and thoggua had disgustingly useful skills, but sooner or later this overdependence was going to land him in trouble.

"You have no idea what you've done today, do you, stranger?"

Oh, he had a very good idea. But he let Dvalinn have his say.

"*Control* is the heartstone of the Asukan Empire. This featherglass, unlike what the Empire has, can change everything. The purity you have shown us can store not just information but *souls*. With this, the Empire could become exponentially stronger. Conversely, with this, Svartalfheim can become power-ful enough to challenge its authority. And yet, here you are, offering this to us, knowing this could mean war, rebellion, and all manner of profitless destruc-tion. Why?"

Lukas smiled. The stick had done its job. Time for the carrot.

"Why is inconsequential. What matters is that we have a way of acquiring more of this sample in small and steady amounts, if only for research purposes."

He was not technically lying given the fact that the featherglass was created by the anomaly he consumed. It was just unavailable to him right now.

Dvalinn eyed him speculatively for a moment. "If that is so, then why are you here? Even in small amounts, you could make a killing by selling it to the Empire."

Oh yes, he had certainly grasped his interest.

"We could, but then we'd become indentured to the Empire. We'd rather hedge our bets on a race that has the best chance of reverse engineering this."

A little flattery went a long way—catching more bees with honey, and so on . . .

Dvalinn sat back upon his throne and tapped the tips of his fingers together, glancing at him. "You're skilled at putting us in quagmires, stranger. You bait us with a priceless treasure and go out of your way to make it appear reasonable. For the power to entrap souls, what are you asking in return?"

And just like that, Lukas knew he had gotten Dvalinn. The trap was set. The bait was taken. At this point, they couldn't pretend it was worthless. Now it was time to finish the deal.

"Oh, quite reasonable things, I assure you. Apart from ten percent of what-ever featherglass you produce, provided you can reverse engineer it, four things really, and weighed against everything we offer you, they are quite reasonable. I just want one simple tool, one simple transaction, one simple clause, and one simple favor."

"How reasonable," Dvalinn said dryly. "Well, we'll see. The tool?"

"I've had firsthand experience with those wardstone pillars you have outside. I believe they can harvest natural energy from the world and use it to fuel everything here. I want one of those things, coupled with everything it needs to work."

Dvalinn's eyes glittered, which Lukas guessed wasn't a good thing. "Our wardstone technology is magnitudes above what Asukans have. We cannot simply *hand* it over to you. The loss would be . . . incalculable."

Lukas could work with that. "Of course. I'm not saying I'd take it with me. It can stay within svartalfar territory. I only require its services for . . . say, the next ten years. I'd be willing to travel all this way to use it, provided the nation allows me to do so unrestricted."

"Luk—"

Dvalinn's eyes gleamed. This was a bait too tempting to pass up. Being so generous also added weight to his claims, as well as built up a trust that had kind of collapsed when these guys had sentenced him to death some minutes ago.

"I wonder . . ." the creature whispered. "Even with a kami capable of absorbing power, I cannot fathom what you plan to do with it."

Oh, he had plans. Plans that involved absorbing enough power to attempt the Rollback Protocol on Blob. With a mere forty-seven percent chance of success, there was no way he'd be willing to bet his reserves on it. No, these pillars would be a welcome substitute for it, even if it required him time and effort to travel all the way to that place, sit, and recharge himself.

Over and over. Until he got it right.

And when he did, he would be able to manufacture featherglass by himself. And it would also get him entry into svartalfar society.

"I believe we understand each other, stranger. We'll have a separate one installed for yourself. As long as it's you and you alone that uses it, we have no issues. Now, about the other three?"

"The transaction next. We want an exclusive job contract with you for the next ten years. Fifteen percent commission on whatever loot we bring. Sound reasonable?"

Dvalinn nodded. "Unexpected but reasonable. I assume you'll want the agreement in writing before you leave?"

"That'd be splendid."

Lukas smiled. "Third. The Clause. It's obvious that I'm the primary party in this deal. As such, the contract cannot be changed without my express permission."

Dvalinn tilted his head. "You fear your own accomplices will betray you?"

Inanna's words came to mind.

"Trust breeds betrayal," he said, "and betrayal has nothing to do with my friendship with them. It's a simple fact of survival. Life is harsh, and if you want to survive, you've got to be practical."

"I see. Easily managed. And the last?"

"A favor, yes," he said, looking around. "In the unfortunate event that I, or my accomplices, feel threatened by the Empire in any form, we seek the right to asylum within your territory for an indeterminate amount of time."

Lukas supposed he was doing pretty good so far, all things considered. His throat was a little dry from all the bullshitting, but he was nearly done now.

"So," he asked Dvalinn, "do we have an accord?"

CHAPTER 10

THE HAND THAT FEEDS YOU

The Otamba Bridge—one of the seven in the entire Llaisy Kingdom—spanned more than a thousand feet across the Delgia River. An emblem of the link between the Graken Mountains up north and the Sea of Mone down south, the bridge was one of the most beautiful in the Empire. To the east, the illuminated facade of the Naowa Palace stood proudly against the bell towers made in reverence to the Goddess Okuninushi. To the west, high atop the Sunder Hill, stood the fortified walls of the Banksi Mansion. And northward, on the other bank of the Delgia, stretched the elegant spires of the Haviskali Ether Forges, the largest in all of the Llaisy Kingdom.

Tanya and Lukas were enjoying lunch under the warm summer sun on a floating hotel near the bridge. In the end, the two of them had left the Zwaray Keep safe and sound, with Lukas grinning like a loon and Tanya sweating buckets out of sheer paranoia. Too exhausted to count the number of things Lukas had fucked up, she had dropped the idea of returning to the Banksi compound and instead chosen to have one last comfort meal.

"I did not expect today, Lukas," she said, pulling his eyes away from the scenery. They were sitting at a table for two on the deck with a few other couples nearby, though none of them were close enough to overhear their conversation.

"One can never know the future, can they?"

There had been absolutely no hiccups after Lukas had offered his proposition. With a speed that defied bremetan comprehension, the svartalfars had a separate pod installed for him just within the citadel walls. They had even gotten an Eztli contract prepared, much to her amusement. Trying to bind Lukas into following a contract using the name of the Great Goddess would be slightly less effective than scolding him, though the lethal blood curse was something to worry about. But what had shocked her most was the casual way with which he had handled the entire matter, and the impossible things he had said during the exchange.

"You really think there'll be no consequences?" she asked, taking a tip from her glass. "The things you demanded from the svartalfars—they butcher people for less. Much, much less. I'm not sure whether to call it bravery or recklessness."

"You mustn't be afraid to dream a little bigger, darling," he said, idly turning a piece of meat around with his fork.

"What I can't understand is how you'll keep your promise to them. You promised them impossible things, Lukas."

He grinned. "Exactly."

Tanya narrowed her eyes.

"The thing about impossible things," Lukas said, still toying with the piece of meat, "is that they are rare and precious and often require equally impossible circumstances, which more often than not, comes with a time factor. An indeterminate time factor."

"I don't understand."

Lukas grinned. "To put it simply, I lied."

The glass slipped from her fingers. Before she could react, wine splattered over her top. Glaring at Lukas, she whispered, "You—you lied? Are you out of your fucking mind?"

Lukas slouched back into his chair with one elbow resting on the table. "Certainly not. I told them it's possible to get small amounts of featherglass but never set a date for delivery. Will those guys not realize that? Yes, they will, but we're giving them some featherglass right now, which means maybe we can drag a year's worth of time from them before having to commit on a date. An entire year of unrestrained access into their borderlands. Even if we don't end up getting them any featherglass and they drop the deal, the fortune we'll make from the borderlands will be massive."

Tanya blinked. "You—you're telling me that all of that back then, was a big scam?"

Lukas just looked amused.

"But then—the requirement for the wardstone? You made it look like it was essential for acquiring the featherglass."

"Oh, that." He bit into his food. "One illusion on top of the other. Makes the entire thing feel more concrete." He let out a soft chuckle. "I need it for an entirely different reason."

"Which is?"

"Irrelevant as of now." Lukas shot her question down. "I'll let you know when it's time."

But Tanya knew. The pillars gathered the World's Energy into them, much like how an anomaly held tremendous amounts of World Energy within it. And she suspected she knew where Lukas was going with it.

"It's your ticket back home, isn't it?" she asked. "That spell you performed in the anomaly. It didn't work out. So this is your way to reattempt it over and over again until you get it right."

She could have been wrong but his eyes appeared somewhat troubled and distant at her words. No doubt he was thinking of home, or maybe—maybe he was thinking about that goddess. Something within her twisted at the thought, but she suppressed it with prejudice. "You're using their greed to get you home."

"Am I, now?" A frown crossed Lukas's face. "Would that be such a bad thing? Maybe I have people waiting for me back there. In my world, you know."

A spark of amusement flickered across his face. "They say that home is where the heart is. And I always carry a bit of my world with me."

Tanya frowned and pushed her plate away and sat up straight on her chair. Despite his casual conversation, Lukas was only half there. Ever since he had regained his focus, he had been . . . different. That confidence she had seen in him back in the anomaly was still there, only it was now tempered with loss and practicality. Often she'd see him stare at the distant horizon, or check his Schema, as if verifying something over and over. Tanya barely looked at her own, except for perhaps the times when she gained a Level. It made her wonder if the Outsider's Schema differed from her own, and if so, how.

She had avoided asking him if he had gained any skills from killing Hreidmar. The sheer concept was silly; the idea of someone "killing" monsters and absorbing their skills into himself was absurd on so many levels that Tanya found it embarrassing to even raise the point. Still, she had seen him replicate the former Guardian's corrosive abilities, but back then, the anomaly had tried to possess him—or something like that. Could anomalies even possess others? Or maybe Lukas hadn't understood what was going on, and it had been the sludge that had possessed him? It'd explain the sudden emergence of those abilities, and the alien, murderous disposition that felt so out of place on that young, scruffy face.

Then why did it feel like he was hiding a deep, powerful secret? That his presence, his strange abilities—they all represented something so terrible and great that even she couldn't comprehend. Was it because he had suppressed her Frost? Maybe, maybe not. He had shown the capacity to drain immense amounts of energy—first from the anomaly, and then from the wardstone, which meant that his body, regardless of how he appeared, could channel vast quantities of energy, enough to make her own capacity seem insignificant. For someone that had always fought an uphill battle to keep her powers restrained, being in the constant presence of someone that overwhelmed her in power felt paradoxical.

And weird.

Definitely weird and—

Lukas snapped his fingers.

Tanya blinked. "Uh, yeah?"

"What's on your mind?"

A hundred and twenty-two different things, and they all had something to do with him. But there was no way she'd admit that out loud.

"Just thinking about Zuken."

"What of him?"

"The contract. I know we got what we went there for, but the wording of the contract . . ." She paused, licking her dry lips. "He's not gonna be pleased."

"And?"

She narrowed her eyes. "He's your benefactor and employer."

"Actually he's only my employer, and I've yet to get that part in writing, so even that's debatable. The only real employment I have now is with the svartalfars. Just look at how far we've gotten. Our very first mission, just days away."

"That's not gonna be enough. He's getting you documentation. Even the overseer knows you're his guy."

Lukas stretched his arms and put them behind his head. "No."

"No?"

He shook his head. "Zuken has only as much claim to my power as I'm willing to allow, and frankly, if he throws a tantrum like a spoiled brat just because I have my agenda, then that's just . . . sad. That said . . ." He trailed off, looking at the ether forges on his right. "I'm not ignorant of his kindness, even if it's done to further his own personal agenda."

He met her eyes. "It's true he gave me this chance of making myself a legitimate adventurer, but the stronger I get, it only helps him."

"But what you're doing will make an enemy out of him."

Lukas eyed her. No matter how much she wanted to look away, Tanya couldn't. It was like . . . gravity. Watching him like this reminded her of his negotiation with Dvalinn and the rest of the councilors, where he had stood in the center, surrounded by soldiers and creatures overwhelming him in strength and yet, maintained his hold at being the power in the room.

"Listen, Tanya," he said, "I don't enjoy starting wars. In fact, I go out of my way to avoid them. But—" His voice became heavy. "—If there's a war, I'll end it."

The way he said it was scary. With no melodrama at all. He might as well just have told her he was going to take out the trash. It reminded her of her own grandfather—a twisted megalomaniac bastard who would stop at nothing once he set his eyes upon a goal. And Lukas Aguilar was, as much as she hated it, a person who donned multiple masks, making the real person behind them impossible to even identify, much less understand. At times, he was an idiot with no sense of self-preservation, or a buffoon that went toe-to-toe with others, drunk on his own strength. And then there would be moments when she felt like she was watching Zuken Banksi in action—a shark at Asukan politics. The way he had gotten the svartalfars eating out of his hands while promising literally nothing was something she was still having trouble wrapping her mind around.

Tanya had been reading people all her life. She considered it something she was good at. And at the moment, Lukas Aguilar radiated with confidence, a belief so firm that it could balance the weight of the world upon its shoulders. Tanya's senses were screaming at her, telling her she was in the presence of one of the most dangerous individuals she had ever encountered—

—and he was only twenty-one years old.

Tanya composed her expression and grabbed her glass again. "It's not about starting or ending a war. Zuken arranged for us to get it done so that you could get into the borderlands and gain a proper kami. But you—"

"Took a cheap shot at him because I could? That he sent me there with good intentions in mind and instead, I leveraged him?"

"That's how it looks, yes."

Lukas scowled. "Well then, he should have had the sense to inform me of what was about to happen beforehand. Neither he, nor you, nor the others—no one mentioned anything about svartalfars, or this deal. I only got the information at the last second, and so when I saw a shot, I took it."

Tanya remained silent for a moment. "If Banksi goes against you—"

"Tattle on me for being an Outsider?" Lukas challenged. "Sure, he can. Just like I can revoke the contract at any point and give the featherglass away to the svartalfars. That should be enough to grant me asylum until I figure a way out."

Tanya pursed her lips, now completely stiff. "You're overestimating yourself and underestimating others. The Empire is a dangerous place, especially for foreigners. And you're—"

"An Outsider, yes, I know." Lukas waved it off. "And I've noticed. Foreigners, other species, half-breeds—they're treated worse, not that I need to tell you about that."

She clenched her fists. "Excuse me?"

Lukas cocked his head. "I'm rather good at studying spiritual information. And I know you're a bremetan and you've a kami, but that's not all. That Frost you have . . . it's something else. Something powerful and dangerous and ancient, almost enough to classify you as a—"

"No!" Tanya gripped the edges of the table. "There is *nothing* else. I was being hunted because I committed a Sin. I destroyed an anomaly, and they wanted to punish me for it."

"And then Zuken hired you to destroy another in exchange for freedom."

"Yes, and that's all there is to it."

Lukas eyed her. His brown eyes gazed at her, judging her. Like she was naked, before that stare. That he wasn't so much looking at her but through her.

"I believe you," he said at last, and looked away.

"Good," Tanya replied, a weird feeling of sadness gripping inside her. Like she had failed at something simple. She felt . . . wasted, like she had broken something beyond repair. She didn't know how, but there was something in that stare that would haunt her in the days to come.

Her life was shitty like that.

CHAPTER 11

FREEDOM TO FALL

By day, Haviskali was a busy town, scorched by the light of the red sun—hard, distinct, and somewhat oppressive. At night, however, the rules changed. The Eternal Light kept up the illumination, but the absence of the sun overhead created a bizarre dichotomy, making it feel colder than it was. If not for the pubs, eateries, and nightclubs illuminating the otherwise grim night, people might have been apprehensive about going out.

And then there were nights like this one, where the sky was covered with purplish fog, blurring and obscuring everything. High-rise buildings became ghostly, looming silhouettes. Streets seemed to grow narrower in the fog, every thoroughfare becoming a lonely, dangerous highway. The cafeterias were closed, the pubs and diners sealed and locked, with the common folk already retreated into the safety of their homes by sundown, save the foolhardy and the desperate. Even the watchers weren't out tonight, unwilling to face the foreboding, misty silence.

This was a night for the mysterious and the strange.

People like us, Lukas thought, standing upon the empty Otamba Bridge, overlooking the town below. They were supposed to head for the Zwaray Keep tonight, but Tanya had some errands to take care of, so he had opted to take a tour of the town by himself.

A cold breeze slipped across the metallic construct, brushing against his fog-dampened cheek like an exhaled frosty breath.

"How did I know I'd find you here?" asked an amused, feminine voice.

"Maybe because we had our date here two days ago and you knew I'd miss you?"

Tanya chuckled and stepped up next to him. Lukas studied her profile. Her hair, normally restrained in a messy bun or ponytail, now hung free over her back, her golden curls emitting a soft, ethereal luminescence that was every bit as eerie as it was beautiful. At the same time, it was a sharp contrast to the feral-looking thing she had been in the anomaly, lean and hyperalert, her eyes trying to watch the whole world at once.

"You look . . . different," he said. "Don't tell me a visit to the salon was the errand you mentioned."

Tanya arched an eyebrow. "It was, actually. Who knows how many days we're gonna be stuck in this new shithole? At least I'm going out in style."

Lukas snorted.

She grinned briefly. "There's also . . . something about the fog. It beckons me. Makes me feel less . . . taut. Unrestrained." At his look, she quickly added, "Not like the Frost, but you get what I mean."

He did. Her eyes had gained a slightly icy sheen, reminding him of the Frost Queen that tried to kill him before Inanna's timely intervention.

Even now, Inanna's spell held her back.

"I know what you're thinking," Her voice carried over the fog. "Very few people have the ability to stomach this fog. Most stay indoors, and those that don't fear the things that come during it."

There was a strange confidence in her tone that Lukas certainly didn't share. "What things?"

"Wraiths. Nameless things. Shades left behind by curses. The kind of thing the Empire tells you doesn't exist."

Lukas felt a shudder go down his spine. He had dealt with some pretty bad shit ever since he had been dropped in this world, and his episode with Solana's ilk definitely topped the list of mind-bending events. He could live with siphoning other monsters and allowing them to possess him. He could stare down predators, angry goddesses, and pretty much everyone else. But there was something utterly violating about that initial attempt at possession—that moment when his body had ceased to be his own and his mind was trapped in an infinite hollowness still gave him nightmares.

It was why, despite how much he smiled at Solana or how comfortable he became in her presence, he never allowed himself to forget that he was dealing with a demon.

"Lukas?"

"Uh," he began, "those are real?"

He had always stayed firm on his apparent lack of knowledge about yokai. It drove Olfric crazy.

"As real as you and me," she said. "Most people are afraid of them. You should see how bad it becomes during the Black Moon. People literally lock themselves indoors for the entire month, fearing something would catch them, devour their souls, and steal their skin for their own."

That was a surprisingly accurate description for Solana. She had described herself as a skinwalker, or as the native term went, a yosuzume. An indescribable, soul-twisting, skin-stealing parasite that wore the flesh of a young, black-haired girl in her twenties.

Even thinking about it made his insides churn.

"How does that help? I mean—"

"We have a system called Kanso, a science that employs storage and redirection of Eternal Light in appropriate directions to cast a spiritual barrier around one's home. The stone walls absorb the power throughout the year and channel the energy when such a situation presents itself."

"But there isn't a Black Moon around."

"No but there are nights like tonight, when the Barrier between worlds is weaker than usual. It's what causes the fog to pass through."

"Something tells me the svartalfars didn't choose tonight on a whim."

Tanya eyed him. "True. The weaker the barrier, the less energy is required to open a well to the borderland. Svartalfars are all about efficiency."

"Speaking of efficiency, what happened to our third member?"

Tanya snorted. "Zuken didn't let him come. Olfric wants a water-type, and we're entering a land of fire. Without a kami, entering this place would be suicide. Besides, all transport ceased by sundown, and he won't get out in the fog."

"No transport, huh? Guess people *are* really freaked out by this stuff." He glanced up at the dark sky, the fog moving around like a living thing. Maybe it *was*, for all he knew.

"You know . . ." He chuckled, strangely nostalgic. "Back in my world, I made a living writing fictional tales about apocalyptic ends of the world. It's—"

He paused at her stupefied expression.

"What?"

"Why would you willingly author tales that inspire dread in others?"

Lukas wondered what Tanya would think of Dean Koontz or Stephen King. "There's a saying back in my world: *Nothing sells like dread*. Maybe it's the adrenaline rush, or about exploring the dark side, or . . . the appeal of shadows. People love it. It's . . ." He paused, gathering his thoughts. "It's like this fog. People fear it, and so it creates rumors and myths. And from them come stories."

"Weird," Tanya made a sour face. "I thought you were a student of diplomacy."

"I was," he said. "This wasn't my profession, per se. It was just something I did to pay my bills, while I was finishing my education. But then other stuff happened, and I found myself inside that underground cave."

"And you desire to be a bard of such abominations?"

Lukas felt amused at the tautness in her tone.

"Uh, I wouldn't *mind* doing it. It'd be a nice retreat from the constant excitement."

"Why?"

"Why what?"

Tanya's frown had devolved into an open scowl. "You have power and potential like few have tasted, yet you speak of an ordinary—no, a *ludicrously pedestrian* life. I mean, sometimes I wonder if you're a natural liar or just delusional."

"Maybe neither. Maybe both." Her irritation sent a rush of pleasure through him. Was this why Inanna enjoyed doing this so much? Being irritatingly cryptic was an art, one that you generally got better at with age.

"So, err . . . no transport. How are we going to get to the keep?"

"I don't know about us, but *I* could obviously fly my way over." She gave him her best condescending leer. "You'd need to chase after me, I suppose. All that lifeforce should get you sprinting at decent speed."

Lukas smiled. "I might surprise you. Just keep looking."

Tanya arched an eyebrow. "I'm watching."

Lukas smiled but didn't say anything else. Instead, he focused inward.

> **Activating Monster Prototype SVARTALFAR**
> **Initiating Consciousness Shift**
> **Enact**

And Hreidmar's instincts took over.

His body began to warm up, and lifeforce rose within. But that was not all. The feeling of being a creature deeply connected to the terrain, to the bonds between all matter, and the feeling that every material force, including gravity, was his to play with, while retaining an instinct that was calmer and infinitely more rational than himself felt . . . unsettling. The closest similarity he could draw was when he had used Shatterpoint Intuition for the first time, but he had to use tachypsychia to vastly increase his perception and keep up with the thoggua's instincts.

The svartalfar prototype needed no such thing. Instead, his senses went blank, replaced with trajectories and strings. A layer of what could only be anti-friction formed around him, isolating him from the world around, except for his feet, to get him the necessary solidity with the ground and not lose his balance. Hreidmar's power lay in subtlety, in understanding the bonds and the interactive forces between all material objects. If Inanna's Kinetomancy was like a hurricane, using the ocean itself and twisting it to one's whim, then Hreidmar's technique was like a ship, playing the natural forces against each other while maintaining oneself afloat in a stormy ocean.

He almost felt bad that such a unique and industrious creature met his end in such a crude way, stuck between the raging fires ascending from below and the invisible barrier halting his escape from every other side.

And now he had his skills. His technique, his instinct and his legacy. In effect, every creature he killed left him their skills. Inanna had called him a *leech,* one that stole skills from others. And if he was going to be a leech, then he was going to be the greatest leech ever. He would combine it with Kinetomancy, to become both the surfer that rides an angry tide, and the ocean that raises those tides in the first place. He would combine it with Shatterpoint Intuition to travel along the most efficient trajectory lines to achieve the best result with minimum effort.

He had killed the seidmadr. It was only fitting that he became the one to take his place.

But until he reached that level, he would have to keep trying. Again and again. Again and again.

Lukas watched the rock chips on the floor. Unmoving. Completely uncaring about what was about to happen. Taunting him. Daring him.

"Well?" Tanya asked, impatient.

Lukas bent down, winked at her and *jumped.*

With a soft whoosh, he shot upward at the velvety night sky. The wind sandblasted against his face, but the force behind it was missing. That, or the layer of anti-friction was deflecting it, reducing it to hollow flaps kissing his face. Before he knew it, the ground and Tanya had gotten lost amidst the purple swirls. He felt the inexorable call of gravity from beneath and suppressed the urge to throw lifeforce at it. He realized it was Alpha Condition trying to snatch the control back from Hreidmar, and for the first time, Lukas fought.

And surrendered.

He didn't want to shoot lifeforce out. The trick was to float, to glide, to use gravity's power against itself. He needed to spread himself out, like a bird did with its wings, and fly.

And fly he did. For a few moments, there was no doubt, no terror of losing control and falling to his death. Not even the sound of the racing wind. Just the soft feeling of the fog, the growing numbness of his limbs as the temperature began to fall sharply with every passing second of his ascent. In a paradox of self-awareness, Lukas sensed that this was death. But he felt glad for it. He allowed the drifting numbness to possess him entirely. He let it carry him wherever it was he would go. What was happening to him, he did not know.

Deactivating Monster Prototype

What? NO—

Reverting Consciousness Shift to PRIME HOST
Enact

The anti-friction flickered out, and Lukas Aguilar plummeted downwards to the ground.

Thump! Thump!

He was dropping like a rock. Feet first. Arms raised. The winds were tearing past him violently. As he plummeted towards the ground, he felt something he had not experienced before—the inexorable pull of gravity during a deadly fall. The faster he fell, the harder the ground seemed to pull, sucking him down. It wasn't a fifty-foot drop into a pool. This one was *thousands* of feet into a town of endless expanse of pavement and stone.

Thump! Thump!

As the reality of his dire situation became apparent, Lukas was briefly distracted by how calm he felt. It took him another second to realize he had instinctively employed tachypsychia to temporarily enhance his perception, and the surging lifeforce within him was temporarily shutting down his fear response. But even at maximum perceptual dilation, he guessed he had less than a minute of subjective time to figure something out before he hit the ground, so panic was the last thing he needed.

Thump! Thump! Thump!

His first and most obvious thought was quickly assessed and discarded. He tried to shoot lifeforce downward, hoping to balance against gravity's pull. That had as much impact as scolding it for its actions. His next thought was to manipulate motion using Kinetomancy, but that had a better chance of tearing him to shreds than halt his descent, and retrying Hreidmar's skills was the last thing he wanted to try. Decreasing friction would only accelerate his free fall, and increasing friction was likely to burn him to ashes. Terramancy would be useless in the air. He knew nothing of Aquamancy. Fire would only aid in immolating him faster.

Thump! Thump!

Lukas frowned at the sensation of his heart beating slowly but not nearly slowly enough under the circumstances, a constant reminder of how little time he had to pull off a miracle. Frustrated that his brainstorming session under tachypsychia had come to an end without any useful ideas, he was further dismayed by how slow his thoughts had become after tachypsychia had run its course. Morbidly, he wondered if some part of him would be stuck in the afterlife thinking about possibilities after he was dead. In desperation, he shut his eyes and used tachypsychia again, throwing everything he could to increase its dilation, his mind flashing through everything he had learned, every skill he had gained, every technique he had studied, every nugget of wisdom he had accumulated from his experience in the anomaly. For a brief instant he nearly lost the dilation as his mind reeled under the onslaught of memories.

Momentum.

Raw Force.

Friction.

Pressure.

Kinetomancy.

And as he plummeted down to the ground, Inanna's voice echoed in the winds.

Do not liken Kinetomancy to a mortal technique. It's the culmination of what allowed me to butcher gods and demons alike. You have no more chance of bearing it than an ant can bear the weight of a mountain.

Even now, she was taunting him. Telling him he still had miles to go. But there had to be something. More out of stubbornness than hope, he forced his mind to continue.

Fire.

Temperature.

Seismic Sensing.

Conjuration.

It was Creation from nothing. Creation. He was falling downward. If only he had a way to slow himself down. Slow himself down. Slow himself—

Imagine what you wish to create. Push the ether into it. Give your imagination form.

—Down.

Lukas opened his eyes, and focused on his palms, releasing ether from them. It didn't work. The ether disintegrated faster than he could conjure it due to the force of his own downward momentum. He had been trying to conjure a flap—nothing great; maybe five or six feet of monster hide to grab on to, the crudest approximation of a parachute imaginable.

Thump!

He had to think of something. Something involving Creation. Something—

Thump!

—something that would work. Something that was tangible yet intangible at the same time. Something that wouldn't shatter from his downward fall. That or he had to conjure something faster. But how could he when he was plummeting down faster than he could *think?*

Disintegration.

Shatterpoint Intuition.

Perception.

Wait. Perception?

The mortal mind is body-bound. That in itself limits what you can think, feel, and act. But the moment you delve into psionics, you irrevocably shatter those limitations.

As the ground grew nearer, a mad and desperate idea began to form. Nothing among his skills could directly help him survive this mess. He could theoretically conjure, but unless he managed to perform it at speeds double the magnitude of his downward descent, it would be useless. And the only way to do that would be to operate at a level that he had never done before. In Inanna's words, *shatter his limitations.*

And if he was going to shatter his limitations, he wasn't going to end up hoping on a crappy parachute to save his ass. He was going to use something *real.*

Something powerful.

If you maintain this altered mental state for more than what your heart can keep up with, you risk a complete breakdown of your brain functions.

Shut up, Inanna! Stop playing both sides. I need to focus—

Never before had he been as motivated to push past the boundaries of the psionic arts as he was right now. His heart was already beating faster and faster, while his mind was growing slower and slower. Just three more beats and it'd trigger a full-scale brain aneurysm. He knew it. He just *knew it.*

Thummmmmp!

"*AAARRRGGGHHH!*"

His mind was frying itself. Breathing was agony. Thinking was agony. His mind was not built to handle this, never mind running at this level in a single go.

It was ridiculous.

Absurd.

Insane.

He did it anyway.

Thummmmmp!

His mind was racing. Ether as an element was, in itself, incapable of materializing by its own power. And yet, in a twist of irony, its domains were along the lines of composition, dissolution, modification, separation, unification, and alteration of shapeless bodies materialized in physical form. He had always thought of physical things to be those that were in a solid state. But he wasn't seeing the full picture. Everything was made of matter. Solid. Liquid. Gas. Each of them had molecules. Each of them held forces of attraction. Each of them exerted *motion.*

And he had inherited a skill that could bend that motion to his will.

It wasn't like he hadn't negated motion before. He had done so with monsters, against Quonnan, and several times against Ryu. He fared considerably better at motion deflection than negation, but even then, it had been against other creatures—people and monsters alike. But to negate his own motion, especially during his free fall, was something he had never done. Never tried. There was no saying if he even *could* do it. Even the slightest mistake would squash him like a bug in midair.

This skill is power beyond what you are built for.

His brain had caught fire inside his skull. A shudder passed through his entire body and Lukas suspected that if he hadn't been dilating, he'd have suffered from a violent full-body spasm or possibly some kind of fit. Pushing both arms outward, Lukas called his power out.

My own belief is that it will destroy you.

It was deafening. The impact of an unstoppable force against an immovable object. His entire body should have been squashed from the power of gravity pulling him down to absolute rest in a fraction of a second. But Kinetomancy was all about breaking the rules—stealing energy from places it wasn't supposed to. Breaking inertia. Taking the laws of physics and throwing them into the trash can.

His bones cracked. His vision went red. Every single nerve ending burned. All of his tendons were snapping. But his fear was gone. As was his doubt and hesitation.

Then everything stopped. Just stopped. The pain was gone. The tension was gone. The descent and even his own body was gone. Rather, inside his mind, his perception remained, multiplied exponentially. The entire universe shrank until it was just within his mind. And in that instant, Lukas Aguilar knew he had done it.

The Screen blinked.

Skill Upgrade Successful		
SKILL	**LEVEL**	**SOUL CAPACITY CONSUMED**
Psychomancy	2	500

He. Could. Do. It.

The pain vanished. Completely. His mind was expanding, his perception growing, sensing, dilating his inner time. Objectively, he knew he'd be a splatter on the ground in a couple of seconds, but in his mind, that felt like *half an hour*. Like he had all the time in the world to think, to plan and execute.

He was done planning, and he was done waiting.

It was time to finish the execution.

Negate motion. Don't stop the wind. Stop yourself. Don't grab. Focus on not falling. There is no force on you. All motion is—

It is a deadly legacy. If you crave it, you must accept what comes with it.

He was willing. And more.

Negate it. You are in control of your motion. All motion is yours, your body included. Remember how Inanna stopped the khorkhoi. Reach out and grab the energy within you. Entwine your power with it. Become one with it.

Give it a yank.

Skill Upgrade Successful		
SKILL	**LEVEL**	**SOUL CAPACITY CONSUMED**
Kinetomancy (Fragmented)	**BROKEN**	**+4679**

He paused.

In midair.

Just like that.

Calibrating Host Body to upgraded Skills requires Level Up

Lukas looked below. He was still hanging in midair, but he wasn't flying. No, instead it was like he had hit an invisible platform where his motion equaled zero. The potential energy he had developed during the free fall had dissipated, shattering the laws of motion in its wake.

That, or he had somehow unconsciously channeled all that energy into the environment without knowing it.

He looked below again.

Yep. Still not falling. Instead he hovered, parallel to the ground.

Just like Hreidmar.

"That's a most unusual style of flight," came Tanya's voice from behind him.

Lukas whirled around and found her floating in the air, right behind him. Unlike himself, she wasn't standing still. Tiny currents of wind spun all around her body, acting both as a buffer against external forces as well as maintaining her weight against gravity. Aeromancy at work, honed through painstaking diligence.

"How do you do it?" she asked.

"Do what?"

Tanya gave him a *Don't-be-stupid* look. "You used the sludge's technique from the anomaly. First against me in those caverns, then against the metal monster doppelganger and recently, against Hreidmar. And now you're floating above the ground, just like he does."

Lukas did his best not to gape his mouth at her. How—*at the anomaly?* Did that mean they already suspected he could steal skills?

But that didn't mean he had to fess up. First rule in such cases—*Always deny.*

"I mess up and fall from a thousand feet, and that's the first thing you ask? Talk about priorities."

She shrugged. "I thought you were doing fine."

Lukas doubled his glare.

"Fine!" she scoffed. "I had a wind funnel ready down there. I'd have caught you in time."

"Just wanted to hear me scream like a child?"

"Maybe. Now quit stalling. *How do you do it?*"

"The usual way," he replied with a half shrug. "My super-secret Outsider powers."

Tanya glided in the air around him, as if the air was a snowy plain and she a skater. "You shot yourself into the air. I didn't sense any mana there."

"If you say so."

"So it had to be lifeforce propulsion. But to *that* level? No, there had to be something else." She cupped her chin and observed him. "Your clothes . . . they aren't burnt. That much lifeforce should've charred them to bits."

She paused, palming her mouth. "Unbelievable. *Friction Modulation.* Easily Level 2 given the altitude. Added with tremendous lifeforce reserves. Are you sure you're not part-vanir?"

"No clue," he said, feeling the first stirrings of annoyance. "Not from around here, remember?"

"But that wouldn't explain this . . . " She gestured at his legs, floating in midair. As if to test, she put one foot next to his, feeling for any barrier. Finding none, she floated away and looked at him again.

"How *are* you doing this?"

"It's not important," he said airily.

"It is," Tanya retorted. "We're going to a borderland together. It's *common sense* to know what my partner is strong or weak at."

"Oh?" Lukas drawled. "Then perhaps we can start with you. How does your Frost work? You're an aeromancer. Are you sure you're fully bremetan, up in your ancestry?"

"Enough!" Tanya snapped. "We are *not* talking about that."

"Wow, so it's only okay when *you* ask questions. You have complicated rules, Tanya."

Tanya looked like she wanted to argue, but then she looked down abruptly. "I see. I suppose only Zuken Banksi can pay for the Outsider's secrets."

As she was saying this, Lukas studied her carefully and even dilated his perception slightly, so that he could review everything he knew about Tanya and her connections with Zuken Banksi. He suspected that the man had told Tanya *some* of his secrets. He doubted Zuken was a man with loose lips, so it had to be planned rather than an impulsive action. Plus, he had him in the lab during the entire time he was "dead." He had plenty of opportunities to inform her about his powers before she and Olfric began to teach him.

But he hadn't.

Which meant that this was a well-planned setup. Zuken hadn't *informed* Tanya to help her be better at teaching Lukas. He had done so with the intention of sowing seeds of mistrust, selling the idea that Lukas was keeping secrets from her but not from Zuken, making her question her own association with him in the first place.

He wasn't actually mad at Zuken for doing that, the same way he wouldn't be mad at a dog for barking at the mailman. It was what they did.

Banksi had made a move. And that was fine. He could up the ante as well.

"Oh?" he asked. "What did he tell you?"

"What makes you think he told me anything?"

He shrugged. "I thought he did. He wanted some background information beyond whatever he could gather from my body. But I thought . . . I thought he told you."

"And why would he?"

"Because he's *your* employer. That's why. It's obvious you're basically being my handler on his behalf. Why would he hide things from you?" He snorted contemptuously. "Doesn't make sense to me."

For a second, a look of terrible rage passed over Tanya's eyes, but then, it faded, and her affability returned.

"Well . . ." she growled, "he didn't. At least, not everything I think." She looked up at him speculatively. "Is it really true that people in your world don't have *any* Soul Capacity?"

He nodded somberly. "Soul Capacity. Lifeforce. Mana. None of it."

"It feels . . . unreal."

Lukas barked out a mirthless laugh. "Honestly, I'm surprised he even believed me."

Her annoyance doubled. "He's confused. Hanging between belief and skepticism. As am I. It certainly explains your obvious lack of knowledge about the things we take for granted. About leveling up. About skills, and so on. That said, I'm also inclined to agree with Zuken that your skill growth is too fast, too impossible for someone who only started learning while being in the anomaly."

Lukas shrugged. "I know. Overachieving is in my blood. Sometimes I just can't help it."

She rolled her eyes. "What makes me skeptical is you learned so much and evolved so quickly, and yet your education feels . . . superficial at best. Even if you can really copy the skills of the creatures you've killed."

"My teacher was the sort of parent who thinks you need to figure things out for yourself."

Tanya blinked. "Those are real?"

He grunted. "But yeah, there's a ton of things I need to know. I'm hoping my deal with Banksi will help on that front. So far, I'm not impressed. Here we are on our mission and he's told me nothing about the borderlands. Makes me wonder if all this is a convenient excuse to get me killed."

Tanya grimaced. "Ah, about that. He kinda told me to make this mission educational for you. There's only like a hundred and thirty-seven things you need to know if you're gonna survive it."

"I'm all ears," Lukas grinned back.

SOULSCAPE	
NAME	**Lukas Aguilar**
Type	**Prime Host**
Level	**8**
Experience	**261**
Current Threshold	**2560**
Utilized Soul Capacity	**22408 / ∞**
ESSENCE	
Maximum Lifeforce Output	**5075**
Replenishment Rate	**700 / hour**
LEY LINE NETWORK	
Maximum Mana Output	**6325**
Synthesis Rate	**810 / hour**

"The nature of Schema is quite simple, really," said Tanya. "It reflects the total spiritual constitution in a format best fit for the person. Different people describe it differently. For most people, it appears in a tabular format, which *sucks*." She pouted. "Literally takes all the artistry and replaces it with cold, hard numbers."

They were sitting at the precipice of the Cantonment's roof, one of the only buildings in Haviskali that could be called a skyscraper, if only barely. After his stunt and subsequent upgrades on Kinetomancy, it had become much easier for him to shoot through the air and keep up with the blonde. Tanya could use the wind to propel herself, while he modified his own motions and accelerated himself, also maintaining an anti-friction bubble around him. His performance was far from perfect, but he was slowly getting the hang of it.

"At least it's efficient."

Tanya tilted her head. "Are you sure you don't have svartalfar in your ancestry?"

Lukas chortled. "Human all the way."

"Yeah, whatever," She grumbled, "I once met a ljósálfar whose Schema was crafted out of shades of color. He said that the colors were words, and words were colors. Too philosophical to get through my skull, but it *sounded* pretty."

Both of them laughed at that.

"What about Experience?"

Tanya giggled. "I'll tell you what my father told me. He said that the world we live in is fond of murder. It rewards those that mimic it, considering them worthy, and feeds upon the rest. When we kill something—a person, creature, or monster—its soul returns to the World, and in return, it grants us a blessing that we call Experience. The bigger and nastier the kill, the more Experience we gain from it, all of which can be accumulated and then exchanged for Soul Capacity when we hit the threshold."

Lukas knew all of that but didn't bother to stop her. It was good to compare his theory with hers.

"Now, leveling up increases both the production rate and output of both lifeforce and mana, depending on what sort of creature you are, I guess, but most importantly, it synchronizes your body with your soul."

"The soul reflects on the body," Lukas repeated Inanna's words.

"Poetic, but the same, basically. Your skills don't change or get better, but your body is now attuned to using those skills. That alone gives you an edge. The negatives: you're probably going to have a tougher time adjusting to skills opposite to the ones you currently have."

Which explained why Kinetomancy and Shatterpoint Intuition came easier to him now than ever. He was hoping that this mission would land him his next Body Level Up. It'd be interesting to see how Hreidmar's skills and the elevated Kinetomancy affected his body.

As for the negatives, he was still to see any of them yet, but that was probably because his body was an anomaly.

"Different people choose to go with this differently. Most will actually delay leveling themselves, choosing to upgrade their skills first. That way, when they finally level up, their bodies are attuned to the upgraded skills instead of their lower variants. The trade-off is that they intentionally stay weaker for a longer time until they level up. Some people actually go the reverse route, choosing to level up faster to acquire more Soul Capacity to gain skills. It has the obvious disadvantage of having a lot of skills at low levels—"

Lukas actually flushed at that.

"—but it gives them a greater number of skills to use. And then there are people who choose a middle ground where they level up quickly but pour all the new Soul Capacity into a single skill or skill set. That's where the majority of us spiritists fall. We gain as much Soul Cap as possible, and use it to elevate our kami's skill levels . . . and is something wrong with my face?"

"Huh—no, nothing," Lukas mumbled, realizing he had been gazing at it for longer than was acceptable. "Just wondering about my skills."

Unlike everyone else, he was no longer subjected to the perils of limited Soul Capacity. It was why he had no problems grabbing whatever useful skill he collected and adding it to his Schema without care.

SKILL ATTRIBUTES		
SKILL	**LEVEL**	**CONSUMED SOUL CAP**
Raw Lifeforce Manipulation	3	5000

Kinetomancy (FRAGMENTED)	APEX	5908
Momentum Manipulation	3	5000
Friction Modulation	2	500
Pressure Modulation	2	500
Innate Gravity Control	2	500

Fire Creation	2	500
Fire Manipulation	2	500

Temperature Modulation	2	500

Earth Manipulation	2	500
Terraportation	2	500
Seismic Sensing	2	500

Conjuration	2	500
Disintegration	2	500

Shatterpoint Intuition	2	500
Psychomancy	2	500

Lukas arched his brow. His Schema had come a long way from what it used to be. The Skills section was neatly arranged in proper stacks, with all related skills grouped together in a single one. Funnily enough, the Seismic Sensing skill he had gotten from the thoggua was placed next to Earth Manipulation and Terraportation, while Innate Gravity Control was placed in the Kinetomancy cluster alongside Momentum, Pressure, and Friction Modulation. Kinetomancy had gotten the newest boost as had Psychomancy. Inanna had described Kinetomancy as a cluster that encompassed every motion-related skill in existence. Momentum, Pressure, Friction, and most recently, Gravity— all of them were tied to force.

"Are you done *preening* over your stats?"

Lukas's face flushed again and he dismissed his Schema when he realized Tanya was staring at him. He glanced at her and was confronted by an arched brow.

"Uh, yes."

The brow rose higher.

Embarrassed, he looked away.

"Given the kind of stunts you pull off with just lifeforce, I assume you've got a Level-3 skill there?"

Lukas stiffened at that for a moment before nodding.

"See?" Tanya reacted, pointing fingers at him accusingly. "Right there! It's *impossible* to gain skills that fast. I've been honing my skills for *years*, and I only have *two* Level-3 skills. For the Goddess's sake, I've seen people take *decades* before they gain a Level-3 skill and you—you know you're pretty messed up, right?"

"Don't I know it?" He took a deep breath, relishing in the feel of the cold, wet wind brushing his face. "Ask yourself, how did someone with no skills and no information become the guy you know in so little time?"

"Before I got to know you, I'd say it was likely a combination of working hard, an arcane skill from this goddess of yours, plus a lot of luck." She took in the fog-covered landscape before her. "Now? I'm gonna add a very high ECR and a superior Schema to that list."

"ECR?"

"Exchange-Conversion Ratio." She began, but the Screen was quicker.

Rate of Conversion of Experience into Soul Capacity

". . ..into your Soul Capacity."

Huh. You learn something new every day.

"Every time you hit the Threshold, you level up and gain a specific amount of Soul Capacity, based on how high or low your ECR is."

What's my ECR?

NIL

Whatever had happened in the anomaly that had unlocked the Prime Host feature had also unlocked its infinite Soul Capacity for his use. It also seemed to have deleted his own ECR.

What was my ECR before the Warmonger Protocol?

68%

Which meant . . . nothing. Not without a relative reference point. "Say, Tanya, what's the average bremetan ECR?"

"The lower ones drag all the way down to twenty and below. The higher-ups are probably in the fifties and maybe in the lower sixties . . . What?" She demanded, noting the surprise flickering through his features. "I'm sure you have a high ECR. What is it?"

"Sixty-eight percent."

Tanya looked at him, impressed. "That's among the top percentile for bremetans."

"You're surprised?"

"Not at the value. After everything you can do, this is just trivial. No, I'm just . . . surprised you told me the true value, knowing what it means."

Lukas shrugged. "Gotta start with trusting someone, right?"

"I thought that was Zuken."

Lukas rolled his eyes. Maybe she was a bit sour about finding things about him from Zuken. Had she grown to think of herself as someone Lukas trusted over the others? It was true she knew him longer than the others and had been vocal in his favor, despite what happened over the dranzithl. Having Zuken tell her his secrets must have felt bitter.

Which was *exactly* why Banksi had done it.

"He and I . . . we have a deal. He helps me out with whatever I want, and in return, I work for him, whatever that entails."

"From what I heard, you chose to tell him things yourself."

Lukas sighed at the petulance in her tone. "Sometimes, a choice isn't a choice at all, Tanya. He already had a ton of information by testing my body when I was in my month-long beauty sleep. In his defense, my own demands were pretty outrageous too, so I had to give away some secrets to even the odds . . . and is it just me, or are you being jealous about it?"

Now it was Tanya's turn to flush. "Jealous? You're crazy."

She looked away.

Yep. Definitely jealous.

"And while we're at it, I don't see you talking about *your* ECR."

The challenge was clear in his words.

Tanya looked hesitant for a few seconds. She was probably considering the pros and cons of giving in to his demand. Finally, she made up her mind and looked him in the eye.

"Eighty-seven percent."

". . . and what level are you?"

"Twenty-two."

". . . I thought the upper percentile lay in the sixties."

Tanya looked away. "You asked. I answered. Leave it at that."

Lukas's eyes brightened as he made a mental note of what she did and did *not* say. If the upper percentile lay in the sixties and she held an eighty-seven ECR, and if she had indeed leveled up *eighteen* times then . . .

"Tell me something," he said. "Does Zuken know exactly what you're capable of?"

Tanya paused, and then after several seconds of consideration, shook her head.

"Then why tell me?"

She knitted her brows and bit her lips. "You told me something about you. Trust has to go both ways, doesn't it?"

He was starting to put things together. Back when he had woken up, one of the first things Tanya had asked was if he was there to kill her. Something in her tone told him that her fears weren't exactly limited to her issues with the Cobalt Army. She was strong and swift and could literally blitz through an entire force and yet, here she was, working for a shady man under a shady deal. Hell, part of why she was trying to establish a solid rapport with him wasn't because of growing feelings or camaraderie, but because he knew part of her secret—her Frost—and was instrumental in subduing it. That and him being an outlier, much like herself, only solidified his worth in her eyes. It was why she had seen him be so carefree towards others, including Banksi himself, but was still trying to establish a stronger bond with him. No, it was more apt to say that she was doing this *because* he was so carefree about others.

This wasn't a person trying to dig into his secrets. This was a girl seeking shelter in a storm.

"So . . ." Her voice broke his reverie. "Was I right?"

Lukas blinked. "In what?"

"Your secret. A High ECR, a superior Schema, and copying skills of your kills?"

"All of that, and one more thing."

"Which is?"

"Compromise."

Tanya cocked her head. "Compromise?"

Lukas laughed. "Yeah, doesn't feel like it, does it? But it is. People say there are no compromises on the path to power, but that's not true. In every step forward, you have to compromise. Choose between what you have, what you can achieve, and what you need to leave behind in return. As long as the compromise is worth more than you give up."

He exhaled loudly. "My teacher once told me that Might makes Right, that I need to grab power, no matter the cost. Had I accepted things back then, maybe I'd have a complete education. But I was naïve . . . idealistic, I suppose. In the end, it came full circle, and despite me agreeing to everything, it was too little, too late. And now, I'm trying to make amends in my own stupid way."

Tanya bit her lip. "Your teacher . . . Was she this goddess you mentioned?"

Lukas stared at her, wondering how much to tell. She had just shared a bit about herself. Something that could land her in danger. Together with the Frost, Lukas was now privy to two of her most dangerous secrets.

Trust goes both ways, she had said.

So be it.

"Yes."

"You were trained by an actual goddess?"

He thought back to Inanna's brutal regimen, her quips, and philosophy.

"It wasn't exactly tutelage. It was a bargain. Everything I received, I paid a price for."

Inanna would not have had it any other way. The least he could do was acknowledge that.

Tanya stared at him with unblinking eyes. "Tutored by a goddess. Has at least one arcane and a Level-3 skill. Doesn't know the fundamentals. Yeah, you're pretty messed up. Still, you've got high lifeforce and mana output, so that has to count for something. Zuken told me to try teaching you different styles of combat and related skills, maybe even some spells along the way. He assured me you could digest all of it." She paused. "You *do* have a large Soul Capacity, don't you?"

Lukas cast his mind to the infinity value in his Schema, the ever-growing number of monster prototypes in his Array. He thought about the hundreds of thousands of skills mashed up together inside Blob and how each and every one of them could be potentially added, used, and upgraded while making zero difference to his overall Soul Capacity.

Then he opened his mouth.

"Yes."

Tanya grunted, oblivious to his thoughts. "Well, that's nice, I suppose. We can make this first job a training session for you."

"Right," Lukas drawled, "is that why you kept your mouth shut whenever I asked you to explain this stuff to me earlier?"

Tanya winked. "Zuken thought you'd learn better this way. Also, it's fun. The borderlands are usually vast and filled with obstacles. It'll be nice seeing where you really stand after they're done with you."

CHAPTER 12

THE BORDERLANDS

The Zwaray Keep was big. The industrial section went on for several miles, but that was only part of the picture. Established around it with meticulous diligence was a township—clean, precise, and neatly arranged to a degree that it would have made any self-respecting civil engineer from Earth green with jealousy.

Much like the town outside, they constructed it entirely out of stone blocks, with tile roofs. Svartalfars weren't big on flaunting wealth through their houses and instead focused on developing their society and population as a whole. Communism on a species level. Intricate rows of spear-like spires and deep archways marked the various subsections of the township, with everything from shops and educational institutions to open grounds and square patches of well-maintained vegetation. Lukas and Tanya had been traveling in one of those platforms at racecar speeds for over two minutes, and they were yet to reach the "Well."

Tanya was correct. The svartalfars really didn't get out of their territory. Why would they when everything they needed was right here?

Finally, after some forty minutes, the platform slowed down. Peaked spires and metallic pillars rose in front of them like dark talons, varying in thickness as they jutted up into the sky. The one standing right before them looked alien, with a twisted, off-center symmetry, an almost-balance. Ash-black, something about it gave Lukas a sudden feeling of intense depression, as if simply being close to this . . . thing was enough to suck away something fundamental from him.

And in the middle of this behemoth was a roughly oval construct, crafted out of several feet of thick stone. It had the appearance of an archaic archway with artistic sigils engraved upon them. No, not sigils. *Runes.* Lukas didn't need to be a scholar to recognize a few members of the Elder Futhark in them, which made sense. These were svartalfars of Svartalfheim. Of course, they'd use runes. He wondered if Inanna would have been able to understand these symbols if—

If she was here.

The thought drained all the enthusiasm out of him, leaving behind a sea of abject loneliness. Inanna—it all came down to her. All of this was ultimately for her.

"Is this the . . ."

"Well?" said Tanya, "Not exactly. It's what we call a Conclave. The actual Well is in the middle of it."

She pointed at the center of the oval. It took him a moment but then he saw what she meant. Shimmering in the air before him was a thin rupture. A bruise, floating in midair, with something pale blue and dense lining it. Now that he saw it, he could see micro-thin rays of light emanating from it, *as if coming from the Other side that didn't exist and yet—*

Lukas looked away.

"You felt it?" Tanya asked. "The strangeness?"

Swallowing, he bobbed his head.

She smiled. "Good. At least that's familiar territory. At least you didn't have a major reaction. There was this one guy I knew who lost his mind by just staring at it for over ten seconds."

Lukas stood still. Something about the bruise—or dare he call it, the rift—felt alien to his senses. It was like staring at Inanna's memory of the Origin all over again.

"What . . . is it?"

"I told you. The Well."

Lukas tried to catch a quick look at it again by simply glancing in its general direction. To his surprise, however, he couldn't find it.

Tanya chuckled.

Annoyed, he turned to her. "What's so funny?"

"You," she said. "Trying to see it from the corner of your eyes . . . It won't work. You have to be specifically looking for it to see it."

She was right. The moment he looked again, searching for it, there it was, beckoning him. Taunting him to stare for just a while longer.

Lukas looked away.

"Wise choice," came a male voice from his right. It was a svartalfar with a companion beside him. The other was female, from what he could guess. The male went on, "Few can overcome the desire to keep looking. Resisting is a sign of fortitude."

"Eh, thanks?"

"I only spoke the obvious. No acknowledgement is necessary."

Clearly svartalfars had excellent communication skills.

"This is Kradir," said the other creature, slimmer with signs of femininity about her. Like Kradir, her eyes were pupilless, pitch-black, and seemed to take in more than they had any right to do. She then pointed at herself. "I'm called Mori. He is an extractor, while I'm the sensor. You'll be providing security to the two of us for this mission, correct?"

"Yes," said Tanya.

Mori continued with her unrepentant drone. "We will travel through the Lava Ridge to extract at least twenty kastrians of lochil ore. That will require several days of travel. We estimate a Level-3 risk factor. Be warned that the area on the inside is a volcanic terrain, with minimum sixty-two percent fire mana saturation, and infested with fire elementals, chiefly ifrit-kind. You may do or collect whatever strikes your fancy during this period as long as it does not hinder your duties. As per your contract, you'll get fifteen percent of our collection post successful completion of the mission. That, or mezals equivalent to its current market value. Standard entry, standard exit. In the event of our demise, our technicians on this side will refuse you exit. We advise you to do your best to protect us."

Lukas blinked. "Hang on a minute. I think I heard something fairly outrageous in there."

Mori cocked her head.

"The demise thing. Not that we want you to die or anything, but why won't the technicians allow us out?"

Mori gave him a blank stare, a slow blink, and then asked, "Is this your first mission?"

"Yes."

"It shows."

"Its standard protocol for svartalfars," Tanya intervened. "They do this to ensure that we take extra care to get the job done."

"And why wasn't I told about this?" he hissed.

Tanya gave him a dry stare. "You speak their tongue. You know their customs. What am I supposed to think?"

His left eye twitched, as he turned to face his protectorates. "You realize we're supposed to protect you, right? This doesn't exactly paint an image of trust."

"We're not paying you for trust," Mori corrected him. "We're paying you for security. The contract ensures you'll protect us from others, but nothing ensures our protection from you."

Lukas blinked.

"It's common sense to be wary of everyone," Mori said without the slightest inflection in her voice. "Even of one's protector."

Tanya grabbed his arm. "Don't think about it very much. It's protocol. Be grateful they're carrying our rations for us."

"Unnecessary," Kradir said, his tone entirely neutral, eyes flat. "Your job is to provide security and handle anything that comes our way. Having to take care of baggage decreases your efficiency."

Lukas glowered at them but to no avail. *These* were his clients? And he was supposed to deal with them for the entire time they'd be on the other side?

Joy.

"What about the pillar I asked for?" Lukas demanded.

"Is that relevant to this mission?" Kradir asked.

"It's relevant to my staying inspired to save your ass."

"The pillar is under construction, Asukan," said Mori in her characteristically bland way. "It should be completed before we are done with this mission. We estimate it would generate seven to eight times the amount of energy you drained out of our wardstone."

Lukas did a quick mental calculation. He had extracted roughly seventeen percent of his total reserves from the wardstone. Assuming this new pillar could pull off what she was claiming, he'd be able to make two Rollback protocol attempts per recharge. That was . . . *awesome*, everything considered.

"Good," said Lukas. "Good. That'll do. How long would it take to recharge the pillar once used up?"

"Roughly three to five days."

Lukas whistled. That was fast. Quickly, he glanced at his Schema.

OMPHALOS ATTRIBUTES	
Energy Reservoir Capacity	∞
Current Energy Level	**686,487,187 units**

Lukas frowned. He had already had an impressive energy level at the crypt and absorbing the omphalos had also flooded him with a minimum thirty-percent rise, making the figure just shy of a billion units. And that was without adding the amount he had drained from the svartalfar wardstone. So, what happened to the extras? Why was his energy level close to half of where it should have been?

"Do you have questions about the mission?" Mori asked, distracting him. "Or any objections?"

Oh, he had. Tons of them. Like how was this Well supposed to work? What were the things he was supposed to keep in mind? And most importantly, what the hell was causing his energy level to fall? But Tanya was traveling with him, and she had promised to make this a training regimen for him. He supposed he could just wait and watch for now.

"I'm good," he said.

"I have a question," said Tanya. "Are we operating on a time limit?"

Kradir shook his head.

Tanya frowned. "I see. Very well, no objections."

That seemed to please the svartalfar. He let out a strange noise from his throat, and the surrounding air shimmered, revealing at least twenty soldiers, several pairs of whom looked like technicians, and a couple of helpers holding large, thick, squarish travel bags. They had camouflaged themselves, only to unveil at Kradir's command.

"Let me guess, protection from one's protector."

Kradir's expression relaxed. He looked like a hyena who'd just finished off a big meal so would only bother giving chase if you attracted its attention. Meanwhile, the technicians hurried, getting the Conclave up and running for what he could only imagine was transportation to this borderland. Olfric and Tanya's descriptions of "lands existing between reality and fantasy" sounded *interesting* but ultimately not very useful for painting a picture he could visualize himself. The closest he had come to imagining was a small zone filled with all kinds of monsters—kind of like the insides of the crypt, only with fewer slimes.

Maybe.

An electric noise grabbed his attention. The floating bruise—or Well, he supposed—was letting out spitting and frothing noises, as the runes engraved upon it began to glow with power. Occasionally, the Well would look like it was being pulled in one direction, only for it to constrict back into the barest shimmer. It was as if it was resisting whatever the Conclave was doing to it.

"They're opening the Well," Tanya said, reading his expression. "That Well is a rift in reality, and the World rejects it. The World's energy is always pushing it from all sides and directions, keeping it closed. What they're trying to do is fight it, constantly drain out the World Energy into those spires, creating a vacuum where the Well can open. Once it opens fully, we can walk through it into the borderland."

"Sounds simple enough."

"It isn't, really."

Lukas frowned for a long moment, his expression taking on several nuanced shades of doubt.

"You'll see."

"I suppose I will."

Meanwhile, the rift had expanded, now nearly the size of a small horse. Enough for a single person to crouch his way through. The crack frothed and spat angrily as the Conclave drained power from the environment into . . . something he couldn't really see. But it felt wrong, if the rising tension inside him was any sign. Whatever this vacuum was, the anomaly inside him abhorred it. It wanted him to act out, to unleash a volley of pure anomalous energy and destroy this—this abomination on the face of Reality.

And the best part? He had no way of knowing how he knew all that. Guess the omphalos was having a greater effect on him than he thought.

"It's time," Mori declared.

The two helpers walked up to them and handed over the travel bags, which they quickly equipped. Both Lukas and Tanya had already brought their own baggage with them, but apart from some tinned food and a bottle of water with two spare sets of clothes, there had been nothing else. The svartalfar pair walked past them and entered through the crackling, spitting portal, Mori heading out first and Kradir following right after.

"Don't panic, and touch nothing," Tanya whispered. "Just walk through it."

Lukas ran his fingers through the pendant around his neck. A sense of strength throbbed within it, as if giving him silent support. It was the only tangible thing left of his world, and the greatest proof Inanna was there and that even though she was gone, she'd be back.

He didn't look at Tanya, but he could feel the sudden intensity of her interest.

"Let's go," she said, and walked into the portal.

"Okay." Lukas mustered a little courage. "Let's do it." He walked up to the portal, feeling the alien energies shifting, contorting, craving to consume. An immense pressure threatened to tear him apart from all directions and then—

He was gone.

The first thing that greeted him was a wafting smell of sulfur.

As the fleeting moment of disorienting pressure passed, Lukas felt a sudden, hot wind driving even more of that scent at his face, pushing his hair back from his forehead.

Then he saw it.

Flames.

They were everywhere. The terrain beneath his feet was hard rock, with thin fissures every fifty feet, oozing out thin streaks of lava, slowly trickling down into the craters on the sides, lava pools frothing angrily and popping out blisters of superheated air. Some fissures diverged from the trend and spat out flames into the air, only for the sparks to fall upon the reddish, igneous floor. Lukas could see shadows of mountains far ahead, and at least one precipice from which lava fell downwards to meet a sea of crimson liquid as it splashed and frothed in chaotic rage—a twisted mockery of a waterfall.

Mori had mentioned they were about to enter a volcanic terrain. She hadn't mentioned jack about traversing through Christian Hell.

Behind him the Well spat out another set of electric noises before collapsing onto itself, leaving them stranded here. And the best part? If these two svartalfars died on his watch, this would become his permanent home address.

"This job just keeps on giving, doesn't it?" he asked no one in particular. "How long do we have before time's up?"

Kradir let out a throaty cackle. "Not only is this your first mission, it seems you know nothing of the ways of the Empire. What rock were you living under all these years, stranger?"

Before Lukas could reply, Kradir turned towards Tanya. "Explaining things to your partner falls under your responsibility, Tanya of the Wind. Allowing his ignorance to affect his performance will put the blame on your head, since you've done business with us before."

Lukas took careful note of that title as he turned towards Tanya. "Told me what?"

Tanya kept her tone neutral. "Remember how I told you there's stuff I need to teach you about the borderlands?"

"Yeah?"

"There are a lot of things you're going to have to learn. Techniques, rules, and exercises. But there are some things that cannot wait for later. Two rules that you need to keep in mind. Number one," she wiggled a finger, "Time flows differently here. For instance, one hour in the real world is a little over two and a half hours in this borderland."

Time Dilation. Great. What else was new?

"We told you. The task will require us to travel a lot. We'll have to go past those mountains," droned Mori. "The technicians will open the Well in exactly three days' time, so we have around eight days to get it done."

"Peachy."

"The second rule—" Tanya gestured. "—is that no one knows *where* the portal will open. Not us, not the technicians out there. When they open the Well next, the Rescue Squad will come in, and send out flares into the air constantly for an entire hour. We'll signal back with our own flares if we can spot it. If that happens, they can keep it open for eight hours maximum, our time. If we can't make it by then, they'll have to shut it down."

"What happens if we can't make it in time?"

"They wait another day to recharge the Conclave before trying again," Kradir replied. "That means two and a half days of waiting before our next opportunity."

"This keeps getting better and better." Lukas scowled. "What if they send their flares and we don't see them?"

"Not a problem," Mori answered. "They stop after an hour, and then open the portal again after a break. Eventually, we'll spot it. Or become dinner for the ifrits and muspels that have made this place their home—whichever comes first. Or is most convenient."

Kradir laughed. "You see, stranger, our jobs aren't for the faint of heart. Most adventurers just perish during our missions. You better bring your A-game, or this will be your last."

"Yeah, I can see that," Lukas replied, quietly wondering why life kept throwing such curveballs at him. "No pressure at all."

CHAPTER 13

DIVINITY

What proof do we have? The words of soothsayers long dead? Texts that have been reworded time and time again across the annals of history? Divinity is such an abstract concept—the idea of entities that have always been and always will be, seems to go against the notions of Potential and Evolution, and yet, no bremetan has ever progressed beyond the mantle of king. Does that mean that the legends are true? That Divinity exists beyond the scope of evolution? That no matter how one progresses, one cannot transcend mortality? Cheat it, perhaps, but not truly transcend it? You can regenerate your lost limbs, you can purge the contamination of your soul, you can soar to the greatest heights of strength, but despite that, you can never touch the gods?

No one has, they say. Not in the three thousand years of the Asukan civilization, they say. Is that not proof enough?

And yet, when one looks at civilizations of the Time Before, the rules change. When I read about the Father of the Aesir sacrificing himself for wisdom and resurrecting himself out of it, suddenly I'm not so sure. Scriptures of the goddess Freyja mention the vast Ginnungagap, the primordial sea of Creation. Yet the Empire professes the existence of Primordials, the creators of the gods themselves. Which is real? Why would gods, masters of the plane by their own right, lie about their origins?

Unless—

Lukas lowered his book, the tent shaking slightly from the furious wind blowing outside. He was glad that Zuken had provided him with a translated copy of an ancient treatise on Divinity before they had left for this trip. There was little else to do.

Fortunately, the book was fascinating. Fascinating and eerie. The author, Kvasir, held a deep mistrust towards the Empire's preaching, classifying it as propaganda, and yet, he couldn't help but notice the proofs that spoke in the

Empire's favor. What was worse was that the Ginnungagap, known as the cradle of Creation in Norse mythology, was referenced alongside the primordial Izanagi and Izanami—the original man and woman of the Shinto mythos. Tales of both existed back on Earth, and yet, *one of them had to be lying*. Kvasir had hit the right question—why would the Shinto pantheon, gods in their own right, lie about their *own* origins? And if they didn't, was it the Norse deities that were to blame? The Ginnungagap—a vast sea of chaotic turmoil from which everything was created—seemed eerily close to an anomaly, or perhaps a singularity or even a realm, however it might appear to be. And all that was without including the Haze, which certainly existed, given he had actually entered it with Solana's help.

Yeah, this was starting to give him a headache.

At the same time, it wasn't exactly the sort of text that would get him anywhere close to getting Inanna back. When not filled with speculations about Creation—something Kvasir was clearly obsessed with—the pages were packed with internal contemplations and lengthy ramblings. Kvasir seemed to have a love-hate relationship with Father Odin, or as he referred to him, "Crooked One-Eye," describing him as a hustler beyond imagining. At the same time, he speculated that the All-Father might have revealed something sinister about Existence, something so dangerous that the Asukan gods went out of their way to destroy the Nordic scriptures post-Ragnarok.

Closing the book, he put it back in his pouch. The pendant's translation ability—as mind-boggling as it was—worked on the written word just as smoothly as it did on those spoken aloud. Obviously, the translator hadn't been able to get everything down pat, for there were scripts that looked Proto-Germanic and were probably parts of the original Nordic script. Maybe, when this was all over, he could use the pendant and get himself the job of a transcriber?

Lukas chuckled at his reverie and grabbed at the single water bottle in his tent, turning it upside down.

Not a single drop fell.

"Empty again," he said, with all the dryness of the surrounding region.

Closing his eyes, he focused on his reserves and began conjuring a small orb of water. He had allowed the marid, or "Shahxith" as Olfric called it, to momentarily take over, and added its skills at Water Creation and Manipulation into his Schema.

Filling the bottle up to the brim, he drank it until it was half empty, and left it where it was.

Exhaling, Lukas muttered, "Show me."

The Screen followed his commands.

OMPHALOS ATTRIBUTES	
Energy Reservoir Capacity	∞
Current Energy Level	**686,487,187 units**

There it was. The unsolved mystery. The drop in his reserves. Lukas had meticulously written down every single incident since he had last checked his reserves and the moment he had found out about the drop. Only three things stood out.

The draining attempt by the svartalfar pillar.

His use of the dranzithl's rejuvenation during the fight with Hreidmar, followed by all that mana he had churned out of himself to burn him alive.

And finally, his use of a form of Kinetomancy that he had never used before.

The first didn't count, especially because the omphalos in him had drained a far greater amount of energy from the pillar during that period.

The second was a reason for drainage, especially because of extreme mana synthesis, but it was nothing special. Hell, he hadn't even felt *exhausted*, and that would have meant production of around ten to twelve thousand units of his reserves. Instead, he was missing *several hundred million*.

That left the final one. His sudden use of an unknown form of Kinetomancy. Of Motion Negation. Whatever he had done, however he had done it, it had also consumed a little less than five thousand Soul Capacity, equal to a Level-3 skill. But leveling up on skills drew on Soul Capacity, of which he had an endless amount. It had *nothing* to do with *omphalos reserves*.

So that wasn't it.

Lukas scratched his head. "What am I missing? Am I wrong about Kinetomancy? Even the Screen shows it as a broken skill."

Inanna's words came to mind.

Do not liken Kinetomancy to a mortal technique. It's the culmination of what allowed me to butcher gods and demons alike. You have no more chance of bearing it than an ant can bear the weight of a mountain.

Yes, yes, he knew all that. But mortal or divine, a technique was a technique. It took form in the body of the skill-bearer, regardless of its origins. He wasn't looking down on the possibilities of the power, but just because he had gotten it from a goddess . . .

The rest of his thoughts died as it hit him.

"A . . . goddess. A skill from a goddess."

Could it really be that simple?

Lukas grabbed his hair and stood up. He had been looking at it the wrong way. At the wrong things. He was looking at Kinetomancy when it should have been the other way around.

The relevant fact wasn't that it was *Kinetomancy* that he had gotten from Inanna. It was the fact that *Inanna,* a *goddess,* gave it to him.

Two very similar things. And yet, they made a world of difference. It was true that Kinetomancy wasn't an arcane skill. He hadn't gotten it by having faith in Inanna. He, or rather, *anyone,* could have Kinetomancy. Inanna had gained it as a *mortal.* She had killed *gods* with it as a mortal. It was the culmination of every single spark, every single development, every single step of growth that a mortal girl went through to become the Supreme Queen of An and Ki.

The same Supreme Queen who had reforged his soul with her divinity. Granted him Kinetomancy.

He had used a Kinetomancy technique that he had previously thought to be beyond him. Unlike any other skill, Kinetomancy was an apex skill. Rising in it was equivalent to leveling up in perhaps a hundred different related skills. All that extra skill-information had to come from *somewhere.*

Yes. That must be it. Like Sherlock Holmes said, when you have eliminated all which is impossible, then whatever remains, however improbable, must be the truth. It was more likely that, just like Blob held the information that once belonged to the Crypt of Fiendish Worms, Inanna's divinity also held information about her—about her skills, her instincts, her powers.

Not unlike a Monster Prototype, only in her case, it was a Goddess Prototype.

Quickly, he went through his Monster Prototype Array.

Yurei. Reiki. Thoggua. Neothelid. Marid. Dranzithl. Svartalfar—

There was nothing about Inanna there. Absolutely nothing.

Tell me about Divinity.

Insufficient Data

Damn it. Okay, tell me about my own soul. Prime Host.

Accessing information about Prime Host
Displaying . . .

PRIME HOST
Unconditionally superlative among all Monster Prototypes
Alpha Condition Raised to Maximum (Level-5) granting an Absolute
Mind free from external influence from Monster Prototypes
Amplified Resistance to mental intrusion and enthrallment

"I *already* know this," Lukas all but growled, punching the ground in growing irritation. He had spent multiple nights at this problem, only to arrive at nothing. And now that he finally had something to go on, something that could actually lead him to understand *something* about Inanna's divinity, the Screen was being stupidly unhelpful. The only thing he knew was that somehow being reforged by her divinity had made him the Prime Host and . . .

Wait.

Why was he supposing that?

What decides if a soul is a Prime Host?

Spiritual Presence

There!

Lukas threw a fist in the air in exhilaration. Spiritual Presence, or in Inanna's case, divinity. His own limited experience said that Spiritual Presence was equivalent to mass, only one was measuring souls. If an omphalos was an array of souls and every soul was just a data chip filled with skills, instincts, and *maybe* memories, then the "spiritually heaviest" soul was the Prime Host.

Now, Lukas knew he was hardly the heaviest thing in his Anomaly Box. The dranzithl alone was far greater in Spiritual Presence than he was. Hell, just being possessed by the yurei earlier on had all but shoved him away from the wheel, and only with Inanna's help had he gotten his body and mind back. He had been a Base Host back then, just the soul that happened to have the best working efficiency with the body (anomaly).

But after being reforged with divinity, he had become Prime Host. That meant—

"Divinity contains information. Skills, instincts, maybe even a prototype for Inanna herself. But . . . how do I get it out? How do I activate it?"

Insufficient Data

Okay. Here's a better idea. Analyze Lukas Aguilar.

Analysis Complete
Rendering . . .

Status	Prime Host
Type	Human
Constituent	Living Tissue
Deciphering Spiritual Constitution . . . **Decoding . . .** **Rendering Complete**	

Nature	Amalgamation
Number of Skills	19
Spiritual Core	Divine
Information Redacted	

"Redacted. Now isn't *that* interesting?"

To his knowledge, the act of redaction was to intentionally obscure certain information citing security or other legitimate reasons. Unless "redacted" meant something entirely different for an omphalos, which he severely doubted, this meant that there was a ton of information in his "Divine" spiritual core, but the information was kept out of his reach by certain protocols.

Kind of like how the Babysitter Protocol had limited his ability to access omphalos functions.

Was it possible that Inanna's divinity was doing the same? An autonomous system that was acting despite being a part of another system? One that had enough Spiritual Presence to make the omphalos unilaterally make him the Prime Host, but enough protocols within itself to keep it out of his reach until he fulfilled certain criteria? And if that was so, just what were these criteria and how was he going to find them out?

Lukas exhaled. Every time he came close to an answer, he found an ocean of new mysteries behind it.

Damn it. I need a break.

Unzipping the flap of his tent, he crouched out, shutting it behind him. Letting the Eternal Light emanate out of the tent would paint a neon sign upon them. Given the kind of creatures that abounded in this region, that would be a very bad idea. His eyes took a few seconds to adjust to the darkness, and in that time, he only heard a strange sound, like an echoing wind . . . but without the wind.

Lukas smiled. Guess he wasn't the only one out there.

He looked on with narrowed eyes, ready for even the smallest movement. One had to be tough and prepared to survive out here, and sometimes, one had to be a merciless fuck.

Something moved in the darkness, amidst the brittle bushes.

Prey Found You

That was enough.

Thrusting out his right hand, he sent a wave of pure force at the bush. Something dark and all too fucking fast jumped out of the darkness behind it, evading his force blast like it was nothing. Lukas tensed his body and readied himself to jump—but the little bastard didn't go for him. Instead it went for the largest yucca tree in his vicinity, slashing through the thick trunk like it was paper with its freakishly strong paw and sending the giant thing crashing down on him.

It might have worked on anybody else. But the creature with fur as black as the blackest night was already moving to attack him from another angle. The fucker was smart but not fast enough to make it count.

Flexing his left hand, he slowed the tree's descent. With his right hand, he grabbed the motion around the creature and yanked it towards him, right in the path of the falling tree.

1 Prey Eliminated
+21 Experience

Lukas breathed hard and felt slightly dizzy, the sudden spike of adrenaline leaving his body. It had been over so fast that he had barely felt the surge of any lifeforce. Crouching, he looked at the creature he had just killed—a janje, this world's variant of a panther, but the size of a large dog, with three pairs of manes sprouting from its head. It was unmoving and most certainly dead—just an average hunter out looking for some food.

The ironies of the world.

He heard the sound of tents flapping and found Tanya and Mori both awake and peering out at him. He glanced back at the creature's corpse, then at the twilight sky above, and then back at them.

"Guess breakfast's served, huh?"

"I hope there are no hard feelings," Kradir told him as they stopped for the sixteenth time during the day.

"Hard feelings?" asked Lukas.

"About this," Kradir said, referring to their system of travel. The svartalfar traveled the same way he did everything—*blandly*. Complete stops. Every time they got the slightest sensation of something under the ground, they would wait and check, with Kradir mapping the terrain, finding the relative depth below which lava flowed, the possible chances of any predator attacking them and so on, while his compatriot sensed for metallic ores beneath the ground.

Wherever they were headed, it was going to take forever to get there.

Journeying through the Lava Ridge was long and arduous, not because of any actual difficulty involved but because of the sheer boredom. Between himself and Tanya, Lukas was sure they could have gotten to those mountains further ahead in another day, maybe two, if they decided to not keep stopping the way. Instead, they were traveling at ridiculously low speeds, with the svartalfar pair walking across the terrain, mapping and sensing it all the way. Meanwhile, Tanya did her best imitation of a passenger pigeon, constantly fluttering in the air, looking around for potential predators.

"Trust me, Kradir," Lukas said, smiling at him—technically. "You don't want me to get in touch with my feelings."

Lukas felt Kradir's eyes shift to him, and a little tension gathered in his body. His shoulder twitched. Maybe he was reconsidering his safety around Lukas. As good as he might be, Lukas had killed Hreidmar in open combat. That alone carried some weight. At least so he thought.

"Don't worry," he told the creature, somehow holding onto that smile. It didn't feel quite right, so he tried a bit harder. "I'm not going to attack you. I'm just questioning if this is indeed the *best* method."

The svartalfar exhaled. "This is important."

"They are Asukans," said Mori, her eyes shut as she sensed around, whatever that entailed. "Dense in the short term. One can only hope they figure things out eventually."

"We can figure out faster if some people stop sitting on their condescending asses and actually explain things for once," he quipped.

That got Mori's attention. She opened a single eye and peered at him. "What do you want to know, Asukan?"

"Why are we doing this?" he asked, cutting to the heart of the matter. "I can easily grab one of you and jump across one hill to the next. I'm pretty sure Tanya can pull off something like that, if not better."

He didn't say that with Hreidmar's skill, he could just take both of them himself and not even sweat, but there was no way he was going to showcase any svartalfar skill in front of the two. God knew he already had enough trouble to begin with.

Kradir scoffed. "We are svartalfars. We do not let Asukans manhandle us."

"*Manhandle?*"

"And it is our duty to map this terrain, topologically by me, and metallurgically, by her. Neither of that is possible without traveling on foot."

"The terrain is quite thin here," added Mori. "We cannot terraport either."

"Walking it is," Lukas mumbled. "I guess that makes—"

His words were drowned in a cacophony of growls and screeches, as a wild, fierce smell hit his hindbrain and straightened the hairs on the nape of his neck. He glanced around and found large, black, fiery shapes materializing around them, surrounding them on all sides. The sound of dispelling wind told him that Tanya had landed next to him.

"Ifrits," he heard her mutter. "Accursed things."

Lukas tilted his head, observing the creatures forming around them. Easily his own height, they were four legged, with bulging bellies and demonic fiery tails, the latter reminding him of Ryu, and monstrous canine heads with tentacles growing out of them. Crimson flames adorned their neck and raced down to their elbows and thighs, their sharp claws scratching the surface of the ground as they growled and screeched. Their toxic musk, smelling eerily like urine, rotten meat, and lots and *lots* of sulfur, filled the air.

"Tanya," he ordered, "take to the skies. Create a thirty-foot perimeter around Mori and Kradir. Whatever comes close to your periphery, turn it back or blow it to bits. I'll deal with everything else." He turned to the svartalfars. "Make sure you stay within her perimeter."

"How did I get elected svartalfar-nanny?" Tanya demanded.

"More importantly," said Mori, "who put him in charge?"

Prey Found You

Yes. Yes, I know.

The ifrits growled and rushed at him. And just like that, Lukas was back in his comfort zone.

He was back at war, and his body was moving with instincts he no longer had to fight to keep under control. The only difference between here and the crypt was that now there were bystanders that could get hurt. He'd kill these ifrits and siphon them, but he had to ensure that the svartalfars were safe from harm. It only brought him the slightest amount of hesitation when he realized that this was the first fight since coming to this world where there were others he needed to keep safe.

He didn't care to wait for her response. His Schema already told him every-thing he needed to know.

IFRIT
Spiritual Parasite. Subspecies of KAMI. Energy Core constitutes mana forge for Fire and Ether. Capable of pyromancy and false construction.

False construction. Just like those yurei, only more real and with fire pow-ers. Wonderful. Enough damage to the shell would probably cause them to disintegrate and then re-form. Or they could go all frenzied and try to possess him, in which case he'd gain some new prototypes. But what if the monsters realized that their attempts at Possession weren't working? Would they keep on trying? Would they run away?

One of the ifrits came rushing at him.

Lukas grinned. *Time to find out.*

Blob followed his mental commands, and instantly divided into two, jump-ing straight into his fists. Flooding it with lifeforce, Lukas hurled it head on, Blob extending out for several dozen feet, while still grabbing on to his hand. Had the ifrit been standing in front of a train, it might have been a bit better off. The aqāru whip, reinforced by several magnitudes by pure lifeforce, smashed into the creature with a concentrated burst of precisely-aimed energy as focused as that of any martial artist. The creature's body *exploded*, with half of it going rag doll, flying back from the impact in an explosive crackling of breaking bone, only to disintegrate fully upon hitting a large boulder.

The shape that fell to the ground from the boulder was kind of . . . amorphous.

The other ifrits saw the encounter and let out a primal scream, as if recognizing him as a challenge that could not be ignored, and dashed in his direction. Lukas was already on his feet, his left hand hurling the aqāru whip, smashing through the bodies of two or three other creatures, injuring if not outright disintegrating them. Aqāru was a horrifically overpowered weapon against metamantic constructs, which the ifrits were beginning to find out the hard way.

Several mists arose from the disintegrating ifrit forms, coalescing together and zooming through the air like an angry wraith. It swooped in his direction.

Here it comes, Lukas thought, readying himself for the mental battle.

But it never came. The Prime Host didn't struggle. Instead, Alpha Condition forced itself against the spiritual intruders with extreme prejudice, pushing them down and exerting Lukas's rationality before he could even feel the shift.

MONSTER PROTOTYPE — IFRIT	
APTITUDE	**LEVEL**
Fire Creation	2
Fire Manipulation (Physical Enhancement)	2
Temperature Manipulation	1
Decoy Creation (Conjuration)	2

Damn it. It was absolutely useless. He had all these skills already. *Remove them from my Schema.*

Delete newly added skills from IFRIT?

Yes.

These were all Level 1, with maybe minor Level-2 skills at best. Cannon fodder, but nothing worth siphoning. Instead, the Experience from his kills kept rising steadily. As all the ifrits attacked from all sides, Lukas spread the whip wider.

The ifrits had noticed the lack of reaction and quickly changed tactics, belching out balls of flame in his direction. Lukas instantly pulled the whip back, just in time to spread it open like a shield, deflecting the barrage of flame-throwers sent to him from another direction, while swatting the whip on his right hand across the ground, tearing one ifrit down after another.

The entire place was clean in less than half a minute.

Lukas turned around and glanced at Mori and Kradir. "So, what do you think? Still gonna walk all the way through?"

The two svartalfars shared a mutual gaze before looking back at him. "Yes."

Lukas groaned.

CHAPTER 14

A Pair of Rule Breakers

Day eleven.

The group had crossed through seven lava streams so far, and the surrounding landscape was slowly changing to an arid wasteland. They had finally reached the mountains, and the terrain was much smoother, darker, and relatively stable. If nothing else, the svartalfars could terraport through these zones, while Lukas and Tanya could just shoot through the air, jumping from cliff to cliff.

It was a good morning.

"We've a good day ahead," said Mori, terraporting next to him. "I'm sensing lochil around."

And there was the second change. Ever since the incident with the ifrits, the female svartalfar's behavior had undergone a radical shift. She still spoke dispassionately, which he expected was a character quirk of her race, but there was a fire somewhere deep down beneath her mannerisms. She would start conversations, seeming to genuinely want to get to know him, timing their interactions whenever Tanya was doing her aerial duties.

Coincidentally, Tanya's disposition had gotten worse over the last couple of days.

"I'm sorry," said Lukas, "did you say you can *sense* it?"

Mori gave him the blank stare he had grown accustomed to. "I'm a sensor. Kradir is an extractor. We said that before we started off for this mission."

Did she? Maybe somewhere between her droning. Or maybe she had said it in that manner specifically to throw him off? One could never really be sure about these people.

"You . . . did. But these aren't just pure metals. These are ores. Particles fused with other metals, dirt, rocks. You can't tell me you can just sense every single particle within the crust." He paused for a moment. "Can you?"

Mori cocked her head, studying him. "You have some knowledge of metal extraction."

"Only in passing."

Mori nodded, as if considering. "What is this knowledge worth to you? You're not a terramancer."

Aha. She would tell him, but was fishing to see if she could get something out of it. And no, she was wrong. He *was* a terramancer. Technically, he could do all the "mancy" that existed in this world as long as he could siphon a creature capable of the same.

"Perhaps you wish to sell this information to other terramancers of your kind?"

That was a valid question. The thing was, bremetan terramancers could do the same. If they *really* wanted to. Bremetans could pull off almost anything other beings could.

Especially when they involved kami into this mess.

He shrugged. "Just idle curiosity."

"I see," Mori said without emotion, "Knowledge for the sake of knowledge. A rare trait that is lost in the race for Potential."

Lukas had the weirdest feeling that he had just managed to avoid a trap. Or at least answered a question without sounding stupid or hostile.

And then Mori did something odd. She grabbed both of his hands and held them open, putting her thin, smaller palms into his, staring at him with her large, dark eyes. "Close your eyes, silence your ears, and *feel.*"

Before he could prepare himself, Lukas was overwhelmed with a rush of images and alien sensations, contacting a power so intense and coherent that for a moment, he thought he was back at the crypt, connecting to its awareness. In that single moment, Lukas saw the ponderous dance of continents clashing against each other to form mountains, felt the slow somnolence of the earth, the immense power that was released upward as lava flowed across the terrain. He saw metals—jewels and coal and endless stretches of basalt and other substances he had never even heard of—being created in the millions and disintegrated in the endless march of time.

Calling upon tachypsychia to its fullest strength, Lukas fought to contain those images, control, and divert them away, instead focusing on what Mori was trying to show him. In his mind, he was diving straight into the crust, dividing into a gazillion different mental branches and furrowing through endless pathways through the labyrinth that was the terrain. One moment, he was caught in a whirlwind of molten stone; the next, he felt a strange, purplish energy oozing out of an orange rock that felt like it would—

Lochil Identified
Creation process available within Heteromorph Conglomerate

And just like that, the spell broke.

Lukas physically pushed himself back, his head seething against the raw pressure he had felt. Had he carried on just a little more, his skull would have probably shattered. Anomaly or not, he was a frail wisp of mortality beside the energy within, which could literally move mountains, level cities, shift river courses and stir oceans in their beds.

Blinking several times, Lukas looked around, shaking his head, and doing his best to ignore the constant hammering against his skull. Neural Suppression salvaged the situation a bit but not enough to ignore it.

"That was—"

"The terrain," Mori replied without the slightest affliction. "I'm surprised you could keep up so far."

"I could feel it," Lukas admitted. The sensation of having his own perception branch away into endless tendrils, each of them sensing a completely different substance with its own unique constitution, energy, and spiritual feel—he would not forget that any time soon. "That was my perception dividing over and over and—"

Mori laughed. It sounded like a weird mix of a cough and a cackle. "That wasn't your perception, stranger. That was *mine.* You were merely feeling the echoes reflected upon your own mind. It takes great fortitude to be aware of the constant branching of perceptions like that. Perhaps you have the potential to be a psion." She tilted her head slightly, studying him. "Perhaps you have already started down that path."

"Uh, maybe," he replied, feeling flustered. The entire geo-sensing episode had thrown him off.

"Perhaps you have a latent talent for sensory skills? The Zwaray Keep is always looking out for those."

"Something wrong?" said Tanya, landing next to him. She did that a lot, especially when Mori was around.

"Uh, Mori was just—"

"Offering him a job."

Lukas almost winced at her bluntness.

"What *job?*"

Mori tuned her out and focused back on him. "I understand you are Asukan and a pyromancer, but in the end, your constitution has . . . more in common with us. There is something *earthly* about you." She gestured with her arm as though to show the terrain beneath them. "You have power, but you wield it crudely. The Zwaray Keep could help you hone it."

And what did *that* little invitation say about him? He couldn't help but wonder. Perhaps she was talking about the anomaly in him, which was—after all was said and done—a world? Svartalfars were creatures of the terrain, and Earth had very much been a physical realm before things went sky high. Still . . .

Tanya seemed to have sensed his hesitation, and he glanced down in surprise as he felt a tug and realized that she had pinched the edge of his shirt. She was looking away, refusing to match his surprised look, a hard expression settling on her face.

Was she afraid he'd accept their proposal?

More importantly, did he *want* to?

Svartalfars symbolized a transition between the new world and the old. They maintained their Nordic roots, their enchantments, and their faith. The Nordic runes were supposed to perform all sorts of mystical enchantments, both physical and esoteric. The sheer diversity of species involved, their culture, and their history—all of it made for a far more lucrative option than the Asukan Empire, who, to his knowledge, were a bunch of control freaks selling their souls for the ability to manacraft.

There was just one tiny problem.

Tanya.

Inanna had invested part of her divine energies in sealing the power within her. She had described Tanya's power as *catastrophic,* something just as ancient and devastating as herself. So long as Tanya stood on the Asukan side, he would too. But if he could convince her to change sides then . . .

Lukas cocked his head. Well, that left multiple possibilities for the future, didn't it?

"I already have a kami, and I've progressed too far to have second thoughts. But tell you what . . . If this mission is a success, we can talk about this sensing thing."

"I figured as much," Mori shrugged, not sounding surprised in the least. "Still, the offer stands."

Fucking hell. Just *what* did she see in him if she was going to give a standing offer to join the Keep? Svartalfars held nothing but disdain for Asukans. Period. You couldn't get simpler than that. And what was with every dubious power he came across in this world that made them always extend offers to join them?

First Inanna, but at least she had her reasons, what with the pendant and the omphalos and everything else. But then Solana entered the picture, with her legends and prophecies about apocalyptic heralds. Tanya—he just encountered her by chance, and, because of Inanna's machinations, he ended up in Zuken Banksi's care, who didn't look like he wanted his fancy Outsider to leave him at any cost . . . and now this.

"I didn't think *poaching* was part of svartalfar protocol," Tanya replied frostily. He wasn't being metaphorical. Her skin actually felt ice cold.

"It isn't poaching if he's a direct dealer. We already have an existing job contract with him and his related associates, *one* of whom just *happens* to be you."

Tanya grabbed his arm tighter. "That may be, but he is with *me*. This mission is supposed to be training for him *while* ensuring your protection. So why don't you focus on your sensing and extracting and leave the *pyromancer* to practice his pyromancy?"

Mori met his eyes and gave him an edged smile. "The offer stands."

And then she vanished into the earth.

"Bitch!" Tanya murmured in a level voice. Narrowing her eyes, she regarded Lukas firmly. "And you should be more careful. It's obvious that they *think* you're the one who can get them more featherglass. They're trying to cut off everyone else by stringing you into one of their *pacts.*"

"Which is why you came to rescue me."

Tanya didn't look up at his eyes as she said, "Yes."

"Great," he replied. "So long we understand each other."

"No kidding," she whispered. "But she isn't wrong. Not completely. Even Zuken noticed it."

Lukas tilted his head.

"You have power, no doubt about that. Probably more power than anyone else I've seen, except for maybe . . ." She paused, hesitantly. "Except my grandfather. I know you have a Level-3 skill, considering some things you pull off. But your control is . . . crude. I've seen spiritists with Level-1 skills that have better control than you do."

Her words sounded harsh, but he had to agree. Inanna had told him it took years, if not decades, for someone to move from a Level 2 to a Level 3. He still remembered the days when he had run around the crypt, having to choose his battles or become food for some monster. And even then, he had the advantage of Kinetomancy and an absurd healing skill.

But things had changed ever since he had gained the Soul Siphon function. With it, skills became something to leech out of his prey after killing them. What took days and weeks and months to develop to even a Level 1, he got for free. Warmonger Protocol had granted him more lifeforce and mana than he knew what to do with. He had deteriorated from a weak but smart fighter to a rampaging berserker demolishing his opponents with pure power. No wonder Inanna held such disdain for his actions. For someone who had to climb the hierarchy leaving a body count in the thousands, Lukas was possibly the greatest mockery of her achievements.

"You say you have the power to use all elements, and I've already seen you use fire, ether, and now Terramancy. Your lifeforce is off the charts. Your healing skills, beyond comprehension. Someone of your resources deserves to *rule* over a nation, not work for Banksi as an adventurer."

Lukas cocked his head. "Pot, meet kettle. You've got an ECR others can only dream about. Your skills in Aeromancy are beyond anything Banksi or Olfric can ever imagine. And your Frost defies comprehension. Think *you* deserve this life? Working under Banksi? Choosing one prison for another?"

Tanya glared at him. "This isn't about me."

"Of course it isn't. It never is."

Tanya turned to leave, but Lukas grabbed her hand. She turned back, surprised.

"My skills are quaint, but I wasn't born yesterday, Tanya. I've seen the life you've chosen for yourself. A slave to masters who deserve to get crumpled underfoot. Instead, you keep your head low. You live like an outcast, mocked by those that are below you. I know. I've faced you at your worst, back in that anomaly. Zuken says you have a powerful kami, but something tells me that your strongest card isn't that, but your *Frost.*"

"We are *not* talking about it!" She hissed, snatching her hand away.

"Of course we aren't. We don't even need to. I already *know* why."

That got her attention. Her blue eyes narrowed at Lukas. "Alright. Why?"

"Because you're ruled by fear. You are afraid."

She threw her head back and laughed. "Afraid? Of what?"

"Of what you could be if you let yourself go astray. Afraid of the power you could use. You've thought about what it might be to wield it and bend the world to your will. What you could have. What you could . . . become. I've seen the way you look at Zuken's house. It's not a look of jealousy or awe. It's *sadness.* Some part of you finds joy in the idea of using your power to take what you wish. And that scares you."

Lukas's life had come full circle. Back in the anomaly, he had stood where Tanya was standing now. He had been the defiant individual, rejecting the allure of power. He had faced the Goddess of Desire and said "no" to her face, denying himself true power because he feared what that would make him. What *she* would make him.

And now, he was standing in Inanna's shoes, talking down to an equally reluctant, self-denying Tanya.

She wanted to refute his words, but she couldn't. Or at least, he didn't let her.

"Don't justify it with lies," Lukas said. "Neither Zuken nor Olfric has any idea what having that sort of power would be like. You might try to mingle with them and pretend you're one of them, but you aren't. Just like I'm not. You, me, we're *rule breakers.* Trying to pretend otherwise is just denial."

Tanya gnashed her teeth. "You—you have no idea what you're talking about. You don't know a single thing about me."

Lukas pressed further. "I think I know enough. More than you allow your-self to know, anyway. After all, *I* was the one who sealed your Frost deep within your psyche, returning you to sanity."

Tanya flinched, like he had slapped her.

Lukas laughed. It was cruel. "You know what's ironic? That *you*, back in the anomaly . . . she tried to enthrall me. Break me. Find out my secrets even if it cost me my life. But guess what? She had more backbone than you do."

Rage flickered in her eyes. "You dare—"

"It's the truth," Lukas continued regardless. "You're hiding in Haviskali, keeping things low-key, because that's what you've always done. *Run.* From your powers, your abilities. From the heritage that birthed that Frost. It's all you know how to do."

"Shut up!" She snarled. "Just. Shut. Up. Don't turn this into something about me. And be mindful of what you say about Banksi. Outsider or not, you might just end up biting off more than you can chew."

"Well, *fuck that!*" said Lukas. "I'm not gonna cower with my tail between my legs. If I stir shit up, then so be it."

Her face fell, and she replied in a morbid tone. "You'll die."

Lukas couldn't help it. He snorted. "Wouldn't be the first time."

With that enigmatic statement, he shot upward into the air, leaving an open-mouthed Tanya to her thoughts.

CHAPTER 15

WARMONGER

The day had finally come. For the fourth time in the past five days, they had witnessed golden flares streak through the borderland sky. But this time, things were different. Kradir had taken out the flare gun and sent out signals. The message was obvious.

We've seen you. We're close. Stay open for the next eight hours.

The moment they received another flare, this one in acknowledgement of theirs, they knew it was time to get muddy. Lukas, in particular, was very excited to see how extraction was really done.

Mori slid out a silvery dagger from one of her deceptively deep pockets and ran it across her palm. She didn't so much as flinch, making Lukas wonder just how common it was for their species to do so. He himself was no stranger to seeing blood—whether his own or his victims—but actively using it for something so mechanical felt a little surreal.

Once enough of it had oozed out, Mori murmured something under her breath and began drawing sigils on the ground using her blood as ink. No, not sigils, *runes.* Every single mark shone as concentrated mana swirled around her own body, caressing her like a lover. Lukas ignored Kradir's chanting in the background as Mori kept drawing one rune after another, until she had crafted two concentric circles on the ground, both of them glowing with eldritch energies. Svartalfars were creatures of the earth, so there was no doubt whatever Terramancy they were about to perform, it would be spectacular. Finally, Mori stepped back, and Kradir's chanting went up a note higher.

Then it happened.

Kradir finished his chant, thrusting both hands upward with a growl, and the ground within the circles *erupted,* revealing four gigantic earthen arms, their palms held open against the sky. The constructs stood head and shoulders above them, easily fifteen feet high, and something tiny, yet powerful and dense, formed in the center of each palm.

Concentric rings of mana manifested around the four arms, oddly reminding Lukas of the fractals he was wearing. The mana particles coalesced, forming the rune circles Mori had drawn on the ground, and began spinning around each arm with surprising velocity.

It was like magic.

Everything he had seen the svartalfar pair do was fascinating. Despite his disposition, Kradir was a skilled sensor. Lukas had seen him predict the topology of the area in vivid detail with extreme precision. His skill probably allowed him to do that at a much larger radius. In the same vein, Mori's ability to divide her focus into multiple parallel mind streams and devote them all to gaining information at the same time was equally mind-boggling. Lukas had a similar skill from the thoggua—Seismic Sensing—but it was crude and only operable on a far smaller scale. And now, he was witnessing them perform an industrial metallurgical operation through Terramancy alone. The way they were churning the ore out of the crust was unbelievable. Between their ability to terraport and the subtler aspects of Terramancy that Hreidmar specialized in, it was painting a neat picture. Lukas could imagine a prototype that held all the above skills within it, ready to be called upon, crafted to serve the whims of its creator. An existence that was both a formula for future proliferation, and a useful skill set in his arsenal. All he needed was a quick siphon—

Lukas blinked.

Then blinked again.

Was he really considering *murdering* the svartalfar duo in cold blood? People he had promised to protect? People that had traveled with him? With whom he'd shared a fire and had conversations into the dead of the night? And for what? For *skills?*

Damn it, Lukas. What's wrong with you?

This had never been an issue before. That part of himself—the anomaly— had its own needs. It had reared its head against Inanna at first, but ever since he had become Prime Host, it had stayed low, deferring to his judgment.

Or maybe he simply hadn't gotten into a situation that attracted its attention.

Damn it. He needed to learn to recognize that influence before someone got hurt.

"Svartalfar blood is an extremely potent medium," said Tanya, standing next to him. "She's magnifying the golem's efficiency using her own blood and power."

Lukas looked at her.

She snorted. "It was obvious seeing your face. I know how you think."

Lukas's lips twitched into the distant echo of a smile. Her assessment was wrong, but he saw no need to correct her. As it was, things had been strained between them since that conversation about her past. Tanya held herself aloof most of the time, but he was glad to see it didn't come at the cost of her professionalism. Regardless of her personal feelings, she still behaved normally. At least in casual conversation.

"By how much?" he asked, switching to Maluscian. There was no need for the svartalfars to know what they were talking about.

"Around . . . four times?" Tanya guessed, effortlessly switching to Maluscian as well. "It varies. Kradir's chanting is basically a pact with the world, sacrificing lifeblood for a temporary gain in power." She snorted. "A lot of Asukans have tried to mimic this, only to end up dying."

He arched an eyebrow.

"Our blood is . . . how do I put it? Less potent? Magically dilute compared to svartalfars, or any of the Old World creatures?"

"I see," he said, glancing at the duo. "I imagine svartalfar blood must be a pretty precious commodity, then."

Tanya froze at that. "Why . . . would you say that?"

What was he supposed to say? Common sense? "Asukans can't manacraft without kami, and even having one comes at the cost of Soul Capacity. If you could just spill some svartalfar blood and cast a spell for, you know, quick and dirty manacrafting, I imagine it'd turn out pretty useful. I mean, they're terramancers, so I imagine it'd be in demand in . . ." He frowned. "Uh, do you have a black market in the Empire? Places where you can deal with contraband?"

"The taverns usually," Tanya said, lips pressed together, "or all of Maluscion."

Lukas smirked at her description. "Yeah, those. I'd imagine svartalfar blood being sold under the table at high prices."

"You're . . . dangerously well-informed about Asukan malpractices."

He sensed the wariness in her tone.

"Don't know about Asukan, but it's a thing where I'm from. The illegal sale thing, I mean."

That didn't seem to pacify her at all.

"I guess that makes sense now," Lukas declared, cupping his chin. "About the warnings. If they die, we won't be allowed to get back. They don't trust Asukans to not spill svartalfar blood and sell it elsewhere."

"Right."

Lukas barked out a laugh. "Idiots."

Tanya arched her brows. "Them?"

"No, the Asukans," he replied, lowering his voice to a whisper. "If I wanted to get a constant supply of svartalfar blood, I'd have just kidnapped several of their species, forced them to breed, and created a colony of them. Maybe even experiment on their blood to see what makes them so potent and try to replicate a synthetic variant, or even try breeding them with Asukans to see if a hybrid—"

He paused, realizing that Tanya had gone white, like she had seen a ghost. Her facial muscles were all strained, and her hands were shaking. If he didn't know better, it was as if she was preparing to strike him down.

"What?"

Tanya didn't answer.

"Tanya?"

She smoothed her face into a non-expression. "Nothing."

He narrowed his eyes. "No. It's definitely something."

She vehemently shook her head. "Nothing, really. Just wondering about what you said. Forceful breeding. Synthetic variants. Experimental bloodlines . . . Is that common where you're from?"

"Yes." Then he thought about how that sounded. "I mean, not that I was involved in that or anything. In my world, synthetic breeding allowed humanity to prosper. Especially through agriculture. Our guys created modified plant species through experimental breeding, and increased crop production. Same for meat, fish, and anything edible, really. Diseases were fought by studying the genetic structure of the pathogen and crafting synthetic vaccines that would teach our body how to fight them."

Her frown deepened. "You did not level up, so you altered your own tissues to make yourselves better?"

That was a little too simplistic, but sure, he could go with that.

"Kind of. Yes."

"I see . . ." she said and looked away.

Lukas snorted and looked back at the ongoing extraction. The area within the runic circles was shining like mercury, frothing and spitting out small chunks of a lustrous, silvery metal into the air, which floated upwards into a bubble of pure energy, almost like it was magnetically attracted to it. Maybe it was, for all he knew. Maybe this was the magical equivalent of ore refining, with the surface acting like an actual refinery unit, liberating the real ore into the bubble above.

"Ugh," muttered Tanya. "I really hate this part."

Lukas glanced at her. "What do you mean?"

"Just watch."

The bubble of pure energy began to spin, creating a sine wave of power, directing the lustrous, pure metal upwards, a tornado of earth mana that was reaching out to embrace the world beneath the crust. He watched as Kradir brought his hands down in a slashing gesture, unleashing the torrent of energy into the crust itself. Lukas didn't need to be a sensor to feel the energy traveling beneath the ground. A feeling of wrongness permeated his person.

A second later, Lukas knew why.

For a single second, gravity vanished from beneath his feet and the land for miles all around them, jerking everything on the surface, Lukas included. And then, that enormous power returned with a vengeance, imploding into itself like a nuclear blast, throwing several giant chunks of what could only be lochil metal out through the ground.

Lukas looked at Tanya in shock, and then back at the ores.

"Yeah," he said. "I see now."

Tanya snorted. "You don't. But you will. Right about now."

She might as well be a conductor waving a baton, directing the scene. For the air was suddenly split with battle cries of several dozen monsters: *giants*—each of them easily twice his height, carrying large clubs of burning rock resting on their shoulders—more ifrits, janje, and feline things that looked too large and too terrifying to be cats. He heard the wild ululations of the ifrits, the strangled moan of the giants, and the chittering screech of those cat-like things, as they all leapt forward at their fastest pace to find and destroy the enemy.

Them.

"Yeah," he grimaced, looking at Tanya with a sour expression. "I see what you mean."

'Told you," she quipped.

MUSPEL
Bipedal, lifeforce-producing organisms with innate fire mana-forges.
Characterized by extreme physical strength and lack of rationality.

Okay. Maybe he had erred slightly in his assessment. This wasn't Christian Hell. This was Muspelheim, or at least, a faithful impersonation of it. And these giants were muspels, fire-breathing, club-wielding monstrosities known for their unmatched capacity for destruction. In fact, Surtr, the mythological figure doomed to become the End of the Aesir in Ragnarok, was a muspel himself.

And he had several *dozen* of those rushing towards him.

Joy.

The first giant—*muspel*—saw them and almost instantly slowed down, legs spread wide like a surfer, slamming its club into the ground and dragging it behind like some berserk plow, rending the stone with an enormous roar of breaking granite as it slowed its enormous momentum.

The ground shook under the violence of their very presence.

"Muspels!" Tanya spat, gritting her teeth. "Hate them." She turned to him. "We've got to leave. As quickly as we can."

He arched an eyebrow at her. "Anything you want to tell me?"

"Muspels stay in herds. If there's a muspel in front of you, it means there's an entire herd around. I'll distract them, and we leave. If even *one* of them dies, the entire herd will be here in no time." Her face twitched. "Trust me. You don't want that."

Lukas glanced back at the svartalfar pair, who were busy collecting the gathered metal and packing them into their deceptively large bags. The giant mana circle was still active, with Mori still sitting at its heart.

"Can't leave without them, can we now?"

A look of frustration crossed Tanya's face. She had already conjured her Wind blades, ready to lash out at a moment's notice. *Not very useful,* he observed. Those monsters right there were flexing muscles the size of tree trunks and moved with a technique perfectly designed to use the full force of their unthinkably powerful bodies. Just one punch would be equivalent to getting hit by a speeding truck in the face.

Aeromancer or no, there was only so much you could take before hitting the bucket.

"Don't die, don't kill, and stall until they give the nod. That's about it, right?"

Tanya hesitated but nodded.

"Fine," he said, stretching his hands. "It'd be nice to test raw strength against one of those guys."

"Lukas," she snapped, before softening her tone. "Just be careful, okay?"

He grinned at her, wondering how impressive he'd look while standing on a hill of muspel corpses. Really, Inanna's curse could be such a pain in the ass. Silently, he analyzed his opponents.

GARM
Quadrupedal, lifeforce-producing organisms with innate fire mana-forges. Weak in strength, but impressive agility and regeneration.

IFRIT
Soul Architecture shows 100% similarity to IFRIT from Monster Prototype Array

"Alright. Same rules as before. Stay up in the air, keep the darlings safe, and bombard anything that gets close. Oh, and try not to kill me."

The corners of her mouth twitched. "Try not to get in my way, yes?"

One of the muspels raised its club in rising fury, the weapon bursting into flame. The creature roared, flexed its muscles, and flung the club, easily several quintals of hard, burning rock, whirling towards him.

Lukas wasn't stupid enough to stop it. It was just too much energy, too much momentum. Sure he could use Kinetomancy to alter its motion, but it'd be like using a medieval shield to block a descending war maul. Possible, but if you did, you'd soon wish you hadn't. No, a few pounds of pressure to the right place, at the right time, would be far more effective.

He chose a third option.

Lukas sidestepped just in time to let the club miss him by degrees, and then grabbed hold of its momentum. With practiced ease, he yanked it around, pulling it out of its trajectory into a wide swing, as if held back by invisible chains. There was an explosion of shattering rock as the muspel's weapon crashed into it with all the might of a freight train, hurling the giant by several hundred feet, knocking it into the ground.

"Oops! Did that hurt?"

The muspel, for its part, tumbled calmly, pushing himself out of the impromptu rock coffin the blow had created, and stood up. It shook its head like a dog, flexed its arms and legs to check if they were in functioning order, and then turned towards him. Then in a voice so deep that he could barely understand the word, it rumbled, *"Seidmadr!"*

Language Identified — Eusmian
Replicating . . .

Its voice sounded like someone had taken a rusty metal rod and dragged it across the floor. But what the hell? Turns out even *that* wasn't beyond the pendant's ability to recognize and translate. Talk about convenient.

"Tiny," Lukas greeted back.

The newly-christened Tiny furrowed its temples, snorting out flames from its mouth. A dark, ugly scar marred its face from the bottom of its left eye, all the way down to its chin. Neon-yellow nerves crisscrossed over its lava-kissed skin, with hands and legs ending in nails sharp enough to serve as daggers. A heavy mantle of fur over a long cloak gave its lean torso some kind of protection as it glared at him.

"This land is ours! Your kind is not welcome here."

"Yeah, that club kind of made that clear," he said, and instantly cursed at himself. He didn't need to look at Tanya to feel her penetrating gaze. Talking to svartalfars in the old tongue was one thing, but muspel? No way she'd dismiss that.

Me and my big mouth.

Lukas watched at the svartalfars from the corner of his left eye. The duo were diligently collecting the metal, but it'd still take some time before they were done. He turned back at the muspel and drew himself up to his fullest height, which meant he was eye-to-lower-quadriceps with it.

Then he spoke.

"The svartalfars are extracting metals there," he said, gesturing with his thumb. "They hired us to protect them. You know what that means?"

"That you'll die protecting them."

"Well . . ." Lukas nodded. "That was the contract."

Tiny lifted its hand. Another muspel threw his own mountain-wrecking club at him. Something told him that the others wouldn't be interfering with this fight. His know-how on Norse culture told him about their rules of combat. Unless he was wrong, the muspel had found him *worthy* of conversation, and would fight him to the death to decide who was superior.

"So much for a club," he murmured, clenching his fists. Not out of panic but preparation. His eyes dilated. *Alert.* Focused. No more reservations. No more holding back for the sake of holding back. This battle was his to win now and he'd guide it to whatever conclusion he deemed fit. Lifeforce surged, and fire arose as well, both in amounts far greater than he normally brought out. Ordinarily, he'd have deployed them as kinetic bursts or bullets, but now they covered his wrists, coiling, slithering, *begging* to be unleashed.

Lukas nodded at the muspel.

Tiny nodded back.

Then it roared and came at him, club whirling.

Lukas dashed in its direction, clashing with the muspel midway. He grabbed the motion around the club and *yanked* it just before the creature could smash him with it. The club slipped out of the giant's hands, only for it to pull it back, but it gave Lukas enough of a window to hammer a kinetic blow on its left ear. Tiny faltered and lost its balance but managed to belch hot, crimson flames in Lukas's direction, which he deflected with a wave of his hand. He could see the flash of surprise in the giant's eyes, before it spun in midair, with a grace that defied all logic and smashed a tree-trunk-sized muscular leg at his abdomen.

Lukas's world went white, as he was flung a good thirty feet back across the ground, slamming against a boulder. If not for Blob instantly covering his upper extremities like a protective sheath, he'd have gotten some serious head injury from the hit. Lifeforce burned hot within him, while his body sent weird tingly sensations to let him know what was going on.

Lukas stood up, shook his head in an attempt to get the damned bells to stop ringing, and looked around blearily. The ground shook as he did.

Oh right, Tiny.

"Good hit," the creature said, laughing for once.

"What do you know?" Lukas grinned back, blood pooling around his jaw. "You too."

He had been wrong in his estimation. Usually, creatures the size of this muspel came without power steering. There was simply too much mass building too much momentum for them to be quick to alter course, kind of like walking on slippery ice. But that was based on Earth physics, not this borderland. The creature before him had slipped past his attacks with a grace that defied all rules. He was reasonably sure that a combination of lifeforce-enhanced speed and Shatterpoint Intuition was enough to overcome the muspel's agility, but he couldn't do that without losing power behind his attacks. Whereas all the muspel needed was one hit and he'd be jelly.

Thump!

The creature's foot slammed down on the granite floor, crushing it into splinters, as it launched forward at him. In less than a second, it had crossed the entire distance, its weapon swung down and—

"HOLD!" Lukas roared defiantly and *snapped* the motion out of Tiny's entire body, freezing it midcourse. The muspel reacted, not in shock, but with red-hot flames, aimed directly at his face. Lukas hastily pulled a force shield to prevent himself from getting scorched, but that cost him his focus. Next thing he knew, Tiny was rushing at him, hammering on his force shield with one arm, not even once trying to go around it even though it'd be ridiculously easy to do so. The impact of the unstoppable force and the unmovable object was deafening as the resulting shockwave made cracks on the ground in all directions.

Lukas had no choice. He had to bring this to an end if he wanted to get out alive.

"Alright," he said. "I've had enough of you."

Tiny howled and dashed at him again, but Lukas took a step and all but vanished, suddenly accelerating and pushing himself to one side, crouching and sweeping his arm out at shin height, catching its enormous leg in the crook of his elbow and arresting its momentum a second time.

A force blast to the face did the rest. Tiny dropped to the floor, its face a violent mix of goo and purple blood. Both its eyes had exploded on contact, the attack tearing through its brain and exploding out of its skull from behind.

Siphoned Monster Prototype MUSPEL

Yeah. Add it to my Schema.

This would be useful. That kind of strength, speed, and agility would come a long way in improving himself as a physical warrior. No doubt this creature boasted multiple Level 3s. It'd be interesting to see the differences between that and—

MONSTER PROTOTYPE — MUSPEL	
SKILLS	**LEVEL**
Fire Creation	2
Fire Manipulation	1
Temperature Manipulation	2
Lifeforce Manipulation (Body Augmentation)	2
Momentum Manipulation (Force Transference)	2

—Level 2?

Lukas blinked.

This was a Level 2? How was that freaking possible? Granted, he had made quick work of the creature, but that was less due to his own strength and more his unpredictability. From altering the motion of his club to negating his own motion, followed by instantaneous self-acceleration and finally, kinetic blasts. It had taken him showcasing four of his techniques just to catch this fellow off guard and end it for good.

If Level-2 skilled creatures were on this level, then just what kind of monstrosities were Level 3?

Still. It was useful, especially the Body Augmentation part. One of the benefits of upgraded Scan and Analyze functions was that they showed the particular areas that the skills affected. Between augmenting his body and Force Transference, he could get some really creative solutions in battle, especially when combined with Shatterpoint Intuition. More importantly, he had killed the muspel in a one-on-one battle. So why was Tanya looking at him like he had done something incredibly stupid?

Oh. Right. He had kinda sorta killed it.

Despite her telling him *not to.*

"They'll come for you now." He heard Mori's dispassionate mutter. Whirling around, he found her standing right behind him. At least they were done collecting the metal.

"You're done?" he asked.

"Yes," said Kradir, bland as always. "But they won't allow us out. You killed them. They will not stop until they've killed us."

"I told you," said Tanya, looking positively ill. *"I. Told. You.* Whatever you do. Don't *kill.*"

"It was crossing the line." He shrugged. "I had to end matters."

"Yeah . . . end it you did," she said, panic vivid in her eyes. "Lukas . . . this wasn't a solution. This was suicide."

"Surely it can't be that bad . . ." His words were muffled in a howling roar among the muspel crowd. The ifrits drowned that with their own wild ululations and scratched the ground with their clawed limbs. And in response came a hundred different roars, screeches, and howls from every direction—the natives all gathering to face a common enemy.

Lukas glanced at Tanya and found her already fluttering above the ground, mana-charged Wind spinning around her. Two tiny spheres of pure energy were already forming in her palms. She gave him a dark look.

"Okay, yeah," he said after a moment of embarrassed silence. "I had to ask."

To say that they were mismatched would be a hilarious understatement.

On one side were two spiritists. Of these two, Lukas was the only one that could match these muspels in a one-on-one battle, and someone had to ensure the svartalfars weren't attacked from behind. Tanya's skills at close combat weren't particularly useful here. She was far better suited to middle-ranged aerial bombing.

On the other side was an army of muspels. And ifrits. And dozens of creatures whose population was growing with every passing second. Just fighting one muspel had taught him that these creatures were pure economies of motion. Each one of them could move to support the other, leaving no backs unguarded and no weaknesses to exploit. Individually, they were strong. Together, they were unstoppable, and that was precisely the scariest factor in the equation.

Lukas knew the truth. His team couldn't win. They didn't stand a chance against this army. If they fought, they'd die. If they tried to run away, they'd die. If they stood where they were, they'd die. Their sole option was to get to the Well as quickly as possible without this entire army on their tail. And the only way to do that was . . .

He exhaled.

"Tanya," he said, "get them out. Take them to the Well. I'll distract this lot until then."

"Are you out of your mind?" Tanya snapped. "I'm not letting you die."

"I'm too young to die now. You get them to safety. Then come back for me."

"No!" she said sharply. "I don't care about them. I'm not leaving you."

"Don't *argue!*" he snarled. "We can't keep fighting forever, and we need them to get on the other side. Get them close to the Well, and then come back for me. I'll keep them busy till then."

"Lukas . . ." Tanya's voice was troubled, which made sense. She didn't know what he was thinking. "I swear if you end up dying while I'm gone, I'll kill you."

"Gotcha!"

He could feel Tanya's hesitation, and the suspicion in the svartalfars' minds. Being the uber-logical creatures that they were, trying to understand his reaction was notably difficult.

He didn't blame them. If anything, he was surprised at himself. All this time trying to gain power, and he was now returning to the fundamentals.

Tanya could fly at extreme speeds. He could jump high and fast enough to follow suit. It was really Kradir and Mori that were at the disadvantage. Even if they managed to terraport their way through, they'd be stopped the moment they left these grounds. The two svartalfars had as much chance of crossing the lava pools as he had of finding a glacier on this borderland.

Which meant, he was going to have to give her time to get them to safety and return.

"We can—" she began.

"Do nothing," he said. "We can't keep fighting forever, and we need Mori and Kradir to get to the other side. Get them to safety, and then come back for me. I'll hold them up."

"And how will you do that?"

Damned good question. Using fire on these muspels would be useless. The dranzithl was an option, but whatever advantage it gave in terms of firepower and regeneration, it took away in terms of rationality. It was a berserker, and perhaps the most difficult of the lot to control. Shatterpoint Intuition was always an option, but he lacked a weapon capable of hacking through muspel flesh. Besides, their flames would be a pain in the ass up close. Lukas concentrated as different images flashed across his mind's eye in less than a second. *Orocoran, neothelid, yurei*—all of them were discarded preemptively for their uselessness. The kasha's Pyromancy was little more than a candle compared to their raging flamethrower, and trying to use the muspel prototype against their kind would end him up six feet under. No matter what creature he sought, none of them were good enough to be the solution.

That left only one option.

Kinetomancy.

The muspels were fast, but nothing was faster than *motion*. Their blows carried enormous force, but no force was greater than inertia. The monsters could belch out flames, but no flame was resistant to the power of redirection.

And all of that was possible through one single skill.

Kinetomancy. A power that brought down gods.

Inanna's skill.

Lukas closed his eyes.

"If you take them away, I can use *everything* I have without reservation."

He didn't need to look at her to feel her hesitation.

"You're just wasting precious time," he asserted. "The faster you leave, the faster you can return. I will probably be too weak to jump so you'll have to carry me out."

"Quit ordering me around, will you?" Tanya scoffed, but the heat from her words was missing. "You . . . are you certain you can . . ."

She trailed off.

Lukas turned and gave her a smirk. "I faced you at full strength and won. Give me a little respect."

With that, all thoughts of her and the svartalfars vanished from his mind as he studied the ever-growing army around them. He had killed the muspel, so *he* was their opponent. So long as he was there on the field, he presumed the muspels would not go after Tanya and the svartalfars. And whatever *did* go after them, she could take care of it.

She was a big girl.

Lukas exhaled, feeling lifeforce flow into him. The first stage of his reinforcement allowed him to move within his body's limits without consuming his stamina or overworking himself. At that level, thanks to the micromanagement of lifeforce he had developed, he could keep going nearly without limits as it took just a drop of his power to get the process started, and then he could continue by fueling it with pure anomalous energy. His resources would actually regenerate faster than what he consumed at that stage.

Stage Two, however, was an entirely different matter. It employed his newly-acquired ability to alter his own motion, allowing him to travel faster than possible, even for his enhanced physique. Hell, he was sure he could easily keep up with a speeding car at this point. Enhanced Momentum Manipulation to reinforce the velocity vector. Friction negation to counter against air friction and resistance. Ether layering upon his body to prevent it from tearing itself apart. And finally, instant bursts of acceleration, coupled with tachypsychia and Shatterpoint Intuition, guiding the blows at maximum efficiency. This wasn't enhancement, this was *self-weaponization*.

It was the style of fighting that Inanna preferred.

Imagine what you wish to create. Push your ether into it. Give your imagination form.

Blob slowly seeped down his hand, forming a thick handle. The tip expanded on either side, forming hard, sharpened edges.

A battle-axe?

Lukas looked at the weapon. No. Not just any axe. *Inanna's axe.* How—*Why* had he chosen *that* weapon of all things? He wasn't an axe-user in the first place.

At the same time, he had a feeling deep in his gut that it was the weapon he *needed* right now.

Ether. True Ether flowed down his palm, percolating into the axe, fusing with it, making it stronger, denser, deadlier. Aqāru was a wonderful material, but nothing was better than ether when it came to instant reinforcement. A hardness, several times that of diamond, was added to the axe's attributes; at the same time, its weight was made perfectly proportional to its size, ensuring minimal loss of power during the swing. His fractals thrummed, supplying him with more power than he needed for his strongest attacks. Tachypsychia merged with Shatterpoint Intuition and Seismic Sense, taking his perception and elevating it to instinctive precognition levels.

"Tanya," he requested—no, *ordered*—her one last time. "I asked you to leave."

"But . . ." the aeromancer trailed, simultaneously conflicted between trying to convince him and awed by the kind of power flaring out of him.

"The muspels are here for a war. I am a *warmonger.*"

"Seidmadr," Mori called out, a strange affliction in her tone. Lukas wondered if she was using that particular term because the fallen muspel had done the same. "You *are* powerful, but no one person can face the might of Muspelheim. You have killed one. There are *hundreds.*"

"The Crypt of Fiendish Worms wasn't an empty anomaly. I left it as one."

And then he smiled. Instincts honed through surviving against a certain goddess overwhelmed everything else. All thoughts vanished. All questions silenced. There was no need to account for lives. There was only the battle, one which he would draw to the best conclusion he would see fit.

"My teacher had a phrase," he said, eyeing the ever-growing army, the weight of the aqāru axe feeling oddly familiar in his hand. "An axe cares not where it falls, only that it is swung."

His fingers clenched the weapon in his hands tighter.

Power emerged.

A strangely modulated shriek of displaced air was the only warning the muspels received.

A black blur hurtled towards them like a bolt of lightning. The two muspels on the left flank hurled themselves back barely in time. The projectile hit the ground, and instantly detonated, the explosion obliterating everything within its vicinity in scant seconds, sending massive shockwaves rippling through the crust. Before anyone knew it, a shaft of pure gray shot through the air and sliced through a muspel's throat.

It was the first to die.

"One done," said Lukas Aguilar. "So fucking many left."

He glanced back at Tanya and the stupefied svartalfars. "Why the hell aren't you running yet?"

Combat had a strange way of playing tricks on the mind. The heat of it was confusing and incoherent, and even afterward it was often difficult to remember the bout in its entirety. The danger of the moment brought specific instances into hyper-focus, those times the situation was at its most perilous, and as a consequence, often these moments were the only instances someone could remember afterward. Raw recruits and grizzled veterans alike described battle as akin to being involved in a series of photo stills, the most memorable moments captured in fleeting images as though frozen in time. Everything else was blurred, made indistinct, unclear, distorted by a brain too busy working in overdrive and flooded with adrenaline.

Lukas would remember every moment of this fight with the muspels with perfect clarity for the rest of his life.

His body was in constant motion. Never stopping. Never halting. Never once giving himself a chance to rest and regather himself. The axe in his hands was a black blur in the periphery of his vision, darting for the muspel's exposed parts in one instant and then changing course to strike another when something rose to block. His body was moving at speeds his normally astute senses couldn't keep up with.

And yet he continued doing it.

The muspel closest to him raised its club and let out a bestial roar. It leapt toward him and thrust it in his face. Lukas took a pair of quick pivoting steps, guiding the club with one hand like he had seen Inanna do so often, and got into the muspel's space, hitting it with a blast of inertia, making it shoot out of its fingers.

And then he promptly spun around and decapitated the creature with one wide swing.

You have crossed the Threshold Barrier.
Level Up Initiated!

Ordinarily that would've been great news, if not for his shit luck. Why? Because he had already leveled up twice before, but neither of them had taken root. Instead, he had this.

A second notification sprang up.

Level Up Delayed until PRIME HOST is not in combat . . .
3 LEVEL UPs in sequence.

Yeah. That's what he meant.

"Fourteen," he panted. "Tell you what? Why don't we take a break for five minutes? That way I can level up and we can have a more awesome showdown?"

The muspels answered by raising their clubs and raining blows on him.

He grunted. Fighting these monsters was like fighting Ryu all over again—only larger, stronger, and more of him. The muspels were now aware of the kind of danger Blob presented and were wary of meeting it head-on. Instead they used their unnatural flexibility to dodge and weave through his attacks and switched to mid-ranged combat, involving fiery clubs, torrents of flame, and minor Terramancy blasts.

Lukas glanced at the sky. Tanya was little more than a pale speck above, her Wind orb carrying both svartalfars with her. Now if she only managed to get them to the Well and returned quickly. But until then—

Lukas spun around and threw up a force shield sidewards, hoping to deflect the tsunami of flames one of the muspels had unleashed on him.

Once upon a time, that shield would have been futile. Kinetic defenses were fairly simple to create, but they had limits. Barely months ago, he had been hard-pressed to deflect the flames shot at him by a half-burnt and fully angry Quonnan.

But times had changed. He was better now. He had learned the lessons the hard way and had the scars to prove it.

So when three of the muspel heavyweights unleashed a firestorm so massive that Quonnan's attack would seem like a small candle in front of this inferno, he wasn't instantly scorched to dust. His shield dribbled with green-gold sparks as it flared out in a quarter-dome of blue-white, light, a barrier of raw, stubborn will merged with kinetic force.

Lukas grinned. "Nice. Here's one of mine."

He threw the axe into the air, mentally commanding Blob to instantly divide into five thin daggers without losing even a fraction of its tensile strength. With speed enough to shock a professional gunman, Lukas launched the daggers at the muspel, Shatterpoint Intuition guiding their trajectories. Two of them were deflected by the clubs, with a third completely missing its target. The fourth ended up slashing through muspel's eye, while the last one made a clean shot right below the nose.

The muspel was dead before it hit the floor.

He barely had time for a victory dance before the ground beneath his feet exploded.

"Seriously?" he yelled, leaping away from the explosion. "Didn't your mom teach you that hitting below the belt is wrong?"

And then his ears suddenly twinged hard, like when the pressure shifts in an airplane, and the empty space behind him wasn't empty anymore. Lukas whirled, calling on Blob to re-form—

—and was flung backwards by several feet by a crushing force too powerful for him to even try to resist. He crashed against several boulders in an explosion of shattering rock that left at least a dozen little cuts all over his face, and several contusions on his limbs. Before Lukas could even try to see what was happening, three muspels were up in the air, clubs raised and slamming down on him. His instincts flared, and a force shield flickered between himself and the clubs.

It stopped him from becoming a thick, gooey paste on the ground, but in return, he was being crushed into it, as if the weight of a fucking building was above him. He gritted his teeth and fought against them, but the muspels kept hammering upon the invisible shield relentlessly like insane lumberjacks. The impact of the unstoppable forces and his immovable shield was deafening as the resulting shockwave sent cracks along the ground and dug him deeper and deeper into the crust.

For fuck's sake, these monsters are going to bury me six feet under!

Lukas felt the shocks from the hit resonate with his body as several of his muscles spasmed under the damage. His chest felt like there was a small elephant sitting on it. Squinting his eyes, he tried to force more power into himself, not with his muscles but with his will. He pictured it as a great, dark hand pressing him down, and his defiance as his own hand, rising to force it away. He poured his will into the image, investing it with power, with reality and life. Gasping, one inch at a time, Lukas managed to get an elbow underneath him and snarled silent defiance upwards, his right hand raised against one of his attackers.

"Get off me!" he snapped.

A titanic wave of pure force erupted out of the shield and punched the living daylights out of his target, hitting him right in the chest. The creature bent in half, spitting blood from its mouth.

Good! Let's see how you like it!

A sudden golden glow in the sky distracted him. Tanya and the svartalfars must have sent it, signaling that they were on their way. Lukas considered escaping, but he needed to do it fast, or he'd be the one stuck here. But no matter what he did, he couldn't manage to get up. Something this strong could not be easily defeated and he was losing time. He needed to do something, and quickly. And in this situation—

Activating Monster Prototype SVARTALFAR
Initiating Consciousness Shift
Enact

One moment he was being crushed into the ground. The next, his instincts and rationality were being substituted by Hreidmar's. The svartalfar's psyche was as alien as it came, and even having used it a few times by this point made the experience no less uncomfortable. A strange earthly power thrummed through his body and Lukas *sank* into the ground, becoming part of the entire terrain.

Man became svartalfar.
Body became terrain.
And Lukas *terraported*.

CHAPTER 16

STORM UNSEALED

Tanya was running late. As always, she had splurged a bit at the spa and was just about to leave for the svartalfar mission. Lukas was probably hanging around the bridge. It seemed like the only place he liked to frequent. But Zuken had suddenly asked her to pay a quick visit before she left, which felt a little strange since the man had hardly spoken a word to her ever since the meeting with the svartalfars.

"I know this mission is vital for our continued business with the svartalfars, but I have some orders. I'd like you to follow them."

Tanya blinked. Zuken sounded so uncharacteristically serious that she was taken aback. She looked up to find him watching her with hard, brown eyes, none of his customary easygoing attitude to be found.

"Three rules. Number One, you and Aguilar return safely. Number Two, the svartalfars return safely. The mission is third in priority. Whatever you need to ensure this, you do it. No matter what happens, do not hesitate. Do not hold back. Whatever comes in your path, let them die for their cause while you and Aguilar live for yours. Under no circumstances can you let anything happen to Aguilar. Understand?"

Tanya gave him a piercing look. She knew Zuken was downright obsessive about Lukas's secrets, but this felt a bit overboard. Even for him. It was almost like . . .

Like there was something he wanted, something he'd go to the very ends of the world to acquire, and only Lukas could give it to him.

"Maybe you shouldn't have let him go for this mission in the first place . . . "

"If I could have prevented it, I would have." His expression was almost unreadable. "Unfortunately, Aguilar is a novelty. Apart from his excessive impulse-control issues, keeping him trapped would only hinder his growth, and that is counterintuitive."

Translation: Lukas would rampage through Zuken's manor and things would get out of hand. Given what she saw of him in the anomaly, it wasn't too far off the list of possibilities.

"You want me to see what he can do. What he can really do."

His eyes wrinkled at the corners. "Yes. I do." His eyes lingered on her for an unnerving moment. "Is that acceptable?"

Tanya nodded. "And if we face a problem?"

"Then ditch the mission. Do whatever you need to get yourself and Aguilar out. Everything else, I'll manage. I cannot stress that enough."

Things had gone to hell.

This mission was supposed to be private training for her companion. She was supposed to show him the dos and don'ts of adventuring and get him accustomed to dealing with missions by himself. At the same time, she'd have the opportunity to spend some time alone with him, which made her feel a flush of warmth for more reasons than one. He was especially good at getting under her skin *and* making her want to tear him to pieces.

Instead, she had left him to fend for himself. All because he had decided to be gallant (or foolish, depending on how you looked at it) and hold the ground until she got them out of the kill zone. She trusted him—well, slightly more than she trusted anyone else, which was saying something— so despite her instincts and Zuken's orders, she had followed through with the plan. Whatever happened, she'd have his back, and he was tough and smart.

And alone, whispered some doubting part of her. *And vulnerable.*

Shut up, me.

What the hell am I doing? She mentally hissed. *Zuken clearly said—*

"Slow down a little," said Kradir, snapping her out of her inner tirade. "The terrain here is better. We can terraport from here."

Tanya gritted her teeth. They had already covered three quarters of the distance. The golden flares in the sky were becoming more prominent. But she knew that the rescuers wouldn't be leaving their ground to come for them. It was up to them to play catchup. Which was why they were zooming towards their destination in her expanded Wind orb.

"Why?" she demanded. "Terraportation is slower. We still have miles to go."

"I'd rather not spend another moment in the air if I can help it," said the extractor.

Tanya wondered if the creature knew how close he had come to getting beheaded. She had no lasting love for svartalfars, and their finicky attitude didn't help matters. But she needed them alive, or else all this would be for nothing.

"My friend is *fighting* to get us to safety back there, and you're having *mood swings?*"

The orb zoomed faster.

"It's not just that," said Mori, her tone apologetic. "Our baggage. We've been employing Terramancy constantly to keep them afloat against gravity. Weight nullification is very draining, exponentially so when we aren't *touching* the ground."

Tanya blinked.

Oh.

Oh.

She had never thought of it that way. She had imagined them to just do their svartalfar hocus-pocus and runecraft to balance the weight. That they were also constantly using Terramancy made a lot more sense.

"We do not give away secrets to Asukans," Kradir snapped at Mori.

"We're in a dangerous situation," Mori said, her voice carrying a tone of wearily familiar annoyance. It was like listening to a husband and wife having an often-repeated quarrel. "The seidmadr took a stand for us. Allowances have to be made."

Kradir made a quiet, disgusted sound.

Tanya slowly descended the Wind orb, traveling down an invisible, inclined plane. Too quick and she risked the orb shattering, which wouldn't end nicely for anyone. Too slow, and they'd run the risk of the svartalfars failing to maintain their spells.

"There is no reason to hurry back," said Kradir. "The pyromancer is dead."

The tempest in her chest suddenly raged at his words. The casual disregard for his life, their sheer indifference, brought Zuken's words back to her.

They are not your friends. Svaltalfars only care for their own kind.

"He. Is. Alive," she said, "and I'm getting back to him."

"A fool's errand," Kradir scoffed. "Your companion was brave, I'll give you that much. But no Asukan, even one as skilled as him, can brave the might of a muspel army and get away with it."

"He's alive," she stressed again. "I'm sure of it."

"How?" asked Mori.

Because if he was dead, she'd have lost control. Because here she was, in a world where the Eternal Light did not penetrate, and yet the Frost's impulses were all but absent. That had he died, the Frost would've taken over and these two would have been butchered before they could have uttered the word "protocol." Because Lukas was no Asukan. Because not even *Death* could claim him. Because he was tutored by a freaking goddess. Because he skirted the rules of the world like changing clothes. And no muspel army, no matter how strong, could kill him.

"Trust me," she said, "I'd—"Tanya began, when the first explosion thudded through the air.

Everyone froze.

A column of flames rose into the air in the southeast, flaring out into the night. The shock wave from the explosion was tangible, even where they stood, and Tanya felt something push through her chest.

"Was that . . . ?" She breathed.

Mori drew herself upright, a cold luminescence gathering around her form in a coronet of glittering motes that trailed a veil of tiny brown particles behind it. Both Tanya and Kradir turned to her, as the sensor lifted her face to the sky and spoke in a voice that didn't so much rumble as resonate with a devastating finality.

"The bylestyr have come. We must flee this place before it is too late."

Tanya's stomach did a nasty little flip.

"Who?"

"Bylestyr," Kradir said. "The wielders of lightning. Most feared among the muspel. Guardians of this realm."

"We've known these lands for a long, long time," said Mori. "Muspelheim is home to a lot of ores. But whenever a bylestyr has taken note of our invasion, we've lost our kinsmen. Believe me, we must leave. *Now.*"

"Lukas—"

"Is dead, or will be dead," Kradir retorted. "Nothing you can do will change that fate. You can leave us right here if you wish. We can make the rest of our journey by ourselves. But be warned, it will change nothing except hastening your demise."

Tanya took a deep breath, closed her eyes, exhaled, and walled away the small ocean of fear that had begun rolling in her mind. Everything had gone to hell, no matter what she did. And she'd face it when it arrived. Compartmentalize and conquer.

Because right now, there was only one thing in her mind.

Get Lukas back.

"Wind-bender," Mori called out. "I ask you to reconsider. If you do this, you'll perish."

"You don't know that."

"Yes I do," said Mori, "and soon."

"The bylestyr are at the zenith of Level 3," said Kradir. "You are skilled, but compared to the bylestyr, you're but an insect."

As he spoke those words, a scream pierced through the air. One so sharp that it threatened to deafen her by sheer volume, but it was far more painful than that. Tanya could feel it pressing against the vaults of her mind, a raging emotion so violent and intense that it would tear her sanity apart if she let even a portion of it in.

The world suddenly went silent, as if reality had taken a deep breath and held it. There was a low quiver in the terrain beneath her feet, a hideous pressure in the air, and then, from the south, a column of red-white energy—pure power—erupted into the sky.

Level-3 Pyromancy. Amplified by several magnitudes inside this volcanic terrain.

Kradir was right. Lukas could not win against this kind of power. A Level-3 creature's wrath was terrifying, capable of causing destruction of untold magnitude. Lukas might have Level-3 skills himself, but his control and experience was still stuck to a hair short of Level 2 at best. Nothing—not his lifeforce, not his skill with motion, and certainly not his Pyromancy—could save him against this.

To defeat that, a power equal to its magnitude was required.

A power that she could conveniently pull up.

A power that would have been beyond her control if not for Lukas Aguilar.

Get Lukas safe. That was her goal. Her motto. *Protect him at all costs. For Zuken, and for herself.*

The Frost had always been a deadly tool. Something that sought to kill, to savor, to tear lifeforce and life out of its victim. But for the first time, she was calling upon its cold, wintry heart for the exact opposite.

To save.

To protect.

And Winter answered.

Her eyes burned an icy blue.

The first noticeable thing was the white spreading over the red terrain. Jagged lines, cracking and spreading in all directions, akin to a world of glass that had suddenly shattered. The lines did not stop, but instead, raced away from each other, rushing to escape Tanya, who stood at the center, a wall of mist and wintry plume acting as a defensive wall against the furious fiery winds that rushed in her direction.

And Tanya spoke.

"Ice is my soul."

The voice that came sounded like a peal of thunder, ragged with inhuman malice, buffeting Lukas with its rolling depth. Thick spears of frost began to form on the surface.

Her eyes turned white.

"Everfrost!"

As if on cue, the plumes exploded, changing from mere white lines to genuine sheets of ice. The freeze extended, stretching between each of the previous lines and thickening, coating everything in near-inch-thick sheets of frozen shelling. The ice erupted in spots, forming enormous tooth-like stalagmites, swelling and erupting with violent force. Anyone else would have questioned how she, despite being an aeromancer, was conjuring *ice* of all things in this environment, but Tanya couldn't care less.

In a few seconds, a veritable Ice Age stood amidst the frothing lava.

"What . . ." whispered Mori from behind her.

Tanya turned and stared at . . . *prey*, a thin sliver of ice forming in her hands almost unconsciously, before the burning terrain reminded her where she was.

"Your protector, should you run away, and predator, should you choose to stay," she murmured. "Get to the portal. I'll get Lukas and join you."

Her icy gaze turned to Kradir and—

"I . . . I did not know."

Tanya blinked, the white haze flickering inside her mind, trying to catch up to the confusion. Kradir was on the ground, on his knees, palms open, head held up, like a prisoner ready to embrace his death, or—

—or a worshiper genuflecting before his god.

"Forgive me. Forgive me, I did not . . . I did not know . . ."

She blinked, shaking her head to dispel the confusion. It didn't help so she just looked away. Frost surged within her, its need to consume everything strangely tempered, leaving the wheels to her rational mind. A true miracle, if she said so herself.

She turned towards the south, where the massive pillar of fire had joined the earth and the sky.

Ever since the calamitous moment of her father's demise, Tanya had always felt her kami inside her and held it back. She had felt the primal drives that were its power, the need to hunt, to fight, to kill and destroy. Its nature was beautiful violence, stark clarity, the most feral needs and animalistic desire pitted against the furious Wind—the will and desire to *shatter* all boundaries.

She had fought against that drive, repressed it, and held it at bay. That savagery was never meant for a world of grocery stores and beauty salons and spas. It was meant for times like this.

So she let it out, and everything changed.

Her weariness vanished. Not because her body was no longer exhausted, but because it was no longer *important*. She had become an extension of a greater entity, a manifestation of the primal force of Wind. Her fear vanished too. Fear was for prey. Fear was for the things she was about to hunt.

Her doubts vanished as well. Doubt was for things that did not know their purpose, and she knew hers. This was a *war*, and there were beasts in front of her.

Beasts that needed their throats ripped out.

A fire that needed to be extinguished.

Tanya's body soared up into the air, an ethereal darkness wrapping around her. Her hands spread out on either side, a thrumming black mist enveloping them before ejecting from her back into massive wingspans of liquid darkness. Wind and Shadow and Frost crawled all over her body, forming a scale mail.

Tanya the spiritist was gone.

What stood in her place, floating in the air, was a warrior angel. A bird of prey. A Queen of Air and Frost and Darkness. Wind buffeted her body, a raging conflagration that made the world less just by existing in it. An unstoppable tide that controlled the very air itself.

A behemoth that was no longer shackled, free to act at last.

She raised both hands forward, and a sphere of pure devastation was born. An orb of nigh infinite pressure, held in place by a madness just as devastating. A core of pure Wind that could destroy anything upon impact. A man. A mountain. Whatever.

Aeromancy amplifying her vision, she saw a giant beast soar into the air, with a small speck of what looked faintly like a man rising further and further upwards, out of its reach.

Tanya smiled as massive blades of Wind formed around her.

She had almost forgotten how good it felt to let loose.

CHAPTER 17

BETS ON THE BATTLEFIELD

Dangerous.

That was the only word fluttering through Lukas's mind, as he tried to keep his knees from hitting the floor. Terraporting had saved him from a gory death for now but it wasn't off the table. He wasn't foolish enough to consider himself *safe*, especially because he couldn't leave the battlefield. Not yet.

And now they know I can terraport.

Information was one of the greatest tools you could hold in a fight, as valuable as any weapon or skill in determining victory. The less they knew of his abilities, the greater his unpredictability and his chances to defeat them. So far, they had discovered he could do Motion Manipulation—both inner and outer—force-shielding, Conjuration, and now Terramancy. They also knew of Blob transforming into whatever shape he desired, so could assume he was a terramancer skilled at Motion Manipulation.

He still had Hreidmar's gravity control techniques, Pyromancy, and Aquamancy hidden up his sleeves. Using his two-bit Pyromancy would be slightly less effective than scolding these muspel, unless he combined it with the dranzithl's corrosion. Maybe as a last measure? Aquamancy . . . He could technically perform it, but here in this fiery environment, he'd be hard-pressed to make it worth anything. Gravity? It could be a last-minute flight attempt if things really went south, but until then, he'd have to keep it hidden.

That pretty much meant the muspels had him figured out.

He still had the muspel prototypes added to his Array. They were useless to him, not unless he got the chance to get the double Level Ups and get his body to better reflect his skill set.

It was like being back at the crypt all over again.

The more things change, he thought, *the more they stay the same. Seriously, Inanna, why do these things keep happening to me?*

As always, there was no answer.

"Earthwalker," he heard them exclaim, *"the seidmadr can terraport!"*

"Yeah," he shot back. "Which one of you saw that coming?"

The muspels looked at each other, as if physically confirming if there was anyone among them that had expected him to terraport. Lukas sighed at their rigid, blank faces. Seriously, his humor was *wasted* upon these creatures. Like . . . *why?* At least *that* could prove as a suitable distraction. For fuck's sake, he needed some distraction if he wanted to stop shaking in fear and take proper action.

"As much as I'd like to give you candy for figuring that out, I really need to leave. There's this portal I really need to catch."

The sounds of growling coming from behind caught his attention. From the corner of his right eye, he could see a group of ifrits encircling him. The muspel in front of him raised his fiery club in the air.

"DIE!" it exclaimed.

"Figures!" Lukas mumbled. Let it not be said he didn't try to be diplomatic. As he slipped into a combat stance, Blob already re-formed into the familiar axe in his hand. He surveyed the arena. There were easily a hundred monsters around. Maybe he *would* need to let the dranzithl run free sooner than he thought.

"Do you really want to go down that road?" he asked. "The more you fight me, the more I kill your people. Just let me leave and we can end it right here."

"We will fight," it boasted. *"And you will die."*

The club smashed downward.

"For someone so tough, you fellas are being awfully sensitive about—oh fu—!"

The world *exploded.*

Fire and burning rock detonated out of the ground. Torrents of flame that could incinerate him with the slightest touch, burning boulders that would reduce him to paste the moment they hit, and a gale of volcanic ash that just had to be bad for his skin—all of them came at him at the same time. And then there was one muspel that wanted to personally maul him.

Kinetomancy took care of the flames, and Lukas was glad to see Blob was hard enough to shatter boulders. He whirled and hacked a muspel's arm off, before hurling it at an ifrit.

But it wasn't enough.

His ability to defend against projectiles using Shatterpoint Intuition was extreme, but even he had his limits. He wasn't fast enough to defend against simultaneous attacks against every point of his body from all sides.

But neither Tanya nor the svartalfars were around anymore. That meant he didn't have to limit himself. He had options. Gathering power in his legs, Lukas leapt straight backwards, employing Friction Modulation to cut past the air resistance in order to increase the distance between himself and his attackers—

—only for another muspel to punch him from the right.

The hit forced all the air out of his legs at once, leaving him bent into a bow shape. Before he knew it, he was flung forward, raw force smashing him into the terrain below, leaving him buried between four feet of rubble.

"Die!" said the creature. *"Die!"*

Lukas would've mocked their cliche Neanderthal war cry, but before he could so much as open his mouth, the muspel threw its club at his face, crashing against his half-formed force-shield like a truck through a wooden fence. The sheer impact was deafening, creating a massive crater, and pushing Lukas several more feet into the dirt.

And then the crater began to *heat up.*

Lukas swallowed. The ground beneath him was going to blow up. And if he didn't get away, he'd be blown up with it. If he tried to stop it, he'd die. If he tried to escape, he'd die. If he stayed where he was, he'd die. He had to think fast . . .

The third hammer of force came thundering down upon him.

Activating Monster Prototype DRANZITHL
Initiating Consciousness Shift
Enact

Lukas was ready. With a sudden leap, he instantly crossed a distance close to a hundred feet.

And then a second force wall came crashing just *inches* away from him.

Lukas didn't wait to see the results. He turned right, and accelerated, shifting through several hundred feet with a single step. Every time his feet left the ground, he crossed another several hundred feet. The muspels rushed after him, yelling and howling, their clubs hammering against the terrain, tearing it apart. Individually, he was faster than any of them, but together, they were. Within the very first minute, his body had already been hit in eight different spots. Several of his muscles were sprained or torn, and his tibia was close to fracturing. If he didn't escape immediately, things would end up very, very bad for him.

Absolutely wonderful.

"Tch!" He grimaced, as he jumped at another corner, mere moments before the ground beneath him exploded in a burst of magma. The molten rock had touched his clothes and burned a massive hole through them. If not for the dranzithl's regeneration, he'd have been short a leg. He'd need to get away from this place as fast as poss—

BOOM!

The ground before him exploded, unleashing a veritable wall of crimson, flames surging higher and higher until they reached the size of a small hill. The sheer force lifted Lukas and sent him hurtling for several dozen feet. His back slammed into one of the craters, with half-melted rock and stone digging into him from behind.

"Urgh!" he groaned. It was the only intelligible sound he could make as he tried to regain his bearings.

His head was pounding and he felt like he had just been spun out of a washing machine. Shifting slightly, he realized that he was half buried in stone and half-molten rock that was slowly corroding through his robes.

"Fuck!" He grunted, and stood up, vainly trying to maintain some semblance of civility on his person. Kind of difficult to do when more than half of your trousers are charred and gone.

Then he saw it.

The blur behind the wall of flames. It was a massive, shadowy figure, larger than anything he had ever faced before.

And it was getting larger by the second.

He saw the face next, an eerie mix of charred flesh and bone. The flesh, if it could be called that, was dark brown with flecks of red and blackened silver, and several horn-like protrusions jutting out at odd angles. The eyes shone with a mad, blue, almost primordial light, contrasting with the bright crimson surrounding it.

Slowly, the demented beast's full form came into view. It took a single step out of the flaming wall, causing tremors on the ground. Then another step. And another. Its body was humanoid, but only just. Its limbs were thicker than oak trunks, and it loomed over him, his head barely reaching above its waistline.

"Um," he said, "you're not . . . their mommy by any chance, are you?"

The demon lifted its head and *roared.*

One moment, there was nothing. Then, *violence* permeated the air. To call the sound merely loud would have been a ridiculous understatement. It seemed to plaster Lukas to the ground, his ears, eyes, and nose bleeding as the dranzithl's regeneration kept healing them over and over again at a spectacular rate. His heart felt like it would burst within his chest, and his hands shook as pinpricks ran along his skin.

The monster tilted its head slightly downward, and Lukas saw its large, blue, demonic eyes.

Something told him, *yelled* at him, that he should run. But his muscles didn't obey his command. His legs spasmed as he tried and failed repeatedly to stand on his feet. None of it seemed normal, and his mind nearly slipped away in fear. He—what was he doing? —he was forgetting something.

Danger.

Right. That was it. Danger. He was in danger—

The *monster* opened its maw again, and its eyes glinted predatorially. It didn't seem to be calculating how to fight him or how to avoid combat. No, it was akin to a starving man looking at an all-you-can-eat buffet, with layers upon layers of delicious, exotic dishes laid out for it to feast upon.

Prey Found You

"Yeah . . ." Lukas mumbled. "Yeah, it did."

Before him, a mere thirty paces away, the monstrous muspel cocked its head. The spikes adorning its skull and neck jutted out at odd angles, frill-like and menacing, making it appear even larger than it actually was. *Lava* trickled down its body like water, an iridescent glare shooting out of its piercing eyes. Jagged, serrated teeth loomed from its jaws, dripping thick, viscid saliva to the ground. It had two pairs of hands, like an ancient Hindu god, and looked like a wrestler who could casually juggle a train engine in his spare time. There was fire within it. Fire outside it. Fire *was* it.

Lukas's attention, however, wasn't focused on those trifling details. Instead, he was gazing into the monster's eyes. There was a feral cunning to those glowing orbs, an inhuman, alien intelligence—primordial and strangely disconcerting.

This wasn't a stupid brute awaiting its turn to mindlessly attack and slaughter, like the ifrit herd. It was aware of its surroundings, to a level perhaps even greater than Lukas himself. It was superior to him, and it knew it.

Lukas had faced impossibly powerful beings before. The Guardian of the Crypt. Solana. Ryu. And of course, Inanna herself. But even with the goddess, he had never lost his defiance.

But standing before this monster, Lukas had to admit he was unnerved.

Yeah . . . Shit's really hit the fan this time.

Like Solana, there was something utterly unnerving about it. Unlike Solana, the power exuding from it was utterly unrestrained. This was a destroyer in the genuine sense of the term. If there was anything that would be an accurate test of his abilities, *this was it.*

Faster than it took a normal person to blink, Lukas went through his Prototype Array, verifying every single monster he knew, right down to their meanest skill, but nothing came even remotely close to being useful other than the dranzithl with its instant regeneration, but even that wasn't enough. Just its will alone had crushed him into a crater. The only option was to run, but how could he outrun something that could attack him faster than he could perceive it?

No. No monster prototype could fight this.

Neither could his strength. Nor his limited Kinetomancy, nor Hreidmar's gravity. Nothing.

As if sensing the turmoil in his mind, it took a single step in his direction, the motion heavy with menace. From the corner of his eyes, Lukas spotted the other muspel standing in ceremony backing down. The ifrit populace had already escaped, their prey instinct overwhelming their desire to hunt.

As soon as it sees me running, it'll scorch me to death, Lukas mused. *It knows it's cornered me and wants me to react. I'm its entertainment. The only option is to keep its flames from touching me.*

The monster clawed another menacing step towards him.

Yes. That was the only way available. He had deflected flames before with minimal knowledge of Kinetomancy. He had grown since then, but the flames he'd face now would be magnitudes—no, a *dimension*—greater than Quonnan's. Nothing he could use—lifeforce, Terramancy, Pyromancy or Aquamancy—would be effective against this monster. None of his monsters would last even five seconds.

Lukas focused on Blob, connecting with its constitution.

Shield me.

Blob rose, expanding in all directions, forming an exo-suit to cover him, head to toe, leaving his nostrils, eyes, ears, and mouth as the only openings available. Aqāru would not be a worthwhile choice of armor against lava and wouldn't last long against flames this potent. Not even when augmented with lifeforce.

But perhaps, he didn't need lifeforce for this. Aqāru was a metal that conducted all elements. And against these flames, Lukas could only think of one.

Earth.

The terrain.

Terramancy.

His fractals went into overdrive, churning out mana in massive volumes, covering every inch of the aqāru armor—reinforcing it, filling in the intermolecular spaces, increasing the attraction between them, the density between molecules, the bindings between multiple molecular layers that made up the aqāru.

What was once a fluid was now denser than diamond.

And yet, still not enough.

Lifeforce burned bright within him. His muscles became denser, more agile, more resistant to tear and fatigue. His bones hardened. His senses dialed up to eleven. His current form was nearly impervious to conventional weaponry, his skin strong enough to deflect Bergott's blades. Even most kami-based attacks designed to kill would bounce off of him now.

But that would all be pointless if he couldn't deflect the flames first.

Lukas braced himself. Reinforced himself to the nth degree. Surrounded himself with a dome of rocks. Created a shield of pure inertia that could stop a running train in its tracks.

It barely halted the first blow.

Lukas was almost knocked back by the sweltering heat, his senses over-loaded by its sheer intensity. Sweat poured down his brow, beads of perspiration clinging to his face and running down his cheeks. Despite that, he didn't falter nor take a single step back. He weathered the heat that would have evaporated a river and faced it with sheer, defiant will.

The flames suddenly stopped. Not because the beast was tired, but because it was observing him. Like it was a scientist and he a guinea pig.

Then came the second blast. It launched from the sides in a wide beam of liquid crimson, scorching the rocks themselves, smashing against the dome in waves of concussive force, buffeting it with fire so thick that it obstructed the world from view.

His eyes watered. His skin blistered. The dome was half molten already.

The monster let out another growl. It came across as mocking in Lukas's ears. A mocking, steely, howling laughter.

"I am not so easily killed, beast," he spat back.

The monstrosity craned back its head. It stared down at the warrior as it challenged, its fiery pupils flashing. With a rumbling growl, it struck with all its might.

The world went red and howling.

Lukas raised both hands, touched upon the reservoir of power that the anomaly had gifted him, and called upon ether.

Ether was the most dynamic element in the universe, capable of changing into all other elements, as well as transforming the unreal into the real. It was what allowed spiritual creatures like ifrits to bear physical form and embody physical properties. Ether was best used to create and protect, and what he had in mind was going to take a lot.

Cold blue light shone from within him. Within his thoughts, Lukas merged the power of ether with raw, undiluted anomalous energy.

If ether was the most versatile element, anomalous energy was the very fab-ric of creation. It didn't make things more potent, but it made them more *real*. And when combined with ether, the results could be pretty interesting. Had he not been fighting for survival, Lukas would have worn a pair of lab goggles, gotten out a workbook, and begun taking notes.

> **Activating Monster Prototype MARID**
> **Initiating Consciousness Shift . . .**
> **Enact**

Instantly, Lukas accessed the marid's skills. He already had them listed in his arsenal, but he was really looking for the kami's instinct more than anything else. Lukas grabbed the surge of anomalous energy and ether within him, and with a command that could only be from the marid's instinct, coupled with a Level-2 Water Creation skill, pushed it out all at once.

Ever seen a tidal wave crash against a volcano? Lukas hadn't either, but if he had, he was pretty sure it would look like this.

His head exploded with raw agony as the energies met and fed upon each other, growing into a thunderstorm in his mind. With a kick, he pushed himself into the air, bent his knees, and went into a crouch, crafting an orb of pure lifeforce all around him, just in time for the wave to crash against the legion of fiery shadows that was the beast's skin, and turned into a great burst of steam. Lukas could see the flames raging all around as the explosive force hurled his orb shield like a cannonball into the sky. The entire area behind him exploded sky high, raining down broken rock fragments and flames all around.

Nearly half a thousand feet above ground, the protective orb reached its apogee and then fell back towards the ground. Lukas hissed in pain from the stress of maintaining and controlling the shield. The marid had no clue what to do in this situation and so Lukas let it dissipate.

> **Switching to Monster Prototype SVARTALFAR**
> **Initiating Consciousness Shift . . .**
> **Enact**

Yes. Level-5 Alpha Condition was a wonderful, wonderful thing.

Seamlessly, the instincts of a kami trapped in midair vanished, replaced by one that was so comfortable standing in midair his fellow compatriots called him a sorcerer for it. Hreidmar's instincts sharpened his focus, and instantly exacted its position with respect to the center of gravity of the terrain. He'd need to make sure he didn't overdo the height or the speed, or else the sudden change of pressure would cripple him. However, even being temporarily disoriented was significantly preferable to being incinerated by that fire demon.

Higher. Higher. Higher.

He rose through the sky at tremendous speed. He couldn't consider what he was doing to be flying. Flying was the action of keeping off of the ground. A process. What he was doing was merely adjusting the position of where he was and keeping himself relative to the ground. His change in location was merely applying velocity to the constant that was Gravity Control. It would be immensely difficult to perform Terramancy like this in the air, with minimal proximity to the terrain, but Lukas had the advantage of drawing from his omphalos reserves. He was moving higher and higher.

He didn't notice that his lungs weren't taking in enough air. They already had trouble with that because of the wounds he had suffered. He didn't notice the damage his body had undertaken in trying to survive the past blows. Instead, his entire focus was down on the ground where the fire demon was looking up from the ground and—

"█████████ ████████"

With an earth-shattering roar, the beast charged forward, hunched down, and then launched itself up into the air at its prey that was rising at speeds that would kill a normal human being.

"Shit!" Lukas swore, seeing the giant rapidly approaching him at an impossibly fast velocity. He'd thought he'd put enough distance between himself and it that he was out of reach. Turns out he had once again forgotten how little such beings cared for the laws of physics. As it stood, Lukas only had a few seconds before it caught him unless he did something quick.

And only one thing came to mind.

"Push!" he grimaced, preparing his already-battered body for the strain that was about to hit him.

A wall of pure force expanded between himself and the beast. Of course, it did absolutely nothing to the beast, but that was expected. Instead, it was the reactive force—Newton's law at work—that pushed him into a parabolic trajectory far, far out of its reach. How he stayed on all fours and managed to not black out nor break his limbs as his body rocketed away, he would never know, but that was exactly what happened. The moment it hit him, Lukas's entire being felt like it was being crushed. His vision went temporarily white from the strain. Breathing was a luxury as the unwanted pressure on his body forced his brain to focus on ensuring his vitals could still function properly, and this was *after* he had reinforced his body beforehand. And the demon was still getting closer and closer and—

It happened in an instant.

A blue blur streaked through the air, traveling so fast it appeared to be a bolt of lightning. It struck right at the giant's chest, ripped through its body, and buried itself deep within its heart before the monstrosity detonated. And when it did, the world beneath Lukas simply vanished, a sea of flames and wind taking its place. The force of the resulting explosion was so powerful that even from several hundred feet above, Lukas was buffeted by a solid wall of air that blew the breath out of his lungs.

The Screen pinged.

<table>
<tr><td colspan="2" align="center">Soul Siphon Success!
Absorbed Monster Prototype BYLESTYR</td></tr>
</table>

MONSTER PROTOTYPE — BYLESTYR	
SKILLS	**LEVEL**
Fire Creation	3
Fire Manipulation	3
Temperature Manipulation	3
Lifeforce Manipulation (Body Augmentation)	3
Momentum Manipulation (Force Transference)	3

Lukas stared at the information in surprise. This was what he was capable of, if he pushed his skills to the zenith? And this was just *Level 3?* He knew that Level 3 required five thousand units of Soul Capacity, compared to the meager five hundred units of Level 2. Even so, this bylestyr wasn't an amalgamation of the power and skill of ten muspel, but far more than that.

The rise wasn't linear or multiplicative.

It was *exponential*.

And if this was Level 3, then Level 4, which required fifty thousand units of Soul Capacity . . . What kind of demons would those be?

It boggled the mind.

<table>
<tr><td align="center">Add skills from BYLESTYR to PRIME HOST?</td></tr>
</table>

"Um, yes?"

<table>
<tr><td align="center">Adding skills from BYLESTYR to PRIME HOST
Initiating Transfer . . .
Deactivating Monster Prototype SVARTALFAR
Initiating Consciousness Shift

Enact</td></tr>
</table>

"WHAT? NO—"

He tried to resist, but he was unprepared for the pain of this sudden assault. Worse, he wasn't prepared for his gravity technique flickering out of existence, as the control over his body was grabbed away from the svartalfar prototype to himself. The sudden shift in his situation dropped his combat mode, allowing Prophylaxis to set in, also setting his nerves on fire. The invisible aerial plat-form beneath his feet vanished, and Lukas plummeted downward like a stone, completely under the inexorable power of gravity, down where a fiery death was awaiting him. He relentlessly tried to focus on reactivating the prototype or trying to use the Gravity skill, but nothing seemed to work. It was almost as if his power had fled right as he needed it most.

Multiple Level Ups in Sequence Detected!
Addition of Multiple Level-3 skills to HOST BODY registered.
Level Ups mandated to complete the process.
Shutting down temporary body functions.

Lukas couldn't give a damn. Here he was, barely clinging to consciousness. The shock and the intense pressure he had subjected himself to was disorienting. He could taste blood in his mouth, which he realized was a bad sign, especially with the recent regeneration and the anomaly's attempts to constantly rejuvenate him. His limbs felt boneless, and there was no way he could stand up with his own strength. With the omphalos choosing to shut down his functions, all he could do was keep falling and hope to survive with his brain intact upon impact. Everything else he could heal but he kind of needed that to live . . .

Ha. Live? What am I worrying about that for? he wondered deliriously.

Initiating Level Ups.

ATTRIBUTE	CHANGE IN PARAMETERS
Level	+3
Soul Capacity	-
Maximum Lifeforce Output	+7550
Replenishment Rate	+600
Maximum Mana Output	+7550
Mana Synthesis	+600

And that was not all.

Assimilating newly gained skills.
Altering HOST BODY to establish perfect synchronicity with new skills.
Establishing bodily changes with LEVEL-3 Lifeforce usage baseline.
Establishing parity with Divine Corruption . . .

What—?

Establishing Evocation System with Level-3 Mana Usage baseline
Enacting . . .

The rest of his thoughts vanished as his eyes burned in their sockets like living coals, with lifeforce and mana rushing through him in incredible torrents. The strength, the power, the abilities—it was more, way more than he had ever experienced. He felt control of his body returning to him and covered his face at the overload of power and physical strength. He felt something being born from him, shaped by his will and molded by the omphalos within him. He felt it wash around him in a single instant—lifeforce, fire, earth, water, and ether swirling around him, felt them become a part of him as his world went white. He closed his eyes from the euphoria of strength and power within, and a terrible joy surged through his heart at the feeling.

Close.

He heard Inanna's voice resound around him.

Inanna—

Not mine to use, whispered her voice sibilantly in his mind as it faded away.

His feet hit the ground.

Lukas opened his eyes.

The muspels were staring at him in complete surprise. Several of the monsters gazed at him with open-mouthed fear and awe, and that made him smirk. Lukas thought back to the attack that had one-shotted the bylestyr. He had no doubts about the identity of its perpetrator, just a lingering question. If she had such weapons up her arsenal, what *else* did she have?

The answer to his reveries came in the form of the sound of . . . *beating wings?*

Before he could even react, the very air around him began shaking, softly at first, but soon violently, as though he were sitting on railroad tracks with a freight train approaching from behind. It filled the air with a discordant hum that grew in intensity until Lukas had to squeeze his eyes shut in discomfort.

Then, all at once, everything simply . . . stopped. The shaking air. The terrible hum. Everything. The silence was so utter and complete that the sound of his own heart beating in his chest startled him. He opened his eyes and, failing to curb his curiosity any longer, looked up.

And up.

And up.

At the sky.

And yet, he couldn't fathom what he beheld before him. He could only stare, transfixed, at the four pairs of wings, each as dark as the blackest night, larger than a bus. The elemental manifestation of all that was cold and dark in the world. He saw the claws. He saw the body. He saw the crystallized center of this . . . leviathan, and in its midst—

Stood Tanya.

"I . . ." said Lukas, "have absolutely no idea what I'm looking at."

The leviathan opened its beak.

"███████████ ████ ███████"

The sound that came was like being thrown into an enormous vat of petroleum. Instantly, Lukas felt like there was no way to get a good breath. He felt pressure against all of his body at once and pain in his ears, reminding him of one very bad dive he'd taken once into a swimming pool. It took all his resolve to not clap his hands over his ears, fall to his knees, and scream.

And then the vision vanished, and Tanya practically teleported in front of him. Lukas idly noticed how her golden blonde hair was all but white right now. Her oceanic blue pupils had also turned a fierce white, and Frost and something else was covering her like armor. Winds spun around her, coiling protectively like a lover's arms. For a moment he feared Inanna's spell had failed and the Frost Queen was back. If that was so, he'd be in deep trouble. Level Up or no, there was no way he could fight that demon and win.

"Ah," she drawled, "you're still alive."

"Surprising, right?" he shot back. "And you got a new look."

The smile on her lips was warm and calming, in contrast to the sheer feeling of wrongness she exuded. Her eyes seemed to glitter with amusement.

"I didn't think the Frost could take over again," he said seriously. "Looks like I was mistaken."

"No," she cocked her head idly. "It's not in control. I'm still me. Only . . . less inhibited, which is *wonderful*. It's far too long since I've had time to . . . how do I put it? *Let my hair down?* Things in the outside world are so fragile. At least here I can *enjoy* myself a bit."

Her tone was musical, beautiful, and *off*, reminding him of the murderous psychopath he had faced in the anomaly. He really hoped that she was still in control of her senses. As good as it was to have her Wind kami on his side, he'd rather not face the Frost Queen again, not in such a condition.

"It was so unfair, you know," Tanya complained, dark amusement ringing in her voice. "Sending me away with those *insects* while you had all the fun . . . No, no, that won't do. That won't do at all."

Her words rippled across the battlefield, the undeniable weight they held giving pause to the monsters surrounding them. In a split second, the air around Lukas writhed, merging with a twisted black mist forming . . .

The silence among the crowd was deafening.

This, Lukas reminded himself, *is what Aeromancy is capable of.*

Wind blades.

They hung in the air, held up by invisible hands, by the dozens, by the hundreds. Enough to match every single monster and more. They lined up row after row, spanning across the circumference of an invisible circle, with himself and Tanya in the center. Lukas didn't need to be a sensor to know that each and every one of those blades had as much impact strength as the dranzithl's corrosive blows.

"Now then . . ." said Tanya impishly. "Let's continue."

The muspel army tossed successive waves of clubs and fire torrents, but for every single attack they could muster, another dozen wind blades flew at them to match it. However, while a single blade was more than a match for their clubs, the same could not be said for the reverse. The price of two or more was needed to be paid to deflect a single blade, and that was without taking into account the implosion of pure power that followed. They were, in effect, miniature vacuum bombs, capable of generating an extremely high temperature explosion, followed by a severe vacuum that pulled in everything within their immediate vicinity.

The toll began to tell.

Gained +1374 Experience!

Gained +2741 Experience!

Gained +1198 Experience!

And so on.

The rules were simple. It didn't matter if he was the one doing the kill or her. Both of them were too close to each other for the world to determine which of them did the task, and hence, awarded both of them with ample amounts of Experience. Experience that led to yet another thing.

You have crossed the Threshold Barrier.
Level Up Initiated!

You have crossed the Threshold Barrier.
Level Up Initiated!

And so on.

> **Level Up Delayed until PRIME HOST is not in combat**
> **2 LEVEL UPs in sequence.**

One thing was clear. This borderland mission was proving to be intensely rewarding. He'd need to volunteer for more of these in the future.

> **Lack of Combat detected.**
> **Initiate Level Up sequence?**

"Yes."

As his body underwent massive changes within, every single Level Up bringing him closer and closer to his skill tier, Lukas idly watched the monsters react to their sudden change of circumstances with commendable alacrity. More and more flanks appeared, trying to overwhelm them with superior numbers, harrying them with unnatural precision, hurling bursts of flame and force with steady accuracy. More than that, they fought with the strength of desperation, with the knowledge that the odds were hopelessly stacked against them. Even then, they died in their attempts.

All of it was depressingly futile.

And then Tanya amped things up.

She raised her right hand upward. More specifically, her index finger.

And on its tip, something flickered.

It danced, a tiny wisp of Wind and black mist so tiny that Lukas had to strain his eyes to see it. A spark, smaller than a single grain, hung in the air, right above her fingertip. The mana it held was so insignificant as to be all but undetectable, lost in the ambient mana saturating the terrain. Even as he watched it, the grain flickered and wavered, as if it were a candle flame about to puff out any second.

Tanya looked at him. "Remember what I said about *control?* Here. Watch."

The wind orb doubled in size.

Again.

And again.

And again and again.

Like a balloon held under a faucet, the spinning orb of Wind and dark mist expanded, swelling as it doubled with each passing heartbeat, until a spinning ball of pure darkness the size of a cannonball floated in midair, glowing with all the majesty of a black sun.

Alarm bells rang in Lukas's head as he took in the amount of mana contained in that little sphere, and realized what that represented. The power wasn't spectacular—he was certain he could dish out more power than that without too much effort. But to see it restrained like that, held in complete stasis? Now *that* was something else.

And then Tanya flicked it off with her finger.

Faster than any mortal eye could track, it shot through the air, a black beam of light tearing its way through the closest muspel and piercing through its head, right between its eyes, like a bolt of lightning.

And then the creature exploded.

It didn't so much as faze the orb as it leaped towards its next victim.

And so on.

Gained +3149 Experience!

Gained +2271 Experience!

Gained +5116 Experience!

She turned to him. "And you! Are you just going to stand there, or are you going to join?"

Lukas cocked his head, his Level Ups already done with, and smiled. "I thought you were doing fine."

Tanya smiled. It was a cruel thing. "If I have to share the Experience from the kills with you, you better bring your weight into this."

Across the horizon, he could see more of them arrive. Ifrits, muspels, creatures of all shapes and sizes. Out of the terrain, out of the lava pools, flying at them from the skies—reinforcements were arriving in every direction. It was like the borderland itself had declared war against them, and was pulling out all the stops.

All lingering doubts vanished from his mind.

"Mori was right," Lukas murmured. "They won't let us out of here. It's like the Crypt of Fiendish Worms all over again."

Tanya gave him an inscrutable look. "You and I remember that place very differently. Say, how about we make a game out of this? I get everything to my left. You, to your right. Let's see who gets to the portal faster."

"Shouldn't take too long," Lukas said, feeling Blob shift into the familiar axe in his right hand. "Let's make this interesting. Only close combat and low to mid-ranged explosions allowed. Getting hit is an instant disqualification."

Tanya rolled her eyes. "Sure but—" She paused, as four pairs of ethereal wings exploded behind her back.

"Can you keep up?"

* * *

The battle turned when Lukas Aguilar bore the brunt of the enemy's combined attacks and shrugged it off with a snap of his fingers. It turned into a slaughter when he started chopping through muspels one after another with his impossibly hard war-axe, with the air of a man sweeping sweat off his brow. It became wholesale butchery when Frost Queen Tanya began throwing out vacuum bomb explosions like they were going out of fashion.

Despite that, the inhabitants of the borderland kept fighting with admirable courage. No, not courage, Lukas realized. Courage was a complex emotion best left for muspels and other superior beings. The ifrits and other kami were just monsters, elemental beings whose instincts were governed by the elemental spectrum. It just so happened that the Fire element both represented and provoked strong emotions.

Most of which were negative ones.

Rage.

Vindication.

Hatred.

The terrain was ridden with malignant growths. An ocean of twisted figures. Crawling on many-jointed limbs, slithering across the terrain, swimming through the lava pools, the creatures were coming at them like a solid avalanche. Creatures clad in armor. Bare-chested, horned demons. Looming, hulking, eight-legged canines. And those were only the ones close to the ground.

From the distant horizon, Lukas could see the raptors coming in vast numbers. Massive reptilian forms, like a plague victim's diseased skin, twisting and contorting as they descended towards them. The sounds they were making were something no sane person should hear.

It was the sound of a world gone mad. A reality trying to destroy itself.

Tanya howled a vicious war cry and shot up higher in the sky, before firing a rain of implosion missiles upon the crust, each of them detonating upon impact. The next moment, she was down on the ground, striking left and right with her wind blades. She made flickering cuts as swift and light as the beating of a hummingbird's wings, leaving nothing but little incisions the depth of a fingernail in spaces of hard flesh, but covering a space as big as her hands around the wounds with vicious, bitterly cold Frost. Wherever she went, a nexus of carnage followed. The abominations closest to her recoiled and were struck with bitter wounds, the alien Frost growing in them and stealing precious lifeforce from their bodies. That left them in a half-frozen state, blocking their allies from getting close enough to strike her. She rode forward into a vacuum of space that could never quite close around her, leaving an opening for Lukas to exploit.

And exploit he did.

With frightening ease, Lukas traversed the battlefield, employing terraportation to devastating effect. He slid out of the ground in front of a monster, grabbed its head, and sank back, burying it upside down. Shooting out of the ground just behind it, he stabbed the next muspel through the neck, decapitating it for good measure.

Every move brought with it an increased aggression. One strike became three. A missed kick created a crater in the ground. The monsters twisted themselves in midair when he appeared before them, and instantly Lukas doubled his speed and sucker punched it in the face, hurling it away by several dozen feet before it skidded to a stop.

Only to find an axe coming for its head.

Blob had forged into an oversized, ornate, double-edged axe, a faithful copy of Inanna's weapon. It was an executioner's weapon, Death in sentient metal, which he held in a familiar, one-handed grip. With flawless grace, it split through muspel and monster alike as effortlessly as a woodsman could chop firewood; it bifurcated twisted forms from head to foot, folding its victims in half with horrifying ease. Such was the speed of his blows that the creatures didn't even bleed until after they hit the ground.

Limbs fell. Heads rolled. Corpses—physical and conjured—paved the way in his wake as he carved a bloody road behind him.

A hundred feet away, Lukas heard Tanya howling in fury, a sound that stunned and weakened everything around her, fully focused on tearing the monsters limb by limb. Parts flew and her wings—all *four* of them—were moving as if they had gained a mind of their own. Pulses of pure pressure, implosions of vacuum, and blades of Wind sharper than steel cut down anything and everything that came within her vicinity.

It was like watching a tornado in action. Absolute, deadly, and bizarrely selective. The yells and shrieks around her were akin to a chorus that rose to an exultant crescendo as she whirled and struck down every living thing that got in their path.

Absolutely everything.

Meanwhile, his Screen kept popping up in the background.

Gained +18127 Experience!
Gained +13111 Experience!
Gained . . . .

Level Up Delayed until PRIME HOST is not in combat . . .
6 LEVEL UPs in sequence.

And so on and so forth.

But the battle was far from over. Up there in the sky, the clouds were shifting, moving, contorting into one another. Sounds of thunder reverberated, but there was no lightning to be seen. Instead, there was a strange throbbing hum of energy that grew in power with every passing second right above him.

His heart rate skyrocketed, and his mouth went dry. As someone who lived in Illinois for over a decade, Lukas had seen his fair share of twisters. People thought they were scary, which they were, but they were also very survivable provided one followed some simple guidelines—warn people early, and when you heard the warning, quickly head for the safest place you could reach.

And right then, his instincts screamed at him to do exactly that.

The heavens were in turmoil. The clouds churned faster and faster. Screams, real and ethereal, exuded into the atmosphere as strange energies soared up into the heavens to join the newly-revolving mandala of power, lighting up the sky with every shade of white, blue, and sea green.

Then came the attack.

Before Lukas could even comprehend what had transpired, something *slashed* through the air, its fury palpable. All he heard was a bloodcurdling shriek of fury and power, before a thunderous fork of lightning streaked through the sky.

Right at Tanya.

The force behind the attack was so immense that Lukas thought it was going to break something. Like maybe the universe. It was a whammy of pure power and pressure so intense that he knew that if it had been directed at him, it'd have compressed his mind into something too inert to function, like a tiny diamond formed out of crushed coal. It wasn't a question of weakness or strength.

Blinking his eyes against the dazzling afterimage of the lightning bolt, he saw Tanya's slender body arch into a bow, curling around the spot where the lightning had struck her, her long, thin-fingered hands clenched around a ball of white-hot vacuum, the edges of her nails blackening and smoking with the heat. Then, with a wail of pure, terrifying scorn, she straightened again and sent that ball of intense nothingness raging through the lightning itself, devouring its power while pushing it backward, resulting in an apocalyptic detonation.

The ethereal manifestation around her faded and Tanya swooped down to the ground, her face splattered with blood, and her left side, from the shoulder to her elbow, was scorched, looking like a meshwork of rotten flesh and bone. Already Frost was beginning to coat those areas. She looked at him and let out a scornful snarl.

"We need to leave. Quickly."

Lukas was in complete agreement, and stood next to her, when his senses were assaulted by a serious, heavy-duty pulse of Pyromancy.

There wasn't even time to shout out a warning. He called upon lifeforce and Kinetomancy for strength and speed. The world around him exploded in a shower of molten rock and lava. Lukas watched in awe as Tanya lifted both arms, slim and pale, fingers spread evenly in a defensive gesture. Frost gathered upon her and expanded outward, as the crimson flares washed over them.

The sound alone, as the two sources of power met, was enough to drive a strong mind mad. He couldn't even tell what it sounded like, specifically. It was too loud and too huge a noise for that. Besides, he was too busy screaming in pure reflexive protest against that sound, and his voice had gotten lost in the din. Fire and lightning and wind whirled in a cyclone centered upon them, but her Frost shield kept everything at bay.

Meanwhile, his shield, covering him in a half dome, was dealing with more backlash than it could normally handle. Blisters were forming all over his skin, but he knew that if the shield vanished, he'd be vaporized in an instant.

Tanya, on the other hand, stood slender and deadly, defying the power around them with a cold, pure light, a sphere of diamond radiance forming around her, dispersing the most vicious efforts of the firestorm. It was like a fast-flowing stream crashing against an obdurate stone. In that withering light and fury, she was a being of distilled determination and defiance—a shadow, an outline, dark and terrible, standing against the tide unmoving.

In that one moment, Lukas realized why Inanna had called her *worthy prey*.

It also reminded him of just how little he understood of Kinetomancy. Even at the peak of her strength, Tanya had been little more than an annoying insect to Inanna, and here he was, standing in awe of Tanya's power.

And then, the massive firestorm faded away, leaving—

"Fuck me!" said Lukas.

Surrounding them were more bylestyr.

Seven of them.

"Oh fu—" Lukas said, just before the storm began.

The Bylestyr attacked, a seemingly endless stream of flame and force. Lukas's ability to block those flames with Kinetomancy was extreme, but he had his limits, and his own weapon simply weren't fast enough to defend against a simultaneous attack against every point of his body. He grabbed their motions and pushed himself against them, using the reaction force and his relatively lighter mass to propel himself out of their vicinity, but he failed to intercept the hastily-thrown punch to his arm.

Crack.

His shoulder shattered.

Regeneration activated.

—and it was back to normal.

Lukas somersaulted above the monster, Blob transformed into a chain connecting both hands, and he wrung it around the giant's neck, right in time for the monster to unleash a wall of force backward in an attempt to blast his face.

Snap!

Soul Siphon Success!
Absorbed Monster Prototype BYLESTYR

Multiple specimens of Prototype BYLESTYR found
Amalgamating . . .
Amalgamation Success!

Nice, thought Lukas. *"One down. Six to—"*

He terraported, just avoiding being incinerated by a pillar of flame that came at him at breakneck speed. He appeared ten feet away, vanished again, then to the right, then left, then right, and right, and kept doing it, as a salvo of crimson rained in his direction, and his rate of terraportation was only getting faster with each shift. He was already moving through the ground fifteen feet away from the latest buckshot, already having dodged eight buck shots while staying underground in rapid succession as he attempted to find a way out.

Only to stumble on the ninth, and be bombarded with innumerable flame blasts aimed for his freaking face . . .

He opened his eyes, and found himself safe and sound, at least several hundred feet away from his opponent.

"Wha—"

"Linear displacement," Tanya said, sauntering over like the predator she was. "Application of pressure and Wind mana to travel at extreme speeds in a linear direction."

"Interesting," Lukas observed, wondering what other skills she was hiding.

"I'm not sure you liked that though," she teased. "You were enjoying yourself a bit too much. Corrosion, Hreidmar's techniques and now bylestyr strength. Using the skills of your previous kills to gain power. Using a combination of all of them with your force techniques to create openings in your opponent's stance to exploit. Targeting their weaknesses with suitable counters from your ever-increasing arsenal of skills and finally adding the skills of your latest kill to your Schema. What a vicious and merciless mindset you must possess to think this way! It's *adorable!*"

As if to underscore her point, she licked her lips.

The difference between the Tanya who he talked to on a daily basis and the seductive and cruel Frost wielder before him made him distinctly uncomfortable. As if she was a different person.

"What happened to running away?" he asked.

"We should," she said, biting her lip, "but I'm having second thoughts. I'm starting to enjoy this. Finally, we've got some time to ourselves. Fighting together, butchering monsters, making a hill of corpses—"

Prey Found You

Damn it.

A second fork of lightning crashed at them, but this time, missed them by several feet. By the time the dust would settle, the bylestyr would be there.

His heart went into his throat as he saw a bylestyr bring its large claws down upon Tanya from above, and dig into the flesh of her naked shoulder, as if she were a block of ice. Tanya contemptuously touched the limb attached to those claws, before slapping it away. The limb shattered into frozen fragments. Casually knocking the now-limbless claws out of her flesh, Tanya let out a chill, hungry laughter before moving to her next kill.

There was no way he could have taken himself through this mess without making it a hell of a lot messier. Tanya made it look *easy*.

"Distract them for a moment, will you?" she asked, shooting up into the air.

Lukas whirled around and slammed his axe against the immediate attacker, slipped down into the ground like it was made of sand, and hacked into the creature's knees. He shot out of the ground from behind and decapitated it with a sweeping slash.

Gained +19218 Experience!

"Well," he said, turning around at the rest, "you heard the lady."

He would be lying if he said his confidence hadn't slightly faltered. This wasn't the first time he'd faced overwhelming might. The khorkhoi took that honor. But this was definitely the first time he'd faced a mixture of overwhelming might *and* numbers. More to the point, the omphalos in him was going berserk. The mantle of the Prime Host didn't just come with access to unlimited Soul Capacity and nifty functions. An anomaly was home to all things related to creation and hunger and savagery. It thought the incoming hordes to be a fantastic idea. That someone needed to butcher their way through them, and it thought that that someone ought to be him. His body was already backing up that concept. Lifeforce was flooding his veins with the same rush that mana surged through his inner ley-line networks. The fractals on his arms began to heat up, and assuming they could all but double his total mana, that was saying something.

He flexed his power. Dust and pebbles began to rise in the air around him, creating a helical sine wave of power. It didn't speak much about his skill, but the sheer power was enough to make his opponents freeze and take note.

"You. Will. Not. Win," spoke one of them, its voice reminding him of heavy, rusted metal being dragged through asphalt.

"Oh, I know that, but guess what? Made you look."

He winked, pressed his feet into the ground, and propelled himself into the air, just in time to see the ebon missile streaking through the air, traveling so fast that it appeared to be little more than a black blur. In a single second, it crossed over half the distance and impacted a bylestyr, with two more standing in its vicinity.

The result wasn't an explosion. It wasn't even a massacre. Both terms implied the possibility of there being more than one probable outcome, but from the instant Tanya unleashed her fury, there was only one way things could end.

This was not an attack. It was an act of God.

The ebon streak hit the fiery defense and *imploded*, power and winds rolling into it like a tsunami, and a wave of blackness and destruction expanded out, devouring the crimson out of the terrain, engulfing everything within its vicinity. The bylestyrs used Fire and then tried to jump back, growing increasingly desperate as the wave kept hungrily claiming the land beneath their feet, consuming it, ripping it down into nothing but raw energy. The bylestyr had defenses in place, their power protecting them like a siege wall.

It was blown away like cobwebs in a hurricane.

The land for half a mile in every direction had vanished, a sea of flames taking its place. The force of the resulting explosion was so powerful that even from where Lukas stood, several hundred feet up in the air, he was buffeted by a wall of air so solid that it sent him reeling.

When the dust settled, the land was gone. The entire zone was destroyed, leaving a giant lava pool in its wake.

Gained +29218 Experience!

Level Up Delayed until PRIME HOST is not in combat . . .
8 LEVEL UPs in sequence.

"So," said Tanya, floating down until she was at his level. "What's next?"

Lukas looked at her blearily. "Get to the portal? Make sure the svartalfars are still safe, and that there's no fallout? It'd be terrible if we did all this and ended up getting one of them killed by mistake."

"There will be no fallout," Tanya said confidently. "The hard part is over. I expect everything to go smoothly from here on out."

Fifteen minutes later—

"I swear the portal was here," said a flustered Tanya, the glacial features now reverted to her normal appearance. "I left those two on solid ground since they could terraport the rest of the way. I told them to hold the Well open until I get you back."

"Well," said an unamused Lukas, "there are no svartalfars. There is no well. And unless my eyes are deceiving me, there is no *solid ground* either."

"But—" Tanya mumbled.

"We're stranded. Aren't we?" Lukas sighed.

Tanya looked at him sheepishly.

"This is gonna suck."

CHAPTER 18

———

THE SHIMIZU'S STANCE

Six years ago . . .

Zuken Banksi resisted the urge to shudder as he stared into the cold, hard eyes of his guest. There wasn't a speck of emotion in those gray orbs—no love, no hate, nothing. For a man who prided himself in reading faces, it was quite a disconcerting thing indeed. And that was without even considering who the man was.

"What can I do for you?"

The man turned toward his sole companion. "Are you sure he's the right person for the job?"

"He is the best, Grandfather," said a twenty-something Ultaf Shimizu. Zuken had known him since his time spent at the Susanoo Shrine in Cyffnar, trying to pick up a very peculiar skill that was seldom used by anyone outside the aquamancer community. A nifty trick that would allow him to develop a rather unconventional Terramancy spell.

Ultaf's grandfather, Mujin, met his eyes. To his chagrin, Zuken found himself almost looking away from his impassive gaze. The White Death, people called him. The most terrifying individual seen since the demise of the man's own father, the Wind King himself. Staring into his eyes was like gazing into a cold void and seemed to suck in all the warmth from the room.

Then the man nodded, and Zuken released the breath he had inadvertently been holding. Had it been anyone else in his stead, they'd already have fallen to their knees, genuflected, and tried to please this titan among men.

Not him.

Zuken, more than anyone else, had a strong resistance against that. He was very familiar with matching gazes with people whose power levels bordered on the ludicrous. Being the unwelcome, nugatory child of the Earth King would do that to you.

"Ultaf mentioned you're in need of my services . . ." Zuken trailed off.

The man slowly nodded. "You have heard about the recent catastrophe that hit the Shimizu settlement."

Zuken nodded slowly. Of course he had. More than half of the Shimizu Clan had been massacred in one night. From the oldest half-blind crones to the crying babies still clenched to their mother's breasts, no one had remained untouched from the devastation that had been unleashed upon the settlement that night. It wasn't clear who or what did it, but rumor was that it was the act of a kami, presumably a Level 4, given the destruction-fest that had followed.

"I'm extremely sorry to hear about that."

"Right," said the man. "You're all broken up over the destruction."

Zuken matched his gaze. "I didn't order it. I didn't profit financially or politically from its destruction. And you survived, so Cyffnar didn't lose the Sacred Eight protection it has enjoyed so far." He shook his head. "A complete waste."

They had already taken a measure of each other. He knew precisely how dangerous the man sitting before him was, and it was why he was making it a point to treat him in as cavalier a fashion as possible. One didn't show dangerous predators weakness or fear. It made them hungry.

Besides, Zuken was Shogun Naowa's wetworks man, and by extension, an enemy of Cyffnar. So when the high and mighty of Cyffnar had come all the way to see him, cockiness was practically obligatory.

Mujin's smile was a wintry thing. "You speak the truth. But we are here on business." He glanced at Ultaf, who pushed a small cube towards Zuken. A memory projection arose out of it, forming the image of a brown-haired, brown-eyed girl. She had an athletic figure, and given the attire, there was no doubt she was a Shimizu herself.

Zuken stared at the projection. The girl was no doubt a teenager but would grow into an eye-turning beauty in the future. There was a strength to her face, a strength normally unseen in anyone that hadn't passed into their thirties.

"What do you want me to do?" he asked, appearing slightly bored. "Kill her?"

"No. We want her alive. Not necessarily unharmed, but alive."

"And you wish to devote your considerable resources towards finding a teenager instead of taking actions to restore your settlement because . . . "

"None of your business," Ultaf growled. "Find the girl. Capture her. Get her back to us. That's all."

Zuken looked at him like he was a slow child. "My services aren't cheap. Just putting it out there. What can you tell me about her?"

"She's sixteen. Her ability with Aeromancy is . . . commendable, and she's gotten Aquamancy training in the past. Her lifeforce reserves are well above average, and she's been trained in assassination, seduction, direct combat, and espionage."

"Sounds like a mercenary-in-training. Someone from your own nest?"

Ultaf clenched his teeth. "Yes. We aren't sure if she has a kami. Our sources tell us that she's currently somewhere along the northern Eaborid border."

Zuken stared at them for several seconds before he said, "Somewhere. Along the northern Eaborid border. That's as specific as you can be?"

"It's as much as we know."

Translation: that was the last place he had heard from his agents before they died. If nothing else, it spoke of the girl's talents. At sixteen, she was quite a gem to be this talented. It was sad that he'd have to capture her and send her packing to the Shimizu, but work was work.

"For what purpose are you hunting her?"

"Why does that matter?"

"It paints a picture of the girl's skills. If you want to simply interrogate her, chances are she'd leave towards Maluscion. You can hide there for years and not be found out. But if there's anything special about her, something that others might notice, then I can use it to track her better."

"There . . . might be," said Ultaf elusively. "But we cannot trust you with that."

His eyes narrowed. "Who is she, Ultaf?"

"Her name is Tanya," Ultaf said, "and she's, my half-sister."

Zuken sat in his office alone, slowly sipping from his glass, as he perused a battered paperback. Unlike his usual habits, this one wasn't from his family library but was rather an old, translated edition of a nine-hundred-year-old text written by a dökkálfar scholar from Karnegrug. Less than five hundred copies had been printed, and the Empire had ended up burning over four hundred and fifty of them. Given how thorough the Empire had been, there was no doubt it contained something worthwhile and dangerous.

Much like the scribblings of *Kvasir*, most of the books from the Time Before spoke of a different world, a different description of the world's geography, one that the Empire taught was *flawed* and *wrong*. Unfortunately, these books were also the only ones that actually tried to put a scientific rationale behind the existence of gods and goddesses, going so far as to suggest that they weren't *born* but made. It was from these materials that Zuken had help in deciphering the mystery of Lukas Aguilar, and he hoped that the same texts would help him find the way to achieve his greatest desire.

That said, if anyone ever found that he had been reading *Ulfhednar Edda*, he might have to eliminate them. Sinners were hunted by the Cobalt Army, but anyone caught even *reading* this book would be instantly purged with Empyreal Fire.

And then the Army would go after their families, their friends, associates, and even pets. Every single entity associated with this criminal would be instantly purged to maintain the sanctity of the Empire.

The perils of living in the Land of Eternal Light.

Zuken was expecting company, so he kept an eye on the door. Because of that, when a nastily familiar face entered, he had time to close the book and slip it discreetly into a private drawer enchanted to be obscured from all five senses and magical scrying. By the time the newcomer abruptly pulled up a chair and sat down in front of him, Zuken had his glass in hand, leaning back, smiling slightly.

"Ultaf Shimizu," he greeted.

The young man looked at him, his expression firmly blank, and posture relaxed.

"Banksi," he finally acknowledged.

Zuken recognized the pose. It was the kind of enforced looseness a true professional used, right before they expected to have to suddenly exert themselves. If he had to hazard a guess, it would be that the Shimizu expected the meeting to end poorly.

He couldn't blame him. Personally, he'd give it four chances out of seven that they'd come to blows before the end of it.

But he wasn't fond of violence. On the contrary, he went out of his way to avoid it. Violence was the tool of the unimaginative. So in return, he maintained his own relaxed posture, knowing fully well how dangerous the man in front of him was. He himself was in a similar field of work and had been for a much longer time.

He was Zuken Banksi. Politeness was part of his arsenal.

"It's been what . . . six years?"

Right outside his office, he saw Elena ask for his permission to enter. He subtly asked her to wait. If Shimizu saw the interaction, he wouldn't respond to it. He simply continued to look at Zuken.

"You have her."

It was a simple statement. An outrageously blunt one, and to the point. There was no doubt who he was referring to, and Zuken couldn't find it in himself to try to play dumb, especially to one he respected on a professional level. That didn't, however, mean that he was going to admit things out loud either. If Ultaf wanted answers out of him, he was going to have to work for it.

"You'll have to be more specific than that."

"Don't you—!" Ultaf began, and Zuken could actually see the exact moment his jaw clenched down, when his breath became slow and long. He could see him mastering his anger enough to keep it restrained. When he spoke again, his voice was cold and measured.

"So?"

"So what?" Zuken prompted.

"So what is this?" Ultaf said. "Are you going to make demands of me? Of Clan Shimizu? After breaking our original agreement?"

"I'm not a demanding person, Ultaf," Zuken said. "A deal for a deal is more to my liking. Oddly enough, I didn't anticipate any dealings between us when you informed me of your arrival."

His tone was light. Playful even. He deliberately kept it so. Ultaf had come for a confrontation, and if he didn't confront him, it'd only make things worse. The trick was to arrange it in a way that suited his purposes.

Which was why what happened next made Zuken pause.

Ultaf went still.

He was just . . . studying him, and for the first time, Zuken had no idea what to expect. It set him on edge. Made him cautious.

It excited him a bit too.

"Why?"

Another demand.

"Why what?" Zuken asked, cocking his head slightly.

He knew this game. He had been playing it for years. Ultaf couldn't accuse him directly, because he had no proof. And if he did accuse him, it could lead to a conflict between two clans, both members of the Sacred Eight. No, the trick was to maneuver Zuken into a confession.

Patience was the name of the game, and the one who spoke first, lost.

"Why," Ultaf repeated. Zuken had to admit, it was an effective strategy. If he had demanded specific answers, he would have been able to find ways around the questions, would have been able to read him and determine what he was looking for and make sure he could find it.

Now though, he was simply demanding an explanation without providing what explanation he wanted. Zuken had to decide what he would say, and he would be able to judge if that was enough.

"And if I don't?" he asked. Ultaf had defined the contest, now it was time to define the stakes. If his explanation wasn't sufficient, would he attack him?

"Then all negotiations will fail, and my army shall breach Haviskali."

Ah.

So that's how it was.

Zuken's eyes narrowed. He had seen this coming but had expected a little more time.

Pity.

"Threatening someone while sitting in their house isn't exactly the best idea, Ultaf."

"Cut the crap, Banksi," Ultaf snarled, apparently no longer willing to play mind games. "I know you have her."

"Her?"

Ultaf growled. "Tanya. Tanya Shimizu. My *sister*. Six years ago, I gave you a job contract. Here in this very room. To find her."

"I'm afraid I disappointed you," Zuken replied. "I couldn't find her."

"Oh I *am* disappointed," said Ultaf. "Not because you couldn't find her, but because you did, and yet, you did not inform me."

Zuken crossed his fingers on the table, and kept his expression bland. "You have me at a loss, Ultaf. The girl you asked me to capture had brown hair, brown eyes. I'll admit I do have a 'Tanya' working for me, but she has golden hair going white, with bright blue eyes."

"An aeromancer."

"Yes."

"Bring her. I wish to see her."

Zuken smiled slightly at his demand. "Unfortunately, she's on a mission right now, a very time-consuming one, I might add. You know how things are with such missions. Why, it could be another month before I see her again. The Goddess knows they don't have enough rations for that long."

"Don't play with me, Banksi. She is her. I *know* it."

"How?" Zuken challenged. First rule of negotiation. Always check your opponent's cards. You never know if they are filled with blanks. "Tanya is not an uncommon name. My employee does not have a family, nor any established clan traits. There is absolutely no proof that this woman is the same *Tanya Shimizu* you hired me for, all those years ago. A job that led to some of my best men killed, I might add. For all I know, this is your attempt to simply bully me into doing you favors."

"You dare to—!"

"Yes," Zuken spoke, a current of warning in his voice. "Your clan isn't exactly known for keeping their hands where they should. Don't pretend it's what it used to be, Ultaf. Your King-Class kami, lost to the wilds. Your settlements? Still trying to become a pale imitation of their past grandeur. And here you are, claiming something that doesn't exist, just to suit your fantasy."

The previously confident and cocky noble gritted his teeth, realizing that things were moving in a direction he didn't anticipate or like. No doubt he was going to try something else now.

"I see," Ultaf said, controlling his tone somewhat. "You're right. There is no proof that can justify that this Tanya is the same creature we ordered you to hunt all those years ago. After all, we did hide her special traits from you."

Zuken narrowed his eyes. He was going to have to be careful here. "Which are?"

"Classified!" Ultaf held his ground. "But I have information. Tanya. Golden hair, blue eyes. A vagrant, likely from Baramunz or Karnegrug. Youngest aeromancer in the Llaisy Kingdom to hit expert rank. Known for mastery at aerokinetic combat. Sinner, infamous for destroying a Class-2 anomaly. Wanted by the Cobalt Army, she remained a fugitive until a special notice from Shogun Naowa freed her from her charges. Does that ring any bells?"

Zuken looked at him in annoyance. "Yes. Same person."

"She's the creature I asked you to capture for me. Regardless of proof, I want her. So perhaps, a trade? What do you wish in exchange for this individual? Name your price."

Zuken stared at him across his steepled fingers. He had already guessed that Tanya's Wind kami was a fully developed Level 3 and was probably bordering Level 4 if not there already. Olfric and the others might have been stupefied from her devastating attack on the Cyffnarian hires in the desert, but as someone in the same business, Zuken had paid more attention to the other things she did.

Maintaining a whirlwind around them for days.

Casual amplification of her pressure-based attack coupled with ironclad control.

And most importantly, the confident motions of a woman that had taken out an entire battalion in cold blood. Zuken was not being egoistical when he had claimed that "Tanya Shimizu" had killed some of his best hires. The girl on his team was the same girl that had decimated his forces all those years ago.

The real question was whether she was the person that demolished the Shimizu settlement. The "Tanya" that worked for him had full control over herself. But throw that away, and he could well imagine what a kami of that level could unleash on an unsuspecting crowd.

And Ultaf Shimizu wanted the girl. Unfortunately, that was a deal that wasn't—*couldn't*—be on the table.

He spoke after a long moment. "I'm not sure if you know this, but I'm not in the business of trading lives, Ultaf. And certainly not people that work for me."

"If you do not, then my army will march to your gates."

"You do that and Haviskali would go to war with Cyffnar."

"Not if we send a formal notice to Shogun Naowa and the Royal Court. I am even willing to drag the Earth King into this matter. Either way, I will have her."

The cold smile returned. "Is that what you think will happen?"

The man laid his hands flat on the table and leaned back slightly. "There is no sense in ruining things over this, Banksi. I do not wish to make you my enemy. Hand Tanya over, and you can get what you want. *Anything*. Wealth. Favors. Subordinates. I am willing to negotiate."

"And what if I say no?"

Ultaf shrugged. "I'll admit it's been *decades* since my grandfather has seen *action*. I'm certain the Shimizu Warlord would like to—shall we say—spread his wings a bit."

Zuken stared at him with half-lidded eyes and said, "Eek!"

Ultaf snorted and stood up. "One month. That is as long as I am willing to give, Banksi. As soon as this woman returns, I expect you to send her packing to me. Or else, you will not like what follows!"

Zuken watched him, his expression never changing. As Ultaf reached the doorway, Zuken called out. "Ultaf Shimizu, if you ever need another job done, send me a letter. Don't try offering me fortune or threats again. Oh, and see yourself out!"

Ultaf paused for a moment, then turned his head.

"One month," he whispered, and then, he was gone.

CHAPTER 19

STORIES FROM THE STRANDED

SOULSCAPE	
NAME	Lukas Aguilar
Type	Prime Host
Level	21
Experience	4163
Current Threshold	17640
Utilized Soul Capacity	41408 / ∞
ESSENCE	
Maximum Lifeforce Output	82750
Replenishment Rate	4600 / hour
LEY LINE NETWORK	
Maximum Mana Output	84000
Synthesis Rate	4710 / hour

It didn't seem real, seeing the changes in his Schema.

Memories of his days spent in the crypt rose to his mind. Running from monsters, choosing his battles, bartering with Inanna over information—back in those days, every single bit of Soul Capacity counted. Every single skill, no matter how inconsequential, was precious. Soul Siphon had made things a lot easier for him, but it hadn't been until he had absorbed the crypt's omphalos that things had truly changed for him.

Level-5 Alpha Condition.

Infinite Soul Capacity.

Those two facts alone had transformed the wary survivor into the consummate warrior he was today. Back at the anomaly, there had been moments when he had to maintain count of how much lifeforce he used in a fight. Now? He had over eighty thousand units at his beck and call. Same for mana. And with those fractals, he might as well double that figure.

And the results were open for everyone to see.

His body had undergone massive changes, both inside and out. The lean muscles were gone, replaced overnight by a meaty weight, giving him a light-heavyweight boxer appearance, the muscles on his forearms feeling like they were made of lean steel cable. He felt slightly taller as well, and his face looked raw and hard, with veins tight against his skin. His brown hair now came down past his neck, but the damn beard felt distinctly uncomfortable. His body felt warmer than ever before, like someone had set up a furnace within it, making it more comfortable in this land of magma than it had any right to be.

But his body wasn't the only thing that had changed.

SKILL ATTRIBUTES		
SKILL	**LEVEL**	**CONSUMED SOUL CAP**
Raw Lifeforce Manipulation	3	5000

Kinetomancy (FRAGMENTED)	APEX	5908
Momentum Manipulation	3	5000
Friction Modulation	2	500
Pressure Modulation	2	500
Innate Gravity Control	2	500

Fire Creation	3	5000
Fire Manipulation	3	5000

Temperature Modulation	3	5000

Earth Manipulation	2	500
Terraportation	2	500
Seismic Sensing	2	500

Conjuration	2	500
Disintegration	2	500

Shatterpoint Intuition	2	500
Psychomancy	2	500

Water Creation	2	500
Water Manipulation	3	5000

It was like what Inanna had said: the body reflects the soul. But like most things with her, it was not the complete picture. The body reflected the soul, but only to the extent defined by the body's limits. A beginner's body could not grasp a Level-2 skill in all its complexity. Even at Level 8, Lukas had been unable to fully comprehend the true scope of what he could do with his skills. It was why despite having a Level 3 at Raw Lifeforce Manipulation and Momentum Manipulation, his abilities bordered a hair short of Level 2's zenith at best.

But now, after the staggering number of Level Ups, his body had evolved, constantly reflecting the skills from the Schema upon itself. Every single Level Up left a tiny addition to his body, and the succeeding Level Up compounded upon that. After a total of *thirteen* Level Ups while also gaining multiple Level-3 skills in Pyromancy, Lukas practically felt like a five-year-old in a grown-up gymnast's body. Was it any surprise he had fallen on his face and ass over seventy times in the first two days since the Level Ups?

Even after weeks, Lukas couldn't help but feel that this power, these skills, were downright surreal. And yet, it only served to twist the knife in his heart.

For even with his Level Ups and his immensely magnified powers, he was completely at sea with his current problem.

They were stranded.

No tents. No food. No clothes except what they had on their person. He already had to divulge his secret Aquamancy powers to Tanya. Given the number of things she knew about him, it probably didn't come as a surprise. If nothing else, she thought it funny and poetic that Olfric had tried to kill him in the anomaly, and he had gotten Olfric's kami for himself in return. They didn't have any of those flare guns to respond just in case the svartalfars attempted a rescue mission again.

Not that they had. He had checked.

In many ways, it was like being back at the crypt all over again. Stuck in an unprecedented situation with a powerful female with more secrets than he could imagine, while trying to figure out the changes occurring within his own body. Where Inanna's supernatural beauty was a constant test of mental fortitude, his raging lifeforce made it equally difficult to stay around Tanya. It blamed Tanya for being such a distraction and had a really primitive way of letting that displeasure known. Much like before, he was back to hunting monsters for nourishment, only this time, they were spending more time flying (for Tanya) and surfing through the air (for him), thanks to Innate Gravity Control and Kinetomancy. There was little reason to fight, and most altercations with the monsters started with decapitation—quick, easy, and to the point. Instead, they used their energies to traverse the skies, looking for potential openings to return to the real world.

Or at least, that was what they did for the first fortnight.

But as days passed, his doubts were starting to creep in. This was not the same as being trapped inside an anomaly. There was no way out, not unless a door opened from the other side. He fervently hoped the svartalfars would try opening another Well soon. But would they? If Kradir or Mori had fallen, chances are those bloodthirsty creatures would abandon Lukas and Tanya to their fates just out of spite.

Or maybe, maybe something else had befallen them. Maybe the sheer destruction had caused faults in the portal. There was always room for error and performance issues when it came to technology. Maybe they were trying to repair it? Maybe it was just taking time. With the time dilation in these zones, that amounted to waiting for more than double the actual time spent in the real world.

It sucked. Big time.

It made him wonder. Would he be able to get out, *ever?* If not, what would he do? How would he get Inanna back? Would his life just . . . end here?

The questions haunted him. Sometimes he'd wake up at night, wondering if he had put his faith in the right people. Maybe if he had tried getting back to the yokai, things would've been different. Sometimes, when he lay looking at the dark skies, he reviewed every single thing he knew about this world and its people, about Zuken, about Olfric and Elena, about Tanya . . .

About Inanna.

He'd search his memory for small, subtle things about them that he might have missed. It scared him, caused him to think he had made some horrible mistakes lately. Tanya had been clear: engage in combat, but don't kill anyone. Yet he had. And that had led to this. Stranded in a borderland with no way out. And with the massive reserves of lifeforce within him, it drove him to *do* something, to act—even if it was just trying to run through everything he *knew.*

"Lukas?"

"Yes?"

He didn't even bother looking beside him. Tanya lay there right next to him, resting her head upon her hands. They had taken off their overcoats and were using them as makeshift pillows. It was a tiny, insignificant thing, but it maintained the illusion of civilization in this barbarian land of flames.

"Not sleepy yet?"

Sleep was the last thing on his mind. He had tried already. Between the raging lifeforce and the constant whispers in his mind, sleep was something that just didn't happen. The growing crankiness was just a side benefit.

"I think the mountains due south have better vegetation. Maybe we could try exploring them in the morning?"

"Nothing's stopping you."

"I was just *saying,*" she replied, sitting up, an undercurrent of anger in her tone. "What's wrong with you?"

Lukas turned towards her. "I think mindless exploration has lost its appeal on me. I'm more interested in finding a way out, not jumping from mountain to mountain and stargazing for nights on end."

Tanya pressed her lips and nodded in acquiescence. "We'll find a way out."

"Yes, like we did in the past weeks."

He looked away.

"Well don't blame it on me," Tanya shot back. "I told you, several times, *not* to kill them. But you can never help but do the exact opposite of what I say, can you?"

Lukas turned around and growled. "Don't you put this on me. I wasn't the one who wanted to participate in this circus. I didn't want to come to the svartalfars. You did all of those things. You and Banksi. You took me to the keep. You kept me in the dark about the plan. You dropped the negotiations on my head. You brought me to this borderland without telling me a thing, despite my asking multiple times."

Tanya looked like she wanted to argue, but instead, she just stayed silent, downcast, her fingers clenched into fists. Lukas watched her for as long as he could stand it, and then decided to break the silence.

"Sorry," he said in a voice softer than he expected, "that was harsh."

"Yes," she nodded, and took a moment to gather her thoughts. "But no less true. I was the tool to poke at your secrets."

"Why do you do it?"

"Do what?"

He just watched her.

"You've got to be more specific."

He just stayed clammed up.

Tanya let out a huff. "Fine. I got what you mean."

"So . . . why?"

"Why . . . ." She looked away, at the distant horizon. "Why do I do what I do? Why do I work for Zuken? Why am I so insistent about figuring you out? If I had to guess, I'd say because it solves both quests for me. The secret of what you did to me, and the secret of your powers."

"Two monsters with one fireball then?" Lukas internally patted himself on the back for the translation.

"I've never heard it put like that, but it fits. I suppose."

"I get it," Lukas said. "You're far more used to this than I am."

"This?"

"This." He gestured at everything around him. "You're used to staying out in the dark. Away from the Eternal Light. Whether it be here in the borderlands, or in that desert. That's why you're so casual about it."

"I'm not casual—"

"You're not freaking out, so that's casual."

Tanya narrowed her eyes but then nodded in acquiescence.

"Why?"

"It's a long story," she said evasively.

"And then you say I have secrets."

Her eyes hardened. "It's not the same thing."

"Looks the same to me."

"Well it isn't," she shot back, irritation rising in her voice. "You're an Outsider, and Zuken's already accepted that as fact. You can break the rules of our world and he wouldn't blink an eye, blaming it on your Outsider powers. Me? I'm a *freak*. Unlike you, I didn't drop inside an anomaly. I grew up in this world. I have . . . *baggage.*"

"And you don't think that sharing that baggage is a good way of establishing trust? Especially when prying for my secrets?"

"Trust gets you killed."

Lukas laughed.

She growled at him. "Do I sound like I'm joking?"

"No," said Lukas, "just reminded me of someone. My teacher."

"The goddess?"

"Yes. She had a sister. She raised and protected her. She paved the way for her to become a powerful goddess in her own right. And then, that sister betrayed her."

"Is that why . . ." Tanya began, hesitant. "Is that why you want to bring her back? This sister goddess killed your teacher, and now you're looking for ways to resurrect her?"

It was a bit more complicated than that, but he assumed it was good enough for now.

"Yes."

"And she gave you those skill-stealing powers?"

"You aren't going to drop that, are you?"

Tanya at least had the decency to look sheepish. "You can't blame me. For all my life, the Frost has been the ultimate mystery I've known but never been able to solve. And here comes this guy out of nowhere, crushes me in battle, shatters the Frost's influence on me and returns me my . . . my rationality. And then I find out that he is not only an Outsider, but he can also *steal* skills from his victims . . ." She looked at him nervously. "Wait. You— you could've killed me. Back then. At the anomaly. But you didn't. You could've taken my Frost powers for yourself."

Damn good question. Could he have? Inanna certainly didn't voice that proposition back then.

"I could have, yes."

"Why didn't you?"

He arched an eyebrow. "Are you seriously asking me why I didn't choose to kill you and steal your powers?"

"Yes," came her adamant response. "I am—*was*—no one to you. I attacked you, and for all I know, tried to kill you—"

"Several times—" Lukas offered.

"Several times," she agreed. "So why save me? You can kill all these muspels and bylestyrs and grow stronger through them. So why not me? Why not Zuken? Or Elena?"

"Because I'm *not* a monster," he said incredulously. "Why is that so difficult to understand?"

"But you'd have grown stronger from it."

His eyes twitched. "Are you attempting to *convince* me to try and kill you? Because I swear, it's working." At her sheepish look, he continued. "Yes, killing monsters grants me their skills, and yes, I'd indeed have gotten stronger if I had killed you. But I'm not a mindless killer, nor do I want to be one. Power for the sake of power means nothing. It needs to be tempered with *purpose*. At least, that's what my grandfather used to say."

"And what *is* your purpose?"

"Get my teacher back."

"The goddess."

"Yes."

Tanya ran her fingers through her hair. "It's blowing my mind. You—you're a bremetan. A mortal. No matter how many skills you get or how powerful you grow, you'll stay a mortal. You will not become a *god.*"

Lukas smiled. "That's where you're wrong. My teacher, before she became the *Supreme Queen* of the Heavens, had a different title. They called her the *Butcher of Gods.* And she achieved that as a *mortal.*"

"No fucking way—"

"And that entity told me I had to take her place. And guess what? She told me there was one person in this world that could do the same."

"Kill a god?" Tanya whispered, disbelief ringing in her tone. "Who—who's that?"

His lips twisted into something predatory. "You."

Tanya had a sudden sinking feeling.

"Me?" she croaked, feeling her fingers go numb. "Your goddess thought that I—that I . . ." She tried to put her growing apprehension and disbelief into words but failed dismally. "She said that I—"

"Had the power that could kill a god?" Lukas offered. "Yes, she described your Frost as something truly ancient, much like herself. That this power was originally feeble, crawling its way into the world, but that given the chance, it could definitely harm a god."

"Harm, not *kill.*"

Lukas sighed. "Now you're just talking semantics."

"It's not semant . . ." she trailed off, unable to keep the shock and awe away from her face. These were some of the most complex, nuanced sentiments he had expressed about her powers. Honestly, it was far, far bolder a claim than she had ever made. It was beyond what she had ever imagined. The Frost had always struck her as something *wrong,* and at the same time, something *truly right.* Like a piece of a puzzle that would fit perfectly under different circumstances, but somehow didn't belong to this puzzle. She had always been content to believe it was a lingering corruption, possibly from the mother she never knew. Maybe she was a deviant, a hybrid from a different race like the himthursars? Maybe some of that corruption had passed into her through her mother.

But a god-slaying power?

"You . . . you must be wrong."

"Maybe. Maybe not." His voice filled with a strange finality. "My teacher did say the power was barely there. I can't guarantee what it can or cannot do as it is now, and certainly not after . . . you know, I suppressed it—"

"If it couldn't even defeat you—"

"Aren't you *listening?*"

Tanya flinched at his sudden snap.

"I told you. It was at its weakest. And even then, you nearly killed me before she stepped in. And before you call *that* weak, remind yourself what you did with just *that*. You decimated Level-3 bylestyrs, multiples of them single-handedly."

"I had Ezzeron's help."

"You massacred your way through the muspel army—"

"You did half of the work—"

"You took a bolt of lightning and deflected it—"

"Yeah, but that's because I used pressure with the—"Tanya noticed Lukas's face begin to twitch. "Fine. I admit. The Frost is powerful. I mean, I really have no way of knowing just how strong it is, though. I know it devours lifeforce and kills, but power-wise, Ezzeron is—"

"Not. The. Point."

Tanya sighed, giving up. *"Fine!* So what?"

Lukas inclined his head and ruffled his fingers through his mussed, tousled hair. "All I'm saying is that there's much more to your Frost than even you know. Which is why I want to know how you got it."

Tanya opened her mouth to speak.

"And no, I have no intention of killing you to steal it."

She shut her mouth. "I . . . I wasn't going to suggest that."

"Listen," he said, with the air of a centenarian, "regardless of my powers, I'm a great believer in solving issues through discussion."

Tanya gritted her teeth. The more this conversation went on, the more uncomfortable she felt. Lukas knowing this much about her was nothing short of alarming. That he had done things to her that she didn't understand ticked all the wrong boxes inside her mind. More than his power, more than his skills and his secrets, it was this . . . uncertainty that he made her feel that scared her the most.

Tanya hated being afraid more than anything else in the world. It took her back to that hill, watching her father die with a smile on his face as he bled out, promising her everything would be fine. A false hope for a girl who had nothing to live for in this world, save her father's one wish. And now Lukas was saying that the power that had been the source of everything bad that had ever happened to her was a—

A—

Lukas got up.

Tanya blinked and got up after him. "Where are you going?"

"Out."

"Out?"

"Yes. I'll fly around a bit. It's obvious you don't trust me."

"I—" She wanted to scream, but the words wouldn't come out of her mouth. How could she? Trust bred betrayal, and every single person she had trusted had betrayed her in some way. And Lukas was asking her to reveal her greatest secret of all. If he knew it, if he told others about it, she'd—

She'd—

"Lukas," she pleaded. "I *can't*. I—I just —"

Her response didn't seem to faze him. Instead, he just sighed. "I know. And that's why I'm going to get some air. Trust needs to go both ways, Tanya, so until you're comfortable enough—"

"Lukas—"

"No, you *listen,*" he emphasized, "I *want* you on my side. Not Zuken's, not Olfric's, not on the Empire's or the svartalfars. *Mine.* You. Me. We're not the same as the others. The only difference is that you're trying so hard to pretend otherwise, and I've been proclaimed as the Outsider. You and me, our destinies are bigger—far bigger—than Zuken's machinations and the Empire's constraints. There is a much larger world outside and so many things to unfold. I certainly don't plan to live my life here, and neither should you."

"That's not your decision to make."

"It's certainly not you that'll be making it."

"How dare you—"

"Speak the truth?" he asked, matter-of-factly. "In all the time I've known you, I've never seen you make a decision. Certainly not a relevant one."

"Take that back!" she snarled.

Lukas met her eyes and said, "No."

"No?"

"No. Tell me Tanya, which decision did you make? Perhaps the choice of killing the anomaly core? Was that your decision? Or perhaps it was to take the Sin on yourself? The same Sin that got you into trouble in the first place? Or was your decision to blindly trust Zuken Banksi when he offered you this job? No, you were a fugitive, and this was your way out. Perhaps it was when you chose to stay on as my nurse? Oh, no, Banksi asked you to do that. The svartalfars, the training, the borderland . . . Tell me Tanya, which of these decisions were *yours?*"

Tanya opened her mouth to retort but words failed her. She couldn't move, couldn't breathe, couldn't think.

Lukas *knew* her. In a way that defied comprehension, he had found her out.

Since when? How long had he known? Hours? Days? Weeks? Could it be that he knew from the very beginning? Was that also a part of his mystical powers? Could he have done what he did, and taken her side every step of the way knowing full well the risk of the choice?

But why?

There was no answer she could come up with. She was left with the knowledge that he was fully aware of what she was, what her powers were, and more importantly, how she'd act. All her preemptive scheming, all the ways she had thought to try to exploit him by playing him against Zuken and Zuken against him, while gaining benefits from both sides, weren't lost to him. He was fully aware of what her angle was, and was fully willing to cooperate. No, not just *cooperate*. He wanted to *trust* her. Wanted to be *trusted by* her.

His blatant admission wasn't meant to say that he was watching her. His casual admittance of her shortcomings weren't an attempt to bully or insult her in any fashion. What he had really told her was something far, far simpler.

You don't have to hide.

For the first time since that accursed day when she had gained ownership of Ezzeron, Tanya had no place and no reason to hide.

It was the second most terrifying experience of her life, immediately after her father's death. The man had asked her to fulfill his wishes, but what she had ended up was becoming a fugitive and a puppet. And yet . . .

It was like a weight had been removed from her shoulders. A burden she had grown so accustomed to bearing for such a long time that she no longer knew it was still crushing her down. Her heart was beating in her chest at an accelerated rate, caught between panic and elation. She wanted to run away from this madman as fast as she could. She wanted to forge a wind blade and slice off his windpipe. He'd be dead before he'd realize what had happened. Secrets and paranoia were always her best weapon and her only armor. Without them, she might as well have been naked, defenseless, and weak.

But run where? Where could she go? She was trapped in this borderland with him—but, more importantly, was there a place where she'd be accepted as herself, with all her Sins and faults? Could she run away from the one person who understood how tainted she truly was but still didn't despise her for it?

I want you on my side. You and I—

You and I.

Such a simple statement, and yet, Tanya couldn't think of anyone ever saying anything like that. All her life, she had always dealt in transactions. A favor for a favor. You scratch my back, I scratch yours. You do this for me, I'll do this in return—that was how it had always been. But Lukas—he didn't want a favor. He wanted *her.*

Her secrets.

Her faults.

Her wounds.

Her.

With him.

No matter how much her instincts screamed at her to act otherwise, Tanya couldn't just walk away from him because—

Because she had been given an opportunity. A chance to become something different. Lukas did not want her to Sin for him. He didn't want to hold something over her head. Tanya already knew she was indebted to him twice over now—first for subjugating the Frost and allowing her to retain her sanity, and second, for standing against Zuken for her. And yet, it felt like he was *begging* her to join him. Not commanding, not coercing, not manipulating, but *begging* her.

Her.

There is a much larger world outside and so many things to unfold. I certainly don't plan to live my life here, and neither should you.

A new world. A new start. A life where she'd be defenseless but not alone, exposed but not despised. Tanya did the only thing her confused mind allowed her to do. For the first time in her entire life, Tanya shed tears. Of relief, or *happiness*, or maybe she was just goddamn tired.

Maybe being *hopeful* wasn't just a word for dreamers and fools, but a distant promise shining down on her like the stars above. Maybe all of this was just a fanciful lie, but so what? At least in that lie, there was a chance that she too could be saved.

"Shimizu," she said.

Lukas turned around. "Excuse me?"

Tanya looked up at him. "Shimizu. One of the Sacred Eight of the Empire. Back then I was called Tanya Shimizu, daughter of Yanric, the *Lord* of the Shimizu Clan, and descendant of the Wind King. And therefore," she preened, "I am technically a princess."

CHAPTER 20

LEGACY

P*rincess?"* Lukas spluttered, before his expression twisted into something devious. "Is that why you order me around?"

"Well, *obviously,*" Tanya drawled. "I have very high standards."

Both of them shared a laugh at that.

"So, the Wind King, eh?" Lukas echoed. "I'm guessing that's more than just another fancy title made by Asukan idiots to hide their insecurities?"

Tanya let out a wicked little laugh. "Only an Outsider could say that. A king is the highest authority in the Empire, right below the emperor himself."

"Bit of a difference, then?"

"More than a little," she replied. "The emperor is a descendant of the Great Goddess herself. People call him a demigod, an immortal. The kings, on the other hand, are people who've gained that strength and reached that mantle."

A look of confusion spread on his face as he sat down next to her. Their shoulders touched. "Hang on, I thought the rulers of the kingdom were called Shoguns. Unless . . ."

"You're right," Tanya said, her voice hollow. She edged away, just enough to move her shoulder away from his. The last thing she needed was to act on her impulses. As it was, her body was reacting like it always did when he was close—a remnant of their first encounter. Employing Psychomancy to ignore such thoughts helped, but now that she was on an emotional high, it'd be exponentially difficult to control herself. Just what was it that he did to her?

So far, she had managed to control herself by maintaining suspicion. Doubt and hesitation came to her naturally, and she used them to her benefit. Every time her fingers wanted to entwine with his, she'd make herself think he'd enthralled her. Every time he did something she found endearing, she'd call it manipulation.

And it worked, mostly, back in the real world. Here, though, with just the two of them, it was less easy. Especially because he wasn't trying to impress or woo her, and often went out of his way to make her uncomfortable. If anything, he wanted her to stop hiding and reveal her true self. And given they were all alone in this borderland and she had sensed the . . .

Tanya shook her head, attempting to clear her thoughts.

"Are you alright?"

She nodded. "Yes, um, the Shogun—he's the bureaucratic head. The emperor's representative for the kingdom. The governor of the army, that sort of thing."

"And a king?"

She flipped her hair, her casual tone returning with every passing second. "King is a title, signifying a mantle of power that isn't chosen, elected, won, or bestowed upon someone. It can only be gained by ascending to the zenith of a particular skill, or if you're talking of manacrafting, a particular element."

"Element," Lukas repeated, immersed in her words.

"Fire, Wind, Earth, Water, and Ether," she said, counting her fingers, "Five kings. Five entities that hold power second only to the emperor himself."

"And they rule five kingdoms?"

Tanya laughed. "You've got it backward, Lukas. Kings are kings not because they have a kingdom but because each of them are *single-handedly* as powerful as one. Not even the entire Llaisy Kingdom can stand against the might of a single king."

Lukas whistled. "So they're kingdom killers."

"They can be."

"But they don't?"

"They can't. All kings swear an oath of fealty to the Empire, and accept the dominance of the Asukan pantheon. They usually stay neutral even during civil wars. If one king decides to involve himself in political matters, then another one will, and soon there won't be a kingdom to quarrel over."

"A deterrent force then, only subservient to the emperor."

Tanya frowned. "Kind of. Plus, two kings fighting would mean large-scale devastation. No one, king or not, wants to bear that much Sin."

At this point, she was moving from her personal knowledge to commonly accepted fact. Tanya didn't know why or how changing the landscape incurred Sin. Modern towns and cities wouldn't exist otherwise. Genocide perhaps? But even that didn't make sense. Genocide was just a fancy name for "massacre," not unlike how she'd massacred the monsters inside the anomaly and only very recently, in this borderland.

And from Lukas's expression, he didn't take her words at face value either.

"You'll need to ask Zuken about that. I was never very much into theology as an apprentice."

"And how does one become a king?"

Tanya narrowed her eyes. "You don't know?"

"If I did, I wouldn't be asking now, would I?"

Tanya grimaced, and looked down again, drawing odd shapes on the sandy floor with her finger. "Guess that makes sense, given your history." She raised her head and met his eyes questioningly, "You know how leveling up skills requires exponentially higher Soul Capacities, right?"

"What about it?"

"In our society, we have two paths to power—the Path of the Scholar, and the Path of the Warrior. Scholars devote their lives to understanding the divine powers, and using them with their blessings. We call them onmyōji."

"Aren't those supposed to be priests?"

Tanya snorted. "Warrior-priests. They worship the gods, but they're also willing to kill in their name."

"Fanatics."

"Yes. If an onmyōji raises a skill to Level 4, we call them a sage." At his nod, she continued. "A warrior on the other hand, becomes a warlord at Level 4. When either reaches Level 5, they become . . ."

"A king?"

"Yes. For spiritists like us, it's a little different. Instead of leveling up ourselves, we level up our kami and use their power."

Lukas frowned. "I see."

"You sound disappointed."

"No. Just . . . wondering."

Tanya had an inkling of what he was thinking. Despite his powers, he had only recently come to use his skills like a full-fledged Level 3. He must have leveled up and synchronized his body better with those skills. Nothing else explained why the difference between the current him and the one that had entered the borderland was like night and day.

"It's one of those things that are exponentially more difficult than it sounds." she said. "Kami are elemental beings, so even a Level 1 can wreck your elemental and emotional balance. The stronger and more powerful the kami, the greater the danger. Being a spiritist is fun, but you don't hear about the sheer number of apprentices who went stark raving mad because their kami fucked up their inner balance."

"Then having a king-class kami would mean—" Lukas began.

"Not only would you need to have enough Soul Capacity to support one, you'd also need to raise your mental and emotional fortitude to an equally absurd level. You've seen what a Level 3 can do. Can you imagine what kind of disaster a Level 4, or worse, a king-class kami, could unleash upon our world if it went insane?"

Lukas winced.

"My great-grandfather, Wakamura Shimizu, was the Wind King. He was the one who gained us our nobility. Made us one of the Sacred Eight. After his demise, it fell upon his descendants to rise up to the challenge and become the next Wind King. The Empire has an unbroken rule about that. It gives the king's clan three generations worth of time—or roughly two hundred years, whichever is greater—to claim the mantle by mastering the kami. If we fail to do that, then the kami—the *king-class* kami—is taken away by the emperor."

The light in Lukas's eyes told her that he knew where this was headed.

"Yes, that king-class kami is *Ezzeron.*"

"You . . . ." Lukas was struggling with words, "You have a Level 5, a king-class kami."

"Yes."

"That means you're a—a king?"

She snorted. "Hardly. I'm a Level 3, with just *one* Level-4 skill, and even that I haven't been able to fully master. I can only do one thing with it, and it's not nice."

"I remember," said Lukas. "That ebon missile you used to one-shot the bylestyrs. That was a Level-4 attack, wasn't it?"

She snorted. "No. It was a Level 3, with a little more juice. I told you, I have the skill, but I haven't been able to fully attune to it. Maybe in a few more years, things could be different."

"This is blowing my mind."

She chuckled. "I haven't even begun. You wanted this, remember?"

"Do you see me complaining?"

She twisted her lips in fond annoyance.

"Back to your story, how does a princess become a fugitive?"

And just like that, all traces of mirth died inside her. "It started when I was nine. I had just graduated from my apprenticeship and begun manacrafting to become an Adept. My teachers at the Shrine told me I'd be a fantastic aquamancer, but my father had other ideas. He wanted me to fulfill my duty as heiress of the clan."

Lukas's eyes narrowed.

"My great-grandfather Wakamura Shimizu raised Ezzeron to Level 5 and became the Wind King, getting us our Sacred Eight title. Naturally, it fell on my grandfather, Mujin, to take his place, but he failed. Same for his son—my father, Yanric Shimizu."

"And your dad thought he'd saddle you with it?"

"He didn't *saddle* me with it. Taking up one's legacy is a great honor. If I succeeded, I'd have become the next Wind King and the *Lord* of my Clan. I'd be one of the Sacred Eight and have the entire Eaborid Kingdom under my thumb!"

"I can see that."

Tanya gave him a steady stare. "Great destinies always carry risk."

"Is that what you tell yourself?"

She glared at him some more. She was good at it, but Lukas had been on the receiving end too many times and was immune to its effects by this point.

"What happens when you—when *one* fails?"

She exhaled. "Then I'm just a failure. *Incapable* descendants of an *incapable* clan. Ezzeron would be taken away, and we'd be reduced to another ordinary clan. And it'd be because of *my* incapability."

"Bullshit!" Lukas snapped. "Your grandpa and your father pushed this on you, but if you fail, it's all your fault?"

"It's not!" said Tanya. "You know my ECR. It's *unnaturally high*. If anyone had the best chance to do it, that would be me. The elders thought I was a blessing from Amaterasu herself. My clan's savior. The future Wind King. Father was adamant that I prepare myself for Ezzeron. That meant developing my Soul Capacity so it would be fit for a Level-2 kami. Obviously my high ECR helped, but it was a nightmare. Getting that much Soul Capacity meant gaining a fuck ton of Experience, and to do that, I had to develop lifeforce skills to be able to fight monsters."

"Quite a conundrum," Lukas observed. "To get those lifeforce skills would mean sacrificing more Soul Capacity, which was probably the last thing you wanted to do."

"Tell me about it." Tanya agreed. "It was a constant struggle. I had to be extremely picky about which lifeforce skills to develop. Too little and it'd leave me impaired. Too much and it'd gorge on my Soul Capacity, pushing me further back on my goals. In the end, I changed from a close combat fighter to a sniper, choosing to bombard from afar and kill monsters before they could get me. My friends, my cousins, they were all training to become spiritists, while I was stuck trying to level up without one. There were days I just wanted to give up, but one look at my father's face and I started off all over again with a new zeal."

"You must have really loved your father."

"Doesn't everyone?"

Lukas shrugged. "No idea. I grew up with my grandfather. I guess he was the closest I had to a father figure."

"And did you love him?"

"Well . . ." Lukas drawled, "he was a pain in the ass, and a nutjob, but I did love him to bits."

"What's a nutjob?"

"A really, really *crazy* person."

"Your grandfather was insane?"

Lukas opened his mouth, and then closed it.

Tanya nodded. "Back to the story. Yes, I love my father."

"Honestly, I think he was kind of an asshole for doing that to you."

"Take that back!"

"No," Lukas retorted. "You're talking about duties, but do you know what he sounds like to me? A douchebag that spits on his daughter's dreams."

"What's a *douchebag?*"

Lukas blinked. "Never mind. Point is, he knew you wanted to be an aquamancer, and he still forced it upon you."

"He was bound by his duty to the clan."

"What about his duty to his child?" Lukas shot back. "I get it. Clan. Prestige. Legacy. But you know what? There are things more important than that."

"Yeah?" Tanya challenged. "Like what?"

His voice lowered. "Like your child's happiness. Like knowing that you have limited time in this world. That somewhere in the race for money and power, you need to give your child a little bit of your time. So what if he's different? So what . . . so what if he chooses a life you wouldn't choose for yourself? They're not you. You're not them. Give them the chance to be what they want, and just be happy for them, no matter what. Because when your time is done, that child will have something to remember you by. And it will actually be good."

Tanya stared at him, as if really seeing him for the first time. All this time, she had pegged him as a man of mystery. An Outsider with myriad powers. All her curiosity had been focused on how different he was, how his powers worked, and how he did what he did. Not once had she ever thought about their similarities. He looked and felt bremetan, spoke similar tongues, and reacted in similar ways. She knew he had a life before this but never gave it any further thought. That maybe he too had a family, and like her, had been cut off from them.

"But he didn't, did he? Instead he trampled your growth, your studies, and your skills, like they were worth *nothing. Just to save his failed clan glory?*"

"We'd have lost the Sacred Eight title." Tanya defended him hotly, her own words sounding like hollow excuses. "That's—that's *important*. Far more than one child's future."

"But that one child was *you.*"

Tanya looked away. "You don't understand, Lukas. Being an heir means something. More than just a fancy title to distinguish me from the rest. My clan, my ancestry, it's our mark upon this world. The legacy of my ancestors is what gives us our purpose. It's the culmination of countless generations, all striving to achieve greatness. Wakamura first gained it, and it's up to his descendants—up to *me*—to carry that torch."

"The same legacy that you've been running away from your entire life?"

Tanya scowled, and crossed her arms. "You just don't get it."

"Sure," said Lukas, lying down beside her, as if she was telling him a bedtime story. "What happened after that? When did you tame Ezzeron?"

Tanya smiled humorlessly. "I didn't. I tried for *years*. The first time was when I had saved up two thousand units of Soul Capacity. The next, with three. I was twelve then. A year later, I tried again, with four and a half thousand."

Her face fell. "It simply wasn't enough."

"What?" Lukas asked, confusion evident on his face. "Why? A Level-2 kami needs only five hundred units of Soul Capacity per skill. With four and a half thousand . . ."

"I don't know. No one did. My father told me that it's the nature of kings to demand unreal expectations on their bearers, but I think he was just making excuses at that point. It wasn't about the Soul Capacity. Ezzeron was Level 2, and Wakamura's scrolls said that Ezzeron had a total of five skills. Just two and a half thousand should've been enough for me to complete the binding successfully. But it . . . wasn't. I tried, over and over, but I kept failing."

"You have him now, so obviously you succeeded eventually."

His words twisted a knife in her heart. "Your words have a bitter irony in them. I was just about to quit. At thirteen, all of my cousins were on their way to successfully mastering Level-1 manacrafting and going on to Level 2. Me? I was hoarding enough Soul Capacity for a single Level-3 skill, but without a kami. It affected me. I'd get nightmares about waking up in the middle of the night, with the Cobalt Army banging at my door. I'd hear my father calling me weak. I'd see the elders pointing fingers at me while trying to keep the army from taking Ezzeron away. I'd beg them to stop, tell them it wasn't my *fault*, that I needed a little more time . . ." She clenched her fists. "Some days I just cried. I'd wake up in the middle of the night from bad dreams that were old hat by then, sobbing my eyes out. I'd get overwhelmed, I'd cry, I'd feel better and go back to sleep. I . . . As months passed, I felt like my future was going nowhere. People were whispering. The days of me being their savior—being their hope for the second Wind King—were gone. I couldn't continue like that." She met his eyes. "It happened when I was thirteen."

"Ezzeron reacted to you?"

"If only," she sighed. "I was abducted."

"Abducted?!"

"I told you. The Shimizu were a falling banner. When the mammoth falls, every wolf wants a piece. I was out on a mission in the Vecchian Plateau to kill some monsters when insurgents captured me. They knew I had no kami and that without me, the Shimizu would be desolate. It was a nightmare."

Tanya closed her eyes. Even thinking back to that day made her want to throw up.

"I remember waking up, chained. I had manacles on my hands and my ankles, suppressing my lifeforce. The Cobalt Army uses those to apprehend criminals, and these people were using it against me. They said something about selling me to desert dwellers, which made no sense. I mean, no one lives there. Except for monsters that can steal your soul and wear your skin and. . ."

The implication of her own words hit her. And from the growing pallid expression on Lukas's face, he had arrived at a similar conclusion. Could it be . . .

"The yokai?" he asked. "They were there in the anomaly. At least, that's what you told me."

She narrowed her eyes. Her instincts screamed that he was hiding something. Lukas had always maintained that he knew next to nothing about yokai. And yet, the yokai had attacked Olfric after he had attacked Lukas. A ton of things just didn't add up. The sudden disappearance of Olfric's kami, her deciding to attack Lukas out of nowhere . . . Frost-influenced or not, Tanya doubted she'd have gone after him on a whim.

If only I knew why.

There were other signs too. For all his claims of dropping into this anomaly from a different world, Lukas was a bit *too familiar* with the Empire. With Maluscion. With the Llaisy Kingdom and Cyffnar. How had he gained that knowledge? She thought about his familiarity with the svartalfar customs and his ability to speak their tongue. The muspels too. Was he lying to her? Maybe he had also been attacked by a yokai and somehow managed to kill it and absorb its powers? Was that how he could perform Conjuration and Pyromancy?

"Tanya?" Lukas asked.

"Huh? Oh, sorry." She cut her reverie short. She had decided to extend a hand of trust to him. He had promised to share his part of the story with her. She'd just have to wait until then.

"It's possible they were talking about yokai, though why insurgents would deal with them is beyond me." A bitter feeling rose in her throat. "They tortured me."

Something dark and frightening crossed his face. "Did they . . . ?"

She didn't miss the implication. "No. Not *that.* They roughed me up a bit, but that was all. Nothing I couldn't heal naturally. I didn't have a kami, and I couldn't use lifeforce. I was bound, with nowhere to go, nothing to fight back with. And then . . . I heard *it.*"

"It?"

"A whisper. A thought. A feeling. I don't know how to describe it. It wasn't angry, it was . . . ecstatic. The next thing I knew, there was a jagged shard of Frost sticking out of one guy's chest."

She remembered it all too well. The long ice spear tearing through his body like wet paper. The glimmer in those mad eyes transitioning from surprise to fear to resignation to . . . nothing.

Killing him had been surprisingly *easy*.

"I felt so serene. There weren't any questions, any worries about right and wrong. No fears, no doubts. Just . . . coldness and a maddening *hunger* . . . "

She looked at him, and noticed his flinch. A dark part of her soul rejoiced at it. "The others were surprised. They made funny little sounds as they attacked me and died. I didn't know how I was doing it. I just did. When my father found me, I was sitting all alone, chained, and covered in blood, with a half-dozen corpses all around me."

She looked over at him and found him distant. Her fears stirred. Was he judging her? Would he think differently of her now? Would he call her a monst—

"What happened after that?"

"They took me home," she continued. "My father later told me how proud he was. That I had, without lifeforce, without a kami, killed people above my Level. The blazing look on his face, the pride in his eyes . . . It made me feel *dirty*. Like I had committed a grave sin."

She stood up, growing restless. "The worst part was that it was true. I got Level Ups, multiple of them, but that wasn't all I got. There was lifeforce, *their* lifeforce. I don't know how, but I had more lifeforce within me than physically possible. Like I had stolen it from them. But that wasn't possible, right? Lifeforce is born in our soul and I had . . . Did I devour their souls? Was I some kind of monster?"

Lukas didn't answer. Instead he asked, "Did you tell anyone?"

She gave him a *Do-I-look-stupid?* look and shook her head. "I wasn't sure who I could trust with this. I ransacked our library, searching for something, anything similar to this strange Frost. I had seen aquamancers create Frost using Temperature Modulation. I read about himthursars—they're like muspels, only they use Frost instead of fire. I wondered if maybe I had gotten infected in some way. Maybe those insurgents had done something to me. It was the only thing that made sense. Because I was an Asukan. Asukans cannot craft mana. Asukans . . . "

Her voice cracked.

"Tanya?"

She didn't respond. Instead, a single tear slowly rolled down her cheek.

"You know you don't need to tell me if you don't want to."

"No!" She shook her head. "No, you need to know. You need to see what I've seen. You need to feel what I felt. You need to . . ." She stopped, unable to continue. She wanted to speak. She wanted to cry. She wanted to leave all of this and fly far, far away.

But she also wanted someone—wanted *him*—to know what happened to her.

"Tanya! Tanya—what's wrong?" She looked up at him, felt his strong arms around her. And she was shaking. Crying. Sobbing. She wasn't normally like this. Afraid. Angry. Scared of being judged, scared of returning to that old nightmare again, scared of her grandfather—it was all eating her up inside. She needed to let it all out. Needed someone to know. Needed someone to *understand.*

"What happened next?" he asked.

"I saw her. My answer. It was always there right in front of me. It was—"

She paused as he grabbed her and hugged her tightly, ignoring all personal boundaries. She felt him caress her back, as his other hand slid through her hair.

Just like her father.

"Whatever it is," he whispered into her ear, "it's in the past! It can't hurt you anymore. And if you still feel afraid, we don't have to talk about it at all."

"I do," she murmured back. "I have to." She was afraid, deathly so, but this was the first time she had trusted someone with her worst nightmares. She wanted to let it all out, once and for all.

"That one night. I remember. There was a Black Moon, just a week after that incident. I was sleeping in my bed, alone. And then . . ."

CHAPTER 21

———

Memories of Ice

The thirteen-year-old girl watched the edge of her bed warily, ready for any-thing to appear, but when nothing happened, she knew she was the one who had to make the first move. Swallowing nervously, she crawled on her hands and knees, slowly making her way forward. But she had barely lowered her head enough to look into the pitch-black darkness beneath when—

"I am not under the bed, young one."

The voice came as a thin whisper, right next to her ear. Tanya could feel some-thing cold breathing down her neck, and she shrieked loudly, before losing her balance and falling headfirst onto the cold wooden floor. Lifeforce flooded into her arms and legs and her instincts kicked in.

"Who—whoever you are, don't come near me!" she cried. "I'll—I'll kill—"

"Of course you will, youngling. That is what you're born to be."

Managing to control her reaction to the barest of flinches, Tanya flooded her palm with lifeforce. It glowed with a familiar blue light, one of the easiest tricks her father had taught her with the esoteric power.

What wasn't familiar to her, however, was the eerie chill that accompanied it.

She couldn't help but shiver as the strange voice laughed in the darkness.

What was happening?

"Stop laughing!" Tanya yelled, no longer holding back her tears. "Who—whoever you are, stop playing your dirty tricks with me."

"Oh, but I am not, youngling."

What was it? Some spirit? She had learned that apparitions and wraiths roamed the mists during the Black Moon. Things that the wards of their homes kept them safe from. Demons, nameless things, spirits, monsters of the vilest kind that made people's skins crawl by mere mention of their name.

"Listen," she intoned, putting on a brave face despite the wetness of her cheeks, "my father is very strong. He'll kill you no matter what you are. So if you want to live, come out and face me!"

A brief silence followed the declaration.

"If you insist."

"Where are you?"

She felt a strange pressure on her skin from her left. Tanya turned, but found nothing except the ornate mirror on the edge of the bed.

"Come closer."

She didn't know why, but she made her way across the bed. Until she was right in front of the mirror.

That was when Tanya saw it.

Frost.

Spikes of ice jutted out from her reflection's right hand, coating the bed in the mirror with sheets of dense hoarfrost. Tanya squealed and looked at her own hand, but found nothing. She looked back into the mirror. The Frost was slowly climbing up her reflection's entire right arm, like rings of thorns coiled around the stem of a rose, contorted into random meandering patterns. Jagged barbs, their surfaces serrated like the edge of a knife, sat in rows across her skin. First her breasts, then her abdomen, then her left shoulder and left hand, until her reflection appeared to be fully encased in Frost.

"This is—this is—an illusion!" Tanya screamed, pushing herself back, touching her own skin. Everything felt normal. She glanced at the mirror again.

Glacial white eyes met oceanic blue.

"An illusion. That's what this is," she repeated. "You hear me? I'm not afraid of you! I'm not afraid—"

Hoarfrost erupted out of her fingernails, coating them in white.

"LOOK AT ME!"

The command in that voice was so overwhelming that Tanya couldn't fight it. Her entire body shook, her heart beating a million times a minute. Every last one of her instincts screamed at her to run away. To her father. To the elders. Someone. Anyone. They'd take care of this Frost. Of this—

Slowly, cautiously, she returned to the mirror.

She'd face it.

Face her distorted reflection.

Face her—

Wait. Where did she go?

The mirror was empty. There was no reflection. Nothing. It was as if she wasn't standing in front of the mirror at all. It was like—

"Looking for me?"

Tanya whirled her head around and followed the sound upward.

The creature looked absolutely fiendish, with two bulbous, blue eyes staring right through her, as if it gazing directly into her very soul.

A pair of sharp, ivory fangs appeared next.

Its arms were too large for its misshapen body. Its hands were too large for its gargantuan arms. Scales the size of kite shields ran up them like overlapping palm trees. Glacial slits filled with malice and an unending rage. It was a nightmare made manifest.

"You—" Tanya pointed an erratically shaking finger toward it. "You're a monster."

"Yes," the monster replied. "And you are me."

Tanya watched as Lukas sat silent, his eyes distant. Her story had affected him, and not just on an emotional level. His sharp, hawk-like eyes would occasionally gaze at her, calculations running through his mind, and then he'd look away, as if staring for a second longer would mess up his train of thought. The Outsider always had an air of mystery about him, wearing it like armor. She knew that his brazenness was often a deception played upon others, shrouding his insight behind the facade of a brawny fool. She hadn't missed the glances he'd given her when he thought she wasn't looking. Glances that had nothing to do with romantic aspirations and everything to do with her powers. He was studying her, and she, him.

"What's going on in your head?"

"Just thinking."

Given how his face was all scrunched up, he was more than just *thinking*. If Tanya didn't know better, she'd say he was going through an existential crisis.

"That thing you saw—" he said slowly, taking the time to weigh each word before speaking, "—did you see it again?"

"Why do you ask?"

He didn't reply.

"No."

His lips twisted into a frown. "Never? Not even if you closed your eyes and focused on it? Or tried to spot it from the corner of your eye? An image, or a dulling of senses?"

Tanya was intrigued. She had never shared these details of her life with anyone else, but she definitely hadn't expected this sort of response. But she'd play ball. For now.

"I don't need to. I could always hear its whispers. Always there at the back of my mind. When I was around others, it'd stay low. But when I was alone, or asleep, it would whisper in my ear."

No one can hear me except you. Just you and me. As it will always be. Everything will perish at your touch. I can see it, the destruction we will bring. Civilizations we

*will turn to ashes. Death will be your only legacy, and with your bloodsoaked hands
I shall—*

Tanya shut her eyes. Just thinking about it sent shivers down her spine. Her
instincts screamed at her to drop the topic, to forget it all and seal it behind her
psionic defenses. There was nothing to be gained by opening old wounds . . .

"Whisper what?"

She pretended not to hear his question. "My father knew something was
wrong with me. He thought I was suffering from trauma from my abduction."
She let out a dry, mirthless chuckle. "I *was*—just not the way he saw it. I began
psionic training, and quickly gained a few useful skills. It was fantastic, and yet
so very useless."

"And cost you more Soul Capacity."

She arched an eyebrow.

"Right. No interruptions. Go on."

"You're right. It cost me more Soul Capacity, but it didn't matter. Because
leveling up had become child's play to me. A casual touch drained lifeforce, and
a single scratch was enough to fell monsters. The whispers egged me on, and I
embraced them. I could fight longer, run faster, throw in more lifeforce without
worrying about my reserves. So long as there was an opponent I could drain, I
could keep going. I was . . . unstoppable."

She paused, taking a deep breath. "At first, it was only against monsters.
Creatures to kill. I was extra careful at using Frost in group missions. In less
than a year, I'd gained two more levels. By the time I was sixteen, I was already
pushing beyond Level 12. I had thousands and thousands of Soul Capacity
saved up, and I had completely mastered my Level-2 lifeforce skills. But Ezzeron just would *not bond with me.*"

"Tough crowd," Lukas murmured.

"You have no idea. My performance amazed and frustrated everyone. I was
the star of my clan, capable of going toe-to-toe with spiritists without a kami.
My cousins all thought I should take another kami and progress, but the elders
were stubborn. They knew that I was their best bet, and so, they did the only
thing they could." She met his eyes with a grin. "They upped the ante. They
started sending me on more dangerous missions. Sometimes with adventurers.
Sometimes solo. Sometimes with the Cobalt Army."

"Must have been fun."

His grin was contagious. "It was. I had long stopped being afraid of the
Frost. I got used to it. The deathly whispers were now a boon. My ECR was
tremendous, and with the Frost, I was leveling up faster and faster. I even had
two Level-3 skills under my belt. It was funny, hearing the guys in the army.
They said I was too fast, too smooth, too quick. They feared me, like they
feared my family. I was no aeromancer, but I was fast. I had no kami, but I

could devastate entire monster herds in no time. Between that and my constant failures with Ezzeron, I grew bitter. My disappointments became harder and harder to handle. I stopped being nice, became more impatient, harsher, and . . . sadistic. The struggle to master Ezzeron was making me arrogant, haughty, dismissive, and demanding. Something had to give."

She closed her eyes and exhaled. "It started with a minor debacle. The new recruits in the Army are always too full of themselves, too proud, as if becoming a glorified slave is a grand accomplishment. I was irritated, and my self-control was slipping, and this asshole was grating on my nerves and . . . I used my Frost on him. In public." She glanced away. "I was stupid. I was crazy. I—"

"You couldn't have known—" began Lukas.

"Couldn't have known what?" she demanded. "That my entire life would go sideways because of that? That years later, I'd look back on that moment and realize that that's when everything went *horribly wrong?*"

He met her glare with a poisonous calm. It was accepting and non-judgmental. For some reason, she kind of hated that.

"They . . . they did things to me. The first time I woke up, I was naked, alone, and hanging from the ceiling by my hands. It hurt a lot. My wrists were bleeding, my shoulders, my waist, my . . ." A sob escaped her throat. "The bastards had tied my ankles with metal cords and there were vine-like things sunk into my body. I don't know why they were there, or what they did. They just . . . hurt. I couldn't use lifeforce, I couldn't use my Frost, I was . . . angry, afraid, helpless, and at their mercy. I remember how I screamed and yelled and cursed their ancestors. I threatened to spill their entrails out if I got my hands on them. I told them I was Shimizu, and how my . . ."

Her voice broke.

"I screamed and screamed until my throat was sore, and then I cried myself to sleep. When I woke up, I was on the floor. There were onmyōji all around me. Before I could do anything, they forced a cloth gag into my mouth, and injected something into my body. I blacked out for hours after that."

Tanya clenched her fists. You'd think that after years of nightmares, she'd get used to it. She hadn't. As the words escaped her lips, the raw horror from her past surged back from the dark pits where she had thought she'd left them.

"When I woke up, I was hanging again. My body—they had washed me, dried my hair, and then hung me back from the ceiling. A feeling of utter violation pervaded my soul. The first few times that happened, I screamed and lashed out in frustration, but after the tenth or eleventh time, I had no more tears left to shed. I'd cry myself to sleep, shutting myself off from reality. I'd dream of my father patting my head, telling me that I made him proud for taming Ezzeron. Every time I slept, I'd have that same dream. And every time I woke up, the same nightmare."

"How long?" asked Lukas in a voice far calmer than Tanya would've thought possible. Something about his face made her go pale.

"Five months," she said. "By the end of the first month, I just . . . came to accept it. Breathing hurt. Thinking hurt. I didn't know how I was still alive, without food and water, but I was. It was like clockwork. Every day the onmyōji would come. They'd paint sigils all over my body in bright red. Maybe it was my blood. I wouldn't know if it was. They'd chant strange things I couldn't make heads or tails of. There was a lot of light and sound, and it hurt terribly. I screamed and begged them to stop, to let me go, to let me die, but they just . . . *Would. Not. Stop.* And all the while, my grandfather stood and watched."

"What?!"

Tanya staggered back at the intensity in his tone. It was like a tangible thing.

"My grandfather," she repeated in a hollow voice. Images of the past swam across her mind. "Turns out he was behind it all. Every night I'd scream until my lungs hurt, and then lull myself to sleep to escape the pain. And I'd dream. Sometimes I'd see strange lights. A woman's face. A man who looked so familiar. Places I've never been to. And then, come morning, the onmyōji would return and wake me up to the same nightmare. Even the whispers were growing silent. I thought I was losing my mind. Maybe I was. When the pain went beyond my . . ." She paused for a second, her eyes glassy. "I thought I'd die, which was stupid. I thought after all this time, the least they could do was give me another chance to bind Ezzeron. Maybe just this one time, I'd get lucky . . ."

He was staring at her in abject horror. A dark part of her rejoiced at his pain.

She probably should try to be a better person.

"Wha—" he croaked, "what about your family? Surely someone, anyone—"

"You think they cared?" Tanya asked with a perversely pleased smirk at the reaction her tale invoked in him. "About me? About a single child's happiness when it meant going against my grandfather? Mujin Shimizu is a *warlord.* A Level-4 aeromancer. You've seen what those bylestyrs did, Lukas. My grandfather can erase a *hundred* of them without batting an eye. That is precisely the sort of monster he is."

"But you're his granddaughter!"

Almost instinctively, her smirk grew wider, relishing the horror he was feeling. "Mujin Shimizu is, has been, and will always be, a *butcher.* He has always been a being of violence and deceit, with an immeasurable thirst for power. In hindsight, it's no surprise that he was a high priest of Yahata, the god of war, murder, bloodlust, and destruction." She smiled softly. "Even when the Wind King was alive, Mujin was his right hand, his executioner. He laid the foundation of Cyffnar upon his blade. Do you think that being unable to gain his father's mantle would leave him more sympathetic to the sufferings of others? Do you think seeing his granddaughter suffer stirred his heart? If anything, time has made him crueler."

"But—" Lukas interrupted, breathless. "You—you're here, and you've got Ezzeron, so that means someone— something—must have saved you."

Tanya hesitated. She was really hoping to avoid that bit.

"Yes."

"Who?"

"Who else?" she asked, looking down to one side, sounding oddly shy, as she whispered. "My father."

CHAPTER 22

FROZEN NIGHTMARES

*T*anya felt nothing.

Touch, temperature, pain—all three had become absent, replaced by a numb, floating sensation that pervaded her mind and body. She didn't know what was happening, only that she had fallen down to the floor, bereft of those chains. She'd have dwelt on that question, if she had enough consciousness left in her. All she could do was mimic the general movements of breathing, just to keep herself from succumbing to that cold, welcoming feeling of darkness.

"—ya . . . —et . . . —up!"

Her body was utterly drained of any and all lifeforce, and the sheer number of sigils on her made it impossible to even try generating more, lest the pain return and leave her screaming. One onmyōji had pierced her tongue and her lips with a strange needle-like thing, and even trying to move her tongue sent jolts of fresh agony through her. But someone was pulling her, dragging her up, asking her to speak.

Speak? How silly! What did she need to do that for? All she needed was—

Was—

Was . . . what?

She tried to move her head. She only managed to tilt it sideways. Drool dripped down her bloodied lips. Or was that blood? She'd have to taste it to be certain.

She didn't care. She did care about her horrifically dry throat though . . .

Thirsty . . .

"—anya, try to walk. It's me, your—"

Your . . . ?

"—will save—"

Step by step, she limped forward. She misjudged the process at least three times, nearly falling down the steps, before someone held her from slipping. Her ears picked up sounds of something exploding, shouts, yells, the roar of the wind, something *cracking and splattering against the ceiling. Other than the sickening sweet stench of decay, death and decomposition, her nose picked up the aroma of rich, crimson blood. Not her own. Her lips were parched. Dry. She needed something fresh. Something that she could stick her Frost-laden fingers into—*

SCREEECHHH!

She felt something cold and familiar form on her face. The someone who was grabbing her let out a groan. Something warm and sticky oozed all over her cold fingers. It felt . . . nice.

Like breathing.

But she was still so thirsty.

Had she not been so exhausted, she'd have noticed that she had not only been judging the correct amount of lifeforce seeping into her body, but also how the Frost was healing her back, and how the sticky liquid on her finger was actually red, and her savior sounded suspiciously like her fath—

Gone. The information was indeed there in her mind for a moment, but as it was deemed too unusable in her hazy mind, the excess simply passed through. Tanya didn't care, so she threw herself into the reflexive action of feeling the lifeforce grow within her.

Then she opened her eyes.

She was sitting, her back against a boulder. Her entire body felt like one big bruise, with the exception of that one finger covered with Frost. Her father sat before her, his face wrought with tiny injuries and blood dripping, like he had been through a war himself.

Her vision flickered.

The image of her father didn't vanish.

Tanya slowly blinked again. The blood oozing out of her forehead was painting her vision red, so that was probably why—

Probably why . . . what?

"Rest, Tanya. Rest."

Rest?

"Don't worry. I'll take care of—"

She tilted slightly.

"—everything."

She opened her eyes again. Her father—he was there, right before her eyes. He was bleeding. She blinked slowly again. Thinking was hard. She needed to focus. She felt a pleasurable tingle in her finger. She looked down at the Frost-covered digit. It had extended outward, like a long monster claw, digging past the flesh and bone of—

"Father."

Tanya yanked her finger out, but Yanric grabbed it and pushed it deep into his abdomen, into his blood.

"Don't worry," he said, a smile tearing through his lips. "Just leave it all to me. You keep taking whatever you need—"

"But—" She wanted to yell.

"It's alright."

It wasn't. She knew what this was. The Frost was digging into his flesh. She wanted to scream "NO!" but grunts and coughs were all she could get out. Jolts of pain, spit, and blood were all she could get out. Her father seeing her like this, her Frost draining his lifeforce . . .

Tanya couldn't bear it.

She yanked her arm out.

Once again, her father grabbed it midway and pushed it back in.

"Let it stay."

There was something odd about him. Like he was sleepy. Like he was fading. Like he was—

"But, Father, I— this is—"

"It's okay." He said and pressed her hand tighter.

"No. No, please don't. Father, you—please don't leave me."

It was becoming easier to speak. Her father's eyes were becoming glassier by the second. His body was stiffening. His eyes were drooping.

There were sounds of people yelling in the background. Now she could see they were on a hilltop overlooking a compound. Smoke was rising from it. Several buildings were wrecked. Who could have done it?

She looked at her father.

"Why are you doing this?" she begged.

Yanric looked at her, and for the first time, his warmth was replaced by a strange melancholy. "You're asking the wrong question, Tanya. The right question would be, why didn't I do this before?"

The smoke continued to rise, now covering the sky.

"I—I don't—"

Yanric pressed his finger to her lips, his usual smile nowhere in sight. "I should've stepped in right away. After they captured you. Instead, I hesitated. It took me this long, and for that, I'm sorry."

"I . . ." She tried again, but he pressed her arm deeper into his stomach. She felt the sharpness tear through something, and blood oozed out of his lips.

"Tanya, don't you see?" he said, utterly indifferent to the pain. "A father's duty is to make his daughter happy. To keep her safe, away from all harm. And if my life can save yours, then it's well spent."

"But, Fath—" She sobbed. "I'm—You're leaving me alone. Don't do this, Father. I—" she sobbed, "—I don't have anyone. I—"

"Shhh!" he said consolingly. "It's already too late, Tanya."

His skin was turning blue.

"It's—it's not! Don't you see you're—"

Yanric caressed her back. That simple action, more than anything else, took her breath away. "Take good care of my daughter for me, will you? Always keep her as beautiful as she is now."

His body seized up. His eyes were all but closed.

"CAPTURE THEM!" She heard a shout from afar, and soldiers rushed towards her. Tanya flinched, readying herself for the pain. "It was . . . difficult," her father murmured, eyes closed. "Ezzeron is . . . strong. So strong. I . . . I always wondered what it would feel like. But now I know. I put you through a terrible ordeal and for that, I'm sorry."

"Father—" She could speak now. His lifeforce had healed her. She could stand up. She could run. She could fight.

"Father, what are you talking about?"

Yanric never told her. Instead, a shadow of a smile formed on his face.

And then his body went utterly stiff.

His eyes flashed open, the warmth in them replaced by an inky blackness, one that would swallow the world if given the chance. His body floated in midair, twisting in unnatural ways, like a marionette being pulled by invisible strings.

And then he opened his mouth.

There was no light. No sound. No show of power. There was . . . Nothing.

And Nothing arose out of his mouth, an emptiness that seemingly swallowed the light around it. Black, transparent fumes poured out of his body, a blackened soot that converged, twisted, morphed itself into a solid presence. The clear sky overhead was suddenly crowded with thunderclouds beginning to rotate directly overhead, faster and faster. The air suddenly became very dense, and lightning with no thunder flickered weirdly through the clouds, which turned every shade of white and blue and black. Amidst them, the behemoth began to form.

It was tall.

Massive.

Larger than the eye could take in, yet still incomplete.

Tanya saw the wings next. Its jaws looked like bone. Its flesh was the blackened mist. Horns sprouted out of its body like demented protrusions. Wings—one, two, three, four pairs—exploded out. A pale, sinister white light shone out of the empty sockets, as if filled with something maddeningly primordial.

Tanya knew its name.

The Beast of the Shimizu. The wrath of the Wind King.

Ezzeron.

Where it touched, the ground disintegrated and flaked away, pulverizing at the edges and dissipating into sand. The sky went dark, illuminated in flashes by the lightning streaking through the heavens, displaying malignant, twisted reflections of the creature. The closest mountain shattered, buildings exploded, and the terrain cracked, a roaring tsunami of pure force thundering through the world, surging out with a frightening amount of energy. The mist fiends screeched and devoured everything that came in their way. Forget the army, this thing was causing reality itself to tear apart. Mist and fog covered the sky, just like the Black Moon.

This was the apocalypse. This was how the world would end.

And she would die with it.

"That you will," said a voice from deep within. "You couldn't save your father. You couldn't save yourself. And now, you cannot fulfill your dream."

"And whose fault is that?" Tanya screamed aloud. It didn't matter if there was no one listening to her. "You made me do this. I'm not weak. You made me a monster! If you hadn't given me this Frost then—"

"Oh, you're going to blame me now? First your father, then Ezzeron, and now me. Who's next? How many until you realize you're the weak one?"

No, she told herself. She was not weak. She was not—

"Weak."

No!

"Weak."

I'm not—

"Weak."

Shut up. Shut up. Shut up.

"You're weak. You're nothing. You're a little girl trying to hide from the Big Bad. You knew you were draining your father's blood but you were too afraid to let go."

Ice pierced through her chest. "No— No, I tried to stop him. I tried to—"

"Stop him from dying? Did you really? Or did you hope he would keep pulling you close, while you drained his life out of him? Serves him right."

Shut up! Shut up! Shut up!

"You're no savior. You never can be."

Shut up! I'm done. It's over. I've nothing left. I—I'm going to die.

She looked at the still-forming figure of Ezzeron. Just being in its presence was suffocating.

"Quitting because you don't have it in you to continue. This creature . . . it could be ours. Ours to wield. Ours to control. Ours to rule over."

She couldn't believe her ears. She could control Ezzeron? That was impossible. Nothing she had ever done, no amount of leveling up had ever made a speck of difference.

"How?"

"Give me control."

"What?!"

"Hand over the reins. To me. Sit back in comfort. Let me, the true part of you, be the one to handle this beast."

Something felt . . . wrong. "Are you . . . " She paused. "Are you really me?"

She sensed something smiling in the darkness. "I am. I am not. I am your other half. The instincts you suppress. The power you deny yourself. We are two sides of the same coin, but that coin is weighted, and one side will always turn up more than the other."

"I . . ."

An icy feeling spread across her chest. The rich, wafting, unmistakable aroma of mana flared against her nostrils. This power was delicious. She had to take it.

"You are a predator, Tanya. And that—" Her own hand rose up, pointing at the titan manifesting in the sky. "—is prey. Let things run their course."

She took a deep breath, closing her eyes.

". . . Alright."

She opened them.

"You . . . you can have control. Just . . . make them pay."

A dark, malevolent laugh echoed in her mind, as her eyes turned glacial white.

"Time to hunt."

CHAPTER 23

TRADE OF SECRETS

Months ago, inside an anomaly, a shard of a goddess did something unexpected.

As Lukas's body lay frozen, stuck on the horizon between life and death, his mind lost in limbo, his soul obliterated, the goddess waited for his return. She was Patience Incarnate, watching as the omphalos kept trying to revive his body in a hundred thousand ways, all of them unique. But none would bring him back.

And so she did something she never would have believed herself capable of doing.

She sacrificed herself.

For him.

A soul for a soul.

A shard of divinity for a speck of ephemeral mortality.

And in so doing, he was reborn. Reforged in divinity, blessed with powers that weren't his to claim. But when he asked her why she did so, her answer was clear.

I was being selfish, she said. The omphalos wouldn't care for me, and you were my only hope.

Lukas wanted to take her words at face value. Inanna was a selfish woman. Nothing she did was without cause, without an agenda that furthered her own goals. Every bit of information she threw his way was aimed to shackle him to her. He knew; he had fought tooth and nail to keep her from laying claim to him. She had said, even as she faded, that she was placing a bet on him. He had come through for her once, so she was trusting him a second time.

Trusting him with her divinity.

Her existence.

Her legacy.

Even if it left her with nothing. No power, no presence, no faith, and—unless he brought her back—no existence.

She called herself selfish, yet why couldn't he believe her fully? Because she was lying? No. He didn't think Inanna could lie. It wasn't her. She always told him the truth, no matter how harsh. Sometimes just a partial truth but never an outright lie. So yes, she was selfish.

And despite what she did, deep within, Inanna really didn't want to die.

But she did what was necessary. Even if it all but guaranteed her demise.

Inanna was a monster. But in the end, sometimes even monsters cry. For all her looking down at him, he was her mortal. Hers. Her hope. Someone that would hold her vigil. And she didn't want him to leave her. That's what she told him.

Could it be that for once, Inanna just didn't want him to die? That in her own selfish way, she simply didn't want to be alone again? That she was afraid? Afraid of being separated from her mortal? And even if it was selfish, even if they deserved what happened to them . . .

Was it so wrong?

"I don't know what happened after," said Tanya, "Maybe I fell unconscious. Maybe the Frost took over. I'm not sure. All I remember is waking up somewhere near the Eaborid border, several thousand miles away from my hometown. I was healed, brimming with more lifeforce than I knew how to handle and multiple Level Ups registered on my Schema. I was stronger, I was free, but, most importantly, I wasn't alone."

Lukas knew where she was going with this.

"I had Ezzeron. Bonded to me. I could feel his power, bubbling beneath that glacier within me. His power frothed and spat, wanting to be unleashed into the world, but it was trapped beneath a world of ice. I didn't know how, but my Frost ruled over him, and Ezzeron *obeyed*. Even to this day, Ezzeron has never truly been mine. It has always been *hers*."

Hers. The Other Tanya. The Frost Incarnate. The one that had wanted to devour him, the one whom Inanna had bound with her divinity, yet continued to slip through every time she used the Frost. The creature that could stand against the might of a goddess.

Yes. The pieces were finally beginning to fall into place.

"*She* has always been there, whispering at the back of my mind. I didn't want to lose control again, so I avoided using the Frost whenever possible. I focused on my mental disciplines, trained myself in the psionic arts, and worked day and night to Level Up and acclimatize my body to Ezzeron's indomitable strength. It was excruciating pain, trying to limit Ezzeron's tides of power without destroying myself. I would cry myself to sleep—from the pain, from the loneliness, from just how goddamn unfair it was. I came so close to giving up so very many times. She'd whisper to me, demanding to be unleashed. Power more intoxicating than anything I'd ever experienced—freedom from pain, from control. But then I'd see my father on that hilltop, feeling the warmth of his embrace before . . ." Tanya looked away. "And I'd push her whispers back."

Tanya met his eyes. "Just like that, four years passed. I traveled past the borders, slipping into Maluscion, hiding myself. I did odd jobs, took missions under the table, somehow surviving, growing, looking out for abductors."

"Abductors?"

"Men for hire," she explained. "My family sent them after me. It was from them that I learned that the Shimizu compound was destroyed. More than half of the people were killed. I heard that my elder brother Ultaf had returned from Asuka and took over the reins of the surviving clan. There was no news about my grandfather. Some said he died; others said he retired after Ezzeron was lost to them. Everyone thought Ezzeron had slipped into the winds, escaping into the Ikai realm. My description and abilities as an aeromancer would inevitably tie me to Ezzeron, so I had to take on a new identity and almost never manifest my kami. Using the Frost made my hair bleed white, so I turned it blonde."

Lukas looked at her hair. Streaks of glacial white were peeking out of her golden curls.

She smiled, as if reading his mind. "Blame the Frost. Nothing survives it. Not even enchantments. I need to reapply it every time I use it."

He nodded.

"I was skilled, both in combat and manacrafting. I was fast. There was no dearth of jobs. My father told me that he wanted me to be pretty. He didn't want to remember me as stained. So I thought, as long as I dressed well, looked pretty, and you couldn't see the bloodstains, I wouldn't be the monster that took his life. I knew it was stupid—a failed dream—but I clung to the idea. Still do."

Lukas swallowed. Tanya was obsessed with looking good. In all the time he had known her, there hadn't been one week that she didn't visit the salons. She spent an enormous amount of money on making certain she looked beautiful and smelled alluring. It was a stark contrast to that feral thing he had met in the crypt, and now he knew why.

"The abductors hunted me across Maluscion and Baramunz. I learned that the emperor had punished my clan for failing to provide a timely descendant to the Wind King and losing the kami. Our Sacred Eight status was all but revoked, and everything fell apart. The abductors stopped coming and suddenly . . ." Light suffused her face. "I was free."

"Why come to Haviskali?"

Tanya looked surprised.

"What?" Lukas asked, shrugging. "You were happy in Baramunz. And from the way you talk of it, you were making a life for yourself. And it's part of the fringes. Why come back, where the Empire could find you?"

The light faded from her eyes. "I was being selfish. With no abductors, with my clan in shambles, I wanted freedom. I thought this was my chance. To get strong. To raise myself to the level where I could use Ezzeron at his peak potential. Become the person my father wanted me to be. I needed access to more difficult missions, and I knew that, if I wanted to climb the ladder, Llaisy Kingdom was my best bet. It was richer than Eaborid and more welcoming to vagrants. Haviskali was a small town, and away from the Empire's politics."

She exhaled. "I came to Haviskali. Registered as a vagrant. Worked my way through the ranks. The Blues noticed me and inducted me into their ranks. That's where I met Olfric. We went on many missions together and then . . ."

Lukas knew the rest. Tanya had mentioned it before. A mission that had gone wrong. A mission where she had committed Sin.

She pursed her lips. "It was a Level-2 anomaly. Underwater. I was no stranger to fighting and killing monsters. It was standard adventurer business. But this was my first time inside an anomaly. Away from civilization, into the jaws of an infant world . . . I don't know how to explain it but the moment we got in, the whispers started getting louder. I wasn't sure what was happening, but down there, underwater, I needed more control than Ezzeron allowed me. I kept pushing and he fought me. The water, the cold, the darkness, the scent of prey . . . it got to me. As I neared the anomaly's core, the whispers kept getting louder and louder and *louder.*"

She closed her eyes and stayed silent for several moments.

"When I woke up, I found myself filled with power. I had leveled up, several times over. The Frost within me had gotten infinitely stronger and, most shockingly, I was *dripping* with Sin. There was a court hearing, and Olfric testified against me. He claimed I had destroyed the anomaly core and killed everyone inside. I wasn't sure what to do. I didn't remember a thing, and so, I ran. I ran and the army chased me. I found asylum in the Zwaray Keep, and then, a month later, Zuken Banksi's letter found me. He made me an offer."

"Destroy the anomaly in the desert," Lukas said.

"In exchange for freedom, yes," she clarified.

"He ever tell you why he wanted it destroyed?"

"I'm a pro. I'm concerned with the task, not the reasons behind it. Zuken gave me an offer I couldn't refuse, even if it meant Sinning again."

Lukas chuckled. "And then you met me."

"Yes," she deadpanned. "You happened to me."

Lukas wasn't sure he liked being described in the same way one would a lethal disease or terrible misfortune but didn't voice it out loud.

"I don't know what you did, but those whispers . . . you made them go away. I had almost forgotten what it was like without them inside my head. The silence was exhilarating, and frightening. I wasn't sure what to do. You made me feel . . . normal again. Like I wasn't a—"

"Monster?"

" . . . Yes."

He couldn't help it. He snorted.

"What?" Tanya asked, confused.

Her expression made him snort again. Tanya watched him with growing confusion.

"It's just that I know a bit about having voices in my head too," he explained. "It's funny, when it first started happening, I was annoyed. I absolutely hated it. Hated her. And then that hate turned to fear when I realized it was the voice of a goddess, a being older than the known universe, trying to lure me into making bargains. But after I got to know her a bit, and then she *literally* sacrificed herself to save my sorry ass, I realized how much I had gotten to her, and how much I . . . miss her."

Tanya watched him.

"But you know what," he said, feeling oddly melancholic, "I know she'll come back. I don't know how, but I know she will, and then I'll remember just how annoying she was. All over again."

The thought brought a smile to his face.

"You really care for this goddess, don't you?"

His eyes met hers. "Yes."

"Do you . . . love her?"

Lukas stilled. Love? A goddess? Inanna wasn't human. She wasn't even a *being*, per se. She could appear in whatever manner she wished—as large as a mountain or as bright as a star. You couldn't love a mountain. You couldn't feel affection for the tremendous power residing within the heart of a volcano. Her beauty was the majesty one saw when they looked at the endlessness of the night sky. Awe, yes. Respect, undoubtedly, and dare he say a feeling of dependency . . . but love?

I got you to laugh, didn't I?

The corners of her lips twitched. ***That you did, mortal. That you did.***

"Well?" Tanya asked.

"I'm a mortal. She's a goddess. She and I had a pact. An accord. I'm just holding to my end of the bargain."

"Do you really believe that?"

"Yes."

Tanya stared at him.

He didn't budge.

Finally, she let out a loud snort of her own.

He shrugged, pushing himself off the ground. But just as he was about to stand up, she grabbed his arm.

"What?"

She met his eyes. "Trust goes both ways, remember? I told you everything about myself. You know me better than anyone else now. I trusted you, so I'll ask, do you trust me?"

Damn it. Reciprocation was a nasty son of a bitch.

"I do."

Her lips twisted. "Good. Because I'm dying to know exactly *what you* are, Lukas Aguilar." Seeing him hesitate, she continued, "I've been completely upfront with you. About my past, my powers, my secrets. Everything. There's no one in this world that knows me more than you. I think I deserve to . . ." she paused, and turned her palms out invitingly, "I think it's only fair that you do the same." She gave him a few moments, but when he still showed no sign of contributing, she twisted the knife. "Unless you still don't trust me after all—"

He held up a hand. "I didn't say I wasn't going to share. I'm just thinking about what I *can* share. You know, without the shit hitting the fan."

"I thought trust went both ways."

He took a moment to reflect. Inanna had invested a lot in Tanya, and this was an opportunity to beat Banksi and get out ahead. And Tanya was right. She had opened herself up to him, and if he didn't reciprocate, things would end badly. But if he did reciprocate and she blurted his secrets to Banksi, he could be in a ton of trouble.

That said, chances of the latter were pretty low. Tanya had entrusted him with a lot of deeply private information. Just the knowledge of her heritage could land her in acute danger. That she wielded the hope of the Shimizu was another. Not to mention her alter ego and ability to become an Asukan nightmare.

Lukas made up his mind.

"All right," he said after some time. "I'll share my story with you. But I should tell you right off the bat, that everything I say is the truth, regardless of how fantastical it might sound."

"Oh, come on," said Tanya, rolling her eyes, "I already know you're an Outsider, and that you were taught by a freaking goddess. I also know you can manacraft all kinds of mana, steal skills from your kills, and are, for all I know, immortal. I can't imagine there's anything you can say that'll beat that?"

"You wanna bet on that?" He grinned.

"One thousand mezals says I won't be fazed," she shot back.

Lukas met her eyes evenly. "My name is Lukas Aguilar and . . . I'm an *anomaly.*"

There was dead silence as Tanya processed his statement, clearly wondering if he was just crazy. After all, his oath didn't necessarily mean what he said was true, just that it was his perception of the truth.

However, he put her disbelief to one side as he turned his attention to his Schema. More precisely, to the omphalos attributes. Much like his skill set, there were considerable changes in the omphalos functions.

OMPHALOS ATTRIBUTES	
Energy Reservoir Capacity	∞
Current Energy Level	**684,985,112 units**
OMPHALOS FUNCTIONS	
Scan	Level 3
Analyze	Level 3
Prophylaxis	Level 2
Soul Siphon	NA
Alpha Condition	Level 5 (MAX) Default for **PRIME HOST**
Evocation	Level 3
Living Anomaly	NA
Territory Creation	Level 1
Capacitance	NA

Another massive drop. This wasn't the first time he had gained new omphalos functions or upgraded the existing ones, so it wasn't due to that. No, this drop had to have happened during the fight with the monster army. Again, he had gained Level Ups but those too weren't a possible source for this drain. No, he had done something unconventional during the fight, just like he had during his flight attempt. Back then, he had channeled motion negation, but this time . . . .

The memory of Blob re-forming into a copy of Inanna's axe came to mind. He had wielded that axe with a familiarity he certainly did not possess. A familiarity that, like Motion Negation, could only come from a single source.

Inanna's divinity.

Had he somehow fulfilled yet another criterion, unlocking more of her memory, her Experience and skills to bleed through? Was her divinity resonating through him?

"What do you mean, an *anomaly?*"

Tanya tilted her head and was now watching him with a penetrating gaze. Lukas gave her a one-armed shrug. "I told you it's gonna be difficult to believe. And it's a long story."

Tanya exhaled. "I think I really need to hear that long story now."

Lukas sat back down, dismissing his Schema, and prepared himself.

Might as well dive right into the deep end. He thought after a moment's reflection.

"As I said, my name is Lukas Aguilar. Back in my world, I was an apprenticing diplomat by profession. The story starts when I woke up to an apocalypse, and found myself in that underground cavern, with this weird screen floating in front of my eyes, and a literal goddess's voice inside my head."

Over the next hour, Tanya listened with rapt fascination as Lukas outlined for her in broad terms what had happened to him. He talked briefly about the earthquake and how he had found himself suddenly capable of using lifeforce, how he had grown from surviving on moss to fighting small monsters for food. He very briefly touched on his encounter with the yokai, limiting himself to his unfortunate battle with the yurei, the possession, and his activation of Soul Siphon. Quonnan became just another yokai monster that was unfortunate enough to end up in his way. Lukas kept his stories broad, beyond himself and his journey, careful not to spill any specific information about Inanna. Not that he felt threatened by Tanya, but he had gotten in the habit of being careful with information. One could not remain with Inanna as long and intimately as he had without coming to learn the value of information. Giving out broad details while holding back relevant points was a key skill, and he had firsthand experience observing a master at work.

"And then I woke up at Banksi's mansion and found you nursing me. You know the rest."

Tanya regarded him in a state of shock as she tried to process what he had said. It was obvious she believed him, and it was equally as obvious that it had shaken her to her very core. She'd gasped audibly as he talked about being possessed by the yurei, and then again when he described how she'd pinned him down with her Frost and proceeded to lobotomize him. The look on her face was one of shock and revulsion, though she never interrupted, letting him finish his story in full. Once he had, she merely stared in his direction without really seeing him.

"Err . . . you're kinda scaring me now," he said.

"I'm just wondering if you can terraform yourself. Can you expand outwards? Grow branches out of yourself?"

Technically, he *could* do that. Anomalous energy was the purest form of Creation, and he had an entire reservoir of that. Already he had some ideas involving Blob and his monster prototypes, but that was neither here nor there. It was why he was so insistent on getting the wardstone built for him as part of the contract. The potential of aqāru, with hundreds and thousands of monster prototypes within it, channeled through anomalous energy was limitless.

"I'm an anomaly, not a tree."

"Anomalies give birth to trees."

"Well this one doesn't," he pointed his thumb at his chest, "this one only grabs the souls of its prey and adds them to its collection."

"Collection," Tanya murmured. "So does that mean those muspels we fought—"

"Yep."

"And the bylestyr we killed—"

"Yep."

"And Hreidmar and that sludge—"

"All stored up in here." He pointed at his head. "Or well, I can access them anyway. I don't exactly have a physical core powering me from within. I think."

"You think?"

"I didn't plan on becoming one, remember?" he threw back. "Half of the time I've spent in this weird world has been discovering what I can or cannot do."

"Says a guy that carries a world within him."

"I did tell you earlier—" He grinned. "—I carry a bit of my world around with me."

"Excuse me for not taking you literally," said Tanya.

She wasn't exactly angry with him, or at least, so it seemed. It was more like she was trying to come to grips with the curveball he'd thrown her way. Her anger was simply the easiest method she had of dealing with it.

She ran her fingers through her hair. "This is blowing my mind."

"I appreciate that."

"Shut up!" She glowered again. "A guy with a world inside him, and a freaking goddess training him. With a semi-sentient piece of metal that turns into whatever he wants it to be—and purrs."

Lukas wondered if he should tell her that Blob was, in fact, a broken culmination of everything that the Crypt of Fiendish Worms was, or that he planned to get it up to snuff soon.

"I'm just thinking back on our talks. The assumptions we made about you, and your responses. All of that was just a complete waste of time."

"Are you gonna tell Zuken that?"

"I should," she admitted. "But I won't. I trusted you with my secrets, and you can trust me with yours. It's just . . . how much of you is you and how much . . ."

"The anomaly? I doubt there's a difference. I'm . . . me, at least in most cases. There are moments when I feel these impulses, prompting me to act in ways I normally wouldn't."

"Oh?" she asked. "Do tell."

Lukas wondered how she'd react if he told her that the anomaly considered her a predator and constantly prompted him to kill her.

"Take Elena, for example. You have no idea how many times I had to turn down the option of siphoning her. There was this time the Screen suggested I was making stupid decisions and needed to revert back to some training wheels protocol or some such shit."

Babysitter Protocol

"Right. Babysitter Protocol. Sorry."

Tanya arched an eyebrow. "Another prompt?"

He groaned. "It's like dealing with a baby. Granted, it's voluntary most of the time, except . . ."

"Except?"

"Except when outside stimuli trigger a reaction from the anomaly system. Like the svartalfar pillar. The Screen kept pinging me about it, but you told me it was safe. So when I tried to cross it, the pillar treated me like the world around it and tried to drain me."

She blinked. "And you damaged it?"

"Drained, not damaged. I have a function—an ability—called Capacitance, that allows me to drain raw energy out of . . . well, I'm not really sure what triggers it. I only used it once in the crypt because we were connected, and then with the pillar, but I haven't had anything similar when I was walking around in Haviskali or here."

"I'd have thought you'd have kept experimenting," she mused.

"It's not as easy as it looks," he admitted. "Testing out my anomaly powers always seems to attract undue attention."

"I can't believe I have a walking, breathing world as a partner."

"You'll get used to it. I know I did."

The days following their mutual revelations were far less frustrating. With both of them getting to know about each other's pasts and powers, their relationship had advanced. Lukas didn't have to wonder if she was constantly angling for something or just how much influence Zuken Banksi was exerting. Tanya seemed freer and more uninhibited. The feeling of someone accepting her, despite knowing her bloodstained history, was probably a novelty she had never experienced. Yes, the world was still as ugly as ever, and they still had no idea about how to get out of this borderland, but at least she had found someone who knew her and still didn't judge her.

Her words, not his.

They had traveled across the borderland. With no need to downplay his abilities, Lukas used Kinetomancy and Gravity Control to simply glide through the air, racing with his aeromancer partner. The borderland was large, easily twice the size of Haviskali, though the lack of topological variety made it difficult to distinguish between regions. After what was probably a week of exploration, they still had absolutely nothing on their hands except the occasional unique creature that they fought and he siphoned away, with Tanya grinning at him knowingly.

And then, *this* happened.

Lukas stared at the *thing* before him—a thin, dented bruise, floating in midair. He had seen something identical back at the keep, only back then, there were bluish energies seeping out of it. Here, it was the reverse: a sliver of pitch dark that seemed to drain everything that entered its reach, even light itself. Unlike the earlier similar bruise that had all but repelled him, this one pulled at his gaze, a gravity that made it impossible to look anywhere but at its swirling, inky blackness.

"Is that . . . ?" Tanya asked.

"Yep."

It was a Well, or what could be a Well as long as it could be opened. He had seen the amount of power the svartalfars used to drag the earlier open, even for a moment. But they were employing raw energy from the world to do it. Why? Perhaps the world itself rejected these bruises, and hence, they used the world's energy to counter it, albeit temporarily? It seemed like a as logical an explanation as any.

"Do you think . . . ?" Tanya began again.

"Can it be opened?" Lukas finished for her, and found her scowling at him. That brought a chuckle to his lips. "Maybe. At least, it's an idea. It's a door. The svartalfars opened it to cross to this borderland, and the thing about doors are, they tend to open on both sides."

He regarded the bruise again.

"I'm just wondering how much energy it'd require to push through."

"Can you do that?"

Good question.

"I think I have a fair chance. The svartalfars use world energy. I am a world, and I have a ton of energy."

He paused.

"What's stopping you?"

"I'm not sure how," he admitted. "When the svartalfars do it, they're opening it from the world's side to the borderland, which is . . . I suppose, *less* than the world we've come from."

"Less?"

"On a world level. So I'd think that when we come in, this borderland resists us. Or maybe, it doesn't. Maybe the world itself just resists us and the svartalfars use the world's energy against itself. But if I try to open it here, I won't be pitting my reserves against this borderland . . ."

"You'd be pitting them against the real world."

Lukas flinched, an unfamiliar irritation filling him at the very concept that the so-called outside world was more *real* and *he* was less.

Tanya noticed his expression and automatically pulled back. The girl had good instincts.

"Lukas?" she prodded.

"Sorry," he apologized. "I guess this was one of the triggers again. You implied that the world back there is more real and I'm . . . less. Honestly, I consider your world an abominable fake, especially with that infernal Eternal Light."

Even up to now, he still found sudden bouts of anger rising within him every time he noticed the lack of shadows. Compared to that, this borderland was closer to how things worked on Earth and was therefore far more palatable.

Tanya looked at him for a couple of seconds before snorting. "Well, that's a first. You probably shouldn't say that in front of Olfric."

"Yeah," Lukas laughed. "That'd go really well."

"Are you going to try?"

"Huh, yes, I think," he said, gazing at the black bruise. "The svartalfars could open it with a couple of pillars, and I think my reserves hold more than enough to match that amount. I'm hoping it should be enough to make a small tear, but where the tear might lead to, I have no idea."

"You won't know until you try," she advised. "If it helps, even if we enter a different nation, I'll know how to deal with things. And it isn't like you'll have problems communicating either, given your ridiculous language translation powers."

He rolled his eyes. Tanya had been practically incensed upon hearing that he had the ability to understand and communicate in every language ever.

A lopsided grin formed on his face, and he raised both arms.

"Here goes nothing."

He pushed both of them into the bruise.

It expanded by a single foot in every direction.

And then the Screen blared out a prompt in blazing red.

Energy Drain Detected **Omphalos Reserves Draining** **73%**

Current Energy Level	184,945,980 units

CHAPTER 24

IGNITING DIVINITY

Lukas stared at the Screen prompt in mounting horror. His reserves hadn't just gone down, they had come close to depletion within a second of connecting with the bruise. Seventy-three percent, and that was only because he managed to pull out. *Fuck!* If he had been another second longer, the bruise would've drained him dry.

"What's wrong?" Tanya asked, worried.

Lukas inhaled and exhaled, giving him a minute to study what had just happened while formulating a reply. "I just got my ass kicked. That's what happened. This thing just drained my power by seventy-three percent!"

"Is that a lot?" she asked.

Lukas gave her a wide-eyed look. "It'd take a svartalfar pillar several days to fill me up from scratch. Do the math."

Her mouth snapped shut.

"Okay," she said after a moment. "That's a lot."

Lukas ran his fingers through his hair. "Okay, at least we now know this is a no-go."

"But it's a Well."

"Yes, and it almost drained me dry. For fuck's sake, I'll probably die if I stick my hand in again."

"But it was working, wasn't it?" she countered. "The Well opened."

"Yes, enough to put a hand through. Not my entire body or yours. And it was open for like half a second. Even if I could open it again, it'd be gone before either of us is totally in. I don't know about you but I'm not in the mood to slice myself off into two dimensions, thank you very much!"

Tanya crossed her arms. "I didn't say that. I just . . ."

"It's useless. I can't even make another attempt without refueling myself, and there are no svartalfar pillars around."

"Yes, but maybe something else is."

He turned to face her. "Something else?"

Tanya shrugged. "You told me you don't know what triggers the energy absorption. So why don't you try it out? It's not like there's anyone here to rat you out or anything."

"Point."

Why hadn't he considered that?

Show me everything on Capacitance.

CAPACITANCE
Absorption of Energy from the World to bolster Omphalos Reserves

VOLUNTARY	Currently Set to OFF

"Switch it on."

Capacitance function Activated! **Identifying Nexus** **Associating relevant Monster Prototypes** **Finding ideal candidates . . .**

A list of prototypes from his Array flashed before him.

Ideal Candidate identified **BYLESTYR**	
Nature	**Fused Prototype**
Soul Capacity	**25000**

Level-5 Alpha Condition denied Consciousness Shift. **Enacting . . .** **Denied!** **Enacting . . .** **Denied!** **Enacting . . .** **Denied!**

"This is just the gift that keeps on giving, isn't it?" He scowled. Alpha Condition, the skill that made him the Prime Host and ensured he maintained his sanity and rationality despite allowing Monster prototypes to take over, was resisting the process. That meant that forming a Nexus would require an original Monster mindset. One that was compatible with the borderland.

Like the bylestyr.

Back when he had done something similar with the dranzithl, the crypt had taken advantage of it and hacked into his anomaly system. What he was attempting now was infinitely more dangerous. If this worked, he'd have access to the awareness of the borderland and maybe beyond. If not, it'd be up to Tanya to snap him out of the trance.

Should I do it? Last time I fucked up badly. But this time . . .

"Where is your sense of adventure?"

"Shut up, Inanna!" he snapped. Turning to Tanya, he said. "I'm about to try something suicidal and stupid. If it works, we'll have a way out. If it doesn't—" He paused. "—Something might happen."

Tanya swallowed, and took several steps back, a familiar hostility returning to her stance. He couldn't blame her. The last time he had poked his nose into another world's matters, it had turned him into a raging berserker with too much power and too little sanity. This time, the stakes were even higher.

On the good side, he hadn't butchered this world's Guardian. Or its equivalent. Whatever.

"Is this the only option?" she asked.

Damned good question.

Show me alternative options for Capacitance.

Insufficient Data

Yeah. That sums it up.

"No other alternative," he said. "It's this way or the highway."

"Highway? What way is that?"

He sighed. This wasn't the time to explain Earth references. "Ignore."

"Okay. Just telling you," She warned, "unlike last time, I have no reason to hold back now."

He gave her a wolfish grin. "If things really go south, the last thing on your mind would be to hold back!"

And this time there would be no Inanna to help him. Come to think of it, had she helped the last time? Or had the connection broken after he had fallen unconscious?

Closing his eyes, he took a deep breath.

"Do it. Deactivate Alpha Condition."

> **Alpha Condition Deactivated**
> **Rewriting spiritual matrices . . .**
> **Establishing Nexus . . .**
>
> **Enacting Consciousness Shift.**

Space splits.

Or is it his senses? They feel everywhere. He senses himself. His body. Human. Mortal. Or is it lostbelt Earth? Omphalos? Pyre of ███████ ████ *—?*

Memories. Events. Impressions. Self and foreign. A human. A lostbelt. Anomaly. Singularity. Real. Unreal. Earth. Fire. Ash—

Cracks appear. Cracks diffuse. Cracks get larger. Brighter. Cracks converge. Diverge. Shatter. Re-form.

His mind devolves.

Instinct arises. Instincts of a human. Instincts of anomaly. Instincts from skills. Instincts of a bylestyr.

There is no pain. The cognition of pain no longer matters. He is swallowed by injury. By his senses. By information. By anomaly. By power. By mind. By—

He falls into a swirling maelstrom of pain.

He doesn't know where he is.

He doesn't know who he is.

He doesn't know what it means.

It doesn't matter.

He sees it now. Like a large integrated circuit. What is a circuit? How does it integrate? What is seeing? Information? Information assimilation? Where would that be? Why would that be? What does—

The complexities increase. They twist. They bend. They form shapes that shouldn't exist. Shapes he knows have always existed. Three-dimensional. Ten-dimensional. Matrices. Lattices.

His vision narrows. What is vision?

The world expands.

He concentrates on needless things. Why? He knows he will split in half otherwise. How does he know?

Unnecessary.

The world is too big for this small body. The Spiritual Presence is too grand to be hidden within this shell.

Yet the world fits. The prototype exists in segregation. Yet the Presence stays hidden. Bound. Forged. Fused.

He is being repelled. He can't be repelled.

He is reaching it. He can't reach it.

He shouldn't reach it. Not reaching it will be unforgivable.

He is reaching out.

He is reaching out.

He is REACHING OUT.

His eyes burn. His brain burns. He extends his arms and they extend and extend and exten—

"Ha—agh—gag!"

His eyes are focused now. Right and wrong. Black and red. Colorful and grayscale.

He is opening his eyes. He is human. He is bylestyr. His perceptions blur. Dim and bright. Pitch-black darkness. And bloodred. He is awake. He is hungry. Raw power enters his body. Power from ley lines. Power from Self.

It cloaks him. Unbridled. Chaos in flesh and blood. Rage without restraint. Force without balance.

An unholy roar emerges from his throat.

It was maddening.

It had been quite some time since he had felt the sensation of a foreign emotion gripping his mind. He had almost forgotten how it felt to allow an alien mind to exert its influence over his own body, have its instincts prevail over his human intellect and rationality. Even when exercising consciousness shifts, the Level-5 Alpha Condition held the majority of the bestial impulses at bay, but now?

Lukas could feel the primal drives that were the bylestyr's power. The need to hunt, to fight, to protect its territory and kill were surging through him. It took all of his inner resolve to not lunge at Tanya in an explosive rage the moment he rested his gaze on her. She was a predator, a destroyer of Creation. Anomaly Slayer. World Killer. She needed to be eliminated. The violence with which he would rip her to shreds would be utterly beautiful and intoxicating; the stark clarity with which he'd carry out his deed was impossible to comprehend with his human rationale. He did not feel fear. He was fire, and fear was for prey. Fear was for things he was about to burn, and he knew exactly what he needed to do.

Rip out her throat.

Nexus Achieved

Registering . . .

Activating Capacitance . . .

The sudden arrival of the prompt acted like ice-cold water, immediately cutting off the feral impulses growing within. Shaking his head, Lukas looked around, a mixture of disorientation and frustration rising within him, and he wasn't sure which was which.

"Lukas?" asked Tanya. "Are you okay?"

He looked at her. As far as opponents went, Tanya was a danger. But he needed her help if he wanted a way out. If anything attacked him, he'd need her on his side. Once he didn't, things might change.

Yes. He could go ahead with that option.

"Stop bothering me," he said, sneering. Guided by raw instinct, he stretched his body, fire and lifeforce surging through them and saturating his fingertips. He flexed his fingers a few times and felt raw energy surge into him from the ground.

Capacitance Function Active
Reverse Shift Active
Energy Absorption
29%

And what a power it was. A storm engulfed his mind, tearing at his perceptions, flooding them with random images and smells and sensations. It was like standing on a mountaintop while it was exploding with boiling, hot lava, only instead of just inflicting pain, every random grain was an experience—a memory—so disjoined, intense, and rapid that it left nothing to hold on to.

Capacitance Function Active
Reverse Shift Active
Energy Absorption
47%

Every inch of his body protested. He could feel blood pouring down his eyes, nose, and lips. His skull felt like it was going to be crushed in from all sides. The raw power roared like a feral wind, ravaging its way into him as endless tides of raw World Energy were siphoned into his human shell.

Capacitance Function Active
Reverse Shift Active
Energy Absorption
71%

He debated what to do. He'd soon be at full capacity, and any more contact with the borderland would utterly fry him. Not unless he managed to drain it while being connected to the borderland. He would have to function like those pillars—drag the World's power and use it against the World's own laws to hold the Well open.

Making up his mind, he pushed his hands into the bruise and *pulled*.

> **Energy Drain Detected**
> **Omphalos Reserves Draining**
> **Capacitance Function Active**
> **Reverse Shift Active**
> **Establishing a bridge . . .**

Everything was happening too fast. The world around him had become a big blur of motion and energy. Sounds tumbled one upon another so rapidly that it was impossible to pick out or identify any given portion of it. Lights were flashing so brightly and at such intensity that he cried out in agony. He thought he heard Tanya yelling in the background, but all he could see was the slowly opening Well that frothed and spat as he forced it to enlarge enough that he could safely push something the size of his fist through it.

More . . .

> **Bridge established**
> **Opening rift . . .**

It hurt so fucking much.

Lukas screamed as his entire body was engulfed in an unyielding tide of energy. Fires roared within him, seeping from the pores of his bloodied, grimy skin in the form of white-hot liquid fire droplets. His eyes burned and shriveled in his sockets, only to heal almost instantly and be burned again, and his hair caught fire. His entire body was flailing about, and an enormous pressure pushed down on his body, crushing him into the hard ground below. For a split second, the little semblance of conscious thought that Lukas had left idly noted that dying was just as bad as he had imagined.

Something cracked from within him and Lukas knew the true definition of the word *agony*.

His eyes opened and he saw—

The Universe.

He saw the great ocean of mist, formless, shapeless, and omnipresent. Spanning and expanding to infinity and beyond. A cosmic maelstrom from which stemmed Existence itself. He saw the celestial bodies—giant, floating worlds, submerged in the eternal ocean of raw power, swirling with a massive vortex in the middle, and in the center of that vortex, with its jaws open sat N█████ —

His world, his entire existence, was suddenly engulfed by a massive surge of something that ripped into his fragile psyche and implanted itself there. Pain itself lost all meaning as this enormous, mind-shattering sensation swept through every iota of his body. The very molecules that made him human shuddered and quaked as something otherworldly settled upon them, fashioning a place within his body for itself. Tachypsychia? What good would elevated perception do if information was pouring into him a thousand times faster than what he could normally handle?

He saw countless worlds. Worlds filled with nothing but flames, a swirling mass of bright crimson in its center. Worlds that radiated a curse so powerful that to even look at them blinded him. He saw the wastelands of frigid tundra, the green slopes, worlds of light and mystery, and the twisting, contorting shapes of liquid metal beaten into shape under the light of the very stars—

Lukas didn't know how long this went on for as time lost all meaning, but it occurred to him at one point or another that this massively overwhelming presence that threatened to tear his mind and soul in half was very familiar.

In fact, it felt as if he had known it all his life . . .

Power. He thought. *So much power. So much power. So much—*

"LUKAS!" He heard Tanya scream in the background. It brought some semblance of focus back into him.

He must have blacked out. It was the only explanation he could think of.

Some people compared losing consciousness to falling asleep. It wasn't like that at all. While there were many similarities between them to an outside observer, they were two fundamentally different states. For one, you didn't dream when you fell unconscious like you did when sleeping. The mind didn't create the brainwaves necessary to dream, so people had no memory of what passed from the moment they fell unconscious to the moment they woke up. For them, it was like no time had passed at all.

Which was why when he opened his eyes and found himself hurtling in a direction away from the bruise, he knew he must have blacked out. And while that knowledge was comforting in the sense that he wasn't completely confused by his situation, it didn't make things any less painful.

The boulder he struck at a colossal speed erupted into splinters. Lukas bounced against the terrain, creating several tin craters before crashing on a hillside, his body tearing a trench in the wall, in which he ended up partially buried.

His skin was burned all over, his bones fractured in multiple places, spikes of agony shooting up and down his spine. It hurt to see; it hurt to breathe; it hurt to do *anything* but lay still in that dust. Somehow managing to raise a hand up, he pulled himself out of the crater he had dug for himself and carefully pushed himself back on his feet.

Only to fall down again.

Okay. What the hell happened?

"Lukas!" Tanya shrieked as she came for him and held him. "We've gotta get out of here! Fast."

Nexus established
LEVEL-5 Alpha Condition Restored
PRIME HOST connected to AWARENESS

"Now!"

Wait! What? Get away? Why? He had finally gotten what he had been aiming for. A connection to the borderland's awareness. This wasn't the time to let his chips down. This was the time to celebrate, for they'd finally be able to—

A tremor radiated through the air, evaporating his thoughts on contact.

"It's coming!" was all Tanya managed to say.

A scream pierced through the air. It didn't even register as a sound. There was just a single, terrible *power* in the air, a sudden titanic burst of disorienting pressure, as if it were a physical thing rather than pure energy. Lukas's limbs didn't bend. The terrain beneath him cracked further, but he managed to withstand it.

The silence that followed lasted a brief second before the world went red and howling. He felt like he was standing in the heart of a sun. Everything around him disappeared, swept in a sea of crimson. They were surrounded. It parted around them like liquid fire, falling to either side as if they were holding back the tides of an ocean.

Or rather, it was Tanya that was holding it back.

A beam of pure light exploded out of the horizon, disappearing somewhere in the distant sky where even his gaze couldn't reach. A tear in the sky appeared in the beam's wake, as if it had punched through the very fabric of reality and sundered it, allowing him to catch a glimpse of what lay beyond. He could see lightning and green and blue mist, with iridescent ripples fading in and out of existence, as the boundaries of the world pulled themselves back together.

His brain finished rebooting and Lukas realized just what had Tanya so freaked out.

The land around them was gone. Half the terrain for miles on end had shattered, sinking beneath the layer of crimson purgatory.

"Whatever you did," said Tanya, in a strained voice, "it made something very, very angry."

Oh yeah.

That.

The anomaly's Guardian had been the sludge. This borderland's Guardian on the other hand . . .

Lukas swallowed.

"And it's coming," she finished.

The world suddenly went silent, as if reality had taken a deep breath and held it. There was a low quiver in the terrain beneath his feet, a hideous pressure in the air, and then, from further north, a column of red-white energy—pure power—hammered in their direction and created a path of utter ruin.

Every single mountain, hill, and plateau in its way shattered like a broken toy.

"If I die while saving your ass," she said, her voice sounding strangely airy, "I'm never forgiving you."

Then he heard it.

"Ice is my soul."

Her words resonated with something deep within him, and her eyes turned glacial white.

"Everfrost!"

The moment she uttered the word, something resonated, a command that was imposed by the will of an impossible force upon the world around it. Wintry plumes that had begun forming around her exploded, covering the terrain with sheets of ice. The freeze extended, stretching and thickening, coating everything in near-inch-thick sheets of frozen shelling. The ice erupted in spots, forming enormous tooth-like stalagmites, swelling and erupting with violent force. In a few seconds, a veritable ice age stood guard against the incoming blast.

And then the powers collided.

Where the red energy touched, the ground melted and flaked away, scorching at the edges and bursting into flame. When it touched the wind, the temperature rose so high that the air itself caught fire. Mountains shattered, hills exploded, and the terrain cracked and belched out lava of the darkest red, as the world around her was pushed beyond limit by an overwhelming pressure. Flames ran rampant. Fissures exploded. A roaring tsunami of pure force thundered through the mountain terrain. Magical energy surged out with it, expanding out in a radial burst, in a wave of such breadth and power that just moments before, Lukas would have considered it impossible.

But the domain of ice held.

Fire was stopped by Frost.

Lukas watched in fascination and disbelief as a cold, blue light formed around Tanya, a sphere of diamond radiance that deflected the incoming wrath, like an angry tide crashing against obdurate stone. And in that withering light, Tanya stood, a silhouette, unbreakable and unmovable against the tide.

And then, it was over. The blast ended. She had done it. She had stopped it. With her Frost. Lukas only had a moment to see the smoke arising from her, remnants of black soot forming all over her, held back from touching her skin by an armor of frigid ice. Tanya turned and looked at him.

Angry.

Her eyes shone bright white.

And then she fell. Boneless. Like a marionette whose strings had been cut. Lukas barely managed to grab her before she fully collapsed, realizing that there was nothing to protect him from another blast. Oh, he had power—a fuck ton of it—and could dish out lifeforce and mana at a magnitude more than he could when he had faced the bylestyr, but something told him that simple *power* wouldn't be able to manage the gap this time around. This energy, this destruction . . . this wasn't an attack.

This was a herald of something awakening.

"We—"Tanya croaked, trying her hardest to get up, "We need to get out of here. We need to—"

But Lukas wasn't listening anymore. A dizziness hit him suddenly, attacking his whole body with nausea.

"Ha—guh!"

His stomach spun around. His senses felt reversed. His vision was engulfed with crimson. As if blood had seeped into his eyes, and everything around him was turning red.

"Ha—ah!"

The temperature hadn't changed, but his body . . . It felt strangely *hot*.

"What is—this?"

His feet were trembling. Whatever was happening to him, it was throwing his body into disarray. Lifeforce, mana—nothing was working. The Screen was going frantic, throwing one crazy contradiction after another. Prophylaxis thought nothing was wrong with his body, which freaked him out even more. Had sucking in that much energy fucked with his anomaly system? There was no way to tell. All he knew was that he was suddenly weakening like a shattered hourglass, sands spilling out the sides, unable to stop it. It was as if he was breathing out his insides with every breath.

He really had pulled the shortest straw this time around.

"GUH!"

A scream escaped his lungs. Just shifting his gaze made him feel like he had run a marathon. Tanya looked like she was suffocating as well. It wasn't just him. But what was causing this?

Why?

How?

His throat hurt like someone had just vanished the very air from his lungs, and left him incapable of breathing more.

"URKUH—!"

An alien rage lit up his mind. Like a white-hot blade it cut into his conscience, threatening to overpower reason, threatening to undo the tranquility within. He struggled, trying to wrestle it back. But it was a living thing, this anger. The entire borderland broiled alongside under this strain, the very air writhing in tormented agony. Whatever it was, Lukas could feel its power surging from every direction, the rage within him giving *it* strength, swimming through his veins and saturating everything inside and outside of him.

After what seemed like an eternity—which couldn't have actually been more than a few seconds—passed, the volatile emotion gradually ceased. The anger ebbed away, gone like a tide, and Lukas, without thinking, looked up and saw—

Primal

TERROR.

"Fuck me!"

The sky simmered, the stench of sulfur overwhelming everything else. And in that mist, among the crimson clouds, a massive *eye* opened, something around it, writhing . . .

A bolt of pure red scythed out, tracing a massive arc through the field of devastation. Wherever it touched, it atomized things. There was literally *nothing* left—no land, no lava, *nothing.* Everything had evaporated. Turned to gas.

Lukas stood up and crossed Tanya's body, standing before her like a shield, raising his arms. It would have been a very sweet gesture, but given the scenario, it was fundamentally stupid. If even a speck of that beam hit him, he'd be incinerated, and so would she.

The bolt came for him.

Throwing all caution to the wind, Lukas let out a yell and threw everything at it.

Their powers collided.

A horrible pressure hit him, a body-crushing agony, like he had suddenly been displaced to the bottom of the sea. He had as much chance of standing against it as a tiny grain of sand had against the might of a rising tide. But the tide had tried to wash him away before, and Lukas had *some* experience battling beings way above his pay grade. It was true he was nothing but a grain of sand compared to that ocean, but pound as it might, the ocean was unable to destroy that grain of sand. Not if it was stubborn enough to hold itself together. The ocean could shove the grain of sand here and there, could batter and rage at it, but when the rage was gone and the water was serene again, that grain of sand would remain.

All he had to do was hold himself together and survive the onslaught.

"Move forward. It's the only way."

So he took the pressure. The snarling, alien rage of those flames threatened to engulf his mind, evaporate him, turn his limbs and brain to jelly. He withstood it. The trick was not to face it. Oh no, he'd be toast long before he even registered it. Instead he did the first thing he had learned from Inanna's skill.

Deflection.

He couldn't stop the energy, but he could always, *always* deflect it. It was the nature of any force to travel the path of least resistance, regardless of its strength. This beast, whatever it was, could have all the power in the world, but it would still have to obey the *laws* of physics.

His job, as a kinetomancer, was to pave multiple avenues for exactly that.

"You wish to stand in defiance of the God of Fire, and yet here you are, trembling before this."

Shut up, Inanna! he thought in protest. He really didn't need her inane commentary to distract him right now. But there was this nagging feeling that it wasn't *Inanna* whose voice he had just heard, but someone else from a half-forgotten dream. The rest of his thoughts vanished as lifeforce—magnitudes more than he had ever used—surged out of his arms, out of his very skin, forming a tangible layer of pure energy, shielding him from the raw heat exuding from that atomizing beam. Inanna's skill helped him to deflect it in two directions, crafting a concave shield before him to bear the brunt of impact. With careful construction, Lukas expanded the surface, decreasing the pressure, and pushed it further and further, increasing the angle of deflection.

And then, just like the receding tide, it was over.

He had done it.

Precious silence reigned for the next several seconds.

Lukas knew better than to trust it. It was the false serenity at the onset of a vicious storm. The eye of the hurricane.

The moment of silence dragged on.

And then . . . .

A long, vengeful howl broke it. It shattered the plane of reality and gutted the foundations of the world.

Dark clawed hands reached out. Grasped the edges of existence. Pulled.

The head came first. Fire meshed with bone. It peered through the hole in reality that its hands had just torn, and laughed. It was a monstrous sound, deep and resonant, rich with bloodstained mirth. The body slipped through. Emerged in all its gruesome glory. The hands erupted into five draconic serpents, each belching flames from its maw. Wings, three pairs of them, dark and scaly and ending in crimson flames. There was no tissue, just bone and fire. Standing, it looked taller than the biggest mountain. The flames twisted and writhed below the rib cage, forming a monstrous tail. The wrongness that emanated from its frame was a physical thing, and just looking at it was enough to drive a normal human insane.

There were no words. No glorified phrases or statements laden with purpose. It did not need them. This creature . . . it proclaimed its intent from its mere presence. Leaked it out just by existing.

This was a destroyer.

A beast of the apocalypse.

A titan.

The beast raised its skull-maw, and a second howl ripped free.

Volcanoes erupted. Hills shattered. Pulverized by the sonic boom. Atomized into fine powder. Ground to dust by sheer, unrelenting force.

"So . . ." he muttered, "this is how it ends. Not with a whisper, but with a bang. Another apocalypse."

He turned his neck to look at Tanya. One last time. Logic would have had him looking around for escape options. He could've used tachypsychia, divided a second into several minutes. There must have been something, anything within his Prototype array that could've offered a way out. Maybe Blob could help. It was aqāru, and the metal was very powerful against the elements. Maybe he could use the bylestyr prototype. They lived in lava—surely that could help him.

But Lukas did nothing. He had given his everything to deflect that hit. And that was just the trailer. This beast . . . it would crush him. It would obliterate him, and he would have no more chance than an ant had against a boot.

The blonde woman met his eyes. He could spot the same resignation in those blue orbs. She knew what was about to happen. He knew what was about to happen. And she knew that he knew it.

This was the end.

His life had run its course. It was time to return to oblivion. There were hopes, dreams, unfulfilled wishes, but none of that mattered. Not in front of *that*.

The apocalyptic beast raised its arms wide, the serpentine limbs hissing in a frenzy, rendering a sound no human should ever hear. As its arms went up, so did the lava. The terrain shattered. So did the sky. Raw, swirling mana of pure flame condensed. Lava bound it together.

Yes. I will die. But I won't go out without a fight. Not before this vermin—

Anomalous behavior detected!
PRIME HOST accessing ▮▮ ▮▮
Breaking existing conventions.
Safety Off.

Lukas could not bring himself to care. Whatever it was, it didn't matter. Not anymore.

The gigantic hands came together. Lukas raised his own in defiance. A universe of crimson crashed on him from all sides.

Lukas Aguilar was gone.

No, it was more accurate to say that the data representing Lukas Aguilar had been overwritten. A viral presence had infected the Anomaly System and the data of the Prime Host had been corrupted beyond recognition. When the anomaly tried to call forth any of the data, all that came to mind were fragments of randomized information from what was once Lukas Aguilar. It was a strange and nigh impossible conundrum, because the Prime Host enjoyed LEVEL-5 Alpha Condition, a state that guaranteed extreme resistance against any forms of mental pollution. Trouble was, like all rules, Alpha Condition too suffered from its absoluteness. It had not counted for three tiny facts:

The presence of divinity inside an otherwise mortal soul.

A relic capable of actualizing a Truth in a world.

And finally, the mortal facing a situation that resonated with the divinity lurking within.

Surrounded by flames on all sides, Lukas Aguilar had resorted to using his strongest card—Kinetomancy, the power of motion manipulation. He had used the bedrock of Inanna's power, and brought it forth in an attempt to protect himself from the strongest fires he had ever faced. The blinding wrath, the impossible heat, the certain death and the extreme helplessness—Lukas had used the power of motion to put up a last stand against them all. And in so doing, reenacted a similar situation to the one that Inanna herself had faced.

An experience that had become the bedrock of Inanna's meteoric rise to power.

What Lukas Aguilar was doing wasn't even something unique. He had done it twice before—first when trying to exert Motion Negation for the first time; the second when facing the army of muspel. In both cases, his instincts had meshed with Inanna's, allowing him to do something beyond his capabilities.

Maybe he had been expecting something similar to happen now.

But it hadn't.

Instead, something more . . . much more happened.

In that one moment, two events existed. The mortal Lukas Aguilar employed Kinetomancy against the fires of the muspels, while in the other, the immortal Inanna had employed Kinetomancy against the fires of the Vikahl Ashlands.

Two distinct events. Yet so similar.

Two distinct people. Yet employing the same skill.

Two different fires. Yet the defiance facing them both was the same.

Each of the above could not be accounted for beforehand. Adding in the factors from earlier, there were too many variables that simply couldn't be taken into account. To begin with, the probability of such a unique meshing of equally unique factors arising was so minuscule that it couldn't even be considered as a possible eventuality.

And yet it happened.

Level-5 Alpha Condition was programmed to protect the Prime Host from all forms of extrusive mental pollution. It did nothing to protect him from what was already inside.

Like the divinity that was used to reforge Lukas's soul after it was sundered apart.

Anything that was considered part of the data belonging to Lukas Aguilar was still Lukas Aguilar, and it was the nature of creatures to alter their constitution through Experience, gaining skills and leveling up. Any corruption from the divinity would also count as change and growth.

Call it a miscalculation of Fate itself. A chance of one in several billions. An eventuality so remote that even the Origin itself would have overlooked it.

And so it happened.

Lukas opened his eyes wide in confusion.

It was natural. He was expecting to be dead by this point.

Instead he was . . .

Was . . .

His thoughts vanished as a strange, blue light attracted his gaze. It was the pendant. Inanna's pendant. His grandfather's gift. His only connection to the world he left behind and the goddess that brought him here. The ornament was glowing with an eldritch sheen, radiating with a power so impossibly hot that the crimson wave felt like a warm shower compared to it. And yet, it left him uncharred, like being kissed by a winter sun.

But that didn't make sense.

"Not everything does. Not everything has to," came an impossible voice. Lukas froze on the spot, his mind unwilling to accept the implications. He must be hearing things, reminiscing about her. He did that a lot. Maybe he had let out another spark of her memories. Yes. That must be it. That *had to be it. There was simply no way—*

"For there are more things in the universe than the paltry laws that govern your perception."

A warm breeze touched his face, as an ethereal hand grasped his own. A warmth surged within him, a feeling similar to being on a lifeforce high, only a thousand times hotter and more intense. He could hear thunder, flashes of lightning, and the chirping of birds—all very disconnected in their own way and yet forming a musical melody that soothed the spirit, like an after tone of some vast gong, or a summer afternoon shower.

He was wrong.

He *had* to be.

Because the alternative meant—

"Mortal."

She stepped up, right next to him. Clad in the heavenly attire that befitted the Supreme Queen, she stood, grabbing a familiar axe in her right arm. Motes of light fell from her as more motes of similar energy kept rising from within, making it appear like her entire form was an ever-constant waterfall.

Lukas opened his mouth to speak, but words failed him. Instead, he watched, dumbfounded, caught in a strange wave of surprise, awe, and happiness.

"Inanna . . ." He breathed. "Is this— Are you—?"

The goddess turned towards him, her expression softening slightly. **"I am . . . not Her, mortal. I am a shade of a shade. A reflection of a reflection. The lingering Presence of the One that holds your faith. An incarnation of the divinity that forged your existence. And yet, I am Her."**

She paused in appraisal, her emerald eyes studying him before a slow smile asserted itself on her beautiful face.

"You did not bow when She offered you tutelage. You did not bow when She offered you powers beyond your wildest imagination. You did not bow when you were at your weakest, and even courted death to allow Her the chance to seek what She wanted. And now, despite Her fading from the greater Reality, you hold Her vigil and seek Her return?"

Lukas shrugged, giving her a lopsided grin. It was surreal how easily he shifted from near-death to conversation. Maybe he was dead. Who knew? And honestly, did he even *care?*

"I gave my word."

That brought a smile to her face. The kind of smile that made flowers bloom and bards create ballads. **"That you did. They say you know a man by his deeds. You've defied Her for no more reason than your own defiance. You've bowed your head to neither power nor manipulation, and have put yourself in harm's way to defend those who you believed needed your protection. And the problems you've invited for yourself in doing so, are hardly inconsequential."**

"Wait! What problems?"

Inanna smiled. **"She used a spell that spanned across the Universe, mortal. Nothing of that magnitude remains unspotted. The gods of this world must have sensed it. The other beings of significant power and presence have as well. The infinite darkness of the In-Between, and Those-That-Dwell-In-The-Darkness have felt it. Many of them can sense the origin of that power within you. You, Lukas Aguilar, have danced about in the shadows at the edge of life. It is no small thing to go into those shadows and come back again, forged in true divinity. Thank** the anomaly within you, for without it, you've no idea the kind of attention you'd have attracted."

"Oh," Lukas said. "Good. Because the pace was starting to slow down so much that I was getting bored."

At that, Inanna tilted her head back and laughed. Then her left hand moved up and touched Lukas's cheek. Just that action made all pains go away, like taking a breath of fresh air after an imprisonment of a lifetime.

"She chose well."

"Not as well as you think. I still have no way of getting her back."

Her lips twisted downward a bit. **"I am not surprised. Especially with your incessant self-crippling nature. Paths of great power lie around you, beckoning you to grasp them. But you, in the same air as a child playing with a pail of water, lie oblivious to the vast ocean before you."**

Lukas wanted to argue; to claim that she was wrong; that he always had Her on the forefront of his mind. Whether it be his dealing with Zuken, or the svartalfars, or even his relationship with Tanya, it had all stemmed from his desire to get Inanna back. It was why he was studying the old gods. It was why he had acquired the deal with the svartalfars. Why he wanted to activate Blob's functions through Rollback Protocol.

"You misconstrue my words, mortal. You've grown since She last met you, but your path ahead is long and arduous. And yet, in your relentless trials to gain what you seek, you've forgotten a very simple truth, one that is the bedrock of your existence."

"Which is?"

Inanna smiled. **"You are a *world*."**

Lukas frowned. "I don't understand. I know I'm an anomaly, but what has that to do with this?"

Inanna said nothing.

"Honestly," said Lukas, "as much as I'm glad to be praised, could I swap these accolades for . . . I dunno, a solution that could bring You back?"

Inanna laughed again. **"She was a reflection of the True Supreme Queen. Just as I am of Her. I sense the Bond you shared with Her, memories of a life I do not remember living. The Scrying Spell claimed that nothing pertaining to the Supreme Queen exists in the Universe. Either that means that all of this is a giant illusion, or someone has gone to extreme lengths to seal the Supreme Queen away from all attempts."**

"Who?"

Her face sobered. **"Only one comes to mind. Ereshkigal."**

"Your sister? I—I don't understand."

She just looked at him. Then she said, **"Let me help you understand."**

And then she *thought* at him.

The flames and the lava ridge around him vanished.

And Lukas found himself standing in a dreary, dark cavern he knew from a half-remembered dream. Bluish flames lit the walls, revealing a maggot-infested corpse hanging from one of them. The next moment, he was down on the ground, gasping like a fish plucked from the ocean.

"What?" He gasped. Even breathing was agony. "What was that?"

"The solution. The answer to your question. My advice is to consider it at your leisure. I cannot aid you any further. What I can do is help you survive."

Lukas stared at her. All she had done was show him a flash of a dream he had once seen. The entire thing had been less than a second. There was absolutely nothing in it that would grant any answer to any of his—

Lukas stiffened.

A flash of memory. Just enough to remember that something had been there, but the rest of the information was absent. Either that or . . .

A different thought struck him. The death of his own world was also a memory he had once experienced, but Inanna had hidden it deep within the recesses of his mind. For his own protection.

Had she done the same thing again?

Consider it at his leisure, she had said. *At his leisure.* Not now. She wasn't being rhetorical, but literal.

So the next viable question could only be—

"Is this where you offer me a deal?"

Inanna let out a throaty laugh. **"The Supreme Queen is not without benevolence, mortal. Especially to those that hold Her vigil. The One you knew promised you power beyond imagination, a promise She could not keep during Her lifetime. To break Her word is beneath Her."**

"She didn't break her word," Lukas defended. "She used her divinity to reforge me. Bring me back to life, sacrificing herself in return."

"It was necessary at that time. An investment with high stakes, made on one She trusted to see things through till the end. That She had to sacrifice herself to ensure Her investment survived does not undo Her word. The Supreme Queen's word is bond, even if the sky falls and the earth shatters on it."

He couldn't believe his ears. "You're going to help me?"

"I am going to keep my word, mortal. You're bold, clever, and, from time to time, lucky. All of those are excellent qualities to have in battle. But against this power, you cannot prevail. The anomaly within you will choose an ethereal Host and survive the day, but you, mortal, will not. With your passing, the Frost girl will perish. And your desire, and the Supreme Queen's plans will be ruined."

"You're saying that my anomaly problems are far from over."

"I'm saying many things. Do you have a chance to master the budding World that has taken root within you? To command its powers like the Origin once did? It is unprecedented and impossibly difficult."

"But it's possible."

"Anything is possible."

"Ah," said Lukas. "We're not really talking about me."

"We are, and we are not."

Inanna smiled at him, and it felt like the first warm day of spring. Her eyes were deeper than time. And then, she just clammed up.

We are? And we are not?

Lukas barely managed to keep a straight face while his inner Neanderthal spluttered and went on a mental rampage. He hated trying to be smart under pressure, but something told him his problems wouldn't be vanishing any time soon.

"Follow your instincts, mortal. And for just this once, let me take the reins. Allow this world to witness Goddess Inanna at war. And when it is done, retreat, reflect, and find the answer you seek." She studied his face. **"Remember, you have what you have for a reason. The power and knowledge and allies She has gotten you. Trust in yourself, and in the Supreme Queen you swore fealty to. The only way to do it, is to *do it*."**

Lukas exhaled. "I'm in trouble, aren't I?"

Inanna smiled. **"Everyone is. Always. The only difference is that now you know it. I will aid you just this once, but beyond that, everything is up to you, Lukas Aguilar."**

"Aid me . . . against . . . that?"

Inanna turned away from him and looked ahead. The world of crimson faded.

A small smile flashed upon her heavenly face. **"It's been eons since I've brought a king down to his knees. I think I shall enjoy this bout."**

CHAPTER 25

INANNA

The world screamed as Inanna cut it in half.

But then it would. Complaining son of a bitch.

It was a scream heard in dreams, on the edge of the wind, and across the wastelands of this lava ridge. A near-silent scream of mercy unheeded, of regret turned into forget. The crimson radiance of the borderland seemed to freeze as Inanna's power cut through its rules.

Lukas wasn't sure exactly what Inanna had done. One moment, the behemoth of flame and lava was rising, its hands converging around them, and the world itself bending backward to manifest its wishes. A sea of boiling lava had risen from the ground to the sky, like a titanic wall, surrounding them from all sides. Kinetomancy or not, it was a weight far beyond anything he could ever imagine.

A man could not hold back a mountain.

It would squash him.

Then Inanna stepped forward. His body, following her command like a marionette, raised his right arm.

And the world *stopped*.

A power strong enough to butcher a god held the mountain in place. What was this demon, or this terrain of crimson, before it?

"What . . ." he heard Tanya croak. "What just happened?"

Lukas didn't answer. He couldn't. For he was floating like an ethereal wraith, both inside and out of his own body. He didn't know if this was what televangelists and mystics referred to as an out-of-body experience, but whatever it was, he didn't think he could ever get used to it.

No matter how many times Inanna shoved him through it.

Instead, he just stared at the surrounding impossibility in sheer wonder.

The world, as Tanya had put it, *stopped.* Just not the way she thought it had. Instead, it was as if everything came at him—at them—and somewhere along the line they just hit an invisible barrier.

Regardless of its mass, momentum, or the pull of gravity acting upon it.

Naturally, the omphalos within him went crazy.

Initiating Parallel Matrices
Safety off! Overclock Set!
Intercepting Routines
Enact

Just like the last time.

Soul Alteration Detected!
Attempting Prime Host Augmentation . . .
FAILED!
Soul Siphon Attempted . . .
FAILED!
Soul Siphon Attempted . . .
FAILED!
No new Soul Prototype Detected.
Rejected.
Adding Altered Data to Prime Host

The last time Inanna had taken over, it had been during the fight against Tanya. Despite being under Babysitter Protocol, the omphalos had thrown a liberal ten thousand units of free Soul Capacity at him, just to grab Inanna's power. Now, with the Warmonger Protocol in place and the endless Soul Capacity at its command, the omphalos had no such restrictions.

It wanted everything Inanna was showing.

Every. Single. Bit.

SKILL UPGRADE Registered!		
SKILL	**LEVEL**	**SOUL CAPACITY REQUIRED**
Kinetomancy (APEX)	4	850000
DESCRIPTION Absolute Manipulation of magnitude and direction of Momentum Vectors		

Whatever shock and disbelief he'd experienced vaporized as Lukas felt the world whimper and whine around him. It was as if Inanna's very presence was a kind of weight on the borderland itself, a gravity that strained space around it. Her Kinetomancy, now in its truest form, was a power older, deeper, and deadlier than anything it could conceive. Compared to her, even the flaming titan seemed as frail and as transient as fleeting shadows.

"What . . . What did you do?" Tanya asked.

"Stay put. Do not strain yourself. This power is beyond you."

The voice was quiet, mellow, and resonant. Though the volume never lifted, it could be heard over the white noise of the apocalypse all around.

"You . . ." Tanya croaked, "You aren't Lukas."

A shadow of a smile flickered on Inanna's—his—face at her words.

"I am he, but he is not Me."

Which, in Lukas's opinion, meant all kinds of bad. If Inanna was describing herself as *him*, then that meant the divinity probably affected him in more ways than he could imagine.

"The mortal would have given you your freedom. He would have you make your own choices, craft your own destiny. To be more than the puppet you're born to be."

What are you doing? he wanted to yell. But Tanya couldn't hear him. Only Inanna could, and she was using this opportunity to speak directly to Tanya. He could only hope that this single conversation wouldn't undo all of his hard work.

"I'm no one's puppet," Tanya declared, slowly pushing herself to stand up.

Inanna laughed at her, her voice resonating with scorn. **"When have you been anything else?"**

"I—" Tanya began, but right then, the fiery beast before them let out an enormous roar and came for them, only to be held at bay by the sphere's power.

Inanna casually waved her hand, and the creature exploded into smithereens.

Only to re-form into a thousand smaller creatures who proceeded to attack the sphere from all sides.

"Do not worry," said Inanna, as if she had not just thrashed a colossal demon around like a weakling. **"I will force you into an accord with the mortal. Bind you to him. His nigh infinite resources will cure you of your pesky limitations. His power will revert you to your truest self and grant you the power to conquer your own demons."**

Tanya staggered back. "How do you—"

"I know you more than you do yourself, pet. I was the one that cut you off from the instincts of that cold hunger."

Lukas watched as Tanya went absolutely still.

The fear in her eyes made Inanna smile.

"Do not fret. I will give you more than you can imagine. I will help you reclaim your power. Make you whole again. Turn you into a force that leaves nothing but a cold, hungry emptiness in its wake. But first . . ."

Her lips twisted. It reminded Lukas of a barbed knife.

"First, I will crush you. Shatter your pride. Drag you into my dominion, kicking and screaming. Crush that defiance from your eyes and turn you into a pliant slave, to go forth and crush the world in my name. Oh, I know it sounds cruel, but after all . . . I can hardly leave a treasure like you alone."

Her words were spoken with absolute certainty, like they were a truth of the universe. A law that she ordained upon destiny itself. It didn't matter what Tanya thought of them. It didn't matter that Inanna would soon fade and not return until Lukas brought her back. It didn't matter that Lukas disagreed with her decision.

"I won't," Tanya argued weakly, still trying to push herself up. "I'll fight you."

"So spirited!" Inanna smirked. **"It's obnoxious, but I can't help but laugh."** Tanya's strained expression made her laugh harder. **"You do not wish to attract my ire, pet. If I accidentally damage you, I will regret it deeply. It would be like blinding a great artist, like cutting off a bard's tongue. Destroying a work of *true art*. Do you know how that would pain me?"**

"You . . ." Tanya stammered. "You. Who are you?"

Inanna smiled. **"A pebble does not need to know the ocean. Be content in your ignorance."**

Tanya clearly wanted to contest that, but one look from Inanna and her jaws shut tightly, as if sealed by invisible hands. She tried vainly to open her mouth, even using her hands to pull her jaws apart, but to no avail.

"Quiet, pet. I will not have you interrupt my entertainment."

As Inanna uttered those words, lightning streaked across the sky. The terrain, or whatever was left of it, exploded. Seas of lava rose to touch the sky like giant leviathans before coming down to crash upon them. Tornadoes swept across the plain. Mountains collapsed. Volcanoes exploded. Chasms formed for hundreds and thousands of miles. The world went *mad* and was coming to devour the sphere Inanna had crafted around them. Reality itself wanted to erase them from existence for daring to shatter its conventions.

It hit the sphere like a runaway truck smashing against a runway barrier.

This was Inanna's power. This was Kinetomancy, and the omphalos had grabbed it. With power like this, he'd be able to—

"Do nothing," Inanna's voice reverberated all around him. **"Not against *that*."**

The colossal demon loomed over them, a creature straight from Lovecraftian nightmares, with a skull wreathed with flames and draconic serpentine creatures arising out of its claws. The lower half had condensed into a fiery abomination, giving it a twisted, genie-like appearance. This . . . Just what was this?

The Screen flashed right then.

IFRIT KING
Fire-Incarnate. Pinnacle of its kind. Natural-born.

"A king?" he mumbled. This titanic demon was an *Ifrit King?* He had learned about warlords and kings from Tanya but had always imagined them as impossibly powerful entities. He had experienced the sheer power of Level 3, both when fighting against it and after assimilating that power for himself. He had felt the acute sense of vulnerability when Tanya had appeared in that giant, avian cloak of darkness with wings spanning out into the sky. Tanya, who had admitted to having a single Level-4 skill, no matter how ill-equipped she was at handling it.

Lukas knew from a theoretical standpoint that a king who boasted at least *one* Level-5 skill would be exponentially more powerful than a Level 4. In his mind, he had conjured an image closer to Inanna—the reflection as he knew her. An entity so powerful that even a tiny fraction of her skill was enough to wreak havoc of untold proportions.

"You are giving it too much credit, mortal," said Inanna, speaking through his lips. **"King it may be, but it is like an infant. As your Schema suggested, a Natural-Born."**

Lukas had not, in all honesty, registered that final bit. He knew that kami, much like monsters of the crypt, were devoid of any and all Soul Capacity. Whatever level they were born into, they stayed that way. That was why they needed to latch onto a proper host and gobble up their Soul Capacity: to evolve and become more. It was why Asukan spiritists always attempted to capture Level-1 or, in rare cases, Level-2 kami, because they'd require a far lesser amount of Soul Capacity to bind. Once that was done, the spiritist used the kami to train and level up.

But to be simply born as a Level 5?

"Spectacular, isn't it?" asked the goddess. **"A most worthy pet."**

An image of Inanna sitting on her throne came to mind, with this monster now shrunken in size and coiled protectively around her, lying on its belly. The demon snored loudly, as Inanna casually petted it on its head.

That he could imagine such a thing so easily told him just how twisted his life had become.

"Will you kill it?"

She shook her head. **"That body is an illusion, conjured out of mana. Destroying that creature would require me to wield my Kinetomancy."**

Lukas looked around at the casual way she held the world around her at a pause. Nothing—matter, energy or anything in between—had penetrated that shell she had crafted around them. If this wasn't the full power of Kinetomancy . . .

"You're a child, mortal. A child staring at the infiniteness of the ocean before him. No matter how much you try, you cannot fit it into your vision."

"Then why aren't you using it?"

Inanna threw her head back and laughed. For Lukas, it was like watching a moving image of himself performing the same actions, only superimposed by Inanna.

"Your greed knows no bounds, mortal. I have already blessed you with a power beyond your wildest dreams, and still you seek for more?"

Lukas flushed at that, embarrassed.

"There is no shame in aiming for greater heights, mortal. But power beyond your capabilities will kill you. My Kinetomancy, even the paltry amount I've granted you, is a legacy far deadlier than you imagine. My belief is that it will destroy you."

Well, *that* wasn't ominous at all.

"While your World shard allows you to hold my skill, your body will break trying to wield it. It is not I that is lacking here. It is you."

Inanna turned towards the Ifrit King, who was constantly trying to grab them. It had gone from raising mountains of lava to turning the air itself to steam, to conjuring bolts of lightning.

"Enough!" Inanna's voice resonated into the sky. **"You're but an infant before me. You seek war but have no idea how to win it."**

She raised her right hand—

"Bow."

—and snapped her fingers.

An overwhelming feeling of *something undefinable* crashed upon the world. The tides of lava were pulled downward with extreme prejudice, and whatever was left of the terrain cracked and imploded downward as well, as if the gravitational pull had been spiked by a thousand. Even the Ifrit King, who had transformed into a hundred smaller forms, was sent crashing into the sea of flames, none of its forms even holding their heads upright.

Bowing before Her.

Lukas stared in awe. Pulling on an object's motion was a task that was difficult even on the best of days. And that went exponentially higher the larger it got. Just manipulating one of the bylestyr's motions *once* had left him short of breath, despite operating within his newfound power levels. Inanna had just manipulated the power of gravity upon a terrain *miles long*, including everything upon it.

And she had done it with just a snap of her fingers.

Meanwhile, a different thought started running through his mind. These creatures were all components of the Ifrit King. A being with Level-5 skills. Nevertheless, it was still a *kami*. And he had a very convenient function that could possibly help him grab a kami.

"Your greed will bring about your ruin, mortal," Inanna admonished, breaking him out of his thoughts.

"But—"

"It is a king," said Inanna. **"Even if you were to siphon it, its presence would overwhelm yours. Your body would be destroyed, your mind unraveled by the weight of its presence, and the omphalos would choose itself over you."**

Lukas clenched his fists. Even with everything he had gained, it was always an uphill climb.

Inanna looked at him, amused. **"And there is the mortal from my memories! Always impatient for more, regardless of what it may cost him. Experience has mellowed you, but it is still there. Look within yourself, for there lies a power more dangerous than anything you could ever imagine."**

Lukas stared at her for a moment. Then he nodded.

"It is time," she said. **"Use the Awareness. Open a rift."**

Lukas blinked. "Open a rift? I can't! I barely tore the bruise open, and it was already—"

"Lukas Aguilar."

Whatever he was about to say died in his throat.

"You carry my pendant. I forged your soul from my divinity. The Supreme Queen's powers are yours to wield. You are a *World*. Opening a rift is not even a challenge compared to what is coming."

A wave of nostalgia hit him as he looked at the familiar glint in her eyes. "You always were a hard taskmaster."

"You have taken it upon yourself to bring me back."

He drew in a breath and let it out. Then he nodded.

Inanna smiled, and a sudden pulling sensation gripped Lukas. He didn't fight it. The next time he opened his eyes, he was back in control. His body was his. The sphere was still holding true, as was the infinite gravity she had exerted upon the world. And Inanna—

"Open the rift, mortal," her voice whispered in his ear. **"It is time. My power will hold the king back until you do so."**

He heard the unspoken implication. The moment he opened a rift, Inanna would fade, leaving him alone again.

His heart rebelled against the idea. He had finally gotten her back. Why must he lose her all over again?

Can't you just stay in my mind again? Or in the pendant? Like before?

The silence that followed for the next two seconds held a beautiful melancholy within it.

"My pendant carried a sliver of the Supreme Queen, manifested by the faith She harvested from the masses. She sacrificed herself to forge a divine soul to hold her vigil. You. And now it is gone."

Why? He wanted to scream. He had used anomalous energy to manifest her. Surely he could do it again in the future?

A soft breeze hit his cheek.

"Perhaps you speak truly. But you must exercise caution, mortal, or your zeal will herald your defeat."

"I—I don't understand."

"The Supreme Queen's divinity forged you. That is true. But you are an ephemeral flame compared to the shining star of her brilliance."

"I was right, then. A part of you still exists within that divinity."

"It is not the divinity that contains me, mortal. It is Me that exudes that divinity. You have reversed the concept."

"But—"

"Back in her day, a defiant mortal Inanna withstood the forbidden flames of the Vikahl Ashlands with nothing but Kinetomancy. And on this day, you, mortal, endured the king born from flame, by the same method. When you used the power of Creation to bring me forth, it manifested Me in all my glory but, in doing so, lessened the divinity that slumbers within you. If you summon me again, the Supreme Queen will perhaps fade away. Forever."

Lukas did not know whether to laugh or cry. His attempts had been in the right direction, his trials vindicated by Inanna's manifestation. Every single time he had felt Inanna's presence rising within him, every single time he had performed something spectacular and unexplainable with Kinetomancy, he was channeling the divinity, sparking its proverbial engine. And finally, he had manifested her completely.

And in so doing, hurt his chances of ever truly bringing her back.

Every single time he succeeded by a tiny amount, he exhausted a fraction of that divinity. And now, there was very little left.

Inanna had put her absolute trust in him. She knew he wouldn't betray her because his faith in his ideals was absolute. If he betrayed her, he would betray himself. And now, despite knowing a way to manifest her again, despite knowing that he succeeded, he'd have to drop it, or else risk losing her forever.

Even when he won, he lost.

Such a twisted irony.

He didn't even notice the tears streaking down his cheeks. "That will not deter me. I will find a different way. I found one, I can find another. Just watch me."

"Perhaps that is why She chose you, mortal." Inanna's voice was growing softer, more distant, like she was drifting further and further away from him. **"She was a rule breaker, as are you. Travel down her path; harness what you have been given. And someday, we might meet again. But until that happens, this is farewell."**

"Lukas—" Tanya whimpered, "Lukas, look—"

He didn't need to. He could feel it. The power of the Sphere was weakening, just like Inanna had said.

"Stay still," he said. "I'll open a rift."

"But—the Well—"

"Silence!" he snapped and narrowed his eyes. He was sure that Inanna was watching. Wherever she was. She had told him he could do that. He would not fail her. He had established the connection before. And he would do it again.

Capacitance Active
Reverse Shift Active
Energy Drain Active

He held out his hands as pure, anomalous energy poured out of them.

Establishing Nexus . . .
Registering . . .

There was no need to perform Consciousness Shift this time around. He had already connected himself with the realm before. He just needed to do it again.

An anomaly of a lostbelt touched a broken realm.

Grabbed the edges of its existence.

And *pulled*.

Bridge Established
Opening rift . . .

He would be lying if he said he didn't hesitate. The information flooded his mind at speeds and quantities beyond what the mortal mind could process. Even with Level-2 tachypsychia, he'd be hard-pressed to process even a *ten-thousandth* of it. This Haze—it was outside of proper time and space, existing in *nothing* between one moment and the next.

Lukas hesitated, even though it could get him killed. He hesitated because to charge blindly forward would surely get him killed.

The Haze—no, the *Ikai Realm*—wasn't a singular existence. It was a reticulum that connected various worlds—borderlands, singularities and maybe even other mini-realms—binding them together in ways beyond his comprehension.

It both did and did not exist. Cascading layers of realities manifested all around him, just a footstep from him and yet an eternity away. It was warm and damp, painfully humid, and bitterly cold. It was magic and it was impossible.

And it was filled with energy.

Endless, unadulterated, potent energy.

And before he knew it, Blob reacted.

> **Rollback Protocol Activated**
> **Attempting Reverse Corruption . . .**

One moment it was acting as a protective vest. Now? The aqāru expanded, covered every inch of his body, and expanded outward, like a large, flappy cape, increasing its surface area as it greedily gobbled the surrounding energy.

It didn't matter. For just a single second of exposure was enough to charge his omphalos reserves several times over.

> **Attempting . . .**
> **FAILED!**
> **Attempting . . .**
> **FAILED!**
> **Attempting . . .**
> **FAILED!**
> **Attempting . . .**
> **FAILED!**

And on and on it went. It tried a hundred times. It failed a hundred times. And on and on and on. The rift enlarged with every passing second. Just a little more and it would be enough. A storm of images and perception hit his mind. Animals, plants, terrain, craters, cities, forests, volcanoes, oceans visible and invisible, worlds of color and utter, utter blackness.

Up. Down. Right. Left. Within. Without. Whole. Disjointed.

And absolutely unending.

Every inch of his body protested painfully. Blood was already pouring down his eyes and nose. His skull felt like it was being crushed like a tomato. Neural Suppression had already lost the battle. So how was he keeping up?

> **Discerning familiar locations . . .**
> **Identifying . . .**

He thought he saw something familiar. Sand. A red sun. An endless desert. A lost kingdom. A woman's face. Solar flares coming down like the judgment of a wrathful god—

"TANYA!"

He couldn't say anything further. His whole body was burning. He could only hope that the physical sensation he felt around his waist were her hands.

> **Attempting . . .**
> **Success!**
>
> **Rollback Complete!**
> **Accessing 16,159 skills . . .**
> **Accessing CRYPT OF FIENDISH WORMS . . .**
> **Establishing Bridge . . .**

Yes. He saw it now. He knew what this was. And with that came an equally horrifying realization. He knew where he was going to emerge, or more importantly, *in whose room.*

No rest for the wicked! Lukas thought deliriously as an impossible vacuum pulled him and Tanya in, a tremendous roar shaking the world he left behind. He crashed into a wall on the other side, his eyes blearily taking in the familiar, dark-haired figure with the jet-black eyes staring at him with a mix of suspicion and delight. The last thing he registered was a notification unfolding itself in an alarming shade of red.

> **Prime Host is no longer in combat**
> **Accelerating Spiritual Augmentation**
> **All Systems Shutting Down for Upgrade**

The Banksi mansion was a tiny thing.

The town of Haviskali alone, between the five distinct zones it encompassed, contained almost half a million souls living their lives in blissful ignorance of the assault taking place in their midst, the wool forcibly pulled over their eyes.

Even the hill upon which the mansion stood, contained four blocks, with roughly thirty houses in each and a population slightly north of six hundred. It was almost inconceivable, if one stopped to consider it, that a singular assault made on a single mansion, housing not more than seven people including residents and staff, might have such an enormous impact on the lives of so many. They were a drop in the bucket, a tiny speck of blackness against the light of society. But that blackness could spread with surprising speed, and on this night, it grew beneath the hill like a cancer, choking out the light.

The wrath of the Shimizu warlord came to this hill, and suddenly, it had a population of zero.

A legion of igriotts, born of a twisted experiment between Wind kami and the igriotts of the Northern Dominion, answerable only to the warlord's call, erupted everywhere at once. Pale, grayish mist rolled off the creatures from the corruption soaked into their bones. They looked skeletal and starved, their animal instincts twisted into a monstrous hunger for bloodshed, their fanged maws ripping through stone and metal alike throughout the settlements on the hill. Individually, they were weak by the standards of adventurer combat. Even someone of Zuken's caliber could kill them in the dozens without much effort.

But against civilians? Normal men, women, and children resting in their homes, just beginning to settle in for a night's sleep? The igriotts moved so quickly that most of the residents within each household were dead before they even realized their homes had been invaded.

Those were the lucky ones. The igriotts were incapable of sadism, but they could hardly help inspiring terror. Far, far too many people woke up to find themselves in a nightmare, fleeing for their lives from shadowy figures that seemed to come out of nothingness and moved faster than they could comprehend. They fled in vain, hunted down like animals with brutal efficiency, and if they managed to elude one invader, it was only to find another waiting in their path an instant later.

And then, once every bed was scoured, every room cleared, and every cradle silenced, the blood-soaked monsters began their true work. They searched the homes, finding the tiny wardstones implanted within each, all of them serving as tiny anchors that maintained the vastly powerful protective barrier that hung over the Banksi mansion.

They'd finish their task. They always did.

This was not how negotiations were done.

When Ultaf Shimizu had come to Zuken's home, demanding that he hand Tanya over to him, Ultaf had granted him a month to think about things. A month that by all rights should have been enough for Tanya and Lukas to return from the mission. Even in a worst-case scenario, Zuken could have sent her and Lukas into hiding, preferably in his private hideaways in Maluscion. Instead, the two had gotten stranded in the borderland after attracting lethal attention from the most powerful inhabitants of the region. If he ever had the fortune to lay eyes on Lukas Aguilar again, he'd have to impress upon the young man the difference between audacity and idiocy.

Either way, he had expected Ultaf to return after a month, demanding that he sell Tanya to him. Zuken had expected him to sit over several glasses of wine and negotiate the terms of the settlement. Maybe he could have convinced him to extend the time period, what with the entire "stranded" situation. He had expected Ultaf to toss around subtle threats. Maybe strongarm Zuken by bringing the Earth King into this mess. By the goddess, the last thing he needed was to see that man's face again.

Zuken even had his cards ready. Lord Naowa, the Shogun of the Llaisy Kingdom was a Lord of the Sacred Eight as well. Certainly nothing compared to the Earth King, but no one to scoff at, either. A diplomatic mess between two Lords of the Sacred Eight was a wonderful way of dragging this matter out for weeks, if not *months*.

He had expected Ultaf to snap at him. Maybe make less subtle threats.

He had *not* expected him to attack him with his army out of nowhere.

But here he was.

Zuken exhaled, and silently sipped his tea. He really hoped that Ultaf was not so lost to barbarism that he'd deny him a final cup of tea before the nastiness began. That the "tea" was actually an alchemical mixture designed to temporarily elevate one's manacrafting abilities by a significant magnitude was a different matter altogether.

He looked down from his rooftop, feeling the slow, subsequent shattering of the wardstones downstream. Unlike other nobles, Zuken didn't place his faith on a singular wardstone. The consequences of having a central point of failure were simply too high. Instead, he had used smaller wardstones and implanted them into the bedrock of the houses downstream, with each wardstone adding its own protection to the barrier placed over the mansion. He did not know how Ultaf had known his strategy, or if he was just plain unlucky, but his monsters were slowly and systematically undoing the barrier protecting his mansion. A second prong of attack, a group of wind spiritists, were rushing uphill, using the forest as a cover. Wind spiritists were hard to track on a good day, and these ones had those monsters as a distraction. By the time his troops had mounted a defense, half of them had already crossed through the outer perimeter.

Despite that, he only had eyes for the single figure that was already airborne, a lance in hand, leaping right at him.

Ultaf Shimizu's charge hit the roof like a bomb, and Zuken raised a barrier just in time to intercept it. The stones beneath his feet shattered as the impact buckled the roof beneath him. He shifted his weight and redirected the charge into a pair of boulders, catapulting them towards Ultaf, who narrowly avoided them, skidding across the roof. The Shimizu had clearly aimed for a lethal blow. Superficial damage to the roof barely counted as a minor problem in comparison to that.

Ultaf turned to face him. "I told you, Banksi. You'll rue the day you went against me."

"I already am," said Zuken, frowning. He hoped Ultaf hadn't seen his hands shake. Just eleven more wardstones and the barrier would fall. "Your army has absolutely no regard for lawn maintenance."

Ultaf threw his head back and laughed. "Witty under pressure. I like that. Tell me, Banksi, what did you hope to gain by crossing me?"

Zuken exhaled. Truth be told, he had been expecting the situation to turn out very differently when he had decided to spurn Ultaf's overtures. Between Tanya's Aeromancy and Lukas Aguilar's unpredictability, he had thought of multiple options if and when the eventual face-off happened.

"You know what they say, humor is like violence. They both come unexpectedly, and the more unpredictable they are, the better."

"I quite agree," said Ultaf, losing his combat stance. "I'm offering you one last chance, Banksi. Call it my Asukan pride. I'd rather avoid killing a noble if I could."

"I can only repeat what I told you earlier, Ultaf," Zuken said tersely. "It is true that I hired Tanya, but she isn't under my protection anymore. She got stranded in a borderland in the last mission. I'm not even certain she's even alive anymore."

He wasn't lying. Getting stranded in a borderland was one of the most dangerous things that could happen to an average adventurer during a mission. That said, Tanya wasn't exactly what one would consider *average.*

Nor Lukas, for that matter.

His thoughts went back to Elena and Olfric, both currently hiding in the emergency room. In the event of a catastrophe, the room was enchanted to sink deep within the crust, all the way to the very base of the mountain. Of course, that was his ultimate failsafe and would only be triggered if all other defenses had failed spectacularly and Zuken had perished.

Not a very attractive thought.

Again, it was the worst possible scenario. Zuken believed that there was a rather substantial number of alternatives that he could insert before things went that far. Any other spiritist in his place would've placed their hopes on the defensive and offensive capabilities of their wards, but Zuken had always been an odd one. To him, manacrafting was just one more set of tools that the mind could use to solve problems.

And his mind told him that the key to his survival lay in convincing Ultaf.

Ultaf Shimizu was a rather simple man to understand once you figured out his logic. He *truly* believed that it was his right to rule, being the only relevant Sacred Eight Lord in the entire region. True, Lord Naowa, the Shogun of the entire Llaisy Kingdom, was a Sacred Eight Lord as well, but he was as docile as they came. Plus, he had the entirety of the kingdom to manage and was probably the last person who wanted to be caught in a crossfire between a Sacred Eight Lord and the outcast son of another over something so trifling. Even Tatun Kinosu, the overseer of Haviskali, would almost certainly turn a blind eye to what was happening.

Hence, Ultaf Shimizu embodied the greatest authority in this region. In Ultaf's mind, the strong stood over the weak and made the rules, and he stood above them all, and therefore had final say in everything. Should there be a subject that he bothered to take interest in, he'd address it as he saw fit with no issues, regardless of the destruction that might cause in his wake if someone attempted something he did not like; he was, in his own mind, obligated to serve as an appropriate judge, jury, and executioner.

It was up to Zuken to make sure that Ultaf did not take up the third role. Dying would be bad for business.

"You can choose to destroy my mansion, Ultaf," he said in as calm a voice as possible. "But the truth won't change. To the best of my knowledge, Tanya has been stranded, along with a compatriot."

Ultaf Shimizu stayed quiet for several moments before smiling briefly, as if amused by a small joke. "You're lying!"

Zuken frowned. He was missing something, a key ingredient in this conversation. Whoever Ultaf's sources were, he must have been mightily confident in them.

"What makes you say that?"

"I have my sources."

"Your sources are wrong," he shot back.

"You're annoying me now," drawled Ultaf. "First you lied about sheltering the creature. Then you stood defiant against me. And now you call my source, Lady Kandra, a liar."

Zuken faltered. Anyone in the mercenary business knew of Lady Kandra. Supposedly, she knew everyone from the bottommost rung of the political ladder to the highest, but no one knew her. Zuken counted himself as one of the rare few that had the opportunity to even *converse* with her. A true ghost, Lady Kandra was someone who could be swayed with neither riches nor resources. She dealt in one thing and one thing alone—information. And that made her dangerous.

And if Lady Kandra was Ultaf's source, no wonder he was being so reckless. The real question was, why would someone like her *lie* to Ultaf Shimizu? Moreso, why would someone that played on the Empire level take interest in something so insignificant?

"I don't know why Lady Kandra thinks otherwise, but it is not true. I do not—"

The rest of his words died in his throat, as the sound of something loud hit his ears. Only, it was less like noise than it was like being thrown into an enormous vat of sludge. Instantly, he felt like there was no way to take a sufficient breath. There was pressure against all of his skin and pain in his ears, like he had just jumped off a high cliff. His defenses failing, Zuken clapped his hands over his ears—not that it did much good. Honestly, it was a miracle that he hadn't fallen to the ground, spasming in agony.

Then he saw it.

Wings.

Six of them.

Each spanning twice the size of an average Jixin, claws that were taller than he was, and a mouth that looked like it could swallow three people in one go. The creature that manifested in the sky above his mansion looked less like a kami and more like a demon.

For the first time since he had seen his father angry, Zuken Banksi felt fear.

For Want of a Friend

Dreams were ethereal things that spoke of your innermost feelings. They could be fears that haunted you in the dark or desires buried so deep within that you yourself did not know what they are. Some dreamt of power, others of pleasure, and then there were those who were ambitious on a smaller scale, constantly seeking modest goals instead of following a larger, time-consuming one.

As far as dreams went, Arah's was a simple one.

He just wanted a friend.

It was easier said than done, of course, what with everyone always *yelling* at him. *Always.* He understood he was a bit on the large side, being an Ifrit King and all, but even *he* deserved to be happy, didn't he? But no one ever *understood.* He'd peek through the clouds and look at the others as the tinier ifrits ran and clashed their claws with each other. It sounded like so much fun. But they never gave Arah a chance to join them. Every time he was near, they just seemed to *know.*

It was a *mystery* like no other.

And then they'd drop to their knees and start *yelling.*

Like it was somehow *his* fault.

Arah had once tried to ask them why, but they just . . . condensed into liquid and seeped into the ground.

Talk about being mean.

It was a good thing that Arah liked to sleep. It wasn't like he needed to eat or breathe or blink. Not that he could blink. You needed *eyelids* for that. Arah wasn't exactly sure what these eyelid things did but those four-armed tiny tots had them. Those had a very disagreeable disposition, but hey, they were friendlier to him, so who cared, right? He had once come down to play with one of them, and it had brought its friends to play as well. Plus, spitting fire was a very boring activity. Why would anyone consider spitting fire interesting when Arah could just . . .Whatever. Life was all about compromise, so Arah had accepted it with a smile.

And for want of a little variety, showed them how to spit fire out of his *eye*.

He thought they'd appreciate the variety he brought to their little game. Instead . . .

Instead, he found them all gone.

Just . . . *gone*.

Maybe they had gotten jealous of his eye-spitting and ran away to sulk? Arah didn't know. He'd never met that crowd after that, despite searching for them, which was where he had come across the next best thing.

Holes.

Okay, maybe that wasn't the best description out there, but Arah wasn't very knowledgeable, was he? All he knew was that they popped in and out, leaking new-color mist, belching tiny creatures from within. Originally, Arah thought that someone was playing peekaboo on the other side, so he rushed in to grab a hole before it closed, but to no avail. Instead, those tiny creatures just *vanished* in flames.

While yelling at him, that is.

It was so weird.

This world that he grew up in didn't have a new-color mist, just red and yellow and . . . black-ish. Arah wasn't the most skilled at remembering colors, but he was sure there was no new-color here. Maybe there were more new-colors on the other side?

Yes. That was the right idea. He'd leave this stupid place. He'd go to this more new-color world and seek new friends. Maybe he'd come back after a while, and play peekaboo with his mean friends here, to see if they were missing him. And then he'd leave them for the new-color world again.

That'd teach them to stop being mean.

Not for very long, though. He didn't want to make them cry.

Yes. Arah was a big softie. He couldn't help it. It was his nature.

It hadn't worked out.

Arah had stopped jumping for the holes, and instead trying to befriend the tiny creatures that came out of them. They were mean too, but less than the mean ones he already knew. They didn't yell at him at first, which was nice for once, and even brought more friends, but then they screamed and vanished when Arah showed them his eye-spitting thing.

In hindsight, he should have tried something else. Maybe he was just bad at this eye-spitting thing? Or maybe eye-spitting was an ifrit thing. These were not ifrits. He'd need to come up with something else.

Another long sleep followed before he came up with a new trick. This time it wasn't a spit. Oh no, spits were ugly, and they splattered all over the place. This time, it was a beam. Like the ones that came from the star above, only thicker. If the star could shoot all that from that far, he'd have to do better, right?

How else would they think *he* was worthy of being friends with them?

At least, that's what he thought. And it wasn't like Arah had a *better* idea.

Imagine his surprise when, the next time he performed his eye-beam trick, his new playmates just vanished. They didn't even bother to yell.

Along with the land they were on.

And the hole.

Arah had thrown a tantrum, kicked those large cone-like pieces of land, and made an absolute mess before heading to another long sleep.

That was some time ago. Arah was bad at counting, but the specifics weren't important, anyway. The important thing was that someone had woken *him* up. He had sensed another hole forming, only this one was . . . well, opening from *this* world.

But it had given him an *idea.*

He could always try opening a hole himself.

Excited, he had pawed through the air, but absolutely nothing happened. The stupid red and yellow stayed. But if this new creature—no, not one, *two.* Two of them were there, and they *knew* how to open a hole.

But wait! He had seen how the creature had yelled while opening the hole. Even though Arah had not shown himself. So, maybe, just *maybe,* he wasn't yelling at Arah but at the hole?

That made Arah think. Maybe the others were *also* yelling at those holes, not at Arah?

That thought led to another thought. Could it be that *yelling* made those holes open faster? It would explain a lot. Armed with this knowledge, Arah knew it was time to experiment. Only through the power of observation could he make the correct inference. Who knew? Maybe Arah would even make a friend in the process?

Gathering himself, Arah let out a nice, loud yell. It wasn't his loudest, but it was louder than the tiny creatures'. So when the world all around him instantly turned darker, Arah knew he was on the right track.

He was on the wrong track. It wasn't working. Maybe if he asked them nicely, they'd be inclined to teach it to him? Arah was a big believer in reciprocation, so he introduced himself with an eye-spitting gesture.

And promptly cheered in victory when the creatures didn't vanish!

Yes! Finally, his efforts had borne fruit. Finally, he had come across some-one that didn't think too badly of his eye-spitting. Excited, Arah moved to his next technique—the eye-beam. Just like before, the creatures stood where they were, and Arah could feel his beam split apart without them vanishing. And the best part? They weren't even *yelling!*

Whooping in joy, Arah manifested himself in all his glory. He was a spiritual being, but he rather liked not being a mass of hot gases and flame. Instead, he had taken a little of everything he had seen from this world and reshaped himself. It was hardly a perfect look, but Arah was open to criticism and experimentation. But for now, it would do. The head, he based on the tiny ifrits, complete with the mane, the bodies upon those four-armed creatures that he had met once and only once. He had seen flying serpents in the sky, but that wouldn't fit in his new body, so he had morphed his claws into those serpents. He could even make them spit flames, which, in his humble opinion, was *insanely cool.*

When his new . . . acquaintances didn't vanish, Arah felt bolder. He had to know just what it was he did right this time around. Not wasting any more time, he went closer, trying to grab them with his hands. The world—big, jeal-ous thing that it was—mimicked him, raising a wall of red and yellow to get to the new friendlies before him and—

—Stopped?

Arah tilted his head, surprised and confused. Despite his surprise at fire not acting like fire and just . . . stopping like that, he just grinned wider and flexed his wings. He wasn't sure if this new creature was using physical force or some new trick, but every bit of flame that fell on him just dissipated.

Arah had never seen a neater trick.

Curious, he extended a hand.

And it stopped too.

Arah pulled his hand back and tried again. It stopped again.

And again. This time with both hands. And again. And again and again. Every time he tried, he would hit an invisible wall and just stop. No matter what he did, no matter how hard he tried, his hand would just not penetrate past that invisible wall.

Arah squealed in exhilaration. This was *so much better* than eye-spitting! This was what *playing* felt like. But Arah was not one to accept defeat. He would break this invisible wall, and he would get them. He flexed both hands and extended them out at full strength.

His appendages crashed against the barrier and disintegrated into flame. Quickly calling them back, Arah tried again, this time with his eye-spitting and eye-beam and a couple more combinations.

It did not matter.

The wall would *Just. Not. Break.*

Was this what his friends could do? No, not friends. *Friend.* Singular. Out of the two, only one was playing with him. The other was just . . . there. Lazing around. Arah hated lazy people. Still, was that *all* he could do? Stop things?

Arah tried to ask his new friend. He doubted that it could understand his tongue, so he had already prepared himself for disappointment. Imagine his surprise when his friend raised its hand and—

—blasted Arah into smithereens.

He hadn't even *felt* whatever his new friend had done before it had happened. Wanting to see the limits of this new trick, Arah quickly re-formed into many, many smaller forms of himself and rushed at his friend excitedly.

He was not disappointed.

Arah only had a moment to look at it in surprise when an invisible heaviness slammed into *all of him* from above. Arah had never felt a weight like this before, and it took everything he had in him to not disperse into mana instantly. Instead, all of him fell down on their hands and knees, crushing several of those claw-snake thingies they had created. The invisible heaviness kept crushing *them* down, no matter what they did to escape it.

If he hadn't known better, he'd have thought this friend was trying to *kill* him. Maybe it was time for him to show some of his own tricks. Reciprocation was key, after all. With a yell, Arah fused the parts of himself back into one, and shattered through the ever-so-slightly-weakening invisible heaviness and dispersed himself into mana, only to re-form himself back into his gigantic form and—

Gone?

Arah blinked.

Yes. His friend was gone. As was its lazy friend.

Disappointed, Arah clumsily sat down in the lava sea that existed instead of the terrain.

Goodbye, friend! he thought. *Perhaps this was all our friendship was meant to be.*

ABOUT THE AUTHORS

T. B. Mare is the pseudonym of the authors of Stranger Than Fiction, a LitRPG adventure series originally released on Royal Road. They are a pair of dreamers who started working together in order to share with readers some of the fun of creating fantasy worlds filled with rich lore and complex characters. Both discovered their love for fantasy and magic at a young age, and the ensuing affairs have carried on well into adulthood. Hopelessly addicted to complex genre fiction—especially the darker kind—they currently work multiple jobs but are looking forward to one day writing full-time.

Podium
DISCOVER
STORIES UNBOUND
PodiumAudio.com